'Boyd Morrison's novel, *The Noah's Ark Quest*, is a stunning thriller with a premise as ingenious as it is flawlessly executed. Lightning-paced, chillingly real, here is a novel that will have you holding your breath until the last page is turned. One of the best debuts I've read this year' **James Rollins**

'When it comes to thrillers, Boyd Morrison has the Midas touch' **Chris Kuzneski**

'A bang-a-minute blockbuster' ***The Times***

'A roller coaster ride of gun-blazing action, fascinating historical references, and a nail-biting battle of wits ... Move over Dan Brown, and give Boyd Morrison a try' **Lisa Gardner**

'A rip-roaring thriller which has the reader entranced from first page to last ... Hold on tight as the pace is akin to that of a white water raft ride – furious bouts of life-threatening action then a spell of calm before the next onslaught on your senses!' ***CrimeSquad.com***

'Heart-stopping action, biblical history, mysticism, a stunning archeological find and mind-boggling evil results in a breathcatching adventure ... a pitch-perfect combination of plot, action and dialogue' ***RT Book Reviews***

'Full of action, villainy, and close calls. Fans of James Rollins, Matthew Reilly, and Douglas Preston take note' ***Booklist***

'The perfect blend of historical mysticism and clever, classical thriller plotting. Imagine the famed Ark rediscovered and reinvented to form the seeds of a modern day conspiracy. Boyd Morrison manages that flawlessly in this blisteringly-paced tale' **Jon Land**

'A perfect thriller' ***Crimesp***

ALSO BY BOYD MORRISON

The Noah's Ark Quest

The Midas Code

The Tsunami Countdown

The Roswell Conspiracy

THE LOCH NESS LEGACY

BOYD MORRISON

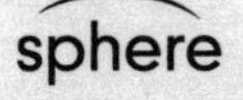

SPHERE

First published in Great Britain in 2013 by Sphere

All characters and events in this publication, other than those clearly in the public domain, are fictitious and any resemblance to real persons, living or dead, is purely coincidental.

A CIP catalogue record for this book
is available from the British Library.

ISBN 978-0-7515-4805-1

Typeset in Sabon by M Rules
Printed and bound in Great Britain by
Clays Ltd, St Ives plc

Papers used by Sphere are from well-managed forests
and other responsible sources.

Sphere
An imprint of
Little, Brown Book Group
100 Victoria Embankment
London EC4Y 0DY

An Hachette UK Company
www.hachette.co.uk

www.littlebrown.co.uk

For Randi. Je t'aime.

PROLOGUE

June, 1827

The jolt against the keel came stronger this time and knocked the tiny rowboat sideways, causing Charles Darwin to cling to the bow gunwale for fear of being thrown into Loch Ness's chilly waters. Steadying himself, he shielded the lantern in his hand to keep the pelting rain from dousing their sole light source.

'Can you see what it is?' John Edmonstone asked as he strained at the oars. The freed slave's eyes were glassy with terror, and his thick Guyanese accent nearly overwhelmed his English.

Darwin angled the lantern downward, but it was no use. The loch's peat-rich water was murky under the best circumstances but completely impenetrable now that the sudden downpour had added its obscuring veil to the gloom of twilight. He swiveled his head to get his bearings.

'I can't even see the shore. Could it be that we're off course?'

Darwin received only a grim frown in reply and went back to searching for a landmark while watching for any sign of the monstrous wake they'd first encountered ten minutes ago. If they weren't able to detect the lights from the village of Drumnadrochit, they might turn in circles for hours. If the boat were upended in the frigid water, their corpses would either wash ashore or sink to the abyssal depths of the loch.

Darwin shivered, his clothes soaked through. He longed for the tropics that Edmonstone had so vividly described during Darwin's private taxidermy instruction back in Edinburgh. He found refuge in those lessons because much of medical school training had quite bored him when it hadn't been making him ill. His stomach had threatened to empty itself every time he observed surgery on conscious patients, performed that way despite his pleas to utilize Humphry Davy's recent discovery of an anesthetic called nitrous oxide, a compound few had taken seriously once it had been dubbed 'laughing gas'. Only the stench of Edmonstone's beloved and pungent saltfish imported from his homeland could match the surgery's sickening effect.

With no hunting or shooting to be had in Edinburgh, Darwin had craved excitement, so it was he who had suggested an exploration of the Scottish Highlands using funds unwittingly provided by his father. Edmonstone, eager to collect new specimens for his taxidermy shop, agreed to be his companion. Their current predicament was the result of an impulsive expedition to the other side of the loch after they found a disused rowboat that the local innkeeper let them borrow.

Now stranded on the loch and under siege by some menace of the deep, Darwin was ruing the decision. To die would be a tragedy; to require rescue would be ignominious. If the Old Man heard of this illicit expedition, Darwin would never know the end of it.

An abrupt noise like a plank slapping against the water split the rain. Darwin wheeled about, but the patter of raindrops made it impossible to discern from which direction it had come.

'What in God's name was that?' he cried.

'It's the beast, Mr Darwin. I'm sure of it.'

Darwin, of course, had heard the tales of a creature living in the loch, though the rare sightings were always made by the friend of a friend. He had quickly dismissed the stories. Even in his short time collecting marine invertebrates on the Firth of Forth, he knew that such second-hand anecdotes were completely unreliable. Direct observation was the only viable scientific method for documenting new species, and retrieving sample specimens was the only way of verifying their existence.

Edmonstone, perhaps because of his upbringing as a slave, was a more superstitious sort. Darwin admired the thoughtful and intelligent man immensely and had trouble reconciling these qualities of his character. But now that he was experiencing such an unusual event himself, he was beginning to see how beliefs like Edmonstone's could be birthed.

Darwin picked up the hatchet they'd used to cut firewood. He had never used the blade as a weapon, and it was comically small when compared to the apparently enormous dimensions of the beast circling beneath them, but it seemed prudent to wield it nevertheless.

A ghostly edifice loomed out of the fading light, and Darwin's heart pounded so hard he feared it would burst. The thudding abated only when he recognized the apparition.

He turned to Edmonstone with a smile. 'It's the tower of Urquhart Castle. We've come south.' The ruined stone tower stood on its strategic promontory overlooking the midpoint of the loch, majestically implacable against the miserable weather.

'Thank the Lord.'

'Steer us to starboard. On our visit yesterday, I noticed a small beach where we can pull ashore until this wretched rain subsides.'

'With pleasure.'

The rowboat slewed around and Edmonstone pulled with even greater haste. If space had allowed, Darwin would have helped him. Instead, he was relegated to lookout.

They were only minutes from reaching shore when the boat rocked again, very nearly foundering. This time Darwin didn't need to search for the source of the disturbance.

A massive shape rose from the water. Darwin's throat closed, making it impossible to draw a breath. A gamey odor emanated from the creature, whose outline Darwin couldn't establish because its great breadth took up his entire vision.

An appendage whirled toward him, and Edmonstone screamed something unintelligible as he swung a gaff hook at the creature. Without thinking, Darwin raised the ax in self-defense and brought it down on what he supposed to be the beast's writhing tail. The blade cut through flesh, drawing a shrill cry from the animal. A piece of the tail's tip flopped to the bottom of the boat, squirming for a moment before becoming still.

Astonished at what he'd done, Darwin looked up and saw a sight he knew he would remember no matter how long he lived.

A huge black eye focused on him, reflecting the light of his lantern like a cat's eye.

Before the creature dipped back below the water, it hesitated for a moment, long enough for Darwin to perceive what he thought was a spark of emotion in the animal's eye, a nobility in its bearing that seemed undeniable. It was reeling back not just in pain, but in confusion. The thing had not expected to be hurt. What he and Edmonstone had experienced was not an attack. The creature had merely been curious.

Then with a splash, it was gone. Only the desperate, rhythmic sound of the oars remained.

As he panted from the ordeal like a foxhound on the chase, Darwin was overcome with sadness. Hunting the abundant pheasant and grouse of England was a sport he relished. But this was different. This beast was unknown to science, perhaps unique.

If he conveyed his story to the world armed with the tangible proof of his find, the terror he'd felt would be magnified a hundred-fold by the fearful town folk who would surely hunt down and destroy the creature. Hearing the tale of a great beast to be captured, Aberdeen whalers would swarm over the loch, harpoons at the ready. Darwin wanted to study wildlife, not exterminate it. This discovery demanded scientific scrutiny, and he vowed to return one day to continue his search.

Now was not the time, but once he calmed, he would speak with Edmonstone about the matter. Together they would determine what to do with their specimen.

The rain ceased as abruptly as it had begun, and the boat lurched toward the shore whilst Edmonstone rowed with all his might. Darwin bent and picked up the fleshy spade-shaped remains that lay at his feet. The smooth, tacky skin was warm to the touch. He tucked the specimen into his coat pocket for safekeeping until he could secure a better method of preservation.

The boat skidded up the beach, and the two men tumbled out onto the rocks. Darwin winced as the jagged stones cut into his hands, but he scrambled through the trees and up the grassy knoll with a vigor he didn't think within him.

Safely at the top of the hill, he and Edmonstone paused to catch their breath, peering at the loch to see if any sign of the creature remained. Not even a ripple of water betrayed that it had ever existed.

LA TOUR EIFFEL

WORLD NEWS

No Decision on Palestinian Issue at Muslim Nation Summit

By MARGARET SIMMONS and YVES BEGNAUD

June 12, PARIS – Syria and Egypt continue to push for an invasion of Israel as other nations at this worldwide summit of Muslim leaders call for restraint in the wake of escalating tensions over Israel's reprisals for rocket attacks launched from Gaza, the West Bank, and southern Lebanon.

Foreign ministers from Jordan, Saudi Arabia, and Indonesia voiced a preference for negotiation and diplomatic intervention by western nations to resolve the current tensions, in direct opposition to the more militant tone set by Iran and Pakistan in response to threats issued by Israel that any incursion into its territory would result in a full retaliatory strike. Given the unacknowledged existence of nuclear weapons in Israel's arsenal, the US and European Union are calling for an immediate ceasefire.

Despite the pleas for peace, armies continue to mobilize on both sides of Israel's borders. The instability of the governments in Egypt and Syria means that the prospects for tensions to dissolve quickly are unpredictable, and supplies of arms from other Muslim nations are flowing into those countries.

With no new talks planned and the summit ending tonight at a dinner atop the Eiffel Tower, the odds of a peaceful resolution to the issue in the next few days are long at best.

ONE

Present Day

A torrent of adrenaline coursed through Tyler Locke's blood like it always did before an impending battle, forcing him to will a calm façade.

'They think we're crazy, you know,' he said, using his vantage point on the Eiffel Tower to scan the Paris skyline for any sign of a threat. The city of lights sparkled peacefully in the last remaining glow of the setting sun, oblivious to menace.

Grant Westfield watched the glittering Seine almost directly below them. 'Of course they do. Who the hell would have the guts to attack a party with this kind of security presence? It's nuts.'

'And yet, here we are.'

Grant smiled, his bright white teeth visible in the window's reflection. 'Maybe we *are* crazy. For being here, I mean. If we're right, this is going to get ugly real fast.'

'Then let's hope we're wrong.'

The Salle Gustave Eiffel bustled with the chatter of four hundred guests in attendance as Bizet's Symphony in C played in the background. With a magnificent view one hundred eighty-seven feet above the ground, the recently renovated private room on the tower's first floor was the setting for the post-dinner cocktail reception. The banquet at the 58 Tour Eiffel restaurant next door had been blissfully uneventful, but now that darkness was upon them, Tyler could feel his muscles tightening with anticipation. This would be the perfect time to attack.

The French government had offered to host the Muslim leadership summit to show the country's commitment to peace in the Middle East and insisted the summit end on a literal high note by taking place in such a spectacular location. The security arrangements, however, had been a nightmare. The tower had been closed to the public for the entire day, unheard of for a sunny June Thursday, and tourists were kept at bay by a horde of policemen and soldiers. This concluding gala was attended by presidents, prime ministers, ambassadors, and sheiks from every Muslim country, which meant no security detail was too small to overlook. Even the floor-to-ceiling windows had been covered with a reflective film so that snipers couldn't target specific attendees.

Still, Tyler felt uneasy and vulnerable, as if they were being displayed as bait.

'The French must not think we're too insane,' Grant said, 'or they wouldn't have let us in here.'

'They wouldn't have if the Turkish ambassador wasn't the former culture minister. I used up my last Noah's Ark chit with them to add us to their guest list.'

Grant tugged at the collar of his tuxedo shirt, which

hugged his neck tightly. 'I just wish it didn't mean wearing this monkey suit.'

Finding a rental tux that fit Grant's shoulders had been a challenge. The coat was stretched to the limit over the muscles of the 250-pound former pro wrestler who had bulked back up to his fighting weight since leaving the Army. Tyler didn't have that problem. Although he'd retired from the Army years ago, he was still trim enough to fit into the same tuxedo size he'd worn since college.

'This way we don't stand out,' Tyler said.

'I don't think it's working as well for you as it is for me,' Grant said, pointedly looking around at the Arabs, Africans, Persians, Pakistanis, and Asians. His mocha skin and shaved head fit right in. Tyler, however, was one of the few Caucasians in the place. In America, it was Grant who normally drew the stares, both for his fame and his broad build, but here he was just another of the many brown faces. Instead it was Tyler's light tan and unruly brown hair getting the sideways glances, aided by the fact that he was six-two and towered over many of the guests.

Tyler shrugged. 'They'll assume I'm one of the French.'

'It would help if you spoke any.'

'*Oui, oui, monsieur.*'

'That's the worst accent I've ever heard.'

'Hey,' Tyler said in mock defensiveness, 'the only words you know how to say are all food-related.'

'What else do I need to know besides croissant, chateaubriand, and beignet?'

'We'll get you some of each when we're done here. Is the DeadEye still scanning?'

Grant checked his smartphone and nodded. 'No unusual activity.'

'Good. Maybe this was all a false alarm.' Tyler spotted a slinky red cocktail dress flash by. 'I'll be right back.'

Grant followed his eyes. 'I have to say, she does look good in that number.'

Tyler couldn't agree more. 'I'm going to check on her progress.'

'Sure. Oh, and grab me one of those little salmon things on your way back. Better yet, send the waiter over with the tray when you see him. I'm starving.'

'The tuxedo isn't tight enough for you?'

Grant looked at him with a raised eyebrow. 'Just because you're scrawny doesn't mean you need to feel jealous.'

Tyler chuckled. At somewhere over two hundred pounds and a couple of inches taller than Grant, few people would call him scrawny. But compared to his friend, almost anyone would look puny.

'I'd better eat some myself, then,' Tyler said. 'Give me a shout if you spot anything unusual.'

'Will do.'

Tyler navigated his way through the crowd toward the bar, which was understandably vacant since most of the attendees abstained from drinking alcohol because of their Muslim faith. The lone person getting a drink was Brielle Cohen, resplendent in a scarlet silk evening gown that demurely covered her top and draped to the floor, but clung to her shape like it was vacuum-sealed. Many of the guests stole glances at her curvaceous figure and long hair the color of burnt sienna, unused to such displays in their countries. Tyler followed suit, noticing that she'd been able to cover up the bruises that had speckled her arms that morning.

The two of them had met when Brielle requested his engineering expertise on an investigation. Her specialty as a private detective was hunting down items lost or stolen during the Holocaust, and her client was in search of a missing artifact. Tyler had been brought in to analyze the wreckage of a structure deliberately obliterated to disguise its original form, and their week together since then had shown him that she was a formidable woman.

As Brielle reached for a glass of wine, Tyler placed his hand on the small of her back and leaned in.

'Any luck?'

She drank half of the wine in three gulps and shook her head. 'Why do you think I need this?' Her British lilt was tinged with exasperation.

'What did the minister of the interior say?'

'The French don't think it's a credible threat. He assured me that his forces have taken every precaution necessary. In his words, the outcome of this summit is too important to interrupt on the hunches of two US Army retirees and a private investigator.'

Tyler was amused at being called a 'retiree'. Both he and Grant were still in their thirties.

Brielle took another drink. 'He also said I shouldn't even be here.'

'What did you say?'

'I told him one Jew wouldn't wreck the bloody summit.'

Tyler smirked. 'What did you really say?'

'I told him to take it up with the Turkish ambassador.'

At least they hadn't been thrown out, but Minister Jacques Fournier had been their last hope of cancelling the event. With the little they had to go on, Tyler couldn't blame the organizers for going forward with the party in spite of their warnings. In Brielle's latest case, her investigative partner Wade Plymouth had sent her a cryptic message that the artifact might have fallen into the hands of a white supremacist group, leading her to a deserted compound outside Oslo, Norway. There she found the destroyed metal framework, at which time she brought in Tyler and Grant to analyze it. What they discovered was much more than they expected. The evidence suggested an impending terrorist event, but Plymouth subsequently went missing, leaving the three of them to follow gut feelings and a thin thread of clues to the Eiffel Tower.

One name from Plymouth, however, convinced Tyler that the threat was real. He had been stunned to learn that the leader of the supposed terrorist group was Carl Zim, a vicious white supremacist focusing his ire on Muslim immigrants. Tyler had testified at the trial that put his brother in prison for murder of a Pakistani five years before, perhaps stoking the flames of Zim's hatred. With a background that engendered an intense fear and loathing toward the spread of Islam, Zim had great motive to kill as many Muslims as possible – the higher profile the better. The Eiffel Tower gathering was the perfect target, and because of his role in provoking Zim, Tyler felt some responsibility for preventing a tragedy. He just hadn't been able to convince anyone in authority that the danger was imminent.

Brielle's eyes locked onto his. 'No matter how this ends up, I've had fun with you this past week.'

'Fun? We almost got killed twice already.' The week with her had entailed a shipyard firefight with Zim's men in Copenhagen and a bar brawl in Amsterdam, during which Brielle had displayed her skill with a weapon. The training she'd received while serving as a Mahal foreign volunteer in the Israeli Defense Forces was something Tyler hadn't shared with the Turkish ambassador.

She took a leisurely sip from her glass, then said, 'Don't you find that the "almost" part is what makes it exhilarating?'

'It does make me think about taking a rest when this is over.'

'Where are you thinking of doing your resting?'

Tyler grinned and leaned closer. 'Do you have any suggestions?'

'I know a nice hotel on Majorca.'

'I thought your parents wouldn't approve, me not being one of the chosen people.'

'They only care about who I marry. I don't share my flings with them.'

'So I'd be a fling?'

Brielle's lips parted deliciously. 'Would you mind?'

'I don't mind being flung once in a while.'

Brielle looked as though she were going to get even naughtier when her gaze slipped past Tyler and the smile faded.

'What is it?' Tyler asked and turned to see what she was watching. Fournier was being escorted out of the party by a young man with a military bearing.

'He just whispered something to him,' Brielle said. 'It didn't look like good news.'

Tyler took her drink and set it on the bar. 'Let's find out what the hubbub is about.'

Tyler caught Grant's eye and signed to him using the American Sign Language they both knew.

There might be trouble. Stay frosty.

Grant nodded, took the smartphone from his pocket, and turned back toward the window.

Brielle held his elbow and they walked toward the door as if they wanted to get some fresh air.

Once they were outside, they spotted Fournier speaking with five policemen in riot gear who were gesturing at the east leg of the tower.

He and Brielle wandered closer until they were in earshot. Brielle translated for him.

'There's something wrong with this lift,' she said after listening for a moment. 'A maintenance crew is on the way up to fix it.'

With only one passenger elevator to the first floor working that day, any malfunction would require the guests to make the long walk down the stairs at the end of the evening.

'That's how they're getting onto the tower,' Tyler said. 'Come on.'

They raced over to the minister, who startled at their sudden appearance.

'You have to stop them,' Tyler said.

'Please go back inside,' the minister said in fluent, accented English. 'This doesn't concern you.'

'Those maintenance men are here as part of a ruse. There's going to be an attack.'

The minister shook his head in annoyance. He already knew Tyler's background – that he was a mechanical engineer with a Ph.D. from Stanford and a former US Army demolitions expert – but calling off the party would be a black eye for the French, so his credentials were overshadowed by more political concerns.

Fournier's eyes narrowed at Brielle. 'Did she put you up to this?'

'Minister,' Brielle said, 'this is a matter of life and death. I suggest you search the maintenance men thoroughly. I think you'll find they aren't who they say they are.'

'You think? They've already been searched. Carefully. Otherwise, they wouldn't have gotten on this tower.'

'They must have concealed their weapons.'

'*C'est incroyable*,' the minister said to the policemen, who shook their heads in disbelief.

'Do you want to take the chance that they aren't who they say they are? Or that they might be carrying a bomb?'

Fournier frowned at the mention of explosives, but said nothing.

At that moment four men dressed in blue overalls appeared, coming out of the small maintenance lift in the south pillar.

'I'll prove they're not lift experts,' Tyler said.

'How?'

'If they are in fact maintenance workers, they'll know details about how the elevator operates, right?'

Fournier looked at both of them for a moment and then must have decided caution was better than getting caught with his pants down.

He said something in French, and the squad of policemen raised their weapons and surrounded the maintenance workers. The four men immediately dropped their equipment bags and put their hands up with shocked looks on their faces.

'Can you interpret for me?' Tyler asked the minister. He took out his smartphone and tapped on the screen to bring up a web page with the Eiffel Tower's schematics that he had researched the day before.

He nodded. 'What do you want to ask them?'

'Just one question. What's the capacity of the lift in kilograms?' It was a simple question that had a very specific and unguessable answer, but an elevator maintenance worker should have known the number without hesitation.

The minister translated, and the lead worker paused at hearing the odd question. Fingers tightened on triggers.

Then the man blurted out a response.

The minister turned to Tyler. 'He wants to know which lift. There are nine throughout the tower.'

Tyler frowned. He was expecting bluster or even a made-up figure.

'The lift in the east pillar that they are supposedly fixing,' Tyler said.

The minister translated, and this time the response was immediate.

'He says it's 9,240 kilograms.'

Tyler looked down at his phone and clenched his jaw when he saw the screen. That was the correct figure.

'Is that right?' the minister asked.

Tyler glanced at Brielle, who tilted her head in frustration. 'You're joking.'

'He's correct,' Tyler said with surprise. He had been so confident this was part of the attack plan.

The minister stared at Tyler, then gestured to the maintenance men as he spoke. They picked up their bags and began to move toward the east pillar.

'Dr Locke, Ms Cohen,' Fournier said, 'you are no longer welcome at this party. Please leave. Now.'

Tyler wheeled around. He couldn't shake the intuition that something wasn't right about this situation. Before he had time to complete that thought, he spotted movement inside the closed gift shop pavilion across from the Salle Gustave Eiffel and realized what was happening.

The maintenance workers had been sent up as a

distraction. All of the police officers now had their backs to the gift shop.

'Down!' Tyler shouted, grabbing Brielle with one hand and tackling Fournier with the other arm.

Automatic weapon fire split the air, killing one of the policemen instantly. The minister was hit in the leg as they fell.

Brielle scrambled behind a metal girder and Tyler dragged the minister with him to join her.

Fournier's eyes were wide with shock. 'What's happening?'

Rounds pinged off the iron around them. Another policeman went down, and the rest were pinned by the withering assault.

Now Tyler realized why the elevator had been disabled. It would take several minutes for the police at the base to climb the tower. By then the attack would be over.

The gunmen didn't have enough manpower to wipe out the guests, but they could keep them inside the reception hall, which Tyler now believed was the real objective. That conclusion was reinforced when he heard the first explosion.

TWO

As Grant picked himself off the floor, shards of shattered glass tumbled down his tuxedo. If he hadn't seen the shadowy shape careening toward the window two seconds before it exploded, he would have caught the glass full in the face.

Panicked party-goers, some of them bloodied, screamed past Grant as they searched for an escape, but between the gunfire on the tower's deck and the explosion outside the window, there was nowhere to find safety. Grant was relieved to see no bodies lying on the floor. The blast must have been timed to blow out the window, leaving an open space for the next bomb to fly through.

Cool air streamed into the room through the gaping hole where the window used to be. Grant blinked and looked for the source of the airborne explosive, but there was no way to see where the attack had been launched from. A rocket-propelled grenade would have left a telltale streak of flame as it rocketed toward its target, but the attackers were using stealthier quadcopters for the assault. The sophisticated flying bombs weren't much bigger than a large garbage can lid and were painted black, making them incredibly difficult to see in the night sky. The quadcopters' bare bones design consisted of nothing more than a central pod carrying the control mechanism and high explosive, with a propeller on each of its four articulated arms.

The only reason Grant had gotten a warning at all that a bomb had been on its way was because of the preventive measures he and Tyler set up in the hotel room they had rented near the Eiffel Tower. They'd left the multi-paned window open so that their proprietary motion-tracking system would have a clear view of the tower.

The portable DeadEye targeting system was a product of Gordian Engineering, the firm the two of them worked for and that Tyler had founded. DeadEye had been developed for the military to help infantry units spot snipers. It took a snapshot image of a scene and then constantly checked that image against new high-definition video coming into the unit. If anything changed, it would alert the soldier monitoring it. Although it was constrained to stationary use due to the limitations of the computer's processing power, it was a powerful tool that could be used even at night.

The DeadEye in the hotel room, a prototype Grant had borrowed from the Gordian labs, was now pointed directly at the Eiffel Tower. When it detected movement in the air around the tower, it would send an alert to Grant's smartphone, and he'd see a visual of the target on his screen.

Two previous warnings had come in, but they were only birds, and Grant had to decrease the sensitivity of the unit.

The third warning came eight seconds before he spotted the quadcopter directly, leaving him just moments to duck.

Now that Grant knew the attack was underway, it was time to fight back. He tapped his phone and launched his own quadcopter, this one built by Gordian for a civilian project called Mayfly. It was an unmanned aerial vehicle developed for hazardous search and rescue missions, like the inspection of the Fukushima nuclear plant that melted down after being flooded by the Japan tsunami. The view on his smartphone was from the camera mounted on the front of the Mayfly drone they'd set up in the hotel room in case of emergency. Grant figured the blown-out window and gunshots outside counted as an emergency.

Normally the camera was the only accessory on the UAV, but Tyler and Grant had spent the past two days weaponizing the Mayfly. They'd given it a stinger. Now Grant would put the jury-rigged contraption to its first test in a combat scenario.

Using the simplified onscreen controls on his smartphone, Grant directed the Mayfly to take off. The screen showed the hotel room as it rose above the bed and threaded its way through the open window. Once it was outside, Grant dialed up the speed to full throttle. The electric motors whisked the UAV up and the Eiffel Tower filled the screen's view.

The DeadEye targeting system was linked to the camera on the Mayfly, superimposing the two images. A new white crosshair appeared on his smartphone screen, which meant another bomb was on the way. Grant directed the Mayfly to intercept.

He sat with his back to the exterior wall. There was no need to try to get a visual on the quadcopter from here. Standing would only reduce his level of control.

The approaching copter was moving so quickly he'd only have one pass to try to disable it. The Mayfly homed in on the target. Grant's finger hovered over the FIRE button. When the target crosshair filled the screen, the Mayfly would be close enough to attack.

This was going to be close. The first floor of the Eiffel Tower, the very spot where he sat, was getting awfully big in the background.

The dot grew larger. Larger. Only seconds now until it reached the Salle Gustave Eiffel and flew right through the shattered window to explode amongst the panicked crowd.

Grant couldn't wait any longer. The target engulfed the screen.

He fired.

Two prongs of a Taser mounted on the Mayfly lanced forward. The prongs latched onto the enemy quadcopter and sent fifty thousand volts through it.

As he'd hoped, the shock from the Taser short-circuited the copter's control mechanism. The quadcopter plummeted to the ground, automatically pulling the leads free from the Mayfly.

They didn't know how many quadcopters were coming,

but if the number exceeded three more, they were in real trouble because the Mayfly had only three Taser shots left.

Another crosshair bloomed on Grant's smartphone. He angled the Mayfly toward it. The two copters converged at high speed.

This time the crosshair grew exponentially. Grant timed it to when he thought the quadcopter would be in range. The crosshair filled the screen and he fired.

Nothing. The Taser prongs missed, and the enemy quadcopter zoomed by. It would be there in seconds.

Grant looked up and saw a red dot playing across the ceiling directly overhead. That was how the quadcopters were being aimed at their target. Someone on the ground had a laser, like the Army used for guiding smart bombs.

And this bomb was going to hit right above where he was sitting.

There were a few other people prone on the floor. He bellowed for them to move, and his deep voice was enough to get them to scramble whether they understood him or not.

Grant sprinted across the room and dived behind the bar.

For a moment he heard the whine of the quadcopter's rotor blades, and then the bomb exploded as it hit the ceiling.

Shrapnel flew across the room, taking three people down with the blast. Casualties wailed like banshees. Shielded by the bar, Grant had escaped injury.

The explosion didn't start any fires, but the smoke was enough to activate the sprinkler system, which doused the entire room.

Grant left the bar's cozy confines to see if he could spot the laser again, shielding his smartphone from the water with his coat as he walked.

The bright red dot was still dancing across the ceiling. There was at least one more bomb to intercept.

THREE

Tyler reloaded the MP-5 submachine gun he'd commandeered from one of the dead security officers.

'Last mag!' he yelled to Brielle.

'Mine too!' she shouted back, unloading another three-round burst at the attackers, who were well-covered inside the gift shop pavilion. 'I think I've hit one, but we're sitting ducks here. We need a better position.'

'The stairs. If we can get to high ground, we can end this.'

There was no reason for the gunmen to leave their positions. Tyler knew their purpose was to keep the guests inside the reception hall so that the explosives could finish the job. They also had a superior position over anyone ascending the stairs. The police would be cut to pieces if they tried storming their way up.

But something about the situation wasn't making sense to him. Tyler's company, Gordian, was well-known for disaster analysis – airplane crashes, oil-rig explosions, building collapses – so he had been Brielle's first choice for reconstructing the steel framework from Oslo. Gordian's advanced computer analysis tools indicated that the structure could be a section of the Eiffel Tower. Small pieces of quadcopter remains had been found amongst the wreckage, so Tyler and Grant had theorized that it could have been some kind of attack preparation against Paris's most famous landmark, the summit event being the most likely target.

But the terrorists couldn't be planning to bring down the entire tower. If that's what they intended, the gunmen and the quadcopters would be superfluous. In addition, collapsing the tower would require a huge quantity of explosives placed in just the right locations, and it would have been noticed by the advance security teams.

Tyler knew he was missing something, but what?

He fired another round and ducked again, turning his head as he did so and catching a glimpse of the maintenance men cowering behind him.

There were only three of them.

'Where's the other one?' he asked Brielle.

'The other what?'

'The fourth maintenance worker.'

'I hadn't noticed,' she said, firing another round. 'I've been a tad busy.'

'Ask them where he went.'

After she spoke, the three men pointed in the direction of the east pillar.

'They say he went downstairs.'

'Why?'

'They thought he ran off because he was scared.'

Tyler looked where they were pointing. To make it over there, the maintenance worker would have had to cover open space, exposing himself to a bullet storm. Staying where he was would have been far safer.

Unless he knew no one would be firing at him.

Tyler suddenly realized what the actual target could be.

The elevator.

'Brielle,' Tyler said, 'ask these guys if they know what was wrong with the lift.'

She gave him a questioning look and then translated. The three of them shook their heads.

If the workmen could fix the elevator easily, the guests would certainly use it to go back down once this was over. A bomb set next to it might be what the attackers were planning all along. No one would think to look during the chaos of an evacuation. Whoever was sending the quadcopters could watch the elevator windows with a telescope to see who got on and then blow up the bomb as the lift passed.

'How long has the missing man been working with them?' Tyler asked Brielle.

The answer came back. 'Two weeks. They don't know much about him, though they mentioned that his accent sounds odd.'

'He must be an impostor. Did you recognize him?'

Brielle shook her head. 'I couldn't see his face very well under the hardhat, but he had glasses, a mustache, and beard.'

A disguise. Tyler was so focused on the lead worker that he hadn't paid much attention to the others.

'We need to lay down suppressing fire so I can make it to the stairway.'

'But I—'

'No time to argue. One. Two. Three!'

Tyler sprinted for the stairs, unloading his entire magazine in the direction of the pavilion as he ran. Brielle did the same with her weapon. Bullets zinged off the metal around him. His luck held out until he was within a few feet of the stairwell.

That's when the bullet hit him in the left arm. Whether it was a direct hit or a ricochet he couldn't tell, but the jolt of pain caused him to drop the submachine gun.

Tyler stumbled against the safety grating and tumbled down the first flight of stairs. He shook his head and held his arm. Given the blood streaming from both sides of his bicep, it seemed like the bullet had passed through his muscle, missing the bone. The only saving grace was that they had been firing relatively small 9mm rounds. His arm wasn't useless, but every time he moved it, agony radiated from the wound like a beacon.

He picked himself up and staggered down the stairs. As he walked he looked for any sign of movement. When he'd gone down five flights and cleared the bottom of the first level, he saw someone crouched on a catwalk directly underneath the Salle Gustave Eiffel. The shadowy figure would have been invisible to anyone not actively searching for him.

The man hadn't spotted him yet, so Tyler had a chance at sneaking up on him. Without the MP-5, surprise would be his only weapon.

He thought he could make the climb over the safety grating encapsulating the stairs. The gunfire and screams would cover any noise he made. But he realized his chance of success was still small. He needed a backup plan.

He took out his phone and tapped quickly, starting a text to Grant.

I'm going to need your help.

FOUR

Tyler's tuxedo was a mess. Ripping his cuff as he climbed over the safety fence was just the latest indignity. The left sleeve of his jacket was saturated with blood. Stains mottled the fabric as if it were black and brown tie-dye. The knees on his pants were torn from crawling around on the deck of the tower while he was under fire. He wondered if James Bond's tuxes had been made of Teflon.

The only reason he was even thinking about the state of his clothes was to keep his mind off his throbbing arm. Several times he had to bite his lip from crying out as he lowered himself gently to the catwalk, careful to minimize both noise and vibration.

He settled into a crouch, putting pressure on his arm to stanch some of the blood flow. In addition to the pain, he was beginning to feel woozy, either from shock or blood loss.

Tyler crept forward, more afraid of losing his balance and falling over the side than he was of the man in front of him. His quarry was still hunched over, intent on some unseen task, wearing black now instead of the gray overalls he'd had on earlier.

Tyler considered what to do, but he didn't have much of a choice. His injury meant a fight wouldn't last long and might end up with him splattered on the pavement below. At this point his best option was simply to get close enough to charge the guy and push him over the side while he wasn't looking. Not a sporting plan, but the one likeliest to keep himself alive.

Although the tower was illuminated by so many lights it could practically be seen from space, shadows from the ironwork played across the catwalk. Every time he took a step, Tyler went from dark to light and then back again, which only added to the disorientation he felt as the blood drained out of him. If the bullet had nicked an artery, he wouldn't last much longer.

Tyler shook off the feeling and kept edging forward. He'd launch himself when he was within two body lengths. Any closer and the man might hear him.

He got within twice that distance when another explosion went off up above them. Grant must have intercepted another drone. Or missed. Tyler couldn't tell. But the shockwave created enough of a tremor that the man in black leaned back to catch himself and turned slightly in the process so that Tyler was now in his peripheral vision.

The man froze. Then his head inched around until he was looking Tyler in the eye. He smiled.

Without the glasses, beard, and mustache, he was now

recognizable as Carl Zim. Tyler had only seen a grainy photo of him, never in person. Zim's wavy blond hair and angular nose lent the Aryan look he worshipped.

'Dr Tyler Locke,' he said. 'You're late.'

'Actually, it looks like I'm right on time.'

Zim nodded at the bullet wound. 'Did Gabrielle Cohen give you that? Jews are so unpredictable.'

'No, it was one of your friends. I see you managed to talk your way onto the maintenance crew even though you're American.' Stalling was Tyler's best tactical play at the moment.

'*Mon français est excellent*. One good thing about having a Parisian mother.'

Tyler rose and Zim did the same. The black he was wearing wasn't a ninja outfit, but rather a tuxedo, stained and torn to make him look like one of the patrons escaping from the party. In the chaos below, he would be escorted to a safe position where he could slip away quietly before anyone realized who he was.

Zim was shorter than Tyler, but wiry and built for speed. Tyler could see cords of muscle flexing along his neck. Tyler's gun was long gone, and Zim couldn't have smuggled a weapon past the security screen. Fists and gravity were all they had to fight each other. Not good odds for Tyler.

'Grant will be here any second now,' Tyler said, 'so you might as well—'

The words had the opposite effect from what he

intended. Instead of hesitating or looking behind him, Zim threw himself at Tyler.

Without the ability to sidestep the attack, Tyler planted his feet and twisted his body so that his good arm would take the brunt of the impact. He planned to use Zim's momentum against him and graze him enough to toss him off the catwalk.

Zim didn't play along. He pulled up short and launched a roundhouse punch at Tyler's injured bicep. Tyler ducked to protect his arm, but that put his ear in the path of Zim's fist.

The jarring impact nearly ended the fight right then, but Tyler was able to grab Zim's arm, throwing them both off-balance. They locked together, each of them grasping the other's lapels to keep from going over the side.

Tyler used the only weapon he had left and head-butted Zim in the face, breaking the man's nose. Blood gushed out, but Zim just grinned, the scarlet sheen coating his teeth. Tyler guessed it wasn't his first broken nose.

Zim kneed Tyler in the gut and then loosened his right hand to sink his fingers into Tyler's arm. Tyler let out a feral scream and nearly blacked out from the pain. He keeled over and fell to the grating of the catwalk. His head cracked into the metal and buzzed from the collision.

Zim spat a mouthful of blood. 'Now you're going to make yourself useful and cause an even bigger distraction when I get to ground level. See you down there.'

He placed a foot on Tyler's chest and pushed. Tyler

grabbed Zim's ankle, but he had no leverage. He felt himself sliding over the side.

The buzz grew even louder. At first Tyler thought he was about to pass out, but he realized that the sound was not in his head. A shadow fell across his eye.

It was the Mayfly. Grant had gotten his text message and made the decision to pull it off protective duty.

Zim braced himself to beat back the quadcopter, which weighed only a few pounds. A hefty swat as it swooped toward him would be enough to send it careening into a girder.

But the Mayfly just hovered there. Zim looked at it in confusion, then shrugged and put his entire effort into one last shove.

Instead, his body went rigid as Tyler heard a new sound: the crackle of electricity. Two shiny metal leads protruded from Zim's neck.

Zim's face contorted in agony and disbelief. With all the strength he had left, Tyler pushed against Zim's foot. Zim tilted back as if he were a mannequin and fell off the catwalk.

Tyler watched Zim's descent. His head hit a girder as he tumbled, sending his body spinning to the ground. A thump was followed by shrieks from an unseen woman. The blood pooling under Zim's head suggested that the impact was lethal.

Tyler lay flat for a few moments while he caught his breath. Then he remembered about Zim's mission. Something he'd been hunched over. Tyler had to check it out and assess whether it presented any danger.

With supreme effort, he pushed himself up. He lurched to his feet and steadied himself before trying to walk forward along the narrow catwalk.

A bright light flashed directly in front of him. Before his brain could even process the sound of the explosion, he was thrown backward.

Tyler's last thought before his mind went blank was that, just like Zim, he was falling.

FIVE

Brielle stretched as she stepped out of the shower, the sudden burst of steam fogging the mirrors in the suite's bathroom. She toweled off, not bothering to wipe the glass. She didn't want to see the bruises that were just starting to fade. She took a sip from the flute resting on the counter. The hot soaks and fine champagne were doing wonders in helping her sore muscles recover.

She'd never stayed in such an expensive hotel room before. Not that she had anything against it; she simply never had been able to afford it. The sumptuous accommodations at L'Hotel in the chic Saint-Germain-des-Prés section of Paris were a thanks from the French government for her part in averting disaster at the Eiffel Tower, and she hadn't protested at all when the gesture was made. She didn't mind a bit of luxury while she planned her next move.

Nearly a week after the assault, the investigation was still ongoing. Only minutes after Tyler went searching for the missing maintenance man, snipers in a French Air Force helicopter took out the gunmen inside the gift shop pavilion, ending the attack. Five security officers had been killed, but Fournier survived, as did all of the guests at the party, though some of those caught in the blasts were still recuperating in hospital.

There were strange aspects of the event that continued to puzzle Brielle. Grant Westfield, an explosives expert in his own right, reported that none of the bombs would have been powerful enough to kill more than a few of the guests. Even if they'd all gone off inside the reception hall, at best the attackers would have killed several dozen partygoers, with no hope of targeting a specific guest. The person who had been controlling the quadcopters from the ground was still at large.

Another unsolved mystery was the segment of the operation on the catwalk under the Salle Gustave Eiffel, where Tyler had fought with Carl Zim. The bomb that had gone off there was just powerful enough to destroy a portion of the tower's utilities, nothing more. The preliminary assessment was that the attack had been meant to disrupt the summit, but that it made little sense as all of the meetings had been concluded before that evening.

No group had yet claimed responsibility, but fingers had started to point. As they'd suspected, Zim had been the leader of the attack, but they weren't going to get much vital info from him since his body lay in the Paris morgue. The rest of the gunmen were identified as members of a French right-wing extremist group who had sympathies with the neo-Nazi movement. It seemed like a clear case of fanatics attacking their new sworn enemies: representatives of the Muslim world that was encroaching on Europe and America.

And then they found out how the gunmen had lain in wait inside the pavilion.

A special exhibit showing rare photographs of the tower's construction had been set up inside the second story of the pavilion, above the gift shop. Three hidden walls had been built into the design. The day before the attack, the five gunmen hid themselves and their weapons inside the display, going as far as using plastic bottles to collect their urine while they waited to emerge after the gift shop closed. Then at the prearranged signal, most likely the appearance of the maintenance men, they opened fire.

Of course, the investigators' first priority was to discover who was responsible for the tower's clever infiltration, and that's where the situation got sticky. Following the money, they discovered that the display had been paid for and the photos supplied by a company based in Tel Aviv. The authorities were trying to sift through the documentation to find out who actually owned the company, information obscured by a series of shell corporations.

With the discovery of a potential Israeli connection, the recriminations in the Middle East were fast approaching a fever pitch. The Muslim nations claimed it was a conspiracy dreamed up by the Mossad as a means of punishing them for attacks against Israel. Tensions had escalated quickly, and armies on both sides were now poised on the brink of war, with planes, tanks, and soldiers massing along the Israeli borders. It would take only a spark to ignite a full-scale attack in either direction, and with rumors of nuclear weapons on both sides, the Western nations, Russia, and China could be drawn into a conflict that would result in the start of World War III.

That's why Brielle drained her glass. No sense in letting it go to waste if nobody would be left to enjoy it next week.

She put on the silver Star of David necklace her grandfather had given her, dropped the towel on the floor, and tiptoed into the suite's bedroom. She slipped under the covers and rested her head on Tyler's chest.

He stroked her damp hair. 'I ordered breakfast for us while you were showering.'

'Croissants?'

'And marmalade, although I never have understood the Brits' fondness for orange jelly.'

'And I never understood how you Americans can eat cold pizza in the morning. It's disgusting.'

'What else can you find to eat in a college dorm at six a.m.?'

'At the University of Edinburgh we had what is called a dining hall. Didn't you have those at MIT?'

'Sure. But they frowned on going down to meals in your underwear.'

'Somehow I doubt that.'

Brielle inadvertently ran her hand across the stitches in his arm. Tyler didn't flinch, but she could feel him tense.

'Sorry. Does it still hurt?'

'I'm only glad it wasn't my pitching arm. As it is, the doctors say I won't be taking the Mariner's mound for a few weeks.'

She supposed that was some American baseball metaphor. Just like a man to play down a gunshot wound and concussion requiring a hospital stay. The blast that Zim set off had thrown Tyler backwards, but through sheer luck he landed on the catwalk instead of going over the side. Three days of nursing in the suite had made him feel well enough for more strenuous activities. He'd recovered quickly and thanked her well for the pampering.

'Grant made it home all right, I expect,' Brielle said as she ran her fingers along the channels between each of Tyler's abdominal muscles. 'He seemed reluctant to leave you until I told him I'd take care of you.'

'Yeah, he got the message after that. He's back in Seattle now. I'm going there myself in a couple of days. When my sister heard I'd been shot, she insisted on meeting me there to make sure my recuperation goes smoothly.'

'Do you see her much?'

'No. Most of the time she's traveling the world doing research into endangered species. She's a zoologist. In fact, we don't get to see each other that often because of our schedules, so it'll be nice to spend time with her. Why don't you come back and meet her?'

Brielle withdrew her hand abruptly, and Tyler stopped stroking her hair.

'We've talked about this,' she said. 'I may not be a strict orthodox Jew, but this isn't something that can be long-term. My parents wouldn't understand. Family is very important to me.'

'It is to me, too.'

'So is my religion. Unless you plan to convert, let's just enjoy our time here together.'

Tyler let out a tiny sigh, but he went back to caressing her hair. 'Absolutely.'

Brielle didn't mention that she would soon be near enough to Seattle to drive there. Wade Plymouth, who had called with the tip that led them to Zim, was the only other employee at Brielle's boutique investigation firm. Her latest information revealed that his last known location was at a bar in a small town south of the Canadian border in Washington state. If she were going to track down her missing friend and colleague, that was the best place to start, and it wasn't Tyler's job to help her. She could tell that spending any more time with him would make it that much harder to tear herself away. A visit to his home would be a bad idea. Better to bask in one last day with him and leave it at that.

Tyler's phone rang. 'Grant,' he said with a smile when he saw the number. He took the call without moving. 'I'm in bed with a beautiful woman, so this better be good.'

After a few moments, his smile disappeared and he sat up. 'You're sure?' He said 'uh-huh' a few times, and then said, 'Okay. Tell them I'll be there tomorrow morning.' He hung up.

'What was that about?' Brielle asked.

'It looks like I'm going to California instead. Grant's already booked me on Air France.'

'How soon?'

Tyler kissed her deeply, sending a shiver down her spine. After a long while, he pulled away and said, 'We have some time left. Grant said the flight isn't for another six hours.'

'What's in California?'

'Pleasant Valley State Prison. The FBI is meeting me there so we can talk to an inmate. He said he'd only speak to the Feds if I was there as well.'

Brielle could see that the thought of the impending meeting troubled Tyler. 'Why you?'

'Because I helped put him there. The prisoner is Victor Zim, Carl Zim's older brother.'

SIX

When the wind blew in their direction, the stench was overpowering. Tyler made sure to close the Suburban's exterior vents as they approached Coalinga on Interstate-5. Located halfway between San Francisco and Los Angeles, the section of freeway was well-known to travelers as the site of Harris Ranch, the largest cattle processing facility on the west coast. Tyler was amused to see that despite the aroma, the ranch had its own inn and restaurant in addition to a small runway. He wondered how well the building's air conditioning filtered out the smell from a hundred thousand cattle. Tyler imagined that Brielle wouldn't appreciate the ranch's nickname. It was dubbed 'Cowschwitz' by animal rights activists because of the two hundred million pounds of beef processed in its slaughterhouse every year.

The central valley of California is among the most productive agricultural regions on Earth, and Tyler had seen nothing but fields and orchards on the three-hour drive from the Bay Area. Special Agent Melanie Harris had filled the time with the region's history as she drove. She joked that the owners of the ranch were no relation, but that she wouldn't mind being adopted.

It would be just the two of them visiting Victor Zim. Zim hadn't provided any hint of what he would reveal, but Harris thought he might be willing to make a deal to shorten his sentence. Tyler wasn't as hopeful. Zim was serving twenty-five to life for premeditated murder, having rejected an offer to plea down before he was convicted. He could have had a change of heart about bargaining now that his brother was dead, but Tyler thought that the word of a man who'd killed six innocent people was worthless.

They turned off the highway at Jayne Road just beyond Harris Ranch and drove past stands of almond and orange groves toward the ironically named Pleasant Valley State Prison. Tyler would bet not a single person at the penitentiary – neither inmate nor guard – would describe the twenty-year-old prison as pleasant.

A mile from I-5, groves gave way to fallow fields, and the sprawling prison came into view. Adjacent to the prison was a mental hospital. The combined units housed more than five thousand inmates, including Sirhan Sirhan, Robert Kennedy's assassin.

Harris drove past the entrance of the hospital and turned left at the next road to take them into the vast prison parking lot. After they passed through the security gate and parked, Tyler opened the door to heat that he rarely experienced in his home town of Seattle, particularly in mid June. The sun blazed through a cloudless sky, baking the asphalt. Thermal waves billowed so thickly that it caused mini-mirages.

A thin but fit blonde, Harris put on her jacket despite the heat. It was her effort to project the FBI's sense of professionalism, a trait Tyler admired. He had specifically requested that she be assigned to this interrogation because he'd saved her life on a Miami cruise ship a few years back, and they'd kept in touch ever since.

'You ready for this?' she asked as they walked toward the visitors' building.

'Sure,' Tyler said with a shrug to give the impression that he wasn't as stressed as he really was. 'Why not?'

'Well, you did send the guy to prison and kill his brother. Any new ideas about why Carl was up on the Eiffel Tower in the first place?'

Tyler had thought about it for the last week and couldn't come up with any valid reason. The bomb he'd planted was too small to do any significant structural damage.

'We don't know yet,' he said. 'Gordian's French unit is analyzing the pieces of wreckage to see if they can find anything revealing. I understand the French authorities will release Carl's autopsy results soon, but I can't see how that will help. What I'd like to know is how Victor Zim found out I was the one who killed his brother. That has to be the reason he would meet with the FBI only if I agreed to come. How did word get to him all the way out here?'

Harris shook her head. 'We're checking into that.

Probably through some French journalist. Carl must have a few men still scattered out there to feed info to Victor.'

'Like the one who was controlling the quadcopter bombs from somewhere off the tower? If he had a telescope, he could have seen me fighting with Carl.'

'We'll get him soon. Once we track down André Laroche and bring him into custody, we'll have no trouble finding the rest of Carl's gang.'

Laroche was a Jewish immigrant from France now living in the Seattle area. The shell corporation that funded the Eiffel Tower display above the gift shop was traced back to him, so he was now the prime suspect for funding the attack. The fact that Laroche had gone missing just a few days after the assault enhanced the suspicion.

Tyler had never met the man and was only familiar with the name because his sister, Alexa, had been working for him on an unrelated project. Tyler didn't like the coincidence, but he couldn't fathom a reason why the attack on the Eiffel Tower and Alexa working for Laroche would be related. He was still trying to figure out how to break the news to Alexa that her patron was the mastermind behind the attack.

'It's hard to believe he's involved. You still haven't found him?'

'We have agents searching his house in Seattle right now. We'll find him.'

'He has a lot of money,' Tyler said. 'It could be a long time before you hunt him down.'

Harris's tight lips told him that she wasn't as confident as she sounded. She stopped and glanced at the prison entrance. 'You clear on how this is going to go?'

Tyler nodded. 'I just sit there and respond only if you tell me to.' He didn't have to say that it would be uncomfortable staring into the face of the criminal he'd testified against, who also happened to be the brother of the man he'd killed.

'Good,' Harris said. 'Interrogations can be tricky, so let me steer the direction of the conversation.'

They passed through more security inside, and Harris handed over her weapon. They were escorted to a private interrogation cell and took their seats to wait for Victor Zim. The room met Tyler's expectations. Gray bars supplementing the cinder-block walls, a metal table topped with a welded steel loop and bolted to the concrete floor, and three aluminum chairs were the extent of the spartan furnishings.

The squeal of unoiled hinges heralded the approach of Zim. Tyler recalled the trial that brought Victor here.

Victor was a gifted chemical engineer working at a plastics plant in Oakland, and Carl was a construction foreman at a different firm. Their baby brother, David, died in the World Trade Center collapse on 9/11. That day he had been waiting tables at the Windows on the World restaurant to put himself through college at NYU. The two surviving brothers tried to join the army in the aftermath but were turned away because both failed psychological exams in which they displayed tendencies toward extremist behavior.

The two of them became heavily involved in militia activities on weekends, traveling to private compounds in the forests of the Sierra Nevada where they received training in weapons and tactical situations. Their constant paramilitary drills for a hypothetical Muslim terrorist attack drove them into the embrace of white supremacist groups.

Victor's pent-up rage and need for revenge reached a peak when he assaulted a Pakistani executive one day at the plant and was summarily fired.

Three months later Victor sneaked back into the plant to sabotage the facility, using his extensive expertise and knowledge of its layout to overheat one of the processing tanks. Six people, including the Pakistani executive, were killed in the subsequent blast. Initially, the police thought it was an industrial accident, and had it not been for Tyler's investigation, it would have been a perfect crime.

Gordian Engineering was one of the foremost forensic engineering and analysis firms in the world. As the former captain of an Army combat engineering company, Tyler had gained extensive experience with explosives. Although he had founded Gordian, Tyler left the day-to-day operations to his former professor, Miles Benson, who became CEO.

Tyler's role was to take the lead in high-profile and unusual jobs as Gordian's chief of special operations, and the chemical plant explosion had been his investigation. During the analysis of the destruction, Tyler determined that the supposedly malfunctioning temperature regulator was an almost exact duplicate that had been installed in place of the original. He was the only one who had noticed that it was the next year's model, different from the previous year's model only in the updated font of the brand's logo.

When they tracked the purchase of the regulator to Victor Zim, Tyler's testimony had been enough to get him convicted. They also suspected that Carl was an accomplice, but there wasn't enough evidence to bring him to trial, and Victor wouldn't testify against Carl to reduce his sentence.

Tyler recognized Victor's combination of methodical planning and desire for violence in Carl's attack. The brothers had the same qualities. The only difference was that Victor Zim didn't look the part. Tyler remembered Victor at the defendant's table as a pudgy man with receding hair, someone who ate a lot of donuts at his desk and spent his exercise time at the militia encampments lying on his considerable stomach to fire guns.

The prison bars slammed shut and two hulking guards accompanied an even larger man between them. This was not the Victor Zim from the trial.

The face was a few years older and the pudginess was gone, replaced by angular creases that would be at home on a marble statue. Every trace of flab had been transformed into coils of ropey muscle that made his prison uniform ridiculously tight across the shoulders. This was a man who spent every minute in the yard at the weight sets, possibly as a way to defend himself from marauding gangs. Someone would have to be extremely confident in his fighting ability to take Zim on.

His hair was shorn to a buzz cut. Black tattoos of skulls and flame-girdled dragons snaked down his arms. Knowing he was going to be in prison for the rest of his life, Zim must have adapted quickly to a regimen that would keep him alive.

Zim strolled in as though he were the one in charge. He stared at Tyler, who returned the gaze with equal force. While Zim had a bemused grin on his face, Tyler kept a stony expression.

The guards shackled him to the table, and Tyler didn't mind the safety precaution. Desperate men with nothing to lose were the most dangerous type. Though Tyler was a combat veteran and able to handle himself in a fight, his current condition meant he wasn't at a hundred percent. No sense in taking chances with this man.

As he'd been instructed, Tyler let Harris do the talking.

'My name is Special Agent Melanie Harris from the FBI, and you know Tyler Locke.'

Zim glanced at Harris and then back at Tyler. 'I didn't know if you'd actually show.'

'We're here because you said you have information pertaining to the Eiffel Tower attack,' Harris said. 'We're in a hurry, so get on with it.'

'No, you're not. If this isn't the most important thing you're doing today, I'd be surprised.'

Tyler didn't look at Harris, but he could feel the annoyance radiating from her. 'Your brother, Carl, was killed seven days ago trying to attack a summit in Paris. Did you know anything about his plan?'

'I know that this guy here was the one who pushed him off the Eiffel Tower.'

'How do you know that?'

Zim shrugged. 'Word gets around.'

'Why are we here, Mr Zim?'

'I'll only talk to Locke.'

Harris shook her head. 'You're talking to *me*.'

'Yeah, and that's over with now. If you don't like it, get the hell out of here. Or is he deaf and dumb now? Should I write it down for him?'

Harris paused, then turned to Tyler and nodded at him.

Zim laughed. 'You need her permission to speak? What, is she your lawyer, too?'

Tyler leaned forward with an unflinching stare. 'What do you want to tell me, Zim?'

'So you haven't gone mute.'

'No, but looking at you makes me wish I'd gone blind.'

Zim laughed again, this time a full guffaw. 'Wow. You weren't this funny in court.'

'Why was your brother on the tower last week? We figured out his plan before he even got there. That's why it didn't succeed.'

Zim sat back in his chair with a self-satisfied smirk. 'Huh. It didn't? You sure about that?'

'What do you mean?'

'You just think you know what this is all about. And here I was under the impression you were a smart guy. MIT grad. Ph.D. in engineering from Stanford. Served in Iraq and Afghanistan. Started your own company when you were thirty. Those are some pretty impressive credentials. And yet, you don't know squat.'

'Why don't you enlighten us, Zim? Carl's dead. No reason to hide it any more. Maybe Special Agent Harris here will even put in a good word for you. You could get out of here in twenty-three years instead of twenty-five.'

'I don't want anything from her.'

'Then what do you want?'

'I want to see the look on your face when I tell you that I'm going to return the favor.'

'What favor?'

'You took my brother from me, and I'm going to do the same for you. It's Alexa, right?'

Tyler jumped up from his seat so quickly that his chair crashed into the bars behind him. He would have launched himself at Zim if Harris hadn't grabbed his arm. Tyler winced as she dug her fingers into his healing wound, which only made him angrier.

Zim noticed the grimace. 'Did Carl hurt you? Looks like he went down with a fight.'

'He went down screaming like a girl,' Tyler growled. 'And I swear, if you have your friends do anything to my sister—'

'You'll what? Send me to prison? Your threats sound a lot stupider than mine. Besides, I don't need friends to kill her. I'll make sure it happens personally.'

It was Tyler's turn to laugh. He shook off Harris and

straightened up. 'Well, that actually makes me feel better. If you ever get out of here, which I seriously doubt, you'll have to be released to a nursing home. Why don't you think about that while you stare at the walls of your spacious eight-by-eight cell?'

'Boy, you really got me there, Locke,' Zim said with a smile. 'Believe me, now that you've taken my second brother from me, there's nothing you can do to scare me.'

'Zim, the minute I walk out of here, I won't think about you another day in my life.'

'Even if I write you letters?'

Tyler didn't answer. He was done with this guy. 'Let's go,' he said to Harris.

Harris nodded to the guards. Tyler turned his back on Zim and waited for the bars to open.

'I'll be thinking about *you*, Locke,' Zim taunted. 'Every hour of every day.'

Tyler ground his teeth waiting for the buzz to sound. When it did, he squeezed through and kept walking until he was outside.

When Harris caught up with him, he was already on his mobile phone. Tyler recognized a real threat when he heard it. Zim wasn't bluffing. He had some kind of plan, and Alexa was the target.

SEVEN

Outside Tyler's house overlooking downtown Seattle from the Magnolia bluff, Grant Westfield rummaged through the back of his Tahoe looking for anything he could change into. After a two-hour weightlifting session at the gym, his workout top and shorts were overly aromatic. Stinking to high heaven was not the most pleasant way to catch up with his best friend's sister.

Grant thought he'd left an old T-shirt in the SUV after he'd washed it one day, but he came up empty. He slammed the hatch. There was nothing to do except hope Alexa could tolerate the smell.

Tyler had called from California to give him the quick rundown on his interrogation of Victor Zim. It would take Tyler at least four hours to get back to Seattle, and he was concerned that Zim's militia colleagues would take the opportunity to go after Alexa, so he'd asked Grant to keep an eye on her until he returned and they could figure out how to proceed.

Of course, Grant agreed to the favor without hesitation. He ran his workout towel over his head to mop up the residual sweat, tossed it through the driver's window, and headed for the front door.

Grant hadn't seen Alexa in years, not since Karen's funeral. Tyler's wife had died in a car accident, and other than their father, his baby sister was the only family he had left. The week of Karen's death had been a blur for all of them, and the somber circumstances meant Grant hadn't spoken more than a few token platitudes to Alexa. Her boyfriend at the time seemed to keep her at arm's length.

She'd been to Seattle only once since then, while Grant was traveling overseas. His vague memory of her was of a pretty, chubby blonde who shared Tyler's square jaw, brace-straightened teeth, and sky-blue eyes.

Normally, Grant would walk right into Tyler's house, but with his sister there, going in unannounced didn't seem like a good idea, especially if the boyfriend were present. He rang the doorbell, an odd sensation.

A few moments later, bare feet padded across hardwood floors. The door opened, and when Grant saw the woman standing in the doorway, he nearly stepped back to make sure he was at the right house.

Instead of a chubby blonde, a svelte redhead smiled back at him. Dressed in a form-fitting V-neck shirt and body-hugging jeans, she bore little resemblance to the woman Grant recalled. Grant couldn't help looking her up and down, and he caught her doing the same to him.

'Grant!' She threw her arms wide and lunged at him, wrapping Grant in an embrace before he could react. She had a surprisingly firm hold on him, and he returned the hug gently.

She pulled away and said, 'Those muscles. Wow! You are even bigger than I remembered. What are you? Two forty? Two forty-five?'

He realized he was gaping and closed his mouth. 'Two-fifty. I'm sorry, Alexa. For a second, I didn't recognize you. You colored your hair.'

'Actually, the blonde was a dye job. This is my natural color. I like to change it up once in a while. I see you do, too. It looks good shaved.'

'Thanks.'

'I've also lost some weight since the last time you saw me. Bought one of those extreme workout DVDs. It got me to drop thirty pounds in three months, but the first week was hell. I see you're still working out.'

'Yeah. Sorry about the stench.'

Alexa eyed his tank top. 'It's not too bad. Nothing that a good shower won't fix. Come on in,' she said, and gestured for him to enter. 'Tyler said you'd be dropping by. I told him I didn't need a babysitter, but when he mentioned it was going to be you, I changed my mind.' She winked at him.

Her flirty behavior was definitely different than at the funeral. Grant smiled wanly and followed her inside.

'Want a beer?' Alexa asked, pulling a Fat Tire from the fridge.

'Sure.' She pulled a second bottle from the shelf and gave him one. They went to the living room and sat across from each other. He forced himself to keep from groaning as he settled into the couch, his joints and muscles aching from the tough workout. The soft cushions were more soothing than he'd ever admit.

Instead of taking in the beautiful view of the city through the huge windows as most visitors did, Alexa focused on Grant intently and smiled.

He took a long swig and looked around. 'Is your boyfriend with you? Bart, wasn't it?'

'Bert. No, he's not around anymore.'

'I'm sorry to hear that.'

'Don't be. He was nice, but kind of a stick-in-the-mud, as I'm sure you noticed when you met him. No, I decided to enjoy the single life for a while. You?'

Grant shook his head and took another drink. He could think of ten smart-aleck things to say – comebacks he wouldn't normally hold back – but this was Tyler's sister. His little sister. His attractive little sister.

'Yeah,' Alexa said, 'Tyler told me you like to keep it fast and loose.'

Grant raised an eyebrow. 'Did he?'

She put up her hands. 'I think he meant it as a compliment.'

The farther the conversation went down this road, the closer Grant was to getting himself in trouble, in Tyler's house no less. He changed the subject.

'What did Tyler tell you about why he asked me to come by?'

'Just that he wanted you to keep me company while he was on his way back. He should be here later this afternoon.'

'Mmmm,' was all Grant said. If Tyler hadn't revealed the real danger just yet, then Grant wasn't going to either. 'How long have you been in town?'

'A couple of days. I thought I'd kill two birds with one stone.'

'How so?'

'Well, first of all I wanted to make sure Tyler was taking care of himself. You know him. Always ready to get back into action before he should. I was worried he was staying in France to head up Gordian's part in the investigation.'

'Uh, no,' Grant said, 'he thought it would be better to relax there before taking the long flight home.'

'Right,' Alexa said, her eyes narrowed with suspicion. 'And then he flies straight to California?'

'Important business. But he promised to ease up for a couple of weeks once he gets back.' Grant took another swig. 'So what's the other bird?'

'I was supposed to meet with a man who lives here. André Laroche. Do you know him?'

Although Tyler had told him over the phone about Laroche's potential involvement with the Eiffel Tower, it was another piece of info he'd let Tyler reveal to her. 'The name's familiar.'

Alexa leaned back and put her feet up on the coffee table. 'He's a timber millionaire. Owns a huge mansion on Mercer

Island. You guys know some of the Microsoft and Amazon billionaires, so I thought you might have run across him. I had a meeting planned with him, but his assistant called to say he wasn't available all of a sudden.'

'Did she say why?'

'No, and that's unusual. Marlo is always a sweetie, but she was very curt about it.'

'What were you supposed to be meeting about?'

'He hired me about a year ago. I'm back because of a video I shot this past April.'

'What video?'

Alexa rolled her eyes. 'Tyler hasn't told you? What a shocker. He's probably embarrassed.'

'He never mentioned it, but I doubt it's because he's embarrassed.'

'I'm the laughing stock of the scientific community. *I'm* embarrassed, why shouldn't he be?'

'About what?'

'About the Loch Ness video. Surely you saw it online sometime in the last week.'

Grant shrugged. 'I'd only consume the news if I could take it in pill form.'

'Too depressing?'

'Nothing I can do about it. I figure if it's important, someone will tell me.'

'Well, I've got something to tell you. Better yet, I'll show you.'

Alexa hopped up and scampered across the floor on her

toes. She returned moments later carrying a laptop and plopped herself down next to him.

'Boy, you do smell. I'll live, but we'll have to get you into a shower soon.' She opened the laptop and clicked on the browser, bringing up a YouTube page titled, *Loch Ness Monster Discovered?*

Grant could see a few comments underneath. 'Fake!' the first said. The second said, 'Spielberg has nothing to worry about.' The one below that, 'How do we even know that's Loch Ness?' It already had over three hundred thousand views.

'The Loch Ness monster? You found *the* Loch Ness monster?'

'That's what Laroche thinks.'

'And you posted this online?' he asked.

'Are you kidding? Without any other evidence? I have a Ph.D. in biology and I'm hoping to get a teaching position somewhere. Do you think it would really help my case to become known as a Nessie hunter?'

Grant understood. Even with a degree from a prestigious university like Northwestern, she would be hard-pressed to find a position if she had a reputation as a crank.

'Then how did the video get online?'

'I'm guessing my colleague posted it.'

'Who's that?'

Alexa burbled out a breath between her lips. 'Mike Dillman, a videographer who was with me at the loch that day. It was supposed to be a short-term gig. I didn't really think anything would come of it, but it was a lot of money and would tide me over while I was writing grant proposals. I also piggybacked some research on freshwater ecosystems I was hoping to publish.'

'And Laroche was your patron?'

She nodded. 'He's seriously into cryptozoology. Says his interest in it started when he saw Bigfoot on a lumber scouting trip in the Cascades.'

Grant frowned. This millionaire was sounding like he was veering from eccentric into full nutcase status. 'What's cryptozoology?'

'It's not a scientific discipline. Pseudo-science, really. The study of mysterious creatures. Bigfoot, the yeti, the chupacabra, the Loch Ness monster.' When she saw Grant's doubtful expression, she continued. 'Like I said, it was a lot of money, and I was just going through the motions. Then this happened.'

She pressed the PLAY icon, and Alexa appeared on screen wearing a wool sweater and cable-knit hat, standing on a small boat. The water visible behind her was choppy. It was obvious that someone else was holding the camera. That had to be Mike Dillman.

This is Dr Alexa Locke, recording twelve, begun at 7:30 p.m., her on-screen self said. *Grid twenty-three seven.*

'I had to record that at the beginning of every video,' Alexa commented in Grant's ear. 'We went out every day in that little motor boat on a systematic search pattern. Laroche's instructions. I didn't argue. His money.'

The camera swung from her and faced the lake. Forested hills rose in the distant background. The gray sky made it difficult to judge distances. No other boats were in the frame. Grant took Alexa's word for it that it was Loch Ness, but it could have been any one of a hundred coastlines for all he knew.

Then a thump came from off-camera, followed by a yelp from Alexa.

Oh, my God! she shouted.

The unseen cameraman's hand came into frame as he was pointing at something. He yelled, *What the hell is that?*

Grant's eyes flicked to Alexa sitting next to him.

'Keep watching,' she said.

The camera slewed around. It took a second to steady and then zoom in on what at first looked like a dark ripple of wave. A tighter frame revealed a hump breaking the surface. It went under again, and the camera tracked its motion. The glistening skin of the hump came up a second time, accompanied by the distinct outline of a flipper.

It was almost as if it were waving to the camera.

Then it disappeared. The camera came back to Alexa, who looked stunned by the sighting. The only thing Grant could hear from the video was Dillman's labored breathing. Two seconds later, the video ended.

'I almost passed out from hyperventilating,' Alexa said. 'We searched for six days after that and never saw it again.'

'That's not computer graphics?' Grant asked.

Alexa shook her head solemnly. 'I swear.'

'Maybe it was a seal or something.'

'I'm five foot eight, and I was standing when that was taken. I used a laser rangefinder to measure the distance to the sighting. By my calculations, that flipper was over four feet high. Whatever that creature was, it had to be thirty feet long.'

EIGHT

Victor Zim grinned as the prison yard melee started right on schedule. All it took were ten cartons of cigarettes and five bottles of smuggled whiskey that he had given to the Aryan Knights. Five minutes after he left the interrogation with Tyler Locke, Zim had been returned to the yard for the daily morning exercise hour. He'd nodded from his position at the edge of the yard and two members of the Knights threw punches at their counterparts in the Black Cobras and the Mexican Border Disciples. Within seconds, dozens of men were at each others' throats, distracting the guards from the parachute floating to the ground.

Not wanting to give away the situation, Zim didn't look up, but he had seen the plane high above as he strolled into the yard and knew exactly where and when the chute would land, controlled by remote adjustments to its cords. Hidden in his palm, Zim held the small laser pointer that had been smuggled in by a laundry supplier. While he waited, he relished the irony that it was Tyler Locke's own sister who had unwittingly set into motion the events that would lead to his escape from prison.

As with any escape attempt, there were dozens of potential roadblocks and mistakes that could ruin the most carefully laid plans, any one of which would result in capture or death. Zim would get only one shot at this, but he was able to breathe easier knowing the first hurdle had been cleared. With a fall of several minutes from the plane's fifteen-thousand-foot altitude, the drop had to commence before the fight even started. If that hadn't occurred on time, the guards would have noticed the parachute long before it hit the ground.

Even so, Zim expected a quick response once it landed, so it was critical to open the package before anyone could stop him.

Between the rioting prisoners, the crowd egging them on, and the guards yelling at them to break it up, it was nearly impossible to hear the nearest tower guard shout a warning about the parachute. Zim was attuned to hear such an out-of-context word, so he caught it right away and knew he had little time left.

Zim raised two fingers and pointed, the signal for the second part of the plan to go into motion. Another Aryan Knight triggered an explosive device made from a bottle and a small amount of smuggled chemicals. It wasn't much more than a pop, but the sudden noise and puff of smoke were enough to draw the eyes of the guards away from the parachute.

In coming up with this idea, Zim had his financial benefactor research other prison escape methods, none of which ended up being adaptable for this enormous facility. Tunneling out would have taken years and could have been discovered many times over the course of the digging. One escapee from Everglades Maximum Security Prison got away when his mother and friends rammed a Mack truck through three fences and an iron gate, but he and his accomplices were caught soon after. And prisoners had escaped numerous times by helicopter, but it was a risky bet because choppers could be heard coming from a mile away, and some of the escapes had been foiled not by the guards but by other prisoners rushing the helicopter and overloading it, preventing it from taking off. For his plan, Zim had to raise the bar.

The silent parachute wasn't seen until the last second. Zim was counting on the guards thinking it was a wayward skydiver from a local club before they discerned that the object hanging from the cords wasn't a person. That's all the confusion Zim needed before the true contents of the package were revealed.

The five-foot-tall pack landed with a thump next to Zim, exposing it for only a moment before the parachute covered it. Zim rushed over to the pack and dived under the parachute. He'd been expecting it to be kited while he snapped open the pack, but the windless day gave him a little bit of extra serendipity. The blue cloak would keep the guards in the tower from seeing what he was doing.

Zim unclasped the metal latches on either side, and the hard plastic covering fell away, revealing the pack's contents:

a stacked quartet of quadcopters identical to the ones used in the Eiffel Tower attack. All he had to do was hit the button to launch each copter and then tag its target with the laser pointer. The autonomous robotic copters would use the infrared sensors to mark the target, store the location in memory, and guide themselves there.

Zim threw the parachute clear. He could feel hundreds of pairs of eyes on him. The melee had stopped, the participants mesmerized by the sight of Zim emerging from underneath the billowing chute. A few of them looked up at the sound of the approaching helicopter, but most of them kept their eyes on Zim.

He pointed the laser and clicked twice, then tapped the pack's GO button. With the target locked in, the top quadcopter whirred to life, its propellers reaching maximum speed even before Zim could take his finger off the button. It zipped away on its fatal mission. Zim repeated the process, and the copter that had been below it followed suit. Within a couple of seconds, all four copters were buzzing toward their victims, one each for the two nearest guard towers and two toward the site of the prison melee.

Even an expert marksman would find it almost impossible to hit such a swift target. But Zim didn't have to worry. Not one guard got off a shot as they simply watched the danger whizzing toward them.

The first copter went straight through the window and blew up in the middle of the tower room. A guard's body went flying across the yard, landing like a rag doll next to the fence.

The second copter turned its target guard tower into a smoking ruin.

With the guard towers no longer a threat, the helicopter shot over the external fence as the final pair of quadcopters plowed into the crowd of men in the yard and detonated. Their screams were drowned out by the sound of the explosions. Those who weren't felled in the carnage scattered in all directions, prisoners and guards united in a frightened stampede toward a safe location.

Time to leave.

The Bell Jetranger set down in the yard next to Zim, who jumped aboard while ducking automatic weapon fire now coming from the more distant intact guard towers.

As the helicopter lifted off, smoke billowed from the back. Zim saw the choking black soot and thought there could be no other conclusion than that the engine had been hit by a stray bullet.

Tyler and Harris were turning onto the I-5 entrance ramp when Harris's phone rang.

'Harris,' she answered, followed by a short pause, then 'What? How?' She dropped the phone into her lap and hit the brakes so hard that Tyler was thrown against his seatbelt. Harris turned in her seat and shifted into reverse to back down.

'What the hell are you doing?'

'There's an escape in progress at the prison.'

Tyler felt his stomach clench. 'Zim. How?'

'Helicopter landed in the yard. One of the guards thinks he hit it.'

'Did they see which way it went?'

'North. The sheriff's office is scrambling their air assets.'

'Then why are you backing up?'

'The Coalinga airport is northwest of the prison. Zim will know that the state patrol will set up roadblocks for miles around the prison. His best chance of escape is by air, and the helicopter will be too identifiable, especially now that it's smoking.'

Tyler thought about it and knew Zim would be more careful than that. 'The Coalinga municipal airport is too obvious. He's got to know that the police would hurry to lock it down.'

'Then where is he going?'

Tyler remembered passing Harris Ranch on the way down. 'There's a landing strip by the inn. He must be meeting someone there.'

Tyler unrolled his window and stuck his head out. Sure enough, a Cessna was on final approach.

'Go!' he yelled. 'We might have time to intercept them.'

Harris put the Suburban back in drive and floored it, activating the vehicle's lights and siren. The SUV screamed up the ramp and hit seventy by the time they were on the freeway.

The Cessna buzzed past. It was only a few miles to the

runway. If they didn't reach the rendezvous in time to stop Zim, the Cessna could fly below radar into the Sierras, where it would be impossible to track. It could then land on any flat piece of land, and Zim would drive to freedom at his leisure. Alexa would never be safe until he was caught or killed.

Tyler scanned the sky to his left to see if he could spot the helicopter. It would be coming in low over the orange groves. For a minute he saw nothing. But he heard it. A low throb grew from the west.

The whirring rotors of the chopper appeared above the trees, and Tyler could see smoke streaming from its rear.

As it approached the highway, the helicopter flew erratically, dipping and weaving as if the pilot were having difficulty controlling it.

The Suburban reached the exit for the inn and restaurant, and Harris yanked the wheel over, streaking down the ramp. The Cessna was already on the tarmac at the end of the runway, turning to face south. All Zim would need to do was land, hop off the chopper, and board the plane, leaving the helicopter behind.

The throb of the rotors pounded behind them. Harris squealed around a corner. She'd have to make three more turns to the runway entrance.

Next to the restaurant was a Shell station where a cattle truck was refueling. Tyler watched as the gyrating helicopter overshot the runway and headed straight for the gas station.

Harris stood on the brakes as the chopper struck the cattle truck dead center.

The Jetranger dissolved into a ball of fire. The truck driver, who had seen the chopper coming, sprinted across the road and dived into a ditch just before the truck's own tanks went up.

'Get down!' Tyler shouted, and he and Harris flung themselves as low as they could get inside the car.

The gas station's underground tank ignited, creating an enormous shock wave that blew out the Suburban's windows, showering them with pellets of safety glass. Heat poured through the open space.

After a few seconds, the explosion dissipated, though chunks of charred and raw meat from the destroyed cattle truck rained down on the SUV, smacking into the roof and hood with wet splats.

Slowly, Tyler and Harris raised their heads and took in the abattoir that used to be the Shell station. The pumps were gone, and the store next to it was a smoldering hulk. Tyler knew it would take weeks to sort through the various body parts strewn around the area, cattle and human mixed together.

Harris picked up her phone and made a call. 'Harris here,' she said, her voice quaking. 'Send fire and ambulance units to Dorris Street and I-5. Forensic units, too. We need to search for Victor Zim's body.'

THE HOUSE OF RIDDLES

WORLD NEWS

Egyptian Foreign Minister Dies from Sudden Illness

By GAMAL HASSAN

June 19, CAIRO – Just a week after returning to Egypt from a summit in Paris, foreign minister Karim Abusir succumbed to an undisclosed disease after being rushed to Dar Al Fouad Hospital in Giza. He was 87.

The death comes at a critical juncture for Egypt. Mr Abusir was one of the few members of the cabinet encouraging the president to refrain from a conflict with Israel as tensions continue to worsen. Although no attendees of the summit were killed in the Eiffel Tower attack on June 12, the repercussions from the incident continue to reverberate throughout the Middle East. Arab leaders are convinced that Israel was behind the assault, despite vehement denials from the Israeli government.

With six armored and eight infantry divisions of the Egyptian army moving into the Sinai desert and with Syrian forces gathering near the Golan Heights, the region is closer to a full-scale war than at any other time in the last forty years.

Part of the urgency seems to be related to the foreign minister's untimely death. The Egyptian government has not commented on the nature of Mr Abusir's illness, but sources in the ministry suggest that foul play has not been ruled out.

NINE

Tyler appeared in Grant's office doorway at Gordian headquarters looking like he'd only gotten a few hours' sleep before taking the first morning flight back from San Jose to Seattle.

Thank God the Victor Zim threat was over yesterday, Grant thought. If it hadn't ended so abruptly, Tyler might have asked him to spend the night at his house to make sure Alexa was safe while he oversaw Gordian's team investigating the helicopter crash. No telling what would have happened then.

Instead, as soon as Tyler had called with the news of the botched escape attempt leading to Zim's death the previous afternoon, Grant was able to go home and take a long, cold shower. After retiring early in the evening, he slept twelve hours, something he hadn't done in years. Even with all the rest, he still felt like he'd run a marathon. All those years in the ring and the Army must have finally been catching up to him.

As Tyler was driving in from the airport, he had called to ask Grant to pick up Alexa and bring her to the office so that Tyler could see her there rather than going home. When Grant arrived to get her, she gave him another hug and a peck on the cheek, one that was a little too lingering. Grant would have flirted with her shamelessly if she hadn't been Tyler's little sister. He restrained himself with only the greatest difficulty. Not wanting to encourage her, he kept his mouth shut on the drive downtown. And he sure as hell wasn't going to let Tyler know.

'Welcome back,' Grant said. 'Find any pieces of Zim?'

Tyler sank into the chair opposite and massaged his injured arm. 'Not yet, but it's a huge mess. It'll take weeks to sort through. Unless we get a DNA match, I doubt we'll identify the pilot from the remains we find. What wasn't flambéed was mixed up with thousands of pounds of steer carcass chunks.'

Grant grimaced. 'Sounds appetizing.'

'It's strictly pasta for me for the next few days.'

'At least Alexa's in the clear now.'

Tyler nodded. 'I think so, but I'll feel better when we have Zim's remains. Where is she?'

'In good hands. I left her with Miles.'

'He's in the office today? I thought he was in Phoenix.'

'Apparently he heard about what happened to you and came back early. He's waiting to get the story.'

'We'll go and see him in a few minutes. Did Alexa give you any trouble?'

Grant's smile disappeared. Normally he could read Tyler like a book, but when it came to his family, Tyler could be cryptic.

'Trouble?' Grant said, trying to act casual. 'What do you mean?'

'Did you see anyone suspicious? Anyone that looked out of place in the neighborhood?'

Grant breathed a sigh of relief and shook his head. 'Nothing unusual. She thinks you're overprotective.'

'With both Zims gone, I'm sure that's the end of any potential vendetta, but I'm glad you were with her all the same.'

'No problem, man.' Tyler smiled, and Grant cringed at what was coming next. *Don't say it. Don't you dare say it.*

'You're one of the few people I'd trust with her,' Tyler said.

You said it. Guilt tore through Grant even though he hadn't actually done anything. The impure thoughts were enough.

Grant cleared his throat and changed the subject. 'I got the report from our French division. The explosion on the tower that knocked you flat also took out the water main feeding the Salle Gustav Eiffel's sprinkler system.'

Tyler frowned. 'Carl Zim was trying to blow up the sprinkler system so that the fire would kill everyone in the reception?'

'Maybe. But if that was the case, his timing was pretty bad. The sprinklers started spraying long before Carl's explosion took place. No way a fire could go anywhere after that. Everything was soaked, including me.'

'Then why blow it up?'

Grant shrugged. 'It might not have been the ultimate target, just collateral damage. The Gordian team was able to partially reconstruct an unusual item from the wreckage.'

'How unusual?'

'In the X-Files range. It's twisted metal from a cylindrical aluminum object about the size of a submarine sandwich. The biggest segments were found on the ground, but they matched bits to pieces on the catwalk where you tangled with Carl Zim.'

'What's so unusual about that?'

Grant turned his computer so Tyler could see the screen. As Tyler scooted his chair forward and leaned on the desk to get a closer look, his phone rang. He looked at the display and said, 'Agent Harris.'

He answered. 'What's the latest, Melanie?' He listened for a few seconds, then said, 'Sure, I'll have someone bring you up to Miles' office when you get here.' He hung up with a puzzled expression.

'What's she doing here?' Grant asked. 'I thought she'd still be working on finding out who tried to bust Zim out of prison.'

Tyler shook his head. 'I don't know. All she said is that it has something to do with the Eiffel Tower attack.'

Grant felt a chill run down his spine. 'I hope it doesn't have anything to do with this thing.' He zoomed in on five pieces that had been laid out side-by-side. The edges were bent and ripped, but they clearly fit together because of the letters that were stenciled across it.

Tyler sounded it out. 'Alt waf fe.'

'One word. *Altwaffe*.'

'That's German, right?'

Grant nodded. 'It means "old weapon". And before you ask, I have no idea why it's called that. Our guys looked it up and couldn't find a reference to it anywhere. Could be a code word.'

'Maybe it means the weapon was considered obsolete.'

'That could be why it didn't go off. Carl might have been expecting a big bang, and it fizzled instead.'

'So we don't know what was in the tube?'

'No. The heat from the explosion destroyed any residue. But you haven't seen the best part.'

Tyler raised an eyebrow. 'Color me intrigued.'

Grant clicked on another thumbnail to show another piece of the same metal.

'This part was on the other side of the tube,' Grant said.

Tyler's eyes flicked from the screen to Grant, the muscles in his jaw tightening. 'It can't be.'

Grant nodded. 'It is. Our guys report that it's the real deal.'

Tyler turned back and shook his head at the screen in disbelief. Though the image on the metal showed faintly through the blackened surface, there was no doubt it was a Nazi swastika.

TEN

There wasn't much more to glean from the report about the Nazi relic. No clue about where it had come from or what its purpose was. Tyler wished he could look at it himself, but there was no way the French government was going to let it out of the country.

Agent Harris texted that she was caught in the Friday morning traffic and was five minutes out. He sent someone down to wait for her while he and Grant headed to Miles' corner office on the top floor.

The door was open, so they walked in without knocking to the sight of Alexa shoving her shoulder with all her might against the back of their CEO's iBOT wheelchair. Miles, a burly retired Marine officer who still sported a high and tight crew cut, smiled at them from his perch in the fully upright position that the gyroscopically stabilized chair made possible and grinned at the full mug of coffee in his hand.

'You can push all you want,' Tyler said, 'you're not going to knock him over.'

Alexa released her stance and smirked at him. 'I wasn't

trying to knock him over, you dimwit. I have twenty bucks that says I can spill his coffee.'

'You'll lose that bet. The motors and gears have been modified by him personally. You couldn't do it with anything less than a forklift.'

She rolled her eyes, took a twenty from her pocket, and slapped it into Miles' waiting hand. He tucked it in his shirt pocket and took a self-satisfied sip from his mug.

'If I'd known your sister was such an easy mark,' he said, 'I would have bet a hundred.'

Alexa rushed over to Tyler and gave him a tight hug. Then she stepped back and inspected his arm. 'I thought you were really injured, you dork.'

'It wasn't as bad as it sounded.'

'It wasn't? You mean getting shot and then almost blown up before nearly falling a hundred and fifty feet to your death wasn't that bad?'

'See? When you put it that way, it sounds like I almost died.'

'You better not,' she said and gave him another brief hug. 'So am I a free woman now or do you want to continue with the nanny bit?' She stared pointedly at Grant and rolled her eyes.

'I'd say you need someone responsible looking after you at all times,' Tyler said, 'but it looks like you're out of danger now.' Without going into excruciating detail, he told Alexa about Victor Zim's threat and his subsequent death.

Alexa's expression went from fear to annoyance to

comprehension in three blinks. She turned to Grant. 'So that's why you rushed over to the house all sweaty.'

Tyler quizzed Grant with his eyes.

'I was at the gym when you called,' Grant explained quickly.

Alexa laughed. 'And he smelled like he brought the whole gym back with him.' She looked at Tyler. 'I'm in the clear?'

Tyler hesitated, so Grant chimed in. 'Unless Zim comes back as a zombie.'

'It's a long walk from California, so I'm not too concerned about that. Well, it looks like you guys have something to talk about, so I'll get out of your hair.'

'Where are you going?' Tyler asked.

'I'm meeting a friend at Pike Place Market for some coffee.'

'Dillman?' Grant said.

Alexa nodded. 'He just texted me. He's not home this morning and thought it would be a good place to rendezvous.'

'Is this the guy who was at Loch Ness with you?' Tyler asked.

'The same.'

Tyler was reluctant to let her go. Though Zim seemed to be out of the picture now, Alexa's connection to Laroche was troubling. Something in his gut was telling him to keep her here.

'Excuse us,' Tyler said to Grant and Miles. He took Alexa aside and lowered his voice.

'Maybe you should wait for me,' he said.

'Until when?'

'Let's go down there for lunch.'

Alexa patted him on his good shoulder. 'You can't keep an eye on me twenty-four seven. Besides, I've traveled to twenty countries without you. I think I can handle downtown Seattle.'

'But if Zim hired somebody to go after you—'

'What are you going to do? Hire a bodyguard to follow me around for the rest of my life? The guy's dead. I'll be fine.'

Tyler sighed. It was tough giving up the big brother routine. 'Okay. How about I meet you at Etta's and we can catch up?'

'Good idea. I'll let you both treat me to crab cakes.'

'Me and Dillman?'

'No, you and Grant. I want to hear his version of Paris, too.'

Tyler shrugged. 'There's not much more to tell.'

She gave him a concerned look and took his hand. 'I know this isn't the first time you've had to kill someone, but it still must have been difficult.'

'It had to be done.'

'Do you want to talk about it?'

'You don't need to hear it.' Alexa had been spared the ugliness of killing, which is why he'd never discussed his missions in Iraq and Afghanistan. There wasn't a common frame of reference, and he was afraid she wouldn't understand some of the things he'd had to do.

'All right,' she said. 'But you know you can tell me anything, right?'

Tyler nodded. 'Oh, I had a question for you. Have you seen André Laroche lately?' Because the FBI's investigation was ongoing, Tyler wasn't allowed to reveal that he was a suspect.

Alexa furrowed her brow at the seeming non-sequitur. 'No. I've been trying to meet with him, but Marlo Dunham – that's his assistant – would only tell me he was unavailable.'

'Has he tried to contact you?'

'Why?'

'Just curious about your plans while you're here.'

'Last I heard from him was a couple of days ago. He sent me an email about our search for the Loch Ness monster.'

'Was there any clue to where he was going?

'No. What's this about?'

'I'd like to meet who you're working for. Has he ever asked you about me?'

'Oh, yeah,' she said sarcastically. 'Your name comes up all the time.'

'I'll take that as a no.'

'You're being really weird.'

'Just let me know if Laroche calls you.'

She looked at him dubiously, then slowly said, 'Okay.'

Tyler loved her naïveté. He'd seen unlikely people do some pretty awful things, so he wasn't surprised by it any more. He wanted to spare her that kind of cynicism.

He smiled and changed the subject. 'Listen. Grant and I will meet you for lunch at noon. Then afterward I can take you on the sightseeing flight I promised.'

'Are you still up for that with your arm and all?'

'I could fly that plane with two fingers. Besides, it's a beautiful day for it.'

She smiled, but her eyes still held worry. 'Sounds great.'

'And be careful on the walk over to the Market. There can be some sketchy people on Third Avenue.'

'If someone messes with me, I can scream with the best of them.'

She walked over to get her purse on Miles' desk. Tyler noticed her whisper something to Grant, who smiled weakly at the comment and avoided her gaze as she waved and left.

'What'd she say?' Tyler asked when she was gone.

'Just that I don't stink any more.'

Tyler sniffed and smiled. 'She's right. You're a veritable flower.'

'Okay, gentlemen,' Miles said as he wheeled himself over to his desk and lowered the chair to a sitting position. 'Now would you mind telling me what happened in California? My PR gal has been working overtime because of you two during the last week.'

Tyler filled him in on the helicopter crash near the Pleasant Valley prison, then Grant brought him up to speed on the report from France.

When Miles saw the swastika, he scowled and said,

'Nazis? Again? I thought we were done with those guys seventy years ago.'

'When I saw the report, I asked Aiden to do a little online research to look for *Altwaffe*,' Grant said. Aiden MacKenna was Gordian's top computer expert and data-mining genius. 'He came up empty on the term, but he sure found a ton on Nazis today. It seems that the neo-Nazi movement has been growing in Europe in recent years, except their hatred is now focused on immigrants from Muslim countries and Africa. Don't get me wrong. They still hate the Jews, but guys that look like me are scaring them even more these days.'

'Yeah, but you're scary for a whole different reason,' Tyler said.

'You mean my amazing physique?'

'The smell. Apparently it's strong enough to knock down a moose.'

'That's because I ooze testosterone,' Grant shot back and then immediately looked like he regretted it.

Miles' intercom buzzed. He picked up the phone, listened for a moment, and said, 'Bring her up.'

Once he put the phone back down, he looked at Tyler and Grant. 'That's Agent Harris. Do you have any other homoerotic banter you'd like to get out of the way before she comes in here?'

Grant feigned shock and cranked a thumb at Tyler. 'Please. You think I spend two hours a day at the gym so *he'll* notice?'

Tyler opened his mouth with a smartass retort, but thought better of it. 'I'll save that one for later.'

'Good idea,' Miles replied.

Harris entered with a grim expression. Her eyes flicked to Grant first, as if she were inspecting him. She nodded to Grant and Tyler, then shook Miles' hand.

'Dr Benson, thanks for letting me come by on such short notice.'

'Not at all. Please have a seat.'

He wheeled around and joined them in the office's sitting area.

'You told Tyler this had to do with the Paris incident?'

She nodded and glanced at Grant again. Tyler sensed her unease, but he had no idea what the problem was.

'Yes, sir,' Harris said. 'I wanted to come to you as soon as I could. This isn't an official call. I thought since I owed Tyler for the incident in Miami – well, that you deserved to hear it now.'

'Hear what?' Tyler asked. Now he was more than a little concerned. 'Is this about Brielle Cohen?'

'What? Oh, no. Nothing to do with her. Well, I suppose in a way. It's about the guests at the party.'

'What about them?'

'I got the briefing this morning. They informed me because of my connection to Carl Zim's brother, in case I learned anything about the attack from Victor.'

'Agent Harris, they're both dead,' Grant said. 'And we saved everyone at the party.'

'Did you?'

'What's that supposed to mean?' Tyler asked.

'Your own report said that the quadcopter bombs were so small that they wouldn't have killed more than a fraction of the guests.'

'True. But we don't know what the attackers' goals were. Maybe they simply wanted to disrupt the summit.'

'Or maybe it was an assassination attempt,' Grant said.

Harris nodded. 'We think you're right.'

'Who was the target?' Tyler asked.

'Everyone there.'

Tyler exchanged glances with Miles and Grant before turning back to Harris.

'You just said that you agreed with our findings that the bombs weren't deadly enough to cause that kind of destruction.'

'They weren't. The bombs were merely a tool.'

'For what?' Miles asked.

'*Altwaffe*,' Tyler said under his breath. He looked up at Harris. 'You know what that is.'

'We think so. Eighteen months ago, a hidden lab was found under Dresden, Germany. It was deep enough underground that it escaped destruction during the fire-bombing in 1945 that killed fifty thousand people. We believe André Laroche came into possession of the weapon.'

Grant shook his head. 'What are the odds?'

'About what?'

'That Laroche also hired Alexa to track down the Loch Ness monster.'

'You're kidding,' Miles said.

'Yesterday I saw the video footage she shot. She says the creature is real.'

Harris rolled her eyes at the mention of the creature. 'I know. He's an amateur cryptozoologist. You should see some of the stuff at his mansion. We've been searching it since yesterday morning, but we've found no sign of him or any reference to the weapon. Did your sister say if she's been in contact with him recently?'

Tyler shook his head. 'She hasn't seen him in a while.'

'When we're done with his house later today, I'd like to talk to her.'

'She's meeting with a colleague right now, but I can bring her by your office this afternoon,' Tyler said. 'But let me get this straight. My sister works for the same man who supposedly plotted the attack on the Eiffel Tower using a Nazi weapon he found, and the person Laroche paid to carry it out was Carl Zim, the brother of the man I helped put in prison? I was willing to chalk some of that up to coincidence before, but not anymore.'

'I agree,' Harris said. 'In fact, the connection with your sister might be why Laroche hired you.'

Tyler was taken aback. 'Hired *me*?'

'We discovered the holding company that financed the display at the Eiffel Tower to hide Zim's gunmen was the same one that hired Brielle Cohen – and subsequently

Gordian – for the investigation that led you to Carl Zim.'

Tyler shook his head. 'That doesn't make sense. If Laroche was behind the attack, why would he hire us and Brielle to stop it?'

'You might have been more efficient than he expected. We theorize that Zim was duped the way you were and was hired unwittingly by the type of people he hated.'

'Muslims?' Grant asked.

'Jews. Laroche's mother was a concentration camp prisoner who survived the Holocaust, only to die later during a Palestinian suicide bombing in Jerusalem. We believe this is a case of revenge against the Muslim leadership that supports the Palestinian cause. The worst part is that Laroche had dealings with the Israeli government. He may have used his connections with the Mossad to get intel about the summit meeting that would have made the attack possible.'

If there was one thing Tyler hated, it was feeling like he'd been fooled. 'And Laroche used us to try to pin the whole thing on white supremacists.'

'If that's the case, it didn't work,' Harris said. 'The leaders of the summit nations think the attack was sanctioned by the Israeli government.'

'It's hard to believe the Israelis would use a weapon designed by the Nazis.'

'Not if you're a Muslim country. They wouldn't put anything past their mortal enemy. Many of them don't even believe the Holocaust happened, so why would they think the Jews would have any problem using a Nazi weapon?'

'You said it was found in a Dresden laboratory. What was the lab's function?'

'It was secretly established to research chemical warfare. *Altwaffe* was some kind of toxin.'

More disturbed glances ricocheted amongst them.

'What's happened, Melanie?' Tyler asked.

Harris took a breath. 'The French say there were three hundred and ninety-four guests at the Eiffel Tower party. According to intel reports coming from the nations that were part of the summit, three of those guests are now dead.'

'My God. Is anyone else sick?'

'Some of the oldest attendees. All three of the people who died were men in their late eighties, including the Egyptian foreign minister. The scientists don't yet know how the chemical works. It seems to shut down every system in the body so that the victims waste away. It's taking longer to affect younger and stronger people, but the doctors think it will prove one hundred percent fatal to anyone who was exposed.'

'How long do they have?'

'A week. Maybe less. Those who are ill seem to hit a wall, and then it ends pretty quickly. If we don't find or create an antidote soon, every person who attended that party will be dead. The surviving leaders will have the excuse and popular support to invade Israel. The forces are already massing. If an invasion happens and Israel can't repel them, they might fight back with their nuclear arsenal. We're looking at the potential start of World War III.'

'Maybe it was bad food,' Grant said. 'Salmonella in the caviar or something.'

'And Grant and I didn't eat because we were keeping a lookout during the entire event,' Tyler said. 'I feel fine.'

'And you would. We don't think you were exposed.'

'I thought you said it was everyone at the party. But wait, it couldn't have been in the food or drinks. Zim was the one with the tube containing the *Altwaffe*, and he never got . . .' Tyler caught himself as he said it. 'The sprinkler system. That's why Carl Zim blew it up. He didn't want us to know why he was there.'

Harris nodded. 'The toxicologists who are working on this – and they are the best in the world – think it was absorbed through the skin. So you wouldn't be sick.'

Tyler's stomach went cold. 'Because I wasn't in there when the sprinklers went off. That was the purpose of the bombs. They were a means to set off the sprinklers. Carl was there to inject the *Altwaffe* into the system.'

Now Tyler realized why Harris had been looking at Grant so oddly. From the moment she stepped into the room, she knew that he'd been poisoned.

ELEVEN

Brielle's eyes adjusted as she entered the dim lighting of Grady's, an out-of-the-way biker bar near Lyman, Washington. She'd tracked Wade Plymouth to this seedy joint, the last place his GPS had located him, right before he texted Carl Zim's name to her. He must have discovered something in this bar that caused him to go missing, and she was determined to find out what happened to him.

Going in with a British accent and a lot of questions wouldn't get her anywhere with the type of men who would spend the morning in a bar. She'd already scouted the location to check out the women. All it took was a stop at a Goodwill store and a druggist's cosmetics counter, and she had everything she'd need to blend in: cutoff jean shorts, cowboy boots, and a black T-shirt torn in the middle to reveal her generous cleavage – enhanced even further by a push-up bra. In a bar like this, it was like wearing a uniform, although much less practical than the one she'd worn in the Israeli Army. The fake dragon tattoo on her right shoulder completed the look. Her Star of David necklace, which would have been a dead giveaway, was safely tucked inside her front pocket.

A new accent was the last piece of the disguise. She'd spent a year studying abroad at Vanderbilt in Nashville. Frequent outings to the city's country and western saloons let her practice her American accent until it was perfected. That helped her blend in when she wanted to, though she didn't use it often once she found that American men went absolutely mental for the BBC shtick. To the college students in Tennessee, nothing was more exotic.

The wood floors of Grady's reeked of spilled beer and the occasional spritzing of vomit. A neon Budweiser sign hung above the long bar, half of its bulbs dark. Grungy booths lined the opposite wall, with beat-up chairs and tables taking up the space in between. A honky-tonk tune blared from the ancient jukebox in the corner. It was thirty minutes before noon, and only a few of the tables were occupied.

Every head turned her way as she sauntered in. As she made her way to the bar, she could feel eyes on her form, as if she were fresh meat to be preyed upon by the boldest hunter in the room.

She took a seat on a stool midway down the bar. The bartender, a craggy old man with a full white beard and a missing left pinkie, looked her up and down.

'What'll it be?'

'Whiskey,' Brielle said.

Without another word, the bartender poured two fingers

of Jack Daniel's into a highball glass and set it down in front of her.

Brielle downed it in one gulp. 'Another.'

The bartender raised an eyebrow, then poured again.

It didn't take long for the first man to approach her. He was a beefy leather-clad biker with 'Mother' scrawled across both biceps. He sidled up to her and leaned on the bar.

'Hey, baby,' he said. 'My name's Big Joe.' He turned to nod to his two buddies who were nursing beers, as if to say this one was already in the bag.

Brielle looked at him for a moment and then went back to her drink. 'Big, huh?'

'Why don't you come party with me and find out?'

'Can't, Joe. Waiting for someone.'

'Yeah, you've been waiting all your life for me.'

'I don't think so.'

'How do you know until you've tried?'

She looked Big Joe up and down and concluded he wasn't the person she was here to find. There was no way someone this undisciplined was part of Zim's group. She went back to nursing her glass.

'You been here before?' Big Joe asked.

'My boyfriend has.'

'Well he's not here now.'

'Look, Joe, I just want to drink my whiskey.'

Big Joe put his hand on Brielle's shoulder and spun her around. 'What if I scare off this guy you're waiting for?'

Now this is where it would get tricky. She had plenty of weapons she could use to defend herself: switchblade in her front pocket and compact Glock in her right boot. But getting into a brawl with a biker and two of his friends wouldn't go well. For them. Then she'd leave with nothing.

She slapped Big Joe's hand away. 'Get your hand off me, you prick!' she yelled.

'Tell me your boyfriend's name, so I know who I'm about to crush when he gets here.'

'Carl Zim!' she shouted a little too loudly, as if she were already tipsy.

At the mention of Zim's name, Big Joe put up his hands in supplication, his eyes wide.

'Whoa, hey,' he said, backing away. 'I didn't know you were with Zim.'

Brielle was surprised by the deferential response. Zim and his militia must have had a tough reputation in this region. 'Well, you know now.'

Big Joe looked at his friends and tilted his head at the door. They scrambled out of there so fast that one of them knocked his bottle onto the floor, adding to the odor.

Brielle turned back to her drink, but she kept her eye on the bartender. He kept looking up at a booth toward the back. Brielle followed his gaze and saw the only two men left in the bar talking to each other. The one facing her, a man in his twenties with long blond hair and no chin, looked at her briefly then back to his seatmate. He shrugged and shook his head.

Brielle took her glass and walked over to them. The second man was slightly older and had black hair, a nose that had been broken a few times, and chubby cheeks. She felt sure they knew about Zim and didn't know what to do with his now ex-girlfriend.

They'd either deny their connection vehemently or they'd fess up and tell her they were part of Carl's group. Either way, Brielle would be able to plant the tiny tracking device in her palm on one of them before he left. Then she'd follow them back to their compound somewhere in the Cascades forest. Once she had the location, she could either try to infiltrate it to find Wade or she could call in the cavalry in the form of a SWAT team. The latter would be preferable if she could collect evidence that Zim had been there and that Wade might still be held hostage. She tried not to think about the likelihood that he was already dead.

'Were you two friends of Carl's?'

They looked at each other, then the older one spoke.

'Never heard of him.'

'Are you sure?'

'Positive.'

'Because he wasn't really my boyfriend.'

'Then why were you yelling that to the biker dude?'

For your benefit, Brielle wanted to say.

'I have some money for Carl,' she actually said. 'For the job he was paid to do.'

Their eyebrows went up at the word 'money'.

'Then you should give it to me.'

Maybe this would be easier than she thought.

'Why?' she demanded. 'I thought you said you didn't know him.'

'My memory came back,' the chubby-cheeked man said. 'Carl was a friend of mine. We worked on the job together.' He showed her a snake tattoo on his left forearm, the same as Carl Zim's.

'What the hell are you doing, Harvin?' the younger one said.

'Shut up.' Harvin turned back to Brielle. 'Is it cash?'

'Wire transfer.'

Harvin grimaced, like he was deciding what to do.

Brielle suspected that whoever pointed the laser at the Eiffel Tower was only one of a few men Zim had used in carrying out the attack. These guys might have already been paid, but they would see more money as a bonus.

'This is for the second job?' Harvin asked.

That pulled her up short. Second job? She covered the falter by coughing.

'Of course,' she said.

'Maybe we should take her to Zim,' the younger guy said.

'I said shut up, Gaither!' He said to Brielle, 'Let me make a call.'

For a moment Brielle was confused by Gaither's remark. How could they take her to see Zim? He was dead. She'd seen the corpse herself, and there was no doubt of the identity. So what was he talking about?

She remembered that Carl had a brother, Victor, his only remaining relative. But Victor had been killed in a prison break the day before.

Something was wrong. She had the intense instinct to get out of there, but if she left now, they'd know she wasn't who they thought. Her plan would fall apart.

'Here,' she said, handing a USB drive to Harvin. She kept her other hand on the switchblade in her pocket. 'Take this to your boss. It has the transfer information.' In fact, it contained the tracking device.

Instead of taking the drive, Harvin grabbed her wrist. 'Who are you really?'

With her free hand, she withdrew the switchblade and flicked it open as she plunged it into Harvin's wrist. He howled a piercing scream.

Gaither moved quicker than she expected and punched her in the gut. The breath knocked from her, she doubled over, but the motion also let her draw the pistol from her boot.

She didn't get a chance to fire it. She'd been so distracted by the fight that she didn't notice the bartender come up behind her. He knocked the Glock from her hand, sending it flying across the room. Brielle swung around, kneed the bartender in the groin with a crippling blow, and ran for the rear exit.

If she got out the door, she could make a dash for her rental SUV. But the exit was locked in defiance of fire codes.

Brielle heard pounding footsteps approach and ducked into the ladies' room, locking herself in the only stall.

Harvin and Gaither burst into the bathroom. She whipped out her phone and opened the first text on the list. She typed furiously but only got four letters down before Harvin kicked the door open. She hit SEND and dropped the phone behind the toilet as the stall door was bashed in.

Brielle got an elbow into Gaither's cheek, but Harvin grasped her in a headlock. She thrashed the entire way as they carried her out of the saloon, the old bartender still writhing on the floor as they passed.

TWELVE

When Harris was finished with her briefing, Tyler and Grant escorted her into the elevator and left her to return to the lobby when they got off at the fifth floor. They ambled down the hallway, the silence thick enough to be sliced by a cleaver. The two of them had been through near-death experiences many times before, but nothing like this. Tyler couldn't recall a single time when Grant had been sick. The guy treated his body like a temple. Sure, he ate like he was force-feeding a tapeworm, but he also took every natural vitamin and supplement on the market. The idea that his best friend would wither away and die right in front of him was terrifying.

Tyler finally spoke, looking Grant in the face. It had an unusually haggard appearance, with bags under the eyes and crow's feet at the corners. 'How are you feeling?'

Grant wouldn't meet his gaze. 'Never better.'

'You look a little tired.'

'Just some latent jet lag.'

'Are you sure?'

'Sure I'm sure. Harris must be wrong. I feel fine.'

Tyler couldn't shake the sense of loss threatening to return. Although he'd never truly banished it after the death of his wife, Karen, he'd finally been able to absorb it into his being and continue on. But if Grant died, too, it would resurface with a vengeance.

'Maybe we should get you to a hospital,' he said. 'Get some tests or something.'

Grant stopped walking and faced Tyler. He looked around to make sure no one could hear them. 'I'm not going to a hospital. I'm not sick. Besides, you heard Harris. There's nothing they can do. I won't lie there waiting for the end. You know me. That's not how I want to go out.'

'I know. I'm here for you. We all are.'

'Don't tell anyone else, okay? I've seen that look of pity before, and I want no part of it.'

Tyler wanted to say he was sorry for bringing Grant into this ordeal in the first place, but that would only make the situation more uncomfortable.

Tyler nodded his assent and tried to gin up a sunny outlook. 'Hey, the doctors might be wrong. Maybe the toxin just affects the elderly.'

They shared a smile to reinforce the optimism, although Tyler didn't think either of them really believed it. A silent look of agreement passed between them that his condition wouldn't be brought up again unless Grant were the one to do it.

They continued walking to the last door, where Tyler inserted his card key. They entered a gleaming room filled with the latest computer equipment. Most of the workstations were occupied by men and women hunched in front of the screens, headphones capping their ears.

Several of the people looked up at their entrance, but only one person didn't go back to work, a lanky man wearing black horn-rimmed glasses. With dark curly hair failing to cover the skull-attached cochlear implant that made it possible for the deaf Irishman to hear again, Aiden MacKenna looked as if Elvis Costello had been assimilated by the Borg.

As he rose, Aiden's hands flew in fluent sign language. 'You wouldn't believe this new girl I saw today. I'm signing because I don't want anyone in here to get a jump on her first. I want to see if you know who she is.'

Tyler had grown up with a deaf grandmother, so he'd known sign language since he was a boy, a skill he taught to Grant when they were in the Army together. The fluency had given him an advantage in hiring Aiden when his impressive computer skills were sought after by every consulting firm and software company in town. Aiden was also a self-styled ladies' man, something he had in common with Grant.

Tyler signed back. 'What does she look like?'

'It's this hot redhead. I met her in the elevator, but she got off before I could get her name. Looked me over, though. I know she wanted me. And she's got the most amazing body.'

'That's not going to happen,' Grant said.

'Don't tell me that sweet young thing is a lesbian,' Aiden said out loud. 'What a shame. Although I'm picturing quite a scene—'

Grant waved his hands to stop Aiden. Tyler, on the other hand, was waiting to hear how far he'd go. Aiden squinted at them and put his hands on his hips.

'Oh, I get it,' he said. 'She's going with one of you. Which one? I bet it's you, isn't it, Tyler?' Aiden edged over and nudged him with an elbow, a sly grin on his face. 'You lucky bastard. Tell me, is she as good in the sack as—'

'Her name's Alexa, and she's my sister,' Tyler said, saving Aiden from putting his foot in his mouth any further. 'My baby sister.'

Aiden turned whiter than a polar bear in a blizzard. 'God, Tyler, I didn't—I mean, I had no way of knowing . . . ' He swallowed hard, but the foot wouldn't go down.

Tyler grabbed his shoulder in a firm grip, just enough to let Aiden know that he meant what he was about to say. 'No worries, Aiden. But you can spread the reminder to everyone in this room that I'm an expert in explosives. I can blow up a house and make it look like an accident.' He smiled. 'How do you think my sister looks now?'

'Like she's radioactive.'

'Good! I can see we have an understanding. Now, I need you to help me with something.'

Aiden nodded furiously. 'Sure. Whatever you need.'

'Can you get into the FBI database?'

'Absolutely. My military clearance works for Homeland Security, which allows me to access—'

'Okay. I need for you to get me the video of the escape from Pleasant Valley State Prison yesterday. Harris told me the cameras had a couple of good angles of the helicopter.' He handed Aiden a piece of paper with the location of the video. Harris couldn't give him access, but she let slip where someone might find it if they were inclined to search.

Aiden took it and said, 'Done. I'll put it up on the Previz screen.' He collected his laptop, and the three of them walked into a glass-enclosed side room outfitted with a screen that took up an entire wall. It was where the Gordian engineers did their pre-visualization design work.

'You think we might get an identity on the pilot?' Grant asked.

'The Feds will have a better shot at an ID. I just want to see how it was done. The report said they used quadcopters at the prison.'

'Sounds like the Eiffel Tower MO.'

'Right. There could be some commonalities. If we can spot something unique, it might give us an idea of who busted Zim out.'

The Cessna pilot who'd landed at Harris Ranch had been useless, a dupe who'd been paid five thousand dollars to land there unannounced. Zim was probably planning to kill him as soon as they landed at their final destination.

'Even if we find them,' Grant said, 'that doesn't mean they have an antidote.'

'No, but they might have more of this *Altwaffe*. If they do and we can find it, maybe the toxicologists can synthesize an antidote.'

When Aiden entered, Tyler stopped talking. He drew the blinds while Aiden launched a video app that was wirelessly linked to the wall display.

'It looks like someone has already synced up the four videos from the different cameras,' Aiden said. 'There's no sound.' The wall screen was filled with a different image of the prison yard in each quadrant.

They watched the prison escape once all the way through, Tyler's eyes flicking from one image to the next. His cell phone dinged, but he was so intent on watching the video that he ignored it.

There was Zim edging away from the main crowd. The fight starting. The parachute landing. Zim pointing some kind of device as quadcopters freed from the cargo pallet zoomed away and blew up in orange fireballs. The helicopter taking a hit and spewing smoke as Zim climbed in. The helicopter taking off and flying out of frame.

'What happened after this?' Grant asked.

'The helicopter seemed to lose hydraulic control as it reached I-5 and rammed into a cattle truck at the Shell station.'

'How long after the takeoff?'

Tyler understood what Grant was asking. 'Not long enough to set down and take off again. Because we know when the escape started in relation to when Harris got the call about it, her phone log let us establish a timeline. Zim's chopper would have had to move in a straight line nonstop to get from the prison to the place where I spotted it from the highway.'

'Imagine the planning that escape must have taken,' Aiden said, 'only to be brought down by a lucky bullet. It had to be a one-in-a-million shot.'

Aiden's words brought a sour taste to the back of Tyler's throat. It was *too* lucky. 'Aiden, play back the escape again.'

The video started over. Tyler pointed at the item in Zim's hand. 'Look at the way he's using that device. He points it and clicks, and a second later a quadcopter takes off in that direction and flies right at it.'

'You think it's a laser?' Grant asked.

'It's got to be. Someone must have smuggled it in for him. It was the only way for him to indicate where the quad-copters should aim. Presetting the targets would have been too difficult. He needed to guide them in real-time. I'll have Harris see who could have brought it in for him. A guard or maybe his lawyer.'

'So?' Aiden said.

'You're exactly right,' Tyler said. 'This was obviously a well-planned escape. Down to the minute. He knew when he'd be in the yard and where that parachute was going to land.'

'Shit happens.'

'I'm sure that's what he wanted the US Marshals to think. Just bad luck for him. Fast forward to the helicopter getting tagged.'

The video sped up until it reached the helicopter landing. Tyler watched as Zim got on. At the same time, smoke billowed from the right side of the chopper, the side away from the view of the closest camera.

'Any idea where that shot came from?' Tyler asked.

'Maybe it's a guard tower we can't see,' Aiden said.

'Or a guard who came out one of the prison doors,' Grant added.

'Maybe. But I don't think so.'

Recognition dawned on Grant's face as he watched the scene. 'That's not right. I can't believe I didn't notice before.' The helicopter spun around as it took off, giving them a good view of where the smoke was coming from: behind the main cabin.

Tyler's stomach churned as he walked up to the screen and traced the line of smoke. 'See that black smoke? It's coming out of the helicopter a foot below where the engine is. Nothing that would smoke is located there.'

Grant came up next to him. 'The helicopter wasn't damaged by a bullet.'

'They wanted us to believe that helicopter crashed accidentally,' Tyler said and pulled out his phone. 'We have to find Alexa before he does.' He dialed her number.

'You mean, that was done on purpose?' Aiden asked.

'It's literally a smokescreen,' Grant said. 'Zim is still alive.'

'Damn,' Tyler said. 'I'm getting her voicemail. We need to go get her right now.' Into the phone, he said, 'Alexa, when you get this, call me. It's extremely urgent. And stay out in the open. We'll meet you at the original Starbucks in a few minutes to pick you up.'

He hung up and brought up the message app to send her an additional warning by text. The first item was a message he hadn't seen until now, the one he'd absent-mindedly ignored during the video.

It was from Brielle. A single word.

Help.

THIRTEEN

The ancient two-door Blazer SUV tore along the desolate fire road, wind whipping Brielle's face. She concentrated on concealing her emotions as her eyes flicked between the two captors, Gaither in the driver's seat directly in front of her and Harvin next to her in the back. They didn't bother to hide their feelings, eyeing her with a mixture of disdain and lust. They had already established who she really was, so she guessed they couldn't stand the idea of being white supremacists who were attracted to a Jewish woman.

As soon as they got to their destination, Brielle would be as good as dead. She didn't want to think what would precede the execution. No way they'd let her go with the info she had. Big Joe and his friends would never confess to seeing her, and the militia compound she'd been trying to find in this operation was still in an unknown location. Her phone was the last link to the outside world, and it was back in the bar. No one would be coming for her.

Brielle gently tested the strength of the rope tied around her wrists behind her back. It was competently knotted but not impossible to remove given enough time. Even if she got it untied, she wouldn't get very far unless she disabled or killed both of them. Harvin and Gaither were armed with M4 assault rifles, and she was now unarmed, verified by a thoroughly distasteful pat-down. The only positive development was that her Star of David hadn't been noticed.

The thick woods on either side of the dirt trail abutted the Mount Baker National Forest, providing their sham militia organization plenty of space to hide its operations. It would take weeks of careful searching to find the compound, and even then these men would kill anyone who trespassed on the property. They called themselves survivalists, but Brielle knew it went much deeper than that. The leaders of this group weren't planning to survive the collapse of civilization. They were looking to start it.

'Come in, Harvin, this is base,' a voice said from Harvin's spread-spectrum handheld radio, a unit similar to one she'd used as a soldier. When it was set to scrambled mode, the coded radio would provide secure communication. They had to be far out of cell phone range.

'Harvin here,' he replied.

'Where are you?'

'Approximately ten minutes out.'

'Roger that. You have her secure?'

'Yes, sir—'

Brielle had only one chance at bluffing her way out of this. She cut in before Harvin released the Talk button. 'I know that's you, Victor!'

Harvin slapped her hard. Brielle had expected something like that and braced herself, but the impact still made her blink back tears.

'Shouting out my name doesn't matter,' Victor Zim said.

So she was right. Somehow Victor hadn't died in the prison escape.

'Given your background, Gabrielle,' Zim went on, 'you should know our transmissions can't be intercepted.'

Brielle's lip curled. Only her parents used her full name, primarily when she brought home someone they considered a schmuck.

'We're going to have a little talk when you get here,' Zim said.

'Better make it quick,' Brielle said. 'My friends are on the way to get me.'

'No, they're not. I know you don't think I'm an idiot, so give it a rest. My men would have been stopped by now if you weren't on your own.'

Brielle glanced at Harvin. The sneer on his face made it clear Zim had covered his bases. She wasn't going to get out of this without taking some drastic risks. The question was when to make her move.

'When the Marshals find out you're still alive,' she said, 'they'll put you in solitary confinement for the rest of your miserable life.'

'Gabrielle, I'll be dead a long time before anyone ever finds your bones.'

'Is that supposed to scare me?' She clenched her jaw to

keep her teeth from chattering from the adrenaline and, she had to admit, fear.

'Yes. But I don't have to ask if it does. I'll see it on your face soon enough. Harvin, bring her to me when you get here. Base out.'

As soon as Brielle reached their compound, escape would be impossible or require luck that she obviously didn't have. That meant her time was now.

Wanting to get their captive to the compound quickly, Gaither was speeding along the winding fire road far too fast. A curve to the right was coming up along a steep drop-off to the left. If she were going to die, it might as well be now.

As Harvin shifted to put the radio back on his belt, Brielle slumped over into his lap. The maneuver was a challenge because she was belted in to restrict her mobility, but neither Harvin nor Gaither were wearing theirs. They both laughed, thinking that she was trying to win her freedom the hard way.

When Harvin put his hands on her shoulders to pull her up, he was in exactly the position she'd wanted, his face above the back of her head. With a lightning strike, she snapped her head backward, and her skull smacked Harvin directly in the nose.

The plates of the skull are many times stronger than the soft cartilage and thin bones of the nose. Even if she didn't kill Harvin by driving bone fragments into his brain, the excruciating pain would leave him in a daze for the seconds she needed.

Brielle popped up and saw blood gushing down Harvin's chin. Before Gaither could react, she sat back, stepped on the seatback release, and slammed the soles of her feet into the back of the driver's seat. Using every muscle fiber in her quads, she jammed Gaither against the steering wheel so hard that he couldn't take his foot off the accelerator, let alone follow the curving road around the bend.

By this time, Harvin had recovered enough to paw at her legs, but the injury to his face had sapped his strength. His arms were no match for her legs.

Gaither, his mouth muffled from being plastered against the steering wheel, screamed as the Blazer flew off the road.

Brielle could see they were headed for a huge Douglas fir. Just before the Blazer's grille met bark, she released her legs so they wouldn't snap on impact.

The SUV's hood crumpled, but no air bags erupted out of the old vehicle. Only the sounds of crunching metal and shattering glass. The Blazer was tossed sideways and rolled twice down the hill before it came to a rest, its wheels tilted against another fir.

Brielle had to shake the cobwebs out to get her bearings. Other than a good smack of her head against the side pillar, she was intact.

The two unbelted men weren't doing as well. Gaither's head drooped at an impossible angle. He was dead.

But Harvin was still alive. The moaning told her so. And if he got his wits back while she was still in the vehicle, he'd make her pay.

Brielle sucked in her breath and reached with her hands until she could touch the seatbelt release. With a press of the button, she was free.

Of course, her hands were still tied behind her and she was stuck in the back seat.

The fir on the driver's side made it impossible to get out that way. The passenger window, however, was open. She had to get as far from the SUV as possible before Harvin could return to his senses and bring his assault rifle to bear.

Brielle fumbled the radio from Harvin's belt holster and awkwardly held onto it as she slithered past him, flopping onto the front passenger seat. She got a good look at Gaither, whose face was a bloody mess.

Brielle wished she could take one of the M4s with her, but with her hands tied behind her back, she couldn't pick up the weapon. Giving thanks for all those yoga classes she'd endured, she contorted herself until she was in a sitting position and then pushed herself up through the window. Harvin made a weak grab for her hair, but she pulled free and fell onto the soft needles of the forest floor, the radio still clutched in her hands. She rolled over and got to her knees.

In another moment she was on her feet and running.

FOURTEEN

Crowds. Grant never liked them much unless they were cheering for him. His days before the Army when he was a professional wrestler meant he got to absorb the adulation of fifteen thousand raucous fans at a time in arenas around the country. It was fun then, but he'd gotten his fill, and after he left the service he never had the urge to go back to that life. Now he was squeezing through the throngs of people in the Pike Place Market trying to find Alexa, who still wasn't answering.

Tourists flocked to the Market, a century-old Seattle institution, almost as much as they did to the Space Needle. Situated on a steep hill overlooking Elliott Bay, Pike Place Market is the home of the original Starbucks as well as the venerable Pike Place Fish Market store where crowds gather to watch fishmongers toss thirty-pound salmon to the register to be purchased. On every day of the year, thousands of visitors stroll through the halls taking in the rich colors and scents of fresh fish and crab from Alaska, produce straight from Washington farms, bouquets of flowers, and crafts from local artisans. Dozens of restaurants and shops are tucked away in the multi-level building.

When Tyler got the message from Brielle, he had a tough decision to make. Grant was honored that Tyler trusted him to find his sister since Tyler was the only one who could go in search of Brielle. Grant had brought along Miles and Aiden to comb the vast market looking for Alexa's eye-catching shock of scarlet hair.

Even with that distinctive mane, finding her would be a challenge, assuming Alexa hadn't been abducted already. Grant had never seen Tyler so stressed. The two of them had been in hairy combat situations and nearly blown up by bombs too many times to count, but the thought of losing his only sister was devastating. Grant himself felt more than his usual amount of nerves, though he didn't know if that was because of the danger to Alexa or because of his own impending death.

Grant denied the effects of the poison to Tyler, but he could no longer ignore them himself. The fatigue, the aching muscles and joints, and the sagging of his skin that had been bothering him for the last few days – all of it made sense now. They were the initial symptoms of his sickness, and he could tell that they were getting worse by the hour, accelerating in their intensity. Even his vision and hearing were starting to fade. It was now only a question of how long he could fight the toxin and stay upright.

The knowledge that he had only a week or so to live made him surprisingly focused on his near-term future.

What could he do with his time left? Help out his friend, for one, by making sure his sister was all right. Two, he could find who was behind all of this. Maybe he wouldn't be able to get revenge before he died, but he could get justice.

And what about his legacy? He didn't think he'd have to face that until he was in his eighties, if he ever did at all. He'd stared down death many times, but it had always been in the moment, without time to consider the implications thoroughly, just pure adrenaline. Now that he could see the scythe raising to cut him down, there were elements of his life that were suddenly out of reach. Working hard and playing hard and going on adventures around the globe meant never getting married or having kids. Did he regret that? Grant reminded himself about Victor Zim's threat to Alexa and decided that attempting any deep reflection – never his strong suit in any case – would have to wait until he was laid up in a hospital bed.

'I'm near the Starbucks, and I don't see her,' Grant said into his wireless headset. He, Miles, and Aiden were conferenced together on their cell phones. 'Anyone else?'

'I'm by the bronze pig,' Miles replied. 'No sign of her.'

'Nothing at the opposite end, either,' Aiden said. 'I'll head back in your direction. Why don't you stay there in case she comes up from the other way?'

'Will do. Grant, did she mention where they were planning to meet?'

'No. And I've tried Mike Dillman several times at the number Aiden found, but it goes straight to voicemail.'

'The last GPS signal from her phone indicated she made it here,' Aiden said. 'But that was fifteen minutes ago. Now the phone is off. She could be gone already.'

'I'm not giving up until we've searched every part of the market,' Grant said. 'It might be nothing more than a dead battery.'

The silence that came in reply told him neither Miles nor Aiden believed that, either.

'Let's all meet at the pig,' Grant said. 'I'll finish my sweep and be there in a couple of minutes.'

Alexa's spectacular view of the snowy Olympic mountain range framing the arrival of a Washington State ferry was spoiled by Michael Dillman's paranoid ravings. The Sound View Café was crammed with tourists, many of whom were from the enormous Celebrity cruise ship docked at the downtown terminal. Because the Pike Place Market restaurant was a short walk from the ship, it was a popular stop for a quick lunch and scenery gaping. Alexa didn't think a single person was paying attention to them, but that didn't stop Dillman from making her lean in close to hear him.

'I'm telling you,' he said with a conspirator's whisper, 'they hacked into my computer, and I'm pretty sure they did the same with my phone.' A ponytail hung from the bottom of his beat-up Seahawks baseball cap and his darting eyes were barely visible behind dark sunglasses. A reed-thin hand nervously picked at the left cuff of his windbreaker.

'Who?' Alexa said, exasperated. 'You're a videographer.

What could you possibly have that's valuable to anyone? No offense.'

'None taken. You're going to think I'm crazy, but it seemed like they were looking through my files on the Loch Ness monster.'

He was right. She did think he was crazy. Someone breaking into Dillman's home to see his Loch Ness files? 'Why would anyone do that?'

Dillman slurped his Coke. 'I don't know. What I do know is that my home office was discreetly disturbed. Believe me, I know where everything is down to the inch. Someone messed around with my stuff and then tried to put it back where they found it. It might even be bugged. And I found key-logging software on my computer.'

'Maybe you downloaded a virus.'

'No way. It was loaded by a USB drive. I think it also infected my phone. They might have done the same to yours. That's why I had you turn it off.'

When Alexa had arrived at their pre-planned meeting place at Starbucks, Dillman had called her and told her to rendezvous with him where they'd first met, which only the two of them knew to be the Sound View Café. Then he made her promise to turn off her phone before she walked over there, claiming it couldn't be tracked while it was powered down. When Dillman joined her at the restaurant, he told Alexa that he'd covertly observed her walk from Starbucks and didn't spot anyone following her.

To say Alexa was dubious would be an understatement.

Dillman had always been somewhat of an oddball, entertaining her during their tedious work with tales of CIA black programs and alien visitations. She'd expected those kinds of stories from someone convinced that Bigfoot and the Loch Ness monster existed. But a conspiracy targeting him personally? Now she was worried about the guy.

'Have you heard from Laroche lately?' he asked her.

'You're the second person to ask me that this morning.'

Dillman's hackles went up. 'Who else did?'

'My brother, Tyler. He wanted to know what I'll be doing while I'm here in Seattle. I've been trying to see Mr Laroche, but Marlo won't tell me anything.'

Marlo Dunham was Laroche's top-notch executive assistant. She knew everything about his business dealings and essentially took care of the long-time bachelor's life. Dunham didn't talk about it much, but Alexa knew the two of them had common tragic histories, which was the reason Laroche had hired her in the first place. They kept a professional relationship, but the bond Laroche and Dunham shared seemed to be strong. For her not to know where he was – coupled with Dillman's story – gave Alexa the first stirrings of concern.

'I did get an email from him a few days ago,' she said.

'What did it say?'

'It was about searching for Nessie, but it was kind of cryptic.'

'How so?'

'It was all over the place. He talked about playing the

opening of the Fifth and about squids and hippos and how I should keep looking for the Loch Ness monster. It didn't make much sense.'

'See? He didn't send anything to me. He probably knew I was compromised.'

'Michael, if you're really concerned about this, I can ask Tyler to go over your computer and cell phone to figure out what happened.'

'Is he some kind of computer hacker?'

'No, he's a partner in an engineering firm. It's his company, really. They have experts who can check out this kind of thing.'

'He'd do that for you?'

'Sure. That's what big brothers are for.'

Dillman scrunched his face in thought, then nodded. 'I knew you were the only one I could trust.'

Alexa stood. 'Come on. His office is only a few blocks away. I'll take you over there.'

'Now?'

'Why not? You tell him your story, and he'll have someone check your phone while we're talking.'

'Okay.' Dillman got up and scanned the restaurant. No one so much as glanced at them as far as Alexa could tell.

'Let me give Tyler a call to let him know we're on the way.'

Dillman seemed about to protest but held his tongue. Alexa turned on her phone as they exited the restaurant into the walkway leading to the main market area.

When it came on, it showed that she had six messages: three from Tyler and three from Grant. She also had a text from Tyler that said, 'Urgent!!!! Call me or Grant now!!!'

She stopped abruptly before they got to the crowd hovering around the outskirts of the store where they were throwing the fish from the iced display racks to the register at the center.

'What is it?'

'I don't know,' Alexa said. 'Something's wrong.'

Grant hit ANSWER as soon as he saw who the call was from.

'Alexa, are you all right?'

'Of course I am. Why wouldn't I be? I tried calling Tyler, but I couldn't reach him.'

'He's on his way north.'

'Why?'

'I can't explain right now. Where are you?'

'I'm at Pike Place Market.'

'Where in the market?'

'Near the fish-throwing place.'

'Okay. Stay where you are. I'll be there in sixty seconds.' He accelerated his pace, dodging people as he walked.

'You're here?'

'Yes. We'll get you out of here and tell you everything in the van.'

He hung up and the phone switched back to the conference call. 'Where are you guys?'

'At the pig,' Miles said.

'I'm inside,' Aiden said. 'Be there in a . . . wait a moment. I think I see Alexa near the Fish Market.'

'Good,' Grant said. 'I'll meet you there.'

'She seems to be chatting with some bloke.'

'Who?'

'Don't know. She's talking to him about you.'

'How do you know that?'

'I used to be deaf, remember? Just because I can hear now doesn't mean I can't still read lips.'

'That must be Dillman.'

'Hold on. There are two other men looking at them.'

'Tourists?'

'Muscle-bound types. Thick jackets and necks. Not here on holiday.'

'Can you see what they're saying?' Miles asked.

'One said . . . oh shite! I think he said, "we only need one of them alive".'

Grant sprinted toward the famous clock sign that read PUBLIC MARKET CENTER, huffing with effort as he ran. The fishmonger was directly underneath it. He could see Miles motoring inside, his iBot wheelchair cranked to its full height.

Aiden's voice went up an octave. 'The two men just went up to Alexa and the bloke. It looks like they have guns at their backs!'

Grant turned the corner. He caught Alexa's eye. The look of fear on her face was unmistakable. Grant and Miles weren't armed, and there were no cops in the vicinity. If these men started shooting in the dense crowd, it could quickly turn into a bloodbath.

The throng watching the fishmongers was so impenetrable that the gunmen steered Alexa and Dillman around it into the morass of people strolling through the market. Running would have been an option for them if the gunmen didn't have hands wrapped around their arms.

'Aiden, you hang back and call the police,' Grant said, trying to catch his breath. 'I'm right behind you, Miles. Can you get the guy with Dillman?'

'He won't know what hit him.'

Grant caught up with Miles but didn't act like he was with him. They put themselves directly in the path of Alexa and Dillman. Alexa was on Grant's left, closest to the crowd watching the flying fish.

Grant fell in behind Miles as if he were waiting for the slow disabled man to move it while the crowd traveling in the opposite direction flowed past. The positioning meant the two gunmen would have to separate and walk around them to either side.

Alexa stared at them, but Grant tried to ignore her. He hoped she was aware enough to keep quiet. If the gunmen suspected anything were about to happen, they'd lose the element of surprise.

As he hoped, the two gunmen shoved Alexa and Dillman apart as Miles approached.

'Pardon me,' Miles said loudly as he jostled Alexa aside.

She stumbled more than the gunman behind her expected.

Miles' right hand grabbed the pistol and twisted it out of the kidnapper's hand. His left hand threw a wicked uppercut to the gunman's jaw, sending him reeling backward.

The distraction caused the man behind Dillman to release his grip and turn toward Miles. Grant was in a perfect position to launch himself at his target. He caught the man's wrists and pushed them toward the ceiling as he shoved the man backward, toppling several tourists as they stumbled toward the ice racks.

Shouts and screams from the surrounding patrons only got louder when Grant's gunman fired several shots at the ceiling. The crowds scattered as the two of them landed on the freezing piles of ice used to chill the fish. Out of the corner of his eye, Grant saw Dillman run toward the street.

'Dillman, come back!' Grant shouted, but even his deep basso was inaudible over the din.

The loss of focus was enough for his opponent to knee him in the stomach, driving the breath from him. Grant took a gulp of air and responded with a head butt. Normally an impact with his skull was enough to incapacitate anyone, but the awkward angle and his protesting muscles reduced the force of the blow. The gunman staggered backward, blood flowing from his brow. He shook his head and brought his pistol up for the kill shot.

Grant was too far away to get to the man before he fired, so he used the only weapon at hand. He grasped the tail of the salmon next to him and whipped it around. The fish smacked into the gunman's hand, sending his pistol flying.

Grant swung the salmon again, but the man backed up enough that Grant connected with nothing but air. Then the man melded with the fleeing crowd.

Grant considered pursuing him, but he didn't know if the gunmen had more friends around. His top priority was making sure Alexa was safe. He found her clinging to Miles, her eyes glassy from the ordeal.

'Where's Dillman?'

Miles pointed toward the street. 'There!'

Grant spotted one of the gunmen pushing Dillman into a grey Suburban. The driver plowed through three fruit stands to make the escape.

A wail of sirens heralded the approach of the police, but by the time they arrived, Dillman was long gone.

FIFTEEN

Victor Zim's Jeep was the first of four vehicles to arrive at the scene of the Blazer's plunge off the fire road. As soon as he'd received the frantic radio call from Harvin, Zim ordered every available man into the search, weapons in hand.

When the Jeep skidded to a halt, he threw open the door and stalked to the edge of the road, where he stopped to survey the damage. The Blazer's grille was caved in from the tree, and the side and roof had been battered during its tumble through the woods.

Gaither's corpse was slumped against the wheel. The remaining live passenger looked pathetic. Harvin was on his butt, propped against the front tire. He glanced at Zim and then looked away in embarrassment.

Exactly the response Zim expected. His stance was intended to provoke awe and intimidation. Legs wide, hands on hips, his muscles flexing in the afternoon sunlight to show off the tattoos snaking down his arms, chiseled jaw set below all-seeing eyes and a hair cut that was two clipper settings from being shaved.

The constant workouts in prison made the bulging veins on his arms stand out even under the skulls and fiery daggers on his biceps. The muscle sculpting was a way to bring his body as close to perfection as possible. As Nietzsche said, 'Become what you are.' Zim had.

The escape from prison had gone exactly as he'd envisioned. In a clearing in the middle of an orange grove, his men had set up an inflatable high fall air bag, the type used by stunt men and firefighters. As the remotely controlled helicopter passed overhead, a dead man at the stick, it slowed long enough for Zim to jump, landing in the center of the air bag. They simply folded it up and drove away as if nothing had happened.

Now Victor would finish Carl's work. His crew, some from his former militia days and some recruited from around the world for this mission by his brother, needed to be convinced that he was now in charge. If there was any man on the team who'd consider disobeying Zim, that man needed to be disabused of the notion immediately.

Zim remained at his vantage point for a few seconds more to see if he could spot any sign of Gabrielle Cohen. Nothing.

Without looking behind him, Zim barked out his orders. 'Davis, you and your men take a mile south. Monroe, you go a mile north. The rest of you are with me.'

He jumped off the edge of the road without bothering to grab a handhold and marched down to the Blazer. The men grunted as they struggled to follow as gracefully.

He didn't need a recap about how Cohen had escaped. He'd gotten Harvin's sniveling account of it over the radio during the ride to the site.

'Which way did she head?' Zim said when he reached the SUV.

'I think she went that way,' Harvin said, pointing over his shoulder in the direction of Lake Shannon.

Zim glared at him. 'You *think*?'

Harvin nodded, a quick bobbing like a nervous Chihuahua. 'I was pretty messed up. The bitch stabbed me in the wrist, and I can tell my leg's broken bad.' The awkward angle of his foot confirmed the self-diagnosis.

'You're not going to be much help on this search then, are you?'

'Are you kidding? I'm probably going to be in a cast for weeks with this thing. I need to get to a doctor.'

Zim sighed and nodded. He reached out to Harvin. 'Let's get you taken care of.'

Harvin took the hand and grimaced as he stood on his one good leg.

Zim put one hand on Harvin's back and snatched the hair on the back of his head. Before Harvin could react, Zim bashed the man's skull against the hood of the Blazer three times, the dull sound of the impacts swallowed by the surrounding trees. Zim released him, and Harvin slumped to the ground, his eyes staring into oblivion.

'Put him in the passenger seat,' Zim said to no one in particular. 'It'll look like the two of them had an accident.'

None of the men moved, shocked into silence. He turned and saw their stunned expressions. Good.

'Now listen up,' Zim said. 'Harvin let Gabrielle Cohen escape, and he became a cripple in the process. If you can't contribute to the mission, you're deadweight. When you all agreed to this operation, you knew the requirements and you accepted the risks. Harvin was a good man, but he would have put everything we're working for in danger.'

He looked into the eyes of each man and saw that they understood. Life was cruel, but those who clearly envisioned what needed to be done could act without hesitation for the good of the cause. If Zim were ever incapacitated and no longer a contributor to society and the team, he would expect someone to do the same for him.

Two men hoisted Harvin's body into the Blazer. When they were done, Zim directed everyone to begin conducting a search grid and instructed his compound's helicopter to fly along the shores of Lake Shannon in case they could spot Cohen out in the open. She didn't have much of a head start and her hands were still tied. She couldn't have gotten far. With the lake as a natural barrier, they would catch her within the hour.

Still, he had to update his own money supplier. Without access to Laroche's land, which they were now searching, and his money for funding, the operation would never have been possible.

He took out his smartphone and made the call using the

compound's satellite hookup and Wi-Max base station. The connection beeped.

'What is it?' A modulator disguised the voice in case anyone was listening in. The effect made it sound as if Zim were speaking to a rasping demon from the pits of Hell. His voice would sound the same on the other end.

'We have a situation,' Zim said. Without using names, he spent a minute summarizing the events.

'Do you have it under control?'

'Yes.'

'If she escapes, she'll be able to lead the authorities to you. You'll have to abandon the compound immediately.'

'We're ready for anything, but it won't come to that. The forest is deserted, and she won't be able to stay out of our sight for long.'

'Any word on the other one?' Zim had already delivered the bad news that Alexa Locke got away.

He took a breath. 'We'll make sure we find the creature before she does.'

'I hope you're right, but I'll see what I can do on my end. I want to be able to count on you like I did your brother. Your planning on the operation last week was brilliant. I rescued you because your talents were wasted in California.'

Zim smiled. 'Once we get these two women in hand, I don't see anything standing in the way of completing the mission as expected.'

'You know you have access to every fund at my disposal. Don't hesitate to use whatever resources you require.'

'I'll make sure they're used well.'

'Good. Now I have some other matters to attend to. Keep me informed of further developments.' The connection terminated and Zim put the phone away.

Hank Pryor, a skinny goateed man who was the electronics genius on the operation, came running up to him, his radio held out in an outstretched palm as if he were offering it to Zim.

'You have to hear this,' Pryor said.

Zim eyed the radio suspiciously, then snatched it from him. 'What is it?'

Pryor glanced toward Harvin's body and back to Zim before clearing his throat. 'It's the Cohen woman. She's calling for help.'

SIXTEEN

The redolent odor of pine needles, moss, and forest-floor decay surrounded Brielle as she sought something sharp to cut through the tough nylon rope tightly binding her wrists, but rocks jagged enough to do the job were nowhere to be found. After running flat out for fifteen minutes to get out of the immediate area of the Blazer – and falling on her face twice along the way – she'd taken a breather to extricate her arms from behind her back, though she nearly had to pull her arms out of their sockets to get them free.

The cooling breeze told her she was nearing the lake. She pressed on, hoping to use the shoreline to guide her south to the highway, which couldn't be more than five miles away. If she could make it there, she'd be safe.

Brielle called again over the radio, using the marine emergency channel in the hopes that a boater on the lake might hear her. 'I'm calling for help from anyone out there. My name is Brielle Cohen. I'm somewhere in the forest west of Lake Shannon. Men are chasing me and trying to kill me. Please respond if you're out there.'

She listened, but all she could hear was the plaintive call of a loon coming from the direction of the lake. No answer. Boaters on the lake might not have radios, or they may simply not have had their radios tuned to her frequency. Any of those possibilities meant that she had to carry on as if she were on her own.

By now she had to assume that Harvin had called for assistance from Zim. Once she headed south, she'd have to be careful not to run straight into his men's waiting arms. But given her inability to contact anyone, she'd have to take that chance.

After another minute, Brielle finally saw water. She threaded her way through the last batch of forest and emerged onto a rocky beach dotted with rotten stumps, some of which protruded from the mirrored surface of the lake that reflected the snowcapped mountains to the north. Though there was a spit of land that would give her a better view down the lake, she kept close to the trees, fearing that she'd be seen if she ventured out there. A couple of kayakers were visible across the mile-wide lake and further north, but they would do her no good. If she called to them and they paddled over, she might even get them killed.

She called on the radio again, but got only static.

Now that she could see how exposed she'd be wending her way toward the highway, she knew her chances of evading Zim's men was minimal at best. Perhaps her best choice was to find a tree to climb. The thick branches would provide cover, and searchers focused on a running target might miss her in a high hiding place. From there she could continue to broadcast until someone picked up her signal. She might be able to lead her pursuers onto the wrong path and backtrack once they'd passed her. If she were lucky, she might even find one of their vehicles and simply drive out of here.

Her heart leapt as the thumping beat of rotors pounded their way toward her. Without knowing if it was friend or foe, Brielle dodged behind a tree. Its low flight path made her think foe. No one who had heard her radio calls would have been able to get a chopper into the air that quickly.

The noise grew until it drowned out the rustling branches above her. She couldn't see the helicopter itself, but she could spot the downdraft of its rotors on the water as it passed. Within a minute, it was out of visual range, its blades a distant thrum.

The helicopter had been so loud that she didn't notice the tinny voice coming from her radio. '. . . in the vicinity. Say again your position.'

At the same time, she heard snapping twigs and hushed voices approaching from the west. Though they were still far off, their proximity made climbing a tree more likely to get her caught than saved.

Then she realized that the voice on the radio might not be a savior, either. It could be one of Zim's men pretending to be a rescuer.

Her only hope was to lead her pursuers astray, and the lake gave her another possibility. She sprinted down the shoreline, talking into the radio as she ran, on the off chance it really was one of the good guys.

'West side of Lake Shannon,' she said between puffs of breath. 'Send the police. Send everyone you can.'

She tossed the radio onto the beach, cracking the case to give the appearance that she'd stumbled and broken it. She kept going. When she saw a massive tree stump in the water that fit her plans, she ripped a piece from her shirt and dropped it, then ran another fifty yards and threw another bit of fabric into the forest. She doubled back, sure that the rocky shoreline wouldn't betray her deception.

When she reached the stump, she took a last look at the trees and could see no one. Steeling herself for the icy embrace of the glacier melt, she waded into the water.

The water sucked her breath away, and Brielle had to clamp her teeth shut to restrain herself from crying out. She wouldn't be able to last long at this temperature, but if she could stay out there long enough and keep her nose above water, she might be overlooked.

She swam to the other side of the stump and found a place that made her least visible from shore. She pressed herself as close to the bark as she could. Her black hair wouldn't stand out. Unless they sent someone into the lake, she would be difficult to spot.

It was unlikely they had a boat since there were no docks on the lake, and the only put-in was at the very southern end. The only danger was the helicopter, but she couldn't do anything about that now.

Her teeth threatened to chatter, but the sound of men picking their way down the beach made her dig deep to keep them quiet.

A shout told her they'd found the radio. Half a dozen men came running along the beach. More yelling when they found the first piece of her shirt and then the second. One of them remarked that she must have gone back into the trees. Then she recognized the voice.

It was the man on Harvin's radio, Victor Zim.

He shushed the men, and they went silent. Brielle held her breath and clung to the trunk.

After a moment, Zim ordered two of the men into the woods. The rest of them were to follow him down the shore. He also radioed the helicopter pilot to turn around.

They took off at a sprint, hoping to catch up with her. By the time they were out of earshot, Brielle's hands were cramping from the cold.

She was about to swim out of her protective covering when she heard a buzz approaching. It wasn't the thump of the helicopter blades. This sound was more like the highly tuned motor of a sports car.

Brielle looked in both directions along the lake but saw no speedboats. Then she realized the noise was coming from above.

She raised her head and saw a tiny white and gray plane dipping toward the lake. It had the sleek lines of a dragonfly, its propeller mounted behind the enclosed cockpit.

At first Brielle thought it was going to crash into the lake, but at the last moment she realized that the smooth underside was designed for water landings.

It was a seaplane. And it was headed straight for her.

She looked back at the beach and saw the plane had drawn the attention of Zim's men, who had stopped to watch this new intruder. They obviously weren't expecting it, which meant the seaplane wasn't theirs.

The problem was that they were now in a position to see her as well, and they did.

Zim shouted for them to open fire. Bullets pinged off the stump and plunked into the water nearby. They were far enough away that any rounds that came close were lucky shots, but it would only take one to kill her.

The plane touched down on the glass-smooth lake as gently as if it were settling onto a feather pillow. It made an adroit turn and plowed through the water toward her.

Brielle quickly figured she had two choices. She could head back to shore and make a run for it through the woods with little hope of outpacing them, or she could take the chance that the seaplane wasn't there by accident.

She was shivering so badly now that a fast run would sap her strength in minutes. A ride in a nice dry seat sounded much better. The seaplane it was.

Brielle pushed away from the stump and paddled toward the middle of the lake as best she could with her hands still tied. Her legs churned furiously to propel her forward, but her progress was achingly slow.

A shadow fell across Brielle, and she realized it was the

plane's wing passing between her and the sun. The engine cut to idle, and the plane was about to glide by her on the right.

The plane's wraparound glass canopy tilted forward, and a man leaped out of his seat. Through blurred vision, she saw a hand stretched toward her from the transom. Brielle was so cold and tired by this point that she just wanted to be out of the water. Without looking to see who it was, she grasped his hand with both of hers and felt herself lifted out of the water like she was holding onto the prong of a forklift.

When her feet were planted on the small outrigger sticking from the plane's belly, she latched onto the man's shirt to steady herself. Bullets zinged around them, a few of them thudding into the plane's fuselage, and she was unceremoniously dumped into the passenger seat.

The man jumped over her, revved up the engine, and lowered the canopy. Brielle planted her feet on either side of the secondary control stick while the plane turned smartly and accelerated.

'Sorry I can't offer you a towel,' a familiar voice said.

Brielle rubbed the water from her eyes. She flinched as a bullet grazed the side window, then blinked in astonishment at Tyler.

'It's you,' was all she could think to say.

Never taking his eyes off the controls, he canted his head and gave her an amused grin. 'I assumed you heard me on the radio. Got your text.'

'I didn't think it went through.' She thought of about ten things to say but decided to keep it simple. 'Thanks.'

'Don't thank me yet. We've got company.'

Tyler glanced in the rearview mirror. Brielle swiveled in her seat and saw the helicopter diving toward them. Muzzle flashes blazed from its side door.

'Better get your belt on,' Tyler said. 'We're expecting a bit of turbulence.'

SEVENTEEN

Tyler pulled back on the stick and the Icon A5 sport plane leaped off the water. He banked right and weaved as he aimed for the nearest valley, making it harder for the gunman in the pursuing helicopter to get a clean shot at them.

Brielle hadn't been able to strap herself into the four-point harness because of the nylon rope around her wrists. With one hand Tyler took the Leatherman multi-tool from his belt, opened the knife, and waved for her to hold out her arms. He steadied the plane with his knees on the stick and sawed through the rope until she was free and could belt herself in.

As he put the Leatherman back, Tyler took a quick glance at her. Brielle was wearing an outfit that looked like a redneck cliché. If he hadn't known her, he would have expected her to speak in a barely understandable drawl.

'I'm glad I found you,' Tyler said.

Brielle brushed strands of wet hair from her face and looped them behind her ears. The dodging back and forth didn't seem to bother her in the slightest. 'Where did you come from?'

'My plane was ready to go and Seattle is only fifty miles away. Your phone was still on, so we tracked the GPS signal. It was smart to use the radio's emergency band.'

A bullet thumped into the fuselage.

Brielle looked back. 'They're getting closer.'

'Not much I can do about that. The bad news is we can't outrun them. This plane is maneuverable, but it's not built for speed.'

'And the good news?'

'We're not dead.'

'Brilliant. How do we get away?'

'We'll try to lose them in the valleys. Once we're out of sight, we can make for civilization.'

'Do you have any weapons on board?'

'Just a flare gun.'

'Where?'

'In the storage bin behind us.'

Brielle reached back and removed an orange box. She opened it and loaded the shell into the gun without hesitating.

'Only one flare,' she said.

'You're handy with a gun . . . Are you feeling recovered enough to make it count?'

She nodded at her open window. 'If you can get us close.'

'I'll see what I can do.'

Getting closer to automatic weapon fire was not his favorite choice, but if the chopper's pilot was any good, losing them in the valleys was iffy at best. Better to rely on offense.

'Here we go,' he said, and pulled back on the stick until they were climbing at a forty-five degree angle. The A5 quickly bled speed as it gained altitude.

The helicopter didn't have any trouble gaining on them, but the radical pitch would make it difficult for the shooter to take aim. He'd wait until the helicopter was in a level position to finish them off.

Tyler increased their climb rate even further, hoping to make it look like he was trying to escape but in reality letting the helicopter catch up more quickly.

When the two aircraft were side by side, Tyler nosed over. The helicopter followed suit.

'Now!' he yelled.

In one fluid motion, Brielle lifted the gun, aimed down the sight, and fired.

The flare rocketed toward the helicopter. Tyler was sure it would be a direct hit. The flare flew right through the open side door of the helicopter, barely missing the shooter, who threw himself backward to avoid the blazing shell.

With luck, the flare would bounce around the cabin, filling it with smoke and making the pilot break off the attack.

This time, however, luck went to the bad guys. The shot was too perfect. It passed through the cabin and out the other side, leaving only a wisp of smoke in its wake.

Brielle tossed the flare gun to the floor in disgust. 'Bloody hell!'

Tyler didn't waste time worrying about the lost opportunity. He rolled left, trying to put some distance between him and the helicopter. Maybe the pilot would be too spooked to continue the chase.

He looked back and saw the shooter waving the pilot on. When the chopper didn't change course, the gunman turned his weapon toward the cockpit in front of him. That must have gotten the pilot's attention because the helicopter immediately turned toward them.

'What do we do now?' Brielle asked.

Without a way to defend themselves, they'd keep taking fire from the shooter until he hit one of them or the engine. Going down in the forest wouldn't turn out well, and landing on water would make the phrase 'sitting duck' uncomfortably appropriate.

Tyler had to take out the chopper. And he had only one weapon at his disposal.

'We need to get them close again.' He put the plane into a turn that would take them back over Lake Shannon.

Brielle gaped at him. 'Why would you do that?'

'A helicopter's main rotor is delicate. If it takes any kind of damage, it'll thrash itself to bits.'

'So? Am I to throw the flare gun at it?'

'No. I'm going to take it out with my wing.'

'But won't that destroy the wing?'

'Believe me, I'm not happy about the idea. This is a brand-new plane.'

'Can we fly without the wing?'

'No.'

Brielle shifted in her seat to face him. 'Don't you think destroying our plane to get away is daft?'

'It would be if we didn't have a parachute.'

'Just one?'

'It's the only one we need.'

'Oh, my God! Have you become a raving lunatic since I last saw you?'

'I should point out that it's a really big parachute.'

'Where is it?'

Before Tyler could answer, bullets raked the left wing. He could see the shooter sneer at him as he calmly reloaded.

Now was his best chance.

He put the A5 into a steep bank toward the chopper. The helicopter had two options, pull up to let the plane pass under it or dip down to avoid the apparently suicidal maneuver. Tyler was counting on the pilot to take the safer move and gain speed by diving, which is exactly what he did, exposing the main rotor.

Tyler snapped the A5 into a barrel roll.

'Are you insane?' Brielle screamed, but Tyler was concentrating too hard to answer. He had to make this work. If he missed, he would have tipped his hand.

The A5 rolled up and over the helicopter, coming down so that the wing tip went through the rotor's radial sweep. The blades savaged the carbon composite skin of the A5's wing, but the damage to the helicopter was even greater. Chunks of aluminum whipped past them, bouncing off the plane.

As the rotor tore itself apart and took the tail assembly with it, the helicopter plummeted toward the lake three thousand feet below.

From the feedback on the stick, Tyler could tell the plane wouldn't be airworthy much longer. He cut the engine throttle, and the hum behind their heads went silent.

Brielle stared at him in shock. 'What in God's name are you doing?'

He reached back and pulled a cardboard panel off a cutout in the bulkhead. 'Pulling our ripcord.' He unfolded the red T-handle underneath. 'Brace yourself.'

Brielle, still confused, took her tiny Star of David from her pocket, put the necklace over her head, and gripped her seat's armrests. 'I'm never getting on a plane with you again.'

'Never say never,' Tyler said, and yanked the handle.

A rocket fired from above the center of the fuselage, eliciting another jump from Brielle. Nylon straps peeled away from the skin of the plane as an enormous blue parachute unfurled behind them. Tyler tried to relax, knowing what was coming next.

As the parachute caught the air, they were thrown forward against their harnesses. The plane went from one hundred thirty miles per hour to zero in less than five seconds.

The plane swayed back and forth in eerie silence as it floated toward the water. Tyler looked down and saw a roiling white eddy to the right, which had to be the helicopter's impact point. By now it would be settling on the bottom of the 280-foot-deep lake.

Brielle was huffing, her knuckles bone white. 'You could have told me it was the plane that had the parachute.'

'I thought it would become self-explanatory.'

The A5 slapped the surface of the lake, and the parachute drifted down behind them. Tyler tilted the canopy forward and climbed out. He unfolded his Leatherman again, this time using the saw to cut through the thick straps. He shook his head as he surveyed the damage to the wing. The plane would never fly again, but that didn't mean it couldn't take them somewhere safe.

He got back in and fired up the engine. A blip of the throttle sent them cruising toward the boat launch at the southern end of the lake.

'Let's hope someone at the put-in can give us a ride,' he said.

'I have to tell you something,' Brielle said. 'The men who abducted me. They were taking me to Victor Zim.'

Tyler didn't think he could be more surprised by the day's events than he already was, but Brielle's pronouncement that Zim was at Lake Shannon stunned him.

'He's here?'

'He was on the beach where you picked me up. He must have escaped from prison.'

'I know. I was at his escape yesterday. He's targeting my sister, Alexa.'

'Is she all right?'

'Zim's men tried to kidnap her this afternoon. Grant radioed me on the flight up and said she's all right, but Zim's men got away with her colleague.'

Brielle unbelted herself to face him. 'Why does Victor want to abduct your sister?'

'I think it's about revenge for killing his brother. You know, an eye for an eye kind of thing. Alexa thinks it's about something else.'

'What could she have that he wants?'

'She has a theory,' Tyler said, 'but you won't believe it.'

'After my week with you, what could I possibly not believe?'

Tyler sighed. She asked for it. 'Her kidnapped colleague suspected that some men were after the files on his computer. Because of that, Alexa thinks Victor Zim wants her to help him find the Loch Ness monster.'

EIGHTEEN

The convoy of five vehicles from the destroyed compound carefully navigated back country roads to avoid any possible police blockades. Once they reached I-5, Zim knew they were safe. Luckily, they were far enough along in their planning that being forced to abandon their base hadn't resulted in a setback. But he'd lost four men today, and even worse it was because of a Jew helped by Tyler Locke.

At the thought of his brother's killer, Zim dug his fingers into his fists so hard that his knuckles threatened to split. Zim had only gotten a brief glimpse of the float plane's pilot, but he couldn't mistake Locke's face. Someday he would make sure both brother and sister would come to regret ever crossing paths with the Zims.

As they approached I-5, Zim glanced at the passenger mirror and watched three vehicles behind him take the exit for the interstate headed north to the Canadian border. The twelve men inside would separate at Vancouver International Airport for their flights to London. The travel was expected to go without a hitch. There was no need to take weapons or other equipment, which would all be supplied once they reached Europe. That helped the evacuation go quickly.

Hank Pryor, the driver next to Zim, followed the SUV in front of them onto the south exit ramp toward Everett, where they would take a motorboat to a small town on the Canadian coast. The two of them were alone in the pickup.

'Looks like the cops were too late setting up any road-blocks,' Pryor said in a squeaky voice that matched his spindly arms and chicken legs. 'Good for us.'

Zim merely nodded.

Pryor looked at him and cleared his throat, as if he knew what he was about to say wouldn't be taken well. 'I know what you're thinking. You can't go making this personal. We've got a job to do.'

Zim slowly turned his head and stared at Pryor. If the man hadn't been an indispensable piece of this operation, Zim would have punched a fist through his squirrely face.

'Are you saying I can't control myself?'

Pryor nodded, so sure of his abilities that Zim wouldn't touch him. 'That's exactly what I'm saying. We're in this for the good of the white race. You want to put all that in jeopardy?'

Zim turned away. 'Do you know why I was in prison?'

'Sure. You were convicted of sabotaging that plant.' Pryor recited the details as if he were recapping the football game from the night before. 'You, of course, denied it.'

'I should have gotten away with it. And that's what I want you to know. Carl and I'd been working out how to do it for three months. We had it planned down to the last detail. No way they should have traced it back to me. I would have come out of it clean as a whistle.'

'Then Locke screwed it up.'

Zim nodded. 'They offered me a plea bargain if I'd give up Carl, but I wouldn't do it.'

'And that's why Carl agreed to this job?'

Zim chuckled, but there was no mirth in it. 'No, he believed in the cause. But he was also a good brother. He paid me back for not squealing. He agreed to carry out the Eiffel Tower mission with you only after he was promised that I'd be busted out of prison once the job was done. This new mission is for one reason: to make sure Carl didn't die in vain.'

Pryor pursed his lips. 'You sure got a raw deal. I feel for you.'

'I don't give a damn what you feel. This operation is bigger than the two of us. After they wipe out Israel, those Muslims will become even more hated than they are now by the white countries. And that Jew-lover in the plane will be joining all of them in Hell.'

'How did Tyler Locke find her?'

'I don't know, and I don't care.'

'Do you think he knows how to find the monster?'

'Dillman claims Alexa Locke doesn't have the Nazi journal, so thanks to him, we have a head start. All we need to do is make sure her brother doesn't catch up.'

Pryor shook his head and laughed. 'The Loch Ness

monster. Who would have thought it was the source for designing a weapon?'

'No one,' Zim said. 'And no one ever will as long as this all goes by the numbers.'

'At least we know the chemical works. I wouldn't have believed it unless I'd seen it happen myself. It only took a few days to kill Plymouth with the dose we gave him. Shriveling up like that didn't look like a fun way to go.'

Zim agreed. He was astounded that such a powerful weapon had lain dormant for almost seventy years, forgotten in an underground lab destroyed during the Dresden air raid that incinerated fifty thousand good German citizens. Just a single container locked away in a storage room, protected from the firestorm that consumed the city and the scientists who'd developed it. The chaotic last days of the war ensured that any official record of the container's contents and its companion notebook were destroyed.

It wasn't until after Laroche bought them from a clueless black market seller that he realized what he'd purchased. It was only by good fortune that the canister found a home with someone sympathetic to Hitler's ultimate cause.

The appropriateness of the situation made Zim smile, and he reassuringly touched the small metal vial in his pocket – the last drops of *Altwaffe* in existence, to be used as he saw fit. What better way to rid the Aryan nations of the blight caused by the lower races than with a chemical weapon created for just such a purpose by the Nazis?

NINETEEN

It took several hours for the authorities to take statements from Brielle and Tyler, a process that was punctuated halfway through by a distant boom and a column of smoke rising northwest of Lake Shannon. They went through the events of the attack in excruciating detail with detectives who wanted to know exactly how the plane had come to be riddled with bullet holes. The two-hundred-foot depth of the water made it impossible for divers without special equipment to probe the wreckage of the helicopter and find their attacker.

Brielle was frustrated because the police doubted her assertion that Victor Zim was the one behind the assault. Despite Tyler's explanation that the helicopter used at the prison was sabotaged, they were operating under the official assumption that Victor had died in the escape attempt.

As Brielle finished eating a protein bar provided by one of the policeman, Tyler showed the forensics team how to fold his plane's wings so that it could be towed back to Seattle for analysis. She could see him cringe every time he glanced at the damaged section, which looked like it had been gnawed by a gigantic beaver.

He patted the plane on the side and walked back toward her, shaking his head.

'It'll take me forever to get another one of these,' he said. 'Do you know how long the waiting list is?'

She shook her head. 'We almost got killed and that's what you're worried about?'

'I'm annoyed, not worried. But at least I know the parachute system works. Money well spent, I'd say.'

Brielle crumpled up the wrapper and tossed it in the waste bin. 'Can we go meet Alexa now? I have some questions for her. My car is back at the bar.'

'Not quite yet. I'm expecting someone.' He looked past her and said, 'There she is.'

Brielle turned and saw a black SUV come to a stop behind her. A thin blonde woman stepped out wearing a neatly pressed suit. She might as well have had 'I'm with the US government' written on a name tag.

The woman strode up to Tyler and shook his hand warmly.

'Sorry to see you again so soon, Tyler,' the woman said.

'Likewise,' Tyler said.

The woman turned to Brielle and held out her hand. 'Special Agent Melanie Harris.'

Brielle took the proffered hand. 'Looks like you know each other.'

'Tyler and I have worked together before.'

Brielle made a mental note to ask about that later.

'The FBI certainly got here quickly,' she said. 'Maybe somebody believes it was Victor Zim after all.'

'There's more to this than I've had time to explain,' Tyler said cryptically, 'so I thought it would be a smart idea to bring Agent Harris up here.'

'It's good you did, too,' Harris said. 'If you'll come with me, I'll take you to the secondary crime scene. I want you to see something.'

Brielle thought the agent meant the Blazer crash, so she sighed and got into the back of the SUV next to Tyler, ready to go over her story one more time. But other than a few direct questions, the FBI agent remained silent. She had obviously been briefed about the incident on the way up.

They drove the same fire road on the west side of the lake, and Brielle's mind flashed back through her earlier ride. But when they reached the scene of the crash they didn't stop. Brielle could make out the blackened frame of the Blazer surrounded by crime scene investigators collecting evidence.

'Where are we going?' she asked.

'There was an explosion and fire reported about two hours ago,' Harris said.

'I know. We heard it and saw the smoke. I assumed it was the Blazer.'

'They happened around the same time. The other fire was at a compound about ten minutes from here.'

'It might be Zim's base,' Brielle said. 'Where they were taking me.'

'That's what we're hoping Tyler can tell us.'

The SUV wound through the woods until it approached a gaggle of fire trucks and police cars, their flashing lights splashing the forest with blue and red. A state trooper waved them down and then let them pass after checking IDs.

They continued down a gravel road to a clearing in the trees. Brielle could see firemen hosing down several structures. The blazes were out but wisps of smoke were still visible. Three of the structures seemed to be the remnants of large wooden buildings that had been burned to the ground. The fourth had the footprint of a trailer home scattered across a huge swath of grass. Thousands of pieces of steel, glass, and melted plastic littered the ground.

They got out of the SUV and Harris led them toward the pile of debris.

'What do you think that is?'

Now Brielle understood why the agent had wanted Tyler's expertise.

Tyler squinted at the wreckage and walked around it to get a look from several angles. Finally, he said, 'Well, they did a pretty good job at blowing it apart, which means they didn't want anyone to know what it was.'

'Any ideas?' Harris asked.

Tyler shook his head. 'It's too jumbled. We'll need to get the pieces back to our facility and try to put Humpty Dumpty back together again. I'll get a team up here to collect it all, which will take a while. We could find pieces up to a quarter mile away, depending on how powerful the blast was.'

Brielle looked at the twisted wreckage and then at Tyler. 'You'll reconstruct this like you did with the metal rig in Norway?'

Tyler nodded. 'We do it all the time with downed airliners. It's like a big jigsaw puzzle.'

'Except you're missing the picture on the box.'

'That's what makes it a challenge.'

Harris pointed at the wooden buildings, now reduced to ashes. 'It might be more than we get from those.'

'Agent Harris,' Brielle said. 'I think Zim and his men abducted Wade Plymouth, a friend of mine. We work together.'

Harris referred to a notebook. 'Yes, I got a short briefing about you on my drive here. Can you tell me more about your investigation?'

'Wade and I were hired to discover the location of a small crate found in Germany that may have been related to the Holocaust. Using the information provided to us, Wade tracked the owners of the crate here. The last text I got from him was from a bar in Lyman, and he had learned that Carl Zim was planning an attack from a base near Oslo. That's how we found Carl's compound in Norway.' Fanatical right-wing sentiments had been growing in Scandinavia over the last few years, so Norway wasn't an unlikely place to find extremists.

Harris glanced at the burned-out buildings and said,

'We'll do what we can to find Mr Plymouth. Let's hope he can tell us more.'

Brielle could see the agent was going through the motions. She didn't think Wade was still alive.

A yell came from across the clearing. 'We've got a body!'

Brielle swallowed hard. They hurried over to the site, where policemen had gathered around two firemen kneeling to examine the corpse. All Brielle could see was that the clothes had not been burned. Her heart raced, knowing that there was only one person Zim would leave behind in his mad scramble to vacate the compound.

'Where did you find it?' Harris asked.

One of the firemen looked up. 'It fell out of the tree. Practically landed on top of me. Must have been caught in the explosion and got tossed into the branches. A leg and arm are missing.'

'Turn him over. Brielle, this might be difficult, but we need to know if this is Plymouth.'

Tyler took her gently by the arm and guided her forward.

The firemen turned the body face up, and Brielle gasped when she saw the face of an elderly man, his skin wrinkled and blotchy. She had to blink and look a second time, but she'd recognize the features anywhere. The scar across the bridge of his nose confirmed it.

'Is that him?' Tyler asked.

Brielle nodded in a stupor.

'Are you sure? This man has to be over eighty. He was an investigator with your company?'

Brielle nodded again more firmly. 'I've known Wade for fourteen years. That's him, but . . . ' She trailed off, not quite believing her eyes.

Tyler looked at Harris and then back to Brielle. 'But what?'

'I met Wade when we were in the same class at university,' Brielle said, the words struggling to emerge from her suddenly parched throat. 'He's thirty-four years old.'

TWENTY

Alexa sat next to Grant in the passenger seat of his Tahoe as they crawled along with the traffic on the I-90 floating bridge toward Mercer Island. She didn't fidget, cry, rant, or moan. The most vocal she got during the ride was a couple of sighs. She had shed some tears of relief and shock on his shoulder at the crime scene before the police arrived, but she had composed herself and delivered a detailed account of events to the investigators.

Grant was surprised at how well she had recovered from nearly being kidnapped, but maybe he shouldn't have been. After all, her brother had gone through much worse without blinking. It had to be a Locke family trait.

'How are you doing?' Grant said, flexing his fingers on the steering wheel. They were still sore from the fight.

Alexa sighed again. 'Oh, I'm okay, but I'm worried about Mike. He's crazy, but he's a good guy. They're going to kill him, aren't they?'

If they haven't already, Grant didn't say out loud. 'They must have followed him to the market, to get one of you.'

'And if you hadn't come to find me, they would have taken both of us.'

'You can thank Tyler for that. He's the one who figured out that Zim is still alive.'

'Zim wasn't there, was he?'

'No, but those had to be his men.'

'How could he have men working for him? He just broke out of prison. And why would they be interested in Mike or our search for the Loch Ness monster?'

'You said Dillman thought someone broke into his computer and downloaded his files on Nessie.' Every time they mentioned the Loch Ness monster, Grant had to restrain himself from rolling his eyes.

'That's what he told me,' Alexa said, 'but I can't guess why Victor Zim would want them.'

'Maybe Zim thought your connection to Laroche could lead back to him. You said Laroche sent you an email a few days ago. Could it be related?'

'The FBI didn't seem to think so. I sent them all my correspondence with André, so I guess they might find some clue. But the last email I got from him was odd. Well, odder than usual.'

'In what way?'

'It was really rambling, like he was drunk or something.' She pulled out her phone. 'Here. I'll read it to you. Even the subject line is weird. It says, "Play the opening of the Fifth," with "Fifth" capitalized. He's a fan of classical music, so I was surprised when the email wasn't about Beethoven.'

She started reading.

Subject: Play the opening of the FIFTH

Dear Alexa,

You must continue our search no matter the obstacles. You of all people should know that doubling the degree to which you work is important to reaching our goal.

At times the creature has been said to resemble a sea serpent, a water horse, a kraken, or a plesiosaur. Dinosaurs are extinct, so the key is in the cells of animals still living.

Hydrophis spiralis, hippopotamus amphibius, and Mesonychoteuthis hamiltoni are all good candidates, but it can't be any single one of those.

However, if you add the structures of these creatures together, that is how you'll find the Loch Ness monster.

I wish you good luck and Godspeed.

André

'What's all the Latin about?' Grant asked.

'Those are species. *Hippopotamus amphibius* is just what it sounds like, a hippo. *Hydrophis spiralis* is the largest species of sea snake. And *Mesonychoteuthis hamiltoni* is the scientific nomenclature for a colossal squid.'

'Colossal squid? Is that the same as a giant squid?'

'Different species, and even bigger than *Architeuthis*.

Only a few specimens of *Mesonychoteuthis* have ever been caught, but the speculation is that they can grow to at least forty-five feet long.'

'The Kraken.'

'Exactly. These squid rarely venture near the surface, but when they did, imagine a fifteenth-century sailor's reaction to seeing one of those floating next to their ship. Remember that Columbus's vessels were only fifty-five feet long.'

'They'd be quaking in their boots that it would pull their dinghy to the bottom.'

'Right. So together that's a water horse – the ancient Greek translation of hippopotamus is "river horse" – a sea serpent, and a kraken.'

'You mean that Laroche thinks the Loch Ness monster is some unholy mashup of those three animals?'

'I don't know. He's certainly eccentric, with his unwavering belief in Bigfoot and Nessie. But he also took a very scientific approach to finding them. That's why he said he hired me. I'm beginning to think he's onto something.'

'Don't tell me you believe in the Loch Ness monster now.' Despite the video evidence, Grant just couldn't buy that there was a dinosaur living in present-day Scotland.

'Unless some elaborate hoax was played on me, I can't dismiss what I saw.'

'But how can that kind of animal live in Loch Ness all this time with no one ever getting a good look at it?'

'I've been thinking about that ever since we captured that video,' Alexa said. 'I have some ideas. First, the lake is rich in peat moss runoff from the surrounding countryside, so it's virtually impossible to see more than a couple of feet deep. Even sonar has trouble resolving echo signatures. Anything swimming under the water is essentially invisible, and it's a big lake.'

'How big?'

'It's twenty-three miles long, a mile wide, and up to seven hundred and fifty feet deep. It contains more freshwater than all the lakes of England and Wales combined.'

Grant nodded. 'That sounds big enough to hide a monster if it wants to stay hidden. What's another reason for the spotty visual record?'

'I don't think Nessie is an air breather.'

'Why not?'

'It would have to come to the surface so often that it would be spotted regularly.'

'So that rules out a dinosaur,' Grant said.

Alexa patted him on the shoulder. 'That's right! I'm impressed.'

'That I know reptiles breathe air?'

'Some people think plesiosaurs are fish. You're a man who knows his biology. That makes you even hotter.'

She chuckled, and now Grant didn't know if she was teasing him or not.

'What else?' he said.

Alexa got a faraway look in her eye, as if she were picturing the creature in her mind. 'I'd also bet Nessie is nocturnal, spending most of its time foraging at night.'

'But you saw it during the day.'

'At dusk. We might have caught it just as it was beginning to feed.'

'On what?'

'That's a tougher question. The loch isn't exactly rich with fish. There's an annual salmon migration, but during the rest of the year, some biologists have calculated that there's simply not enough biomass to support a breeding population of large creatures in the loch. If my size calculations are correct, Nessie could weigh two tons or more. Multiple creatures would empty the loch of food in months and starve to death.'

'So it doesn't exist? I'm confused.'

'I tend to agree with a theory espoused by some other Nessie hunters. It could be a single animal. Specifically, a sturgeon.'

'As in beluga caviar?'

'Right. Most photographic evidence of the creature is completely false. The famous surgeon's photograph from 1934 – you know, the one showing what looks like a plesiosaur rearing its head next to Urquhart Castle? – most analyses show that to be a hoax, which was corroborated by someone claiming to be in on the prank.'

'I'm shocked,' Grant deadpanned.

'But the sheer number of sightings is hard to dismiss, and a sturgeon fits all of the parameters I've named. It's a bottom feeder, so it would rarely be seen at the surface, especially during the daytime. They can grow to well over four thousand pounds. And they are called the Methuselah of fishes because they can live a hundred years or longer.'

'It's not a native species, is it?'

'Not in Scotland, no.'

'So how did it get there?'

'Who knows? Maybe some visitor to Russia brought breeding stock back with him and dumped it in the loch. André would be so disappointed if it turns out to be something that mundane.' She looked down at the mysterious message on her phone. 'It's as if he were trying to tell me something but had a few too many before he wrote the message.'

Grant had Alexa read the odd email again as he exited the highway onto Island Crest Way on Mercer Island, one of Seattle's wealthiest suburbs. They were on the way to Laroche's lakeside estate, where Tyler, Brielle, and Harris were planning to meet them.

'I'm worried about him going missing like this,' Alexa said.

'I hate to tell you, but Laroche might be one of the bad guys.' Since Alexa was now caught up in the aftermath of the Eiffel Tower plot, Grant explained that Laroche was the prime suspect responsible for funding the attack. He left out the part about his exposure to the chemical weapon.

'That can't be true,' Alexa said, shell-shocked by the news. 'He may be an odd duck, but he's not a mass murderer.'

'His mother was Jewish. The Muslim countries think he's in league with the Mossad to assassinate their leaders.'

'And what do the Israelis say?'

'They deny it, which is exactly what the Muslim countries would expect them to say.'

'Maybe he was kidnapped like Mike was.'

'Or he's gone to ground because he knows he's been implicated in the attack. He's got enough money to make it happen.'

Alexa shook her head. 'I don't believe it. Not André.'

The sadness in her voice made Grant's heart sink, almost as if she were readying herself for the inevitable. She was a trusting soul. It was like he was watching innocence lost.

'We'll find out what happened to him,' he said. 'I promise.'

Alexa grabbed his hand and gave it a squeeze. 'Thanks.'

Grant turned down a heavily wooded lane that took a steep decline toward the western side of the island. They wound through the twisting streets until the navigation system announced they'd arrived. All that was visible was a white iron gate with a speaker box. Grant pulled up and pushed the intercom button.

A woman with elegant diction replied. 'May I help you?'

'Grant Westfield and Alexa Locke.'

'Oh, yes. Please park to the right of the fountain. I'll meet you at the door.'

A buzz sounded, and the gate swung aside.

Alexa crinkled her lips. 'Fountain?'

'You haven't been here?'

'No. Just to his office downtown.'

The driveway curved as it descended. When the forest parted, it was as though they'd emerged through some kind of wormhole into the French countryside. Laroche's mansion was built in the style of a French chateau, with ornate accents along the eaves, three cylindrical towers topped by needle-sharp spires, and a steeply pitched slate roof.

'*This* is where Laroche lives?' Grant marveled.

'Why? Have *you* been here before?'

'No, but I've seen it. From the lake, every year when I come down to watch the hydroplane races from my boat. We call it the Disney Castle.'

'It does look like where Cinderella might live,' Alexa said. 'Of course, after she marries her Prince Charming.'

A six-car garage sat to the left of the circular masonry driveway that wrapped around a twelve-foot-high fountain.

Alexa peered at the geysers spouting from the waterworks. 'I know I've seen that before.'

'The fountain?'

'Yes, but I can't remember where.'

Grant parked, but didn't see Harris's government-issued SUV, only a BMW sedan. She must have already dropped Tyler and Brielle off and left to pursue other leads. According to Tyler, the FBI finished their search of the house and found nothing. Laroche had vanished into thin air.

Grant and Alexa got out and went to the front door, which opened as they approached. A woman in her late twenties waited there, smiling at the sight of Alexa. Her painstakingly highlighted coif, tailored Armani suit, and heels that looked more expensive than a semester at Harvard shouted that she was a woman of means. *Laroche must pay his people well*, Grant thought.

She waved them over and closed the door before grasping both of Alexa's hands with hers.

'I'm so glad you could come, Alexa.'

'Not at all. I just wish it weren't true.'

'I know. I feel the same. I've been with Mr Laroche for four years, and I find it unbelievable that he would plan something so callous. The FBI have been through the entire mansion and finally left twenty minutes ago.' She turned to Grant. 'Mr Westfield, I'm Marlo Dunham, Mr Laroche's executive assistant.'

'Pleased to meet you. Is Tyler here?'

'In the living room. If you'll follow me.' She turned and marched away, her heels clacking on the marble floors.

Grant had been in mansions before, but he couldn't help gawking at the intricate tapestries and artworks that lined the spacious foyer. He assumed it all was original, collected from Laroche's ancestral homeland.

But other touches were quite odd and seemingly out of place. One in particular made him stop when he passed. Set into an alcove was a nine-foot tall hairy ape-man. At first he thought it was a Chewbacca costume set there as a joke, but a second glance confirmed that it was actually a replica of the Bigfoot that was videotaped in the famous grainy footage he'd seen so many times. It was even posed in the act of walking. Next to it was a plaster molding of a footprint, set into the floor as if it were a celebrity's at Grauman's Chinese Theatre. Grant hovered his boot over it. This was the first time his foot had seemed tiny.

'I told you he was odd,' Alexa said.

'When you have this much money, I believe the word is "eccentric".'

Dunham, who stood at a doorway further on, said, 'Mr Westfield?'

They followed her to an enormous living room like none he'd seen before. On one side of the room, hundreds of pieces of metal seemed to hang in mid-air. They didn't conform to any particular shape or apparent pattern. It wasn't until he got closer that Grant could see the pair of ultra-thin wires suspending each piece in its place, done so as to keep the fragments from spinning. The mobile was set in a corner against one blank stone wall and one etched with lines.

The rest of the room was furnished with ornate red velvet chairs and settees positioned around polished wood tables inlaid with cloisonné designs. A grand piano sat majestically among them. A third wall was a series of glass doors that opened onto a patio with a lavish garden and pool below. The doors framed an incredible view of the lake, with the tips of Seattle's skyscrapers visible in the background.

Tyler and Brielle stood at the opposite end of the room, huddled in discussion. She had changed out of the getup that Tyler had told Grant about and was now back into slacks and a light sweater. Behind them was a painting of a lake scene with a moody gray sky and green rolling hills in the background. It looked like any other pastoral scene that caused Grant to glaze over on an art museum tour until he spotted a small shape swimming in the water next to the ruins of a castle. It was a spitting image of the Loch Ness monster from the famous surgeon's photograph that Alexa mentioned, showing the creature's long neck rising above the surface.

Things were getting weirder and weirder.

Tyler saw them and rushed over to Alexa, hugging her then holding her out to look at her.

'Are you all right?' he asked her.

'I'm fine.'

'I'm sorry I couldn't come look for you myself.'

'I understand. I'm sure glad that you're a smart guy and that Grant knows how to punch people.'

Tyler clapped him on the shoulder. 'Thanks. I owe you.'

'Happy to do it,' Grant said. 'It's too bad Dillman made a run for it. Any word about him?'

Tyler shook his head. 'Nothing. And we've got a lot to talk about.'

'I know. You couldn't even wait to trash your new plane until *after* I'd gotten a ride in it?'

'Sometimes my will to live depends on destroying stuff. I just wish it wasn't *my* stuff.'

Tyler introduced Brielle. For a moment, Alexa glanced back and forth between Brielle and Tyler, but she said nothing.

'The FBI couldn't find anything?' Grant asked.

Tyler shook his head. 'They gave up, but I wanted to look

around a while longer, so thanks for coming to get us. With Zim gone, Laroche is our only lead now. We'll try his office next.'

'No luck?'

'Nada. I thought we might notice something they didn't, but they were pretty thorough ...' Tyler stopped talking abruptly and focused on Alexa.

She was staring intently at the piano. She examined it for a moment, deep in thought, and then took out her phone. After a few moments looking at the screen, she turned to Grant.

'That has to mean something,' she said.

'What?'

'The subject of André's email. "Play the opening of the Fifth". He hoped I'd come here eventually to look for him.'

Grant shrugged. 'Can't hurt. Give it a try.'

'I don't play the piano.'

'I do,' Brielle said. 'What do you want me to play?'

'The opening to Beethoven's Fifth Symphony.'

Brielle walked over to the keyboard and played four chords, tapping out the familiar dun-dun-dun-duh.

Grant heard a clunk near the picture of Loch Ness. They collectively gasped when the painting swung aside, revealing a gigantic steel door of the size found in a bank. There was no keypad, keyhole, or combination lock. Just a huge wheel shaped like an old sailing vessel's helm.

'It's good you brought Alexa with you,' Tyler said as he stood agog in front of the vault. 'Now, how do we get it open?'

TWENTY-ONE

Tyler phoned Agent Harris about their discovery, but she wouldn't be able to make it back for an hour. While they waited, he wanted to tell Grant and Alexa about what he and Brielle had found at Lake Shannon, but it couldn't happen until they were out of earshot of Marlo Dunham. The only reason that Brielle had been brought up to speed about the Nazi weapon was because of the revelation about Wade Plymouth's death.

The *Altwaffe* designation now made sense. 'Old weapon' wasn't a code word. It was the literal description of the poison's effects. The Nazis had developed a chemical weapon that somehow sped up the aging process. In effect it was an artificially accelerated form of progeria, a genetic disorder that causes children to age rapidly, with few living past their teens. The Third Reich had been hoping to unleash this secret weapon to turn the tide of World War II. If Laroche possessed the records of *Altwaffe*'s development, it might provide information that the toxicologists could use in creating an antidote.

As he considered their next move, Tyler stood next to

Brielle at the patio doors and studied the statues that dominated the lawn below. Three enormous white marble carvings of horses and men flanked an even larger statue of women bathing the feet of a seated godlike man in robes. All of the people had the strong features and curly hair he'd seen in Greek-style statues that didn't seem to fit in with the French motif of the mansion. The only flaw was the missing outstretched foot of the pampered man. Given all of the other strange elements of the house, Tyler supposed that he shouldn't consider it odd.

'Ms Dunham,' he said, 'does Laroche have any other safes?'

'I didn't even know about *this* vault,' she said.

'So you don't know what he kept in here?'

'No, but I can't believe that Mr Laroche would be behind something so heinous.'

'Then let's hope what we find inside the vault will exonerate him. Any other surprises in this room?'

'The only one I know about is this,' Dunham said. 'I showed it to the FBI yesterday.'

Dunham picked up a remote control with a touchscreen display on it. She tapped on the screen, and a segment of ceiling slid aside. A device that looked like a LCD projector lowered with a mechanical whine. When it came to a stop, a white light bloomed from the lens.

Tyler turned, expecting to see a video. Instead, he saw a shadow.

The hanging metal mobile, which had appeared so random,

now cast a silhouette on the wall that clearly depicted the outline of a dragon, yet another mythical creature. The spotlight was placed in the only position that could produce the shadow. Alexa couldn't resist the urge to pass her hand in front of the light.

Dunham walked over to the mobile. 'There are two things Mr Laroche is passionate about. One is his French heritage, as you can see from this house. The second is cryptozoology, which led to his hiring Dr Locke. I mean, this Dr Locke,' she said, indicating Alexa. 'He had this mobile commissioned after he'd seen the work of artists Tim Noble and Sue Webster, who create a similar effect with piles of trash.'

'Similar effect?' Alexa asked.

'Noble and Webster arrange refuse in a distinct way. What looks like a collection of garbage in normal light is transformed when a single light source is projected from the exact right location. The result is a shadow of, say, a couple embracing. They also have a sense of the macabre, creating the silhouette of two heads on pikes using the carcasses of dead animals.'

Alexa screwed up her face at the description. 'Lovely.'

'It looks like Mr Laroche has a taste for the peculiar as well,' Tyler said. 'He never mentioned this vault to you?'

Dunham shook her head. 'He's a private man. I have to say I'm disappointed he didn't trust me enough to tell me about it.'

'Enough with the games,' Brielle said, throwing her

hands up. 'Can't we cut it open? Find a specialist who opens bank vaults?'

Tyler shook his head. 'Not in the time we have. It would require delicate work with a thermal lance. It might take days, and even then the lance is so hot that it might destroy any document inside. We have to figure out the code.'

'Do you think it's the piano?' Alexa asked.

'It opened the painting, so that's a good bet,' Grant said. 'And it's a great way to encode something. There are eighty-eight keys. It's better than 256-bit encryption. Even a supercomputer wouldn't be able to crack it.'

'There must be a coded acoustic receiver in the room,' Tyler said. 'And I doubt it would be a common tune. Too likely that someone could happen upon the code by sheer luck. Do you have any idea how to get inside it, Ms Dunham?'

'No clue. Obviously I didn't know a piano tune could move the painting.'

'The email!' Alexa shouted, clapping her hands. 'The rest of it must tell me how to get inside the vault. He was giving me the code.'

'Mr Laroche sent you a code?' Dunham asked, mystified.

Alexa nodded, pulled out her phone, and read the email to them.

Dunham pursed her lips. 'Why do you think the rest of it is a code?'

'What other reason could he have for making it so cryptic?'

'Do you know how to interpret it?'

Alexa frowned. 'Uh, no.'

'Read the first part again,' Tyler said.

You must continue our search no matter the obstacles. You of all people should know that doubling the degree to which you work is important to reaching our goal.

Tyler pointed at Alexa. '"You of all people", he says. Something you in particular should know.'

'So she needs to double the work she does on this?' Grant said. 'How is that relevant? His message is, "Work harder"?'

Alexa shook her head slowly. 'André was always saying that he was so proud of how much effort we were putting into the job, taking our work to the nth degree. It has to be what he meant. He said it all the time.'

Grant turned to Tyler. 'Didn't we have equations about nth-degree polynomials in linear algebra?'

'Yes, but I doubt Laroche was giving her a math equation to solve. He was aiming this puzzle at Alexa. That means it should be something in her area of expertise.'

'Which is what?' Brielle asked.

'Zoology, with a specialization in taxonomy and genetics.' When she saw Brielle's confused look, Alexa continued. 'I study the classification and heredity of animals. That was the reason André said I was the best candidate to search for Nessie. Once we found it, he wanted me to figure out how to classify it in the animal phylum.'

'Keep going with the message,' Tyler said.

Alexa read the next paragraph.

At times the creature has been said to resemble a sea serpent, a water horse, a kraken, or a plesiosaur. Dinosaurs are extinct, so the key is in the cells of animals still living.

'About the only thing he left out was a yeti and a unicorn,' Grant said.

'He was making a juxtaposition with the mythical creatures,' Alexa said. 'André must mean that the key is literally in the cells of these animals.'

'How?' Tyler asked. 'Is he talking about genetically combining them?'

Realization dawned on Alexa's face. Tyler knew the look well.

'Doubling the nth degree,' she said. 'Double n, meaning 2n. The key is in their cells.'

Brielle looked confused again. So was Tyler. 'What's 2n?'

'It's the diploid chromosome number for any living thing. It varies widely. Humans have forty-six chromosomes. Chickens have eighty. Fruit flies have eight.'

She read the next part of the message.

Hydrophis spiralis, hippopotamus amphibius, and Mesonychoteuthis hamiltoni are all good candidates, but it can't be any single one of those.

'It has to be what he means. The chromosome numbers for the sea snake, hippo, and colossal squid.' She tapped furiously on her phone touchpad. 'There's an online database at Harvard that I have access to. It'll take me a couple of minutes to track all three down.'

Tyler shook his head in wonderment. 'Laroche would have known that only a zoologist could have connected the dots.'

'But why send a scrambled message to Alexa?' Dunham said.

Brielle stared at the massive vault. 'And what the hell is so important for him to protect?'

'Got 'em!' Alexa said triumphantly. 'The sea snake chromosome number is eighteen, the hippo's is thirty-six, and the colossal squid's is a hundred and eighty-four.'

She read the last part of the message.

However, if you add the structures of these creatures together, that is how you'll find the Loch Ness monster.

Tyler did the addition in his head. 'That's two hundred thirty-eight.'

'That's way too short to be a code,' Grant said.

Brielle jotted the numbers on a notepad. 'What if we put them side by side?'

'If we go in the order he used in the message,' Alexa said, 'that's 1836184.'

Grant looked at the baby grand. 'How do you play that on a piano?'

Brielle shook her head. 'Those numbers don't correspond to notes. Besides, we wouldn't know what key to play.'

Tyler stared at the mobile and the shadow it cast on the blank wall. Why was that wall bare and the wall next to it lined? It almost looked like a . . .

He suddenly whipped around, looking for a seam in the ceiling, but there was so much detail in the woodwork that it was impossible to see where Laroche might have hidden a recessed light projector.

He pointed to the lines and asked Brielle, 'What do those look like to you?'

Brielle scrutinized the lines, which weren't all evenly spaced. They were slightly separated every five lines. Her eyes widened when she recognized the pattern.

'Those are musical staves.'

Tyler picked up the remote. 'And I'll bet we can get some music from those lines.'

The touchscreen had a numerical keypad. He plugged 1836184 into it.

The light projecting on the mobile went out and rose back into the ceiling. At the same time another light lowered from a spot opposite the lined wall. When it clicked into place, the spotlight shone on the mobile from the perpendicular direction.

Dots appeared on the wall, perfectly spaced within or on the lines. Some of the dots were formed by two or more of the irregularly shaped hanging metal pieces. If Tyler hadn't seen it with his own eyes, he wouldn't have believed they could blend together so flawlessly. Some of the dots even had lines extending from them, indicating quarter- or half-notes.

Tyler turned to Dunham. 'Have you seen that before?'

Dunham shook her head slowly, a stunned look on her face.

'Can you play that?' he asked Brielle.

She squinted at the notes. 'The chords are fairly complex for me, but I'll give it a try.'

Brielle sat on the bench and flexed her fingers. The rest of them went back and forth between watching her and the vault door.

She played three slow chords, followed by two quick ones. Nothing happened.

'Why does that sound familiar?' Alexa said.

'Are you kidding?' Grant said. 'That's the opening theme from *2001: A Space Odyssey*.'

'It's called *Also Sprach Zarathustra*,' Brielle said. 'Everybody learns to play it. But it's several keys off the normal one, so nobody would have played it by accident. I got some of the notes wrong. Let me try again.'

She played it twice more, getting more comfortable each time until she got it note perfect.

The third time did the trick. A deep hum emanated from the vault. Tyler could almost feel its huge steel bars being drawn from the door. The hum ceased, and the door swung open, a light blazing from beyond. A recording of the *2001* music played from the interior. Laroche certainly had a flair for the dramatic.

When the door was fully open, the music ended. Tyler and the others crept forward until they were at the entrance.

'Oh, my God!' Alexa shouted and dashed inside.

'Wait!' Tyler ran after her. She was already kneeling by a figure propped against a display case.

'He's alive,' she said, her fingers pressed against the carotid, 'but barely breathing. We need an ambulance.'

André Laroche wasn't on the run. He had locked himself inside his own vault.

TWENTY-TWO

Brielle stood back while Tyler and Alexa tended to Laroche and Grant called emergency services. She looked around and saw that one person was missing.

'Where did Ms Dunham go?'

She didn't wait for a response and went to look for her. It wasn't a good sign when the loyal assistant didn't stick around to see what was inside the safe.

Brielle backtracked her way toward the entrance and saw Dunham emerge from a side hallway. Without hesitation, Dunham raised a semiautomatic pistol and fired.

Instinctively, Brielle ducked, and the first two shots went wide. As bullets whistled past her, she dodged left and took refuge behind Bigfoot in the alcove. Several more rounds slammed into the stuffed beast, and then heels clacked in triple-time toward the front door.

Brielle poked her head out to see Dunham climb into a BMW. It laid patches of rubber on the stones and was gone.

Tyler yelled from around the corner. 'Brielle, are you all right?'

Brielle emerged from her hiding place. 'I'm fine. It's clear now.'

Tyler stepped out from behind the wall. 'What happened?' Grant followed, inspecting the bullet holes in the wall.

'It was Marlo Dunham. She shot at me and took off. Silver BMW. I didn't get the plates, but it's probably her car.'

Grant shook his head in disbelief. 'Why?'

'Because of what we found in the vault. She must have left the room when she realized we were about to open it and would find Laroche inside.'

'I'll call the police and tell them to be on the lookout for her car,' Grant said. 'With only two directions off Mercer Island, she should be easy to spot.' He made the call while they walked back to the vault.

As they waited for the ambulance, they checked out the vault's contents. Display cases ringed the interior. Each held an artifact, all of them labeled. One claimed the item was a lock of Bigfoot's hair. Another was the tooth of a Tasmanian wolf, dated 1956. The biggest display case was at the back and held a six-foot-long fish that had been stuffed and mounted. It was labeled a coelacanth.

'What is all this stuff?' Grant wondered aloud.

'It must be André's treasure,' Alexa said as she cradled Laroche's head in her lap. 'He believes that Bigfoot and the Loch Ness monster are real, out there waiting to be discovered. Like the Tasmanian wolf, which was declared extinct a hundred years ago, but there are people who think a few still roam the wilds of that island.'

'And the big ugly fish?'

'The last coelacanth was thought to have died in the Cretaceous Period, but fishermen caught one off the east coast of Africa in 1938, proving the species was still in existence after sixty-five million years. Since then, they've been caught regularly. I had no idea he had one. I've only seen it one other time, at the Smithsonian National Museum of Natural History in DC.'

'So he thinks the Loch Ness monster is like the coelacanth?' Tyler said. 'It's been around since the time of the dinosaurs, and we just haven't seen it all these years?'

'It might not be a dinosaur, but the coelacanth does show we could be surprised by more species yet to be discovered. That's what makes my job interesting.'

'I think *I've* found something interesting,' Brielle said, standing at a small pedestal with a case on it.

Tyler and Grant looked over her shoulder as she carefully flipped through a notebook. The pages were yellowed with age.

A single word was emblazoned on the cover above a swastika: *Altwaffe*. Old weapon.

Brielle felt a chill as she thought of her friend, Wade Plymouth, who had aged fifty years in little more than two weeks.

Sirens wailed in the distance. The paramedics and police would arrive at the mansion any minute.

'Grant,' Tyler said, 'did you bring that high-res camera?'

'Just like you asked.'

'Then let's get a picture of every page in the book. We're going to have to turn it over to the Feds, but I don't want to be cut out of the loop.'

Brielle picked up the notebook to hand it over and felt a piece of paper underneath. She didn't want to cede anything to the police that she didn't have to, so she deftly swiped it to her side as she gave Grant the book.

Tyler flipped through the pages rapidly for Grant to capture the words on video.

'I'll bring the paramedics in,' Brielle said and left them to finish documenting the notebook.

The ambulance stopped in the driveway, and two paramedics jumped out with their gear. She led them to the living room and pointed them to the vault. She stayed behind to read the page she had acquired.

Dear Alexa,

I pray that you are the one who found this note. If you are reading this, then you understood my email and discovered my body. I'm sorry for the mysterious email, but I couldn't let Marlo Dunham know that you were the sole person with the code to get into the vault. If she had realized what I'd sent, she would have killed you. She has held me captive for nine days. I know she planned to kill me when she no longer needed me, and I thought locking myself in the one place she couldn't get to me was the only option left.

I know she betrayed me and planned to unleash the

Altwaffe. When I bought the canister and notebook, I thought it was simply a way to find the Loch Ness monster, and so did the unwitting seller. But when I realized what it was, Marlo convinced me not to turn it over to the authorities, fearing that it would be turned into a potent weapon by the government. Instead, I locked it away, unsure of how to destroy it safely myself. Little did I realize that I was being deceived by my trusted assistant.

She took the weapon, but left the notebook, possibly to implicate me. She didn't know that the notebook also contains the formula for an antidote. It's a fairly simple process, once you have the key ingredient, but no one on earth has it.

The reason is simple. To make the antidote, you must have a tissue sample from the Loch Ness monster.

As police rushed past her, Brielle shook her head and read the sentence three more times to make sure she had read it right. The next sentence was even stranger.

The Nazis claim to have acquired a sample taken by Charles Darwin himself. I know that's difficult to believe, but you must. It's the only way to undo the damage that I have done by not destroying the *Altwaffe* when I should have. If only I had recognized Marlo's insanity sooner.

I can't take the chance that Marlo has found a way

into the vault, and that it is she instead of you reading this note. I can't lead her to Nessie and help her destroy any hope for a cure. On the back of this page are clusters of numbers and letters. You must follow in the footstep of the Sun King's Apollo. Place the sheet so that Apollo's hallux is aligned with the 2n of your favorite animal and his lateral one is aligned with the 2n of that animal's most feared enemy. Starting at three, the resulting connected code will lead you to a book at the current home of Darwin's intellect. There you will learn how to locate the creature and find a cure.

I'm sorry to burden you with this quest. I wish I could have seen you again, my dear, but it was not to be. Please understand that I only had the best of intentions.

Your friend,

André

Brielle flipped the sheet over and saw hundreds of numbers and letters speckling the page. There was no identifiable pattern to it, as if it were a connect-the-dots drawing.

'What are you reading?' Tyler asked, startling Brielle. She was about to come up with a lie, but Tyler stopped her. 'I saw you take it from the vault. You need to work on your sleight of hand.'

She pulled him aside and whispered to him. 'We have to keep this quiet.' She handed him the note.

He read it, then looked at her. 'This is incredible.'

'I know. It's hard to believe.'

'That's the problem. We need the antidote within the next week.'

'Why?'

Tyler glanced around to make sure no one was listening. 'The weapon's already been deployed. Through the sprinklers inside the Salle Gustave Eiffel. People are already starting to die.'

'My God. Wasn't Grant inside at the time?'

Tyler nodded solemnly. 'And they don't have any idea how to treat it.'

Wade Plymouth's wrinkled face flashed in front of her. 'Then this is our only hope.'

Tyler was taken aback. 'You really think going after a mythical creature is the best use of our time?'

'Your own sister made a video recording of it.'

'She made a video recording of something. Why don't we go after Bigfoot while we're at it?'

'The Nazis obviously believed it,' Brielle said. 'And Victor Zim does, too. Why else would he try to abduct Alexa?'

'I don't know. But I'm certain there's no sea monster living in Loch Ness. It's a legend perpetuated by cranks and hoaxers.'

'So certain that you're willing to bet Grant's life on it?'

Tyler went silent, then said, 'Why are you so quick to buy into this?'

'Because I saw one of my closest friends turned into an elderly man virtually overnight. That makes me ready to believe almost anything, especially if it helps me get the bastards who did that to him. Do you have a better idea?'

Tyler scratched his temple in thought. After a full minute, he cursed under his breath. 'All right. I can try convincing Agent Harris, but how does she ask her superiors to put resources into finding the Loch Ness monster? I can imagine sitting in their position and thinking it's nuts.'

Brielle nodded at his point. Despite her confidence in presenting her case to Tyler, she wasn't sure if they'd find anything at all. 'Then we have to do it ourselves.'

She saw Tyler wrestling with the thought of keeping information from the Feds. He was a big boy scout; doing things the right way was in his blood.

Finally he said, 'We know Alexa and Grant will go along with this, so we'll keep it to the four of us until we have irrefutable proof.'

He pocketed the sheet. Once Laroche's comatose form was carried away to the hospital, Harris arrived and they spent the next hour answering her questions about the vault, Dunham, and the notebook. Neither Tyler nor Brielle mentioned the letter left by Laroche.

Dunham's gunshots were enough to implicate her. Her car was found abandoned at Mercer Village Shopping Center. She was on the run with a BOLO issued. The be-on-the-lookout alert had every Washington law enforcement agency on the hunt for her, so they were confident about catching her, but Brielle thought she might have been ready for such an eventuality.

When the FBI was done with them, the four of them finally had the privacy of Grant's SUV to discuss the note. Grant looked especially hopeful that there was now something he could do to prevent his own death.

Alexa read it twice.

'Laroche may not be any help for a while,' Tyler said. 'The paramedics said he might have suffered a stroke and don't know if he'll make it. Alexa, do you understand his clues?'

'The stuff specific to me, sure. I told André that the harp seal was my favorite animal. So cute. And the harp seal's most feared enemy is the polar bear. So those chromosome numbers are easy to find. But then I'm not sure what we're supposed to do with it.'

'What's the current home of Darwin's intellect?' Tyler asked her.

'Where his brain is,' Grant said. 'We need to find where he's buried.'

Alexa shook her head. 'No, André specifically said his "intellect". We have to go where his thoughts are preserved.'

'How can his thoughts be preserved?'

'Of course! The largest collection of Darwin's letters, notes, and books is at the University of Cambridge library in England. The numbers must point to a specific document in the library. We'll need to find the right combination of numbers. There must be millions of possibilities on this page.'

Brielle leaned forward. 'What's a hallux?'

'It's a big toe. The lateral one must refer to the little toe.'

'So we need Apollo's big toe and pinky toe,' Grant said. 'Great. That makes no sense.'

An image of a foot flashed in Brielle's mind. 'The statues in the backyard!' she shouted in triumph. 'That has to be what Laroche meant.'

'Because one of the figures was missing a foot?' Tyler asked.

'It's a statue of Apollo. I've seen it before.'

'We can't use it obviously, but then neither could Marlo Dunham,' Tyler said. 'Laroche must have traced the foot to make the clue and then he destroyed it or threw it in the lake.'

'So we're back to zero,' Grant said.

'No, we're not,' Brielle said. 'The reason I recognized the statue is because it's a replica.'

Alexa snapped her fingers. 'The fountain in the driveway! That's a replica, too!'

Brielle nodded. 'They're both from the same place. We have to go to France.'

Tyler furrowed his brow at her. 'Why?'

'Because the original statue was designed for the Sun King, Louis XIV,' she said, 'and it's now sitting in the gardens of Versailles.'

TWENTY-THREE

Zim allowed himself to enjoy the steady breeze while the thirty-five-foot power boat motored toward the town of Sidney on British Columbia's Vancouver Island. The late afternoon sun was starting to fade over the Strait of Juan de Fuca, but they would reach port before dark. Then it was onto a flight from Victoria International Airport to Calgary, then to Heathrow in London and on to Paris after that. Zim wanted to absorb as much of the open air as he could before being crammed into a plane for the next fourteen hours.

The vessel reminded Zim of the one his father had owned when he and his brothers were young boys, the days when they'd gone out on long weekend excursions on Lake Michigan, the days before his father's job at the auto parts factory was destroyed by the company owned by a Saudi sheik who bought the plant merely to shut it down. Those were the last happy times Zim could remember, and it was his first taste of how ruthless Arabs could be. The family had sold everything and moved to California looking for work, where his father was reduced to pounding out dents at an auto body shop until he drank himself to death.

Despite how much he reveled in the motion of the boat on the waves, Zim knew he couldn't return to that life on Lake Michigan. He was a wanted man now and always would be. Stepping onto the dock in Everett was probably the last time he'd set foot in the United States. Europe would become his new home. If he ended up dying on this operation, at least he'd be going out in the birthplace of the white race. And he'd do it while making the Arabs pay for what they'd done to his family.

Pryor was down in the bunk napping while Marlo Dunham lounged next to him in a sweater and jeans that hugged her slim body. Pryor had been lusting after her ever since they'd picked her up on Mercer Island, but Zim felt no attraction to her. Brunettes didn't do it for him. If he ever took a wife, she would have to fit the Aryan ideal of a tall blonde Viking goddess. Maybe he'd settle in Norway. Carl had said it was filled with his type of woman.

'How long until we arrive?' Dunham asked.

'A couple of hours,' Zim said. 'We'll be in plenty of time for the flight.'

'I'm not concerned about that. You both need to alter your appearance to match the passports or we'll be arrested the moment we go through security in Victoria.'

'Don't worry about it. We've got the disguises in the cabin. We'll put them on before we dock. What about you? You're as wanted as we are now.'

'I've got a blonde wig, a different nose, and glasses.'

'Blonde, huh?'

Dunham sneered at him. 'Don't even think it. I'm not interested.'

'What if I don't care?'

'What if I don't show up at the airport and you have no plane tickets? Remember, I funded your jailbreak, and I control the purse strings on this mission. Without my money, your friend Pryor over there wouldn't be able to build a flashlight.'

Zim gritted his teeth. He didn't relish being in thrall to this or any other woman. 'Relax. It was a joke. Besides, I don't want Carl's sloppy seconds.'

Dunham gave him the finger, leaned back, and put on her sunglasses.

She had hooked up with his brother four years after Victor was sent to prison. Carl told him it was fate, but Zim always thought it was a little convenient that she latched onto him just before presenting her plan to attack the summit with this old Nazi weapon. He later learned that she had found out about the tragic Zim brothers and seen an opportunity. Carl was too much of a stooge to realize what was happening. Dunham pushed all of his buttons in precisely the right way.

She had used their mutual tragedies to reel Carl in. Years before, Dunham had fallen in love with some kind of peacenik who joined an aid organization supporting the Palestinian cause. Just like a woman, she was so head over heels for the guy that she went to Gaza with him. When an Israeli airstrike hit the apartment complex they were living in, her boyfriend was killed, and Dunham was injured so badly that not only did she lose the baby she was carrying, she lost the ability to ever have children.

Zim didn't like Dunham, but he could identify with her sudden change of attitude. Tragedy could do that in an instant.

Dunham returned to the US stewing in hatred and convinced that both the Israelis and Palestinians were scum. Laroche kept a close watch on Israeli news and, unaware of her pathological grudge, took pity on Dunham because his own mother had been killed in a Palestinian suicide attack. He offered her a job to take advantage of her education in archaeology, which she had planned to indulge when she moved to the Middle East. Laroche hoped her background would dovetail with his cryptozoology passion. With no other job prospects, she took the position and worked for him faithfully for the next three years, despite his allegiance to Israel.

Laroche's fortuitous purchase of the Nazi chemical weapon reignited Dunham's need for revenge, but her plan required muscle to make it a reality. When she met Alexa Locke, she briefly considered Tyler for the job but quickly found out what a do-gooder he was. He would never agree to it. She needed someone who would understand her desire for vengeance, and when she heard about Tyler's involvement with Victor and Carl Zim, Dunham sought

Carl out and convinced him to join forces with her. Carl's only condition was that they would free his brother once the job was done.

Carl was totally dazzled by Dunham and wrote about her in glowing letters to Victor that his attorney was able to bring in uncensored during regular visits. Victor suspected there was some fabrication and embellishment of the story on Dunham's part, but it didn't matter. Their goals were aligned perfectly: now Dunham would get the destruction of Israel and Zim would make Islam a dirty word in the western nations while taking out all of their leaders at once.

Zim put the boat on a heading that would take them around Orcas Island. 'How are you going to keep the money flowing now that they've found Laroche?'

'Embezzling from that old fool was easy,' Dunham said. 'I've got enough cash stashed away for whatever we need.'

'Are you sure they won't find it? You thought they wouldn't find that vault for weeks and look how that went.'

'And they wouldn't have if your men hadn't screwed up and let both Alexa Locke and Brielle Cohen get away.'

Zim shifted in his seat. 'I'm down four men because they had help. Tyler Locke and Grant Westfield rescued them.'

'I realized that when they showed up at Laroche's estate.'

'Which wouldn't have been a problem if you had killed Laroche when I told you to.'

Dunham had Laroche locked in a room at the mansion,

delaying the inevitable need to kill him because of some misguided sense of pity. She learned her lesson when he broke out of his room long enough to send the email to Alexa and lock himself in the vault.

Zim looked at Dunham with undisguised disdain. 'Why didn't you kill them all at the mansion?'

'There was no point in giving myself away if they didn't get into the vault.'

'You should have had the gun with you.'

'How was I supposed to know they'd open the vault so easily? I've been trying to figure out the code for days. The only reason they could do it was because of the clues Laroche sent to Alexa.'

Zim grunted but said nothing. It sounded like a bunch of flimsy excuses to him. If he had been there, all their adversaries would be dead, and he would have destroyed the notebook, making the rest of this mission unnecessary.

'We should split up in London,' Dunham said.

'Why?'

'Because if they get to Versailles before you do, we'll have to stop them in England. You'll take Pryor with you to France and meet up with the men there. I'll take the other half of them and stake out the library at Cambridge.'

Zim scowled at her. She was getting too used to ordering him around. 'Are you sure you can handle it?'

'You're so sweet,' she said with a mock baby voice. 'You're worried about me getting hurt? Please. Carl trained me on weapons. I'm ready.'

'I'm worried about you getting captured and losing our money,' Zim said.

'I'm not going to sit back in a hotel while the Locke siblings and their friends screw up a year of planning. If they find the Loch Ness monster in time to make the antidote, then your brother died for nothing.'

'And if we find the monster first?'

'Then not only do we have to kill it,' she said with a shrug, 'we have to make sure its corpse will never be found.'

VERSAILLES

WORLD NEWS

Rocket Attacks Depleting Iron Dome Missile Shield

By RIMONA BENESCH

June 20, TEL AVIV –The Israeli defense system known as Iron Dome has been so active over the past week that a shortage of missiles could render it ineffective in a matter of days, according to sources in the military. If that happens, Israel's major population areas would be at the mercy of a massive rocket and artillery bombardment.

Some officers in the Israeli Defense Force are concerned that depletion of the missiles is the goal of the repeated attacks. Iron Dome is also an effective anti-aircraft system. If it is not available to defend against incoming airstrikes, they fear that Egyptian and Syrian forces – supplied with advanced Chinese and Russian weapons by sympathetic countries in the Muslim world – will be emboldened to launch an all-out invasion.

As rumors of Muslim leaders dying from a poison supposedly administered by Mossad agents continue to spread, the threat of just such an invasion is not being taken lightly. Speculation continues unabated into the cause of the illness, but doctors are still at a loss for how to treat the deadly affliction. If no cure is found, sources say that the affected countries will feel obligated to strike back against the perceived aggressor.

Israeli Prime Minister Elijah Alfandari has issued a statement that any incursion will be met with massive force and did not rule out retaliating against countries supporting the invasion, raising the risk that such a conflict could expand to a war engulfing the entire Middle East.

TWENTY-FOUR

When the RER C train pulled into the Chateau de Versailles station, it was already five in the afternoon. Rather than struggle through the clogged Paris traffic, Tyler decided that they'd reach the palace faster using rapid transit. Brielle had purchased a book on Versailles at the airport and buried her nose in it for the entire train ride.

Normally, Miles would have been happy for them to use a company jet for their air travel, but one was in Afghanistan and the other was undergoing maintenance. Instead, they took a late-night nonstop flight to Charles de Gaulle airport, while Alexa and Grant flew to London Heathrow. Upon landing, Tyler had gotten the message that the two of them were on their own train to Cambridge. He and Brielle stopped only to leave their bags at a hotel, where the concierge gave them complimentary tickets to Versailles.

The plan was simple. Tyler and Brielle would find the statue of Apollo and get the exact dimensions of his foot by taking a photograph of it next to a ruler. Tyler would then email the photo to Grant, who would print out the photo at the appropriate size and overlay it on the copy of Laroche's note to get the next clue. Alexa would figure out what they were looking for in the library, and hopefully that would describe how to find the Loch Ness monster. He also had Miles divert two Gordian GhostMantas intended for a North Sea oil rig to Loch Ness.

Simple, but as Tyler went through the plan in his mind, it sounded ridiculous. When he'd presented Special Agent Harris with the idea, she felt the same way. She acknowledged that the Nazi notebook was valuable and might provide some insights for the toxicology teams working on an antidote in Washington, London, and Frankfurt, but there was no way she was going to ask the French or British authorities to help in the search for a mythological creature. She said she had neither the time nor the resources to go on a wild goose chase.

Harris even thought Laroche might have gone to these lengths to divert attention away from his own involvement. If he was in on the plot with Dunham, she might have double-crossed him, leading him to concoct his wild story. However, they wouldn't be able to get answers from him any time soon. Doctors said he had neglected to take his blood pressure medication with him into the vault, and because of the ensuing stroke and brain swelling, they had no idea when or if he'd ever wake up.

Under most any other circumstances, Tyler would have agreed with Harris and not even considered pursuing this path. He'd seen some unbelievable things in his life, but his innate nature as a skeptic made the whole thing hard to swallow.

This was one time, however, that his logical side was kicked to the curb. Other than Alexa's three-second video, there was nothing concrete to suggest that something unknown to science was alive in Loch Ness, no matter how hard Zim and Dunham were trying to stop them. If that's all he had, Tyler wouldn't be in France now.

Instead, Tyler was here because he was clinging to hope. His best friend was dying. If having a shot at saving Grant meant believing in an outrageous story, he'd need to have a little faith. The alternative was too terrible to contemplate.

Tyler took a deep breath and focused himself on their work.

'Do you know where we're going?' Tyler asked Brielle.

She looked up from her book. 'Yes. The statue of the Baths of Apollo was originally in the Cave of Thetis, an indoor bathhouse. Now it's in one of the twelve *bosquets*, or groves. They're rectangular stands of trees with paths cut through them to clearings, statuary, and fountains. The statues will be roped off, so we'll have to cross illicitly to get close enough for the photo.'

'We'll have to wait a while until the grove is clear of tourists.'

'It may not be much of a problem. At this time of day, more people will be exiting than entering.'

The train lurched to a stop, and they had to jostle their way through the passengers waiting to get on. Brielle was right about people leaving; the station was jammed with tourists spent from their day at the palace.

They made their way through the station and turned right when they got outside. According to Brielle, it was a short walk to the chateau. No clouds were present to blot out the warm afternoon sun. A T-shirt and jeans were all Tyler needed, while Brielle wore cargo shorts and a loose-fitting top. They fit right in with the tourists.

Seeing so many couples and families returning from a day of sightseeing, holding hands and laughing, Tyler felt the urge to put his arm around Brielle's shoulder. But considering the task at hand, it didn't seem right.

'I haven't been to Versailles in twenty years,' Brielle said. 'Came here with my parents when I was in high school. It's a magical place. Elegant. Inspiring. I always thought I'd return someday on a romantic holiday.'

Tyler smiled. 'This doesn't qualify?'

'I don't know if that statement makes you a hopeless romantic or just hopeless. Have you been here before?'

'No. Karen always wanted to come here, but she died before it happened.'

'I'm sorry.'

'Thanks. I guess we both thought we'd be here under different circumstances.'

Silence descended. Ever since Tyler plucked Brielle out of Lake Shannon, they'd been all business. Even the flight to Paris had consisted of little more than planning and sleep. After the Eiffel Tower incident, Tyler never thought he'd see Brielle again, let alone three days later. They'd said their final goodbyes and gone their separate ways at the hotel, expecting that would be the end of it. It was like sleeping with someone during a spring break fling and then returning to college to find out your one-night stand lived in the same dorm.

'I went out with a gentile once,' Brielle said. 'Dated, I mean. So I've been down that road before. It doesn't end well.'

'For whom?'

'For either of us. No sense in trying again, although it does seem like someone is determined to put us together.' She turned to him. 'Do you believe in fate?'

Tyler shook his head. 'I like having a little more control over my life than that.'

'What *do* you believe in?'

'Living in the moment. If there's one thing I've learned, you never know when your time is up.'

'You mean, dying is just bad luck?'

'If you want to call it that. But I like to think of luck as where preparation meets opportunity.'

Brielle chuckled at that. 'And what an opportunity we have before us now. I'm back at Versailles because of a quest to find Nessie so that some boffin in a lab can extract an antitoxin to a Nazi superweapon.'

'Well, when you say it like that, it sounds absurd. Are you buying into Laroche's letter?'

'Dunham thinks the Loch Ness monster is important, so

there must be something to it. Whether that means we find Nessie or something else, I don't know. I guess we'll find out together.'

They rounded the corner and there ahead of them loomed one of the largest residences ever built, the chateau of Versailles. At over 700,000 square feet, it is fourteen times the size of Bill Gates' enormous mansion in Seattle. The gardens are even larger, encompassing two thousand acres.

As they approached, passing a statue of Louis XIV astride a horse, Tyler couldn't take his eyes from the ornate stone and brick palace that encircled a gigantic cobbled courtyard. The façade was lavishly appointed with sculptures and adorned with gold filigree along the eaves of the slate roofs. Even the gate and fencing were gilt. Clearly Laroche had borrowed many of Versailles's themes when designing his own estate.

Even at this late hour, a pack of visitors waited in line to get into the palace.

'We don't have to get in line because we're not going inside,' Brielle said, and then nodded to the left. 'The entrance to the gardens is over here.'

They went through an alcove and presented their tickets. On weekdays the gardens were accessible for free, but on weekends there was a fee because tourists were treated to the Grandes Eaux, the only days the fountains were in operation.

They emerged into the rear courtyard, which was perhaps even more spectacular than the front. Opulent gardens and forests stretched as far as Tyler could see. The terrace's gravel and sand hardpan, split by two huge pools, gave way to steps that led down to a jetting fountain. Past the fountain was a promenade that extended along a manicured lawn to another fountain and then the Grand Canal. Nearly a mile long and bisected by an equally long basin, the wide pool was dotted with rowboats for hire.

Tyler wasn't prepared for the number of vehicles that were flitting about the gardens. In addition to the smattering of utility carts used by the gardeners, trams were shuttling people between the main palace, the Grand Trianon where the king kept his private residence, and the Petit Trianon, where Marie Antoinette once lived. Rental golf carts whizzed by, and in the distance he could see people on bicycles.

A Mozart concerto lilted from hidden speakers to accompany the waterworks. If it weren't for the modern clothes and vehicles, Tyler might have thought they'd been transported back to the eighteenth century.

Brielle consulted a map in her book. She looked up and pointed at a grove to the right. 'The entrance should be on the other side.'

As they went around the pools, Tyler looked up to see people on the second floor of the palace staring down at the view.

'That's the Hall of Mirrors.'

'I've heard about it,' Tyler said. 'I'd like to see it someday.'

'Maybe someday I'll bring you back.' Brielle immediately

looked away, as if she regretted saying it, and Tyler pretended not to hear her.

They got to a path between the groves, and as soon as they entered, the clamor from the hordes of tourists faded. The closest person was a quarter-mile down the pathway. To be isolated so quickly was surprising, but Tyler supposed that few people explored off the main paths. Only the sound of the music remained.

He and Brielle walked between the groves, which were blocked by green fencing to discourage adventurous visitors from diving into the thick foliage. It didn't stop a calico cat from squeezing out through a small break in the fencing. The cat must have been startled by Tyler's footsteps because it darted back into the grove through the same hole.

'The king's pets?' Tyler asked.

'There are neighborhoods all around the park. It's probably looking for a tasty mouse.' After a minute more of walking, Brielle said, 'It should be the next left.'

At the turn, they stopped abruptly. A closed iron gate blocked their path, marked with a sign: *Le Bosquet des Bains d'Apollon est fermé.* The English translation was below: 'The Grove of Apollo's Baths is closed.'

'Did your book say anything about this?' Tyler asked.

'No. They must be doing maintenance.'

Tyler examined the gate, seven feet high and topped with short spikes. 'Ready for a little breaking and entering?'

Brielle looked both ways. 'We'll be in and out in five minutes. No one will ever know.'

'Assuming no one's working in there.'

'On a Saturday? Come on.'

She put her foot on the cross bar and started climbing.

Lyle Ponder watched his targets climb over the gate to the Baths of Apollo and took out his phone. Norm Lonegan waited behind him.

The call was answered on the first ring.

'Yeah?' Zim said.

'They just went into a closed area.'

'You sure it's them?'

'Positive.'

'Think you can get them without being seen?'

'No problem,' Ponder said, as he felt for the small gun in his jacket pocket. He had been watching for Locke and Cohen in case they showed up and spotted them from his observation point outside the main gate. He was relieved to see them head straight for the gardens; if they had gone into the palace unexpectedly, he and Lonegan wouldn't have been able to pass through the metal detectors.

'Then do it.' Zim said. 'By the time the police figure out where the gunshots came from, they'll have bigger things to worry about.'

TWENTY-FIVE

Marlo Dunham sat in a black Range Rover outside the University of Cambridge main library. If Locke or any of his group came, it would be to this building. Most likely it would be Grant Westfield and Alexa Locke, as Zim had just called to tell her that Tyler and Brielle Cohen had been sighted at Versailles. Zim was prepared to destroy the Apollo statue, knowing exactly where to place the explosive because of the three-dimensional computer rendering Laroche had acquired so that he could build a duplicate fountain on his estate.

Dunham sat in the passenger seat next to a long-haired man whose name wasn't important enough to remember. Two more men were behind her.

Their ability to lay in wait for their prey was thanks to Laroche himself. When he escaped from his room, he must have realized he couldn't leave the house without setting off the alarm and alerting her, but he had enough time to write his note on a computer and build his little code. After he locked himself away in the vault, Dunham found the files that Laroche thought he'd trashed, making it easy to reconstruct them.

The guns she and the men were carrying had been supplied by local white supremacist contacts who had smuggled them in from Italy. The underground network of neo-Nazis made it surprisingly easy to get weapons. It took money, but she had plenty.

If all she'd wanted to do was retire to a life on the beach, she could have done it months ago with the cash she'd siphoned from Laroche's businesses. The fool had put so much trust in her that she transferred the money right under his nose, doctoring the ledgers on the computers to which she had unfettered access.

But retirement alone wasn't going to satisfy her. Not until she did something to earn it. If Ken had only known how ungrateful the people in Gaza could be, if he'd known how ruthless the Israelis were, he wouldn't have taken her and their unborn child to such a hellhole. He'd want her to settle the dispute once and for all, and that's exactly what she planned to do. The Muslim nations would finally have their rationale for the Israeli annihilation they craved.

The key to making that happen was in allowing the *Altwaffe* poison to run its course. Once the Muslim leaders were dead, there would be no turning back, no negotiations, no peace. It would be a war that would live in infamy. She knew the Israeli government would take out their enemies' leaders if they only had the balls, so Dunham was letting them borrow hers.

Now she had to stop the Lockes from destroying her dream. She knew they would be looking for a book inside the library, but because she was missing the puzzle piece about Alexa's favorite animal, she couldn't decipher what book they were looking for. That meant letting them find the book, and then killing them here in Cambridge. If Zim didn't take care of business at Versailles, she'd take back the balls she'd let *him* borrow and finish the job.

Geoffrey Ashburn, an affable man in his fifties with white hair and a shaggy beard, puttered behind a bus while continuing his ongoing narration, infuriating Grant with his sluggish pace. When Ashburn heard that Alexa was a biologist visiting the library to get information about Charles Darwin, the drive from the Cambridge train station became a tour of landmarks dedicated to showing them the university with an entire college named after the legendary scientist. Grant fumed silently in the back seat, his back stiffening up and his head pounding from the blood pressure that had skyrocketed during the trip over.

Grant wanted to go directly to the library, but Ashburn insisted on showing them his city first. The place was undeniably charming with tea rooms and shops lining narrow alleys, stately stone buildings, and green lawns bordering a narrow river carrying visitors on flat boats called punts that were pushed along with poles by men standing on the back. They reminded Grant of Venetian gondoliers, except these men were dressed in casual tees instead of black hats and striped shirts.

Gordian provided Ashburn, a mechanical engineering professor, with a good portion of the funding for his research into high-energy storage batteries to power low-emission vehicles, an offshoot of the university's famed solar racing team. Grant knew that he and Alexa wouldn't be given access to the library's oldest documents without a sponsor, so he'd let Ashburn go on as long as it took to get the information from Tyler at Versailles.

'As I'm sure you are aware,' Ashburn said, 'Cambridge is the fourth oldest university in the world, after the universities of Bologna, Paris, and to our continued chagrin, Oxford. I find it refreshing to know we have some stability in this world. When I think of that awful attack at the Eiffel Tower or those vandals who spray-painted walls inside Windsor Castle to protest austerity measures last week, it's comforting to know that our institutions can stand the test of time. Just a few years ago, Cambridge celebrated the eight hundredth anniversary of its founding.'

'That is incredible, Professor,' said Alexa, who was sitting in the passenger seat. She patted Ashburn's arm to punctuate her amazement. She sure knew how to butter up someone, but Grant felt a twinge of jealousy. Not because he thought she might be flirting with the professor, but because now he wasn't sure if she had been flirting with him.

Grant yawned. Insomnia wasn't typically a problem for him. He could sleep almost anywhere. During the flight, Alexa had nestled against his shoulder as she slept, but

Grant couldn't get more than a few winks. It left him plenty of time to ponder the progression of the chemical weapon coursing through his system, noting the progressive deterioration of his body. His inability to do anything about it was maddening.

'You say you're a Darwin expert, Dr Locke?' Ashburn asked.

'Please, it's Alexa. Well, all biologists are well versed in his theories, but my expertise is in endangered species.'

'Oh, really. What research brings you to our hallowed halls?'

Alexa flicked her eyes at Grant, who shrugged in response.

'I'm, uh, investigating his time in Scotland.'

'At the University of Edinburgh or his trip to Glen Roy?'

Alexa squirmed in her seat. She obviously hadn't been expecting probing questions. 'You know Darwin that well?'

'I'm fascinated by all of the geniuses who have graced our campus. Darwin. Sir Isaac Newton. Watson and Crick. Charles Babbage. I hope to stand among them someday. Perhaps I'll even have a building named after me like we did for Stephen Hawking. Speaking of our facilities, when you are finished at the library, I insist on showing you our laboratory, Mr Westfield. The students would love to show off their progress.'

'Please call me Grant,' he said through gritted teeth. 'And yes, I'd love to.' What else could he say? The man knew their train schedule.

'And do call me Geoffrey. In fact, we're going to be putting the experimental vehicles through their paces in a race tonight if you'd like to stay and watch, though I don't want to press you. There's a track right outside of town.'

'We'll see.'

'Brilliant. Now is it Darwin's exploration of Glen Roy that you're interested in, Dr Locke?'

'What happened at Glen Roy?' Grant asked. When he saw the questioning look from Ashburn, Grant added, 'I don't know what she's talking about. I'm only along for the ride.'

Ashburn looked from Alexa to Grant and said, 'Oh, I see. I see.'

'Yes, Grant's my boy toy. He keeps me company on these research trips.'

Grant gaped at Alexa, and she winked back.

Ashburn cleared his throat. 'I see.'

'We're just friends,' Grant snapped. When he saw Ashburn's surprised reaction and Alexa's hurt look, he took a breath and calmed himself. 'I mean, her brother is Gordian's chief of special operations, Tyler Locke.'

'Of course! Alexa Locke. I should have made the connection. Please give him my regards.'

'I will,' Grant said. 'Now tell us about Glen Roy.' If Darwin's visit to Scotland could support the idea that he had interacted with the Loch Ness monster, Grant wanted to hear it.

'After Darwin went around the world on the *Beagle*,'

Alexa said, 'he spent two years analyzing his data. Remember that this was still more than twenty years before he wrote *On the Origin of Species*. You'd think his next destination would be to the jungles of the Congo or the Sahara Desert. Instead, he went to the Scottish Highlands to develop a geological theory about why three parallel shelves ran the length of Glen Roy. Darwin spent a few weeks there gathering data and returned with the theory that the valley had actually been an inlet of the Atlantic Ocean, and the parallel shelves were formed as the sea level subsided when the land was thrust upward.'

'Of course,' Ashburn said, 'it turned out to be the biggest mistake of his scientific career.'

'Why?' Grant asked.

Alexa turned to face him. 'Because Darwin didn't know that glaciers had blocked the ends of the valley, causing water levels to rise and fall over the millennia. Darwin's theory had been completely wrong and a source of some embarrassment for him.'

Ashburn pulled into a parking spot in front of a huge brick building with an imposing central tower. They exited the car and walked toward the front entrance.

'I'll take you inside and get you set up with the librarians,' Ashburn said.

'Where exactly is Glen Roy?' Grant asked.

'It's to the southeast of Loch Ness.'

'Do you think the same thing could have happened to Loch Ness? That the glaciers dammed it up?'

'It's a possibility,' Alexa said. 'That would cause it to be isolated from the open ocean. If his exploration found any unusual creatures up there, Darwin might have thought it would confirm or contradict his evolutionary theory.'

'Yes, perhaps Darwin was searching for Nessie's ancestors,' Ashburn said with a guffaw.

Alexa and Grant looked at each other, then Grant half-heartedly laughed along with him, and Alexa joined in.

'That would be funny,' Grant said. 'Darwin looking for the Loch Ness monster? Crazy.'

Ashburn held the door for them. 'I don't mean to make light of your research, Dr Locke. I'm sure it's focusing on something far more serious than mythical beasts.'

As they went inside, Ashburn didn't seem to notice that he was the only one laughing.

TWENTY-SIX

The fragrance of the garden's floral bounty was overpowered by the stink of stagnant water. As she and Tyler entered the clearing in the center of the grove, Brielle could see that this fountain hadn't been in operation for months, and the pond at the front of the statuary display was green with algae.

Otherwise, the exhibit was largely as she remembered during her last visit. The same three statues from Laroche's backyard were featured within the backdrop of a stone grotto designed like cave openings. When it was in service, water cascaded down the wide pedestal distressed to look as if it were a craggy rock face.

The statues to the right and left depicted grooms attending to Apollo's steeds, while the center marble composition portrayed the daily ritual of nymphs bathing the god. One was in the act of washing his right foot, the same that was missing back in Seattle. Scaffolding had been erected around the central statue. Brielle could see evidence of the moss-covered façade being scrubbed clean, and a bucket dangled from a rope attached to the top of the scaffold.

She and Tyler were alone in the grove. He extracted his phone and a tape measure from his pocket.

'Piece of cake,' he said.

They edged around the pond and scrambled up to the statue.

When they were next to it, Brielle could see how intricate the carving was. Even the portion of the statue not visible from the front was crafted to the last detail.

'Magnificent, isn't it?'

'This whole place is amazing. I can see why Laroche is proud of his heritage. Here. Hold this next to the foot.'

Tyler gave her the measuring tape. She unfurled it, knelt, and laid it lengthwise along the outer part of the sole.

'Perfect.' Tyler got behind her and raised the phone, snapping several photos. 'Got 'em.'

Brielle stood and turned to leave, but Tyler continued looking at the foot.

'What's wrong?'

'The dimensions seem off. Hand me the copy of Laroche's drawing.'

She dug the sheet from her pocket and unfolded it before giving it to Tyler. He placed it beneath the extended foot.

'What were the chromosome numbers again for the polar bear and harp seal?' he asked.

She checked the notes on her phone. 'Seventy-four and thirty-two. Why?'

'Because they don't line up. Look.'

She bent over and saw that the dot next to seventy-four

was aligned with the big toe, but the dot by thirty-two was nowhere near the little toe. She frowned at Tyler, who looked as puzzled as she was.

'We've been had,' Tyler said. 'Laroche did lead us on a wild goose chase.'

'Do you really think he'd go to all that trouble?'

'If he wanted us to spin our wheels on this instead of tracking down the Loch Ness monster some other way he would. The note very specifically said "the footstep of the Sun King's Apollo". Then he chopped off the foot of his version of this statue. Unless there's another Apollo around here, he's pulled one over on us.'

Tyler's words jarred Brielle's memory. 'Bugger,' she said, and snatched the book on Versailles from her pocket.

'What?'

'There *is* another statue of Apollo. I was so fixated on this one that I didn't even consider it.' She flipped through the pages until she found it.

The image showed a bronze figure seated on a chariot being drawn by four horses through a pool of water. Fish and horn-blowing tritons surrounded the bucking stallions. The caption read, 'The Fountain of Apollo'.

'Laroche claimed he was being held prisoner and feared that Dunham would figure out a way to open the vault,' Brielle said. 'Perhaps this was another way to throw her off, to make sure she didn't decipher his code.'

'We'll only know if we can see the dimensions of his foot. Where is it?'

'Straight in front of the Grand Canal.'

'It looks like the only way to see the foot directly from above is to climb into the fountain.'

Brielle shrugged. 'What's the worst that could happen? They throw us out?'

'Or arrest us for trespassing.'

'I'll think of a distraction.'

Tyler smiled. 'Maybe you could fall in.'

'Ah, another romantic dream of mine fulfilled. Getting dunked in a fountain at Versailles.'

Brielle turned to climb back down to the clearing when Tyler said, 'Huh. The cat got spooked again.' Before she could see what he meant, he grabbed her arm and yanked her off her feet, dragging her behind the statue. Bullets ricocheted off the stonework.

'Bloody hell!' she yelled.

'Zim's men,' Tyler said, as he crouched back to back with Apollo. 'They must have seen us enter.'

'How did they know we were coming here?'

'I'm not sure, but our feline friend gave that guy away. He must have been setting up to ambush us on the way out.'

'How many men?'

'Can't tell.'

'They've got us pinned,' Brielle said.

'And it's only a matter of time before they can get into position for a kill shot.'

'Any ideas?'

He looked around the cave, his gaze settling on the bucket, then following the rope up to the top of the scaffold.

'You're not thinking of climbing that?' Brielle said. 'Those pistols may not have much accuracy at that range, but they'll pick us off eventually.'

'I was thinking more of a Tarzan escape.' He untied the rope from the bucket. 'If we get some momentum, the trajectory should take us to the other side of the scaffold, and we can duck into the woods. Once we're out of the grove and into the open, they can't run around with guns drawn.'

'Are you serious?'

'Unless you have a Smith and Wesson tucked in your shorts, I think this gun battle is a bit one-sided.'

Brielle almost suggested they call the police, but the next round of bullet impacts made the notion absurd. They'd be dead before anyone arrived.

'I'm in favor of not dying,' she said. 'Are you sure the scaffold will hold our weight?'

'No.'

'All right then.'

He took the rope in hand and wrapped it around his wrist.

Brielle saw that there was no way for her to grab it as well. 'Wait a minute—'

'Climb on.' He knelt so that his back was to her.

'You are deranged.'

'I can handle it. You're pretty light.'

'*Pretty* light?'

She peeked through the arms of Apollo. One of the men was running to a flanking position. The other one fired. More rounds pinged off the stones.

'Very light!' Tyler shouted. 'Get on!'

Brielle climbed on his back. 'Ready!'

Tyler burst out of his crouch and dashed forward until the rope went taut. Brielle felt the heat of the bullets as they zinged past her. Tyler launched himself off the pedestal and the rope swung them around, the scaffold teetering on two of its legs. If it gave out or tipped over, they'd be thrown into the pond, where they'd be at the mercy of Zim's men.

The scaffolding held. They swung in a wide arc over the water and toward the side statue.

'When we land, keep going!' Tyler shouted.

The rope completed its arc, and his feet came down on the pedestal only a few yards from the trees. Brielle dropped and had her legs moving as soon as she touched the ground. They dived into the woods, bullets clipping branches and leaves behind them.

They didn't stop until they reached the outer fence. Tyler went first and heaved her over with him. They landed on the path in front of an elderly couple who gaped at them in astonishment.

'*Qu'est-ce que c'est . . .*' said the woman.

'*Bonjour*,' Tyler said, dusting the dirt from his jeans. He continued with his fractured French. '*Ou est les toilettes, s'il vous plait*?'

The man mutely pointed behind him at the chateau.

Tyler grabbed Brielle's hand and ran in the opposite direction with her in tow. The couple called out that they were going the wrong way.

Brielle sprinted beside him. 'Your first thought was to ask where the bathroom is?'

'It's the only French I know. And I do have to go at some point. But we need to get to the fountain first.'

Two gendarmes darted around the corner. Brielle put on her best shrieking act and told them in French that two men were shooting guns in the *Bains d'Apollon*. One of the policeman got on his radio to call it in while the other drew his sidearm and approached the section of woods from which they'd emerged.

Tyler and Brielle kept running. She looked over her shoulder and saw one of the gunmen come over the fence right into the arms of the waiting policemen. The second man, his blond hair rumpled and dirty and his jacket torn, fell back over the fence but dropped his weapon on the path. One of the policemen climbed the fence to pursue him.

'Well,' Brielle said, 'you've got your distraction.'

They jogged on, turning at the next corner. Just as they reached the end of the path that spilled into the main promenade, the blond gunman leaped over the fence in front of them and took off toward the Grand Canal, not noticing Tyler and Brielle in his haste. She expected the gendarme to appear as well, but there was no sign of him. She guessed that he'd lost sight of his prey.

When they entered the promenade, Brielle saw the Apollo

Fountain a few hundred yards ahead spewing water from a dozen spots and showering the entire statue in a fine mist. The tourists seemed more curious than afraid about what was happening, possibly because the gunshots had been muffled and no one had seen anyone shooting. The gunman raced away, but she had no idea where he thought he was going.

A thrum droned from the same direction. Sunlight glinted off a silver plane flying low. Too low, as if the pilot were going to crash. Brielle blinked twice before she realized that it wasn't an accident about to happen.

A float plane was coming in for a landing on the Grand Canal.

Passengers in their boats frantically paddled to get out of the way of the aircraft, which settled onto the smooth pool. It pivoted at the end of the canal, and the passenger door opened.

She and Tyler skidded to a halt. Standing there on the pontoon like a king surveying his realm was a grinning Victor Zim.

TWENTY-SEVEN

Tyler was astounded to see Zim hop off the pontoon and run over to the fountain.

'What's he doing?' Brielle asked.

'Maybe the same thing we are,' Tyler replied. 'I think it confirms your theory that the fountain is our target.'

An electric utility cart driven by a gardener pulled up next to them from a cross path. The gardener got out and spoke on his radio as he stared at the plane idling in the canal. Tyler nodded toward the cart, and Brielle hopped in. Tyler got in the driver's seat and floored the accelerator as the gardener cursed at them and gave a half-hearted chase before giving up.

Tyler kept his eyes on Zim, who waded out into the pool. Tourists were pointing and taking photos of him walking into the mist, but he didn't seem to care. He got to the center where Apollo sat on his chariot and bent over. It looked like he had something in his hand, possibly taking a photo like Tyler was planning to do.

'I'll take Zim,' Tyler said. 'You get the photo and send it

to Grant. Who knows how long we'll have before the entire place is swarming with cops.'

As if in response, the music abruptly stopped, and a voice replaced it, speaking first in French and then English.

An incident at Versailles requires evacuation. Please go to the nearest exit.

Many of the tourists simply ignored the plea and kept watching the events unfolding.

Zim finished his task and waded back toward the canal. By this time the blond gunman was at the float plane and climbed aboard.

The cart reached the front of the fountain, and Brielle jumped out and into the water. Tyler drove around, reaching the rear of the fountain as Zim pulled himself out. Tyler aimed the cart at Zim, hoping to run him down, but Zim saw him at the last moment and sidestepped the speeding vehicle.

As he passed, Tyler reached with one arm and grabbed a handful of Zim's shirt, pulling Tyler out of the cart and both of them to the ground.

Zim reached into his jacket and drew a pistol. Tyler dived for his hand and deflected it before Zim could get a bead on Tyler's head. The gun went off, and now tourists started running and screaming.

Tyler dug his fingers into Zim's wrist tendons as he wrenched it sideways. The pistol went flying and slid under the cart.

'You're a dead man, Locke,' Zim hissed. He backhanded

Tyler in the temple, setting off a cacophony of bells in his head. Tyler shook it off and elbowed Zim in the face, connecting with his eye socket.

He had the upper hand until Zim punched Tyler in his healing bicep. Tyler cried out in pain and rolled off him. Zim jumped to his feet and attempted to deliver the final blow by stomping on Tyler's head, but he rolled again, the foot missing his head by no more than an inch. It was so close that water from Zim's boot sprayed Tyler in the face.

'Come on!' came a shout from the plane. Zim looked around, and Tyler saw policemen racing down from the palace.

'I'll finish you next time,' Zim said as he ran off.

Brielle ran up and knelt beside him. 'Are you all right?'

Tyler nodded. She thrust something at him. 'I found this next to the foot of Apollo. Can you disarm it?'

He could make out a red timer counting down inside a sandwich-sized plastic baggie. It was mounted on a small block of C4 plastic explosive.

They had two minutes.

At a party once, an annoying acquaintance found out that Tyler had disposed of bombs and complained about movies, asking him why they always showed bombs with a convenient red LED timer counting down.

'If I put a bomb in your car and activated it,' Tyler had replied, 'I'd want to know when it was going off.' That shut the guy up.

Disarming a bomb, however, wasn't a simple matter.

Unless you had time to examine the device so you knew exactly what you were dealing with, cutting a wire was inviting a premature boom.

The goal now was finding somewhere to place the bomb so that it wouldn't harm anyone when it went off. Tyler saw Zim climbing onto the plane's pontoon and had a brainstorm.

There was a nylon rope in the back of the utility cart, the kind used to cordon off areas that the gardener was working on. Tyler took one end of it.

'Tie the other end to the cart,' he instructed Brielle as he put the top of the baggie between his teeth and ran for the plane. If he couldn't put the bomb on the plane, he could at least keep it from taking off.

Zim had already closed the door, and the plane's engine revved up. If it got any speed, Tyler wouldn't be able to catch it by swimming.

The plane turned and Tyler hurtled off the edge of the canal. He landed on the pontoon and promptly slipped off. With his single free hand, he grasped the rear strut connecting the pontoon to the fuselage. He pulled himself up so that he was straddling the pontoon like a saddle.

Using two half-hitches, he knotted the rope to the strut. He looked back and saw that Brielle had tied the other end to the frame of the cart.

With all of the boats and passengers now evacuated from the canal, it was wide open. The plane roared as it attempted to take off, and the rope became taut. The extra weight was enough to curb the aircraft's acceleration, and Tyler looked for a spot to tuck the bomb in the fuselage. He saw a small access panel toward the rear and stood to open it but was pitched backward and nearly fell off when the plane began to move forward again. The pilot had compensated for the drag, and the utility cart was now rolling toward the canal.

Brielle got in and hit the brakes, but the cart was already on the grass. The tires bit but then slid along the slick surface. The back tires went off the edge, and the cart tumbled into the water with Brielle still inside.

The cart was slowing the plane so that it couldn't take off, but Brielle was trapped as the cart was dragged through the water. If he didn't cut the rope, she might drown before he could free her.

Tyler didn't need to slow the plane any more. The bomb would take care of Zim. He flicked open his Leatherman tool's knife and sliced through the rope. He used the blade to pry the access panel open and took the bomb from his teeth.

Thirty seconds left. Perfect.

He put the tool away to jam the bomb in the cubby hole, but he almost dropped the baggie when he was kicked in the leg. Tyler collapsed to the pontoon and saw the blond gunman prepare for another blow.

Tyler leaned forward and grabbed the man's jacket before he could follow through on the kick. He realized he wouldn't be able to hide the explosive in the access panel now. But he had a better idea. While he had a hold of the coat, Tyler pushed upward against the guy's chin and surreptitiously slipped the bomb into the side pocket. The man shoved him back, causing Tyler's foot to slip off the pontoon. He fell into the water and came up to see the unwitting bomb carrier smiling before he climbed back into the plane.

Tyler stood in the shallow pool with his shoulders above the surface and waved goodbye. He counted the seconds down. There couldn't be more than five left.

The plane rose from the water five hundred yards down the canal. Just as it did so, the passenger door flew open, and the gunman tumbled out of the plane, pushed by Zim's boot. The door closed, and the man somersaulted into the water with a splash as the plane banked hard.

A geyser of water erupted from the canal with an earsplitting crack. The plane zoomed away low over the trees.

Tyler waded back to Brielle, who was already out of the water. She extended a hand and helped him out.

'Are you all right?' she asked him.

'Yes, but my plan didn't work. Either Zim or his man must have noticed the wet bomb soaking the guy's pocket, and Zim threw him out. How about you?'

'Fine. I got the photo off to Grant before I saw the bomb.'

'We need to warn him that they're on to us.'

'I don't think my phone's any use now.'

'Mine's soaked, too.'

Two gendarmes ran up to them with guns drawn. Tyler

didn't have to guess what they were yelling. He put his hands up, and Brielle did the same.

Tyler leaned over to her. 'It's good Minister Fournier owes us a favor. Who knew we'd be calling it in so soon?'

TWENTY-EIGHT

Once they had their library cards, Professor Ashburn left Alexa and Grant alone and went back to his lab, telling them to call when they were ready to leave. Although they now had access to the library, they wouldn't be able to check anything out without him present.

Alexa was happy that she and Grant were alone again. She enjoyed spending time with him and making him uncomfortable. She'd always found him attractive, and her new self-confidence in her body made the teasing even more fun. But she'd reined it in when she saw that he was crabby and a little haggard looking.

Shortly after Ashburn took off, Alexa was surprised to see the texted photo from Brielle because the foot next to a ruler was bronze, not the marble she was expecting. While Grant adjusted the size of the photo on a borrowed computer, Alexa leaned in next to him.

'Tyler's not answering,' she said.

Grant fidgeted in his seat, as if he couldn't find a comfortable position, but he kept his focus on the screen. 'From the look of the photo, Brielle was in the middle of a fountain when it was taken. Maybe his phone got wet and shorted out.'

'Still, it bothers me.'

'Don't worry about Tyler. He can handle himself.'

'You've been through a lot together, haven't you? He's told me a bit about his adventures with you, but I get the feeling he's leaving out the good parts in some brotherly urge not to scare me.'

'I don't know if they could be called the good parts. He does what he needs to get the job done, and he always puts others first. When things get hairy, he's the guy you want on your side.'

'Of that I'm sure,' Alexa said. 'I may not have gone through what you have with him, but I've known him a lot longer. He's always stood up for people. I remember one time when he took me to a car race – you know how into racing he is. Since I made him ride horses, much to his regret, Tyler got to introduce me to his passion. I was fourteen and he was sixteen. We were walking through the concourse at the race track, and two older teens started harassing me. Tyler told them to back off, and he received a punch in the nose for his efforts. He got right back up off the ground and went at them until track security arrived and took the boys away for beating him up.'

'Sounds like the Tyler I know,' Grant said.

'Except now he looks the part. He wasn't always the man's man that he seems to have become during his time in the military. He was as skinny as a flagpole in high school.'

Grant finally took his attention from the screen. 'You're kidding.'

'You didn't know?'

'We've never whipped out his old photo albums from childhood.'

'Oh, yeah. He couldn't even do a push-up. He didn't build any muscle until he reached his full height in college. His metabolism was through the roof. I was so jealous.'

'Why?'

'Because he got all the good genes. Smart, tall, good-looking in a geeky way, the ability to gorge himself on Big Macs without gaining an ounce. I've always been pudgy.'

'You're more like him than you think, *Doctor* Locke. And you definitely aren't pudgy any more. You look . . . very fit.'

'Aren't you sweet?' She rubbed his arm, and he turned away. 'Thanks, but it required two-hour workouts and a steady diet of cottage cheese and rice cakes to get rid of the fluff.'

'Well, it worked.' He pursed his lips as if considering his next line, then said, 'Listen, I'm sorry I barked at you earlier. That wasn't called for.'

'That's all right. I didn't mean to embarrass you.'

'You didn't. I'm just . . . not myself right now.'

Alexa stared at Grant as he went back to resizing the photograph. 'We should go out when we get back.'

The mouse stopped moving, and Grant sighed, with more dejection than exasperation. 'Alexa, I don't think that's a good idea.'

'Why? Because Tyler's my brother?'

'No, because he's my best friend.'

'Then we won't tell him.'

'That's an even worse idea.' The mouse started moving again.

'Oh, come on. The guys I meet in university biology departments or at conferences are so dull or gay or married or dorky or insecure. I know you like me. You may have been a good pro wrestler, but you're a terrible actor.'

'There's no point, anyway.'

'Why not?'

'We . . . we don't have time.'

'I don't mean this minute. I'm talking about when this whole business with Loch Ness is over.'

Grant shook his head. 'Believe me, Alexa, you've set your sights on the wrong guy.' He hit PRINT, and a page spooled into the printer.

'I don't know,' Alexa said. 'I have pretty good aim.' She grabbed Grant by the cheeks and pulled him to her, kissing him softly on the lips. At first, he kissed back but then drew away.

'Alexa.' He hesitated. 'Ask me again next week.'

She smiled and winked at him. 'I knew I could be convincing. Now let's find us a manuscript.'

She took the printout from the tray and laid a white

sheet of paper over it, tracing the outline of the bronze foot. When she was done, she laid Laroche's numbered sheet over that. The big and little toes were perfectly aligned with the chromosome numbers for harp seal and polar bear.

Alexa circled all the numbers and letters that touched the outline. She wrote them out in order starting with the big toe and going clockwise starting at the three as Laroche instructed.

3 74 c 91 32 5 6

'Type this into the catalogue,' Alexa said.

When the computer returned no results, Grant said, 'Are you sure that's the number?'

'Positive. No other letters or numbers come close to the outline of Apollo's foot.'

'Well, nothing in the library matches it.'

She peered at the screen. 'If this is a catalogue number, it looks like the last set of digits is too long. Let's try truncating it.'

'How?'

'Try 374.c.9.13.'

Grant typed it in. Still no result. He tried a few more combinations. 374.c.91.325. 374.c.9.1. It wasn't until he input 374.c.91.3 that they got a title.

Practical Taxidermy: The preparation, stuffing, and mounting of animals for museums and travelers by Henry Bosworth, pub. 1935.

'Taxidermy?' Grant huffed. 'Laroche sent us to find a

book on stuffing animals? Does he think Nessie is mounted on someone's wall?'

Alexa jotted the number on a note card. 'Let's find out.'

They made their way up to the fifth floor and found the book in the stacks. The cover had a picture of a rhino on display in an exhibit with a child pointing it out to his father.

'What are we looking for?' Grant asked in a low voice.

'There were three digits left over from what we used in the catalogue identifier. Two, five, and six. I think that's a page number.'

She flipped the book to page 256. The header atop the page read, *Taxidermy Through History*. The section was labeled *John Edmonstone*.

'This has to be it,' Alexa whispered.

'It is? How do you know?'

'John Edmonstone was a taxidermist in Edinburgh in the early eighteen hundreds. He was a freed slave from Guyana.'

'A brother in Scotland?'

'Darwin was friends with him during his medical school training. He even took some lessons in taxidermy from Edmonstone, which not only fueled his interest in biology, but also taught him valuable information about animal preservation that would come in handy during his voyage on the *Beagle*.'

'So we've got our Darwin link. What does it say?'

Alexa skimmed down the page until she saw a paragraph

with the words she was searching for. 'Listen to this. "One story that was passed to me is especially interesting given the recent photo of a creature in Loch Ness taken by surgeon Robert Kenneth Wilson and featured in many newspaper articles in 1934. During an interview with noted Scottish taxidermist Ewan Stewart, I was regaled with a tale that he alleged had originated with John Edmonstone. Edmonstone claimed that he and a college student had been attacked by a fantastical beast on an outing to Loch Ness and speculated about why it had been drawn to them."'

'So Edmonstone had a Nessie hunting call?' Grant asked.

'I doubt he would name it that if he was attacked by Nessie.'

'True. It would be like having a grizzly bear whistle. Not something you'd want to use again.'

'The rest of this is even better,' Alexa said, and continued reading. '"An unnamed companion was said to have cut off a part of the beast, which can only be supposed to be an ancestor of the creature photographed by Mr Wilson. Although we can't attest to the veracity of Edmonstone's story, Mr Stewart also claimed that the entire account was recorded in a journal that Edmonstone kept secreted inside a mounted stag head that adorned his flat, accessed by a latch cleverly hidden under the fur at the base of the stag's neck. No one knows what happened to Edmonstone's possessions upon his death, so we may never learn more about his tall tale."'

'No problem,' Grant said sarcastically. 'Assuming the

story is true, all we have to do is find a two-hundred-year-old stag head that may not even exist any more and hope that no one has already removed the journal. What could be easier?'

'There has to be a way to find it or Laroche wouldn't have laid out all of these clues. He must have read this book and begun a search for the stag-head trophy. He might even know where it is. Stop being so pessimistic.'

'Well, we're not going to be able to ask Laroche. Last I heard, he was still in a coma.' Grant knocked his knee against the bookshelf, and his face contorted in pain. He held his leg for a few moments until he relaxed again.

'You don't look so good, either. Are you all right?'

'Just a little joint soreness. Probably got it from all the plane travel in the past week.' He wasn't very convincing, but before Alexa could probe, he went on. 'Tyler and Brielle are coming back to London tonight. We'll put our heads together at the hotel and see if we can make sense of this.'

'Are they a thing? I got a weird vibe when I saw them together.'

'It's complicated. She's Jewish.'

'That shouldn't be a problem for Tyler. We were raised Presbyterian by our grandmother, but neither of us has been much of a church-goer since we were kids.'

'I think it's more a problem for her.'

Alexa frowned. 'That's too bad. Even though she's kind of gruff, I like her. She seems like a good match for him.'

'Sometimes it doesn't work out like you want it to,'

Grant said, looking intently at Alexa. He took out his phone. 'I'll call Ashburn to pick us up.'

Alexa stuck the note card in the page as a bookmark. When they got to the lobby, Ashburn was waiting for them and checked out the book. Alexa wanted to read it more closely to see if there were any other clues. She tucked the book in her purse, and they got in his car for the two-minute ride to the engineering lab. Ashburn assured them that they wouldn't miss their return train to King's Cross.

They pulled into a gated car park and Ashburn swiped his card to lift the barrier. Once they were parked, Ashburn escorted them to a garage-type roll-up door. Alexa could make out all kinds of equipment inside the lab where two students were working, but Ashburn waved his arm at four go-karts lined up in front of the open door. Each one was painted in a different color: black, red, green, and yellow, with wraparound black rubber bumpers.

As Grant and Alexa approached, the students dropped what they were doing and gathered at the door.

'Lawrence and Penelope,' Ashburn said, 'I would like to introduce you to senior Gordian engineer Grant Westfield and Dr Alexa Locke, the sister of Gordian's founder, Tyler Locke. Lawrence and Penelope are two of the students responsible for developing the HydroSpeed project for which Gordian has so generously provided funding. Unfortunately, the rest are in class at the moment.'

The students smiled and nodded.

'You may not be aware, Alexa,' Ashburn continued, 'but the intent of HydroSpeed is to perfect a simplified hydrogen fuel cell vehicle that would be affordable enough for emerging markets. It was your brother's suggestion that we put our ideas to the test using go-karts before we move on to a full-scale car.'

'Are they operational?' she asked.

'Absolutely. A full twenty horsepower. We expect a top speed of fifty miles per hour. They'll be put through their paces during an endurance race at a local track tonight. We'll be loading them onto the transport lorry within the hour. I do wish you could stay to watch.'

'I'm afraid we don't have time,' Grant said.

'Of course, of course.' Ashburn clapped his hands. 'I know! Perhaps you'd like to take one for a short jaunt around the car park.'

'I don't know . . .'

'We test them out here all the time. It's really very simple. The accelerator pedal is on the right and the brake on the left. To reverse, you hold back the lever in the center.'

'Aren't I a little big to fit in one?'

'Nonsense,' Ashburn said, patting his considerable belly. 'You can't weigh more than I do, and I've driven them myself.'

'Come on,' Alexa said to Grant. 'Take it for a spin. I want to see what these things can do!' While she had never developed the passion for competition Tyler had, racing go-karts with him as a teenager had given her a taste for speed.

As an adult, she drove a Mini Cooper, the closest she could get to a street-legal go-kart.

'All right,' Grant said. 'Just once around the lot.'

'Excellent,' Ashburn said. 'We'll put you in the red one. Lawrence, please fetch a helmet for Mr Westfield. Penelope, please keep an eye on the gates to make sure we don't have anyone drive in during the run.'

The students scattered, and Grant eased himself into the seat of the go-kart, the stiff suspension groaning under him. Grant buckled himself in as Ashburn switched the engine on. Unlike the noisy gas-powered karts Alexa had raced before, the fuel cell on this one merely hummed like a fan.

Her phone chimed. She looked at the display and saw an unfamiliar number.

'Hello?' she answered.

'Alexa, it's Tyler.'

'Where have you been? We've got some incredible information to—'

'Tell us tonight. You need to know something. Zim was here.'

'Zim? At Versailles?'

Grant looked up at her when she mentioned the name.

'Yes,' Tyler said. 'I don't know how he knew we'd be here, but we have to assume he knows you're in Cambridge as well.'

Alexa spun around, scanning the area around the car park. Her eyes settled on a Range Rover idling in the street.

There was no mistaking the woman sitting in the passenger seat.

Marlo Dunham.

She stared back at Alexa with utter contempt, then spoke something over her shoulder. Two men burst from the SUV, guns drawn, and ran toward them.

'Shit,' Alexa hissed.

If they chased Grant and Alexa into the building, Ashburn and his students would be caught in the crossfire and might be killed before the police could arrive. She and Grant had to get away from the others and put some distance between them.

Alexa pocketed the phone without bothering to hang up, scrambled into the black go-kart, and switched the power on. She hoped Ashburn's students had been as good with the execution as they had been with the design.

'Call the police!' she yelled at Ashburn, who was stunned at her sudden action. When he didn't move, she pointed at the running assailants and shouted even louder. 'Now!'

He turned heel and ducked into the lab, herding Lawrence, who had arrived with the helmet.

Alexa snapped the harness together. Grant, still belted into his low go-kart, craned to see what had alarmed her.

'Dunham's men,' she said to him. 'Follow me.'

She mashed the accelerator, and the go-kart rocketed forward. She twisted the wheel to head for the gate opposite from where Dunham's SUV was. The kart pirouetted like it was on toe shoes, and Alexa zipped under the barrier while bullets carved divots in the asphalt.

She peeked back. Grant got the message and wasn't far behind her.

Unfortunately, two of Dunham's men got the same idea and jumped into the green and yellow karts. Before she even turned the corner, they were in hot pursuit.

TWENTY-NINE

No matter how hard he stood on the gas, Grant couldn't keep up with Alexa, who had to continually slow down for him to catch up. It was really a simple matter of physics. Their go-karts had the same horsepower, but he outweighed her by over a hundred pounds. He could feel the inertia slowing him every time they made a turn, and it was letting the lighter men behind them close the gap.

Grant was impressed by Alexa's skill and fearlessness. Tyler must have taught her a few driving tricks because she didn't show any hesitation darting around cars, drawing honks from the normally polite British drivers. The only problem she had was remembering to drive on the left. Twice she swerved into oncoming traffic, which might not have ended well for the tiny go-kart.

Grant struggled to set himself in a better driving position, but it was no use. Although the kart could handle his weight, his wide shoulders spilled out from the molded seat, making him lean forward. The suspension had no give, which meant that every seam, bump, and crack in the road was transferred directly to his pelvis, causing him to grimace in pain. Without the helmet, his eyes watered as he squinted to see through the wind, and there was nothing he could do to avoid bugs and the stench of auto exhaust fumes that were at nose level.

An engine roared behind Grant. A look over his shoulder revealed the black Range Rover coming up on him. It wasn't nearly as nimble as the kart, but its top speed was far higher. If they spent much longer on the main road, it would flatten him.

Alexa turned and saw the same thing. Grant pointed to a side alley ahead of them that wasn't wide enough for the SUV. The Range Rover was so close now that the sound of the V8 was deafening.

Alexa juked left, and the go-kart threaded through concrete pylons placed to prevent vehicles from using the pedestrian walkway. Grant followed and nicked the bumper, causing the wheels to skid sideways. The Range Rover kept going down the street, but the green and yellow go-karts followed them.

The cobblestone surface made the go-kart buck like a bronco. Without horns, they couldn't beep at the pedestrians sauntering through the shopping arcade. Alexa's shouts of warning were the only thing keeping bystanders from getting run down.

They shot out of the arcade and into the street, cars screeching and spinning to a halt as they blasted through the traffic. Out of the corner of his eye, Grant caught a glimpse of the Range Rover pacing them on a parallel street. He'd seen an earpiece on one of the pursuers, so Grant assumed he was in cell-phone contact with Dunham, giving her their position.

They needed to thin the number of their opponents.

They flashed into another narrow shopping arcade. Dumbfounded faces in shop windows whizzed by. Grant shouted Alexa's name. When she turned, he motioned for her to let him catch up. She slowed and he pulled even with her.

'I have an idea!' he yelled over the wind. 'Remember those concrete pylons?'

'Yeah.'

'Let the guy behind us catch up.'

'What?'

'We'll herd him.'

Alexa gave him a confused glance at first, but then lit up and nodded.

'One! Two! Three!'

At the same time, they hit their brakes and went to either side of the arcade, Grant barely missing chairs at an outdoor café. The green go-kart nearly raced past them, but he slowed to keep from overshooting. Grant gunned the engine and yanked the wheel over, aiming for the green go-kart like he was in a high-speed bumper car. He rapped the side of the kart, sending it careening sideways into Alexa, who bumped him back.

The steering wheel was so jittery that it required both

hands to use, which was why neither of the men in the pursuing karts had taken a shot at them. Driving with only one hand would be suicide. But now that he was boxed in, the grinning man between them went for his pistol, thinking he had the perfect opportunity. He lowered his arm to take a bead on Grant, never noticing that they were reaching the end of the arcade.

Three short concrete pylons blocked the entrance, and the gunman was headed straight for the center one. Grant wrenched his wheel to the side, and Alexa did the same. Both of them missed the pylons by inches.

The gunman wasn't so lucky.

He hit the pylon head-on at forty miles an hour. Worse, he hadn't taken time to latch his harness. The go-kart jolted to a stop, but the gunman flew into the air, his arms pinwheeling as he tumbled. He landed head first on the asphalt, and his body rolled through the street like a ragdoll before coming to rest.

They were out of arcades, so Alexa turned left onto the road. Grant had become disoriented in the winding alleys, but he recognized the boulevard as Trumpington Street, the same road where the department of engineering was located. If they followed it back south, they would return to the lab where surely the police would be by now.

'Keep going straight!' he shouted. Alexa raised a thumb in response.

The Range Rover blew out of a side street and nearly ran Grant over. He turned sharply and slammed on the brakes to keep from going through the front door of a tea shop. The yellow go-kart whooshed by him, intent on getting to Alexa. Dunham must have been aware that she was the key to finding the Loch Ness monster. Without her, their plans would be destroyed, not to mention the grief her death would cause Tyler.

Watching the Range Rover and go-kart converge on her, Grant was consumed by an overwhelming sense of protectiveness at the danger Alexa faced. He'd lost a woman close to him before. He wasn't going through that again.

Grant focused his entire being on catching up with them. He stood on the gas and willed the go-kart to go faster. Alexa was weaving all over the road in an attempt to shake her pursuers, which gave Grant the slim hope that he could make up the distance.

The man in the go-kart pulled next to Alexa and grabbed for her in a bid to take her hand off the wheel. He was only able to latch onto her purse strap instead. He pulled hard, and Alexa leaned awkwardly to the right. A parked car two hundred yards down the road had to be his target. If he steered her into it, she'd be killed, seatbelt or not.

Alexa shrugged out of the strap as her purse was ripped away from her. She regained control but had no room to maneuver with his kart in the way. The Range Rover was now next to the yellow kart, and Dunham had the window unrolled. She waved for the man to throw her the purse.

All of this distracted them from Grant's pursuit. He was right behind the yellow go-kart and rammed it with his right front bumper just as the man tossed the purse up. Dunham caught it, but the action had required the man to take his hand off the wheel.

Grant's nudge was enough to push the man's kart sideways under the rear wheel of the Range Rover, crushing the go-kart. Its driver screamed for an instant and went silent.

At the last moment, Alexa was able to dodge and missed the parked car by inches.

The Range Rover pulled up to finish the job, Dunham brandishing her own pistol through the open window, but without warning Alexa threw the go-kart into a hard right turn and Grant followed. They raced through a gate labeled The Fitzwilliam Museum. The entryway was far too narrow for the SUV to follow. The driver kept going instead of stopping, no doubt scared off by the sound of sirens now ringing throughout the town.

Alexa circled around in the opposite direction and came to a stop next to the museum entrance. She threw off her belts and sprang wildly from her seat as if she were planning to take off at a sprint. Grant exited the go-kart and stopped her, pulling her to him.

'They're gone! They're gone. We're safe. Are you all right?'

'I'm okay,' she said, gulping in breaths as if she'd run a marathon. 'I'm okay. I'm okay.'

Grant smiled at her. 'That was some amazing driving back there. You could be a pro.'

'Tyler taught me well.'

'Who knew he was good at something?'

'They took my purse.'

'I know. I couldn't get to it in time. We'll get you a new passport and phone in London.'

'It's not that.'

Grant looked at her in confusion and then realized what she meant before she uttered it.

'They've got the book,' Alexa said. 'Marlo Dunham now knows what we know.'

THIRTY

It was eight p.m. by the time Victor Zim and Hank Pryor filed off the P&O ferry at Dover with the other foot passengers. Using the fake passports provided by Dunham, they didn't have any trouble getting through British customs.

Zim's original plan had been to drop into the Versailles estate using a helicopter, but since his only chopper pilot died over Lake Shannon in Washington, he took a page from Locke and hijacked a float plane instead. Pryor, an experienced aircraft pilot, was able to fly it without much trouble before they abandoned it at a local lake to make their final getaway.

Leaving Norm Lonegan behind to be questioned by the French police didn't bother Zim. He was a hired gun and didn't know anything useful about their upcoming plans. And Lyle Ponder, bringing a bomb back into the plane without knowing it, deserved to be thrown out and blown up.

Pryor was the big concern. The former airplane engineer from Kansas was Zim's greatest asset. If he were killed or taken by the cops, they'd lose their electrical genius and pilot. He wasn't going to be able to assist in any fight and was barely passable with a weapon, but his prowess with machines had made Zim's prison escape possible. The remote-controlled helicopter and quadcopters were works of art.

However, once this was all over, he wouldn't mind saying goodbye to the twerp. He was an arrogant pain in the ass.

'I still think we should have stayed to kill them,' Pryor said as they walked to the pick-up area.

'For such a smart guy, you're pretty stupid sometimes,' Zim said. 'Locke and Cohen had already sent the message to his sister and Westfield. That's how they found the book. If we had stayed, we would have gotten ourselves caught or killed for nothing.'

'But they're telling the police everything. I'm surprised we didn't get nabbed on the ferry.'

'I'm surprised, too. In Calais you were sweating like a pig.'

'This entire mission is now in jeopardy. They're edging closer to getting what they need for the antidote. If they find it, then months of work will go down the drain.'

'Pryor, if you don't stop your whining, I'll kick your face in. We'll see how well you can blubber through a set of broken teeth.'

'You can't,' Pryor said, defiant. 'You need me.'

Zim stared at him as they continued walking. 'I don't need anyone that much. You've known me long enough. Do I sound like I'm bluffing?'

Pryor opened his mouth, then closed it.

'Good,' Zim said.

The black Range Rover was in the pickup lane. Dunham nodded at them as they got in, and the driver pulled away.

'Nice job in France,' Dunham said from the front seat, her voice dripping with sarcasm. 'Two men lost, huh?'

'Yeah, you did so much better in Cambridge.'

'At least I got the book.'

'Do you know if they read it?'

'It looks like they did and bookmarked a page about a taxidermist named John Edmonstone. I know where we have to go.'

'How?'

'Laroche. He had me bid on two stag heads that were found in Glasgow last year. They were being sold during an estate sale. Laroche had me do some research and found that each of them was inscribed with the initials, "J.E." and they were presented as gifts to the prince to be hung at Balmoral. When the Scots realized they'd once been owned by Prince Albert, husband of Queen Victoria, they were declared important historical objects, the stags presumably shot by the prince himself. They were taken off the market by the government so they could be put on display. One of them could be the stag head referred to in this account. Once we get access to them, it's a simple matter of destroying what we find inside. Then this is over.'

'And we can all go our separate ways,' Pryor said.

'Thank God for that,' Zim said.

'Look,' Dunham said. 'I'm not happy about this alliance either, but we're stuck with each other. You'll both get your money as promised, and then I never want to see you again.'

'No problem. But you better not stiff us. It's going to take a ton of cash to live on the run.'

'Don't worry. You'll have every cent owed to you.'

'Good. How long will it take to get to these stag heads?'

'We'd better stay off trains and planes. It's an eight-hour drive, but the buildings where they're displayed won't open until nine thirty tomorrow morning anyway. We'll plan how to get access to them during the drive. The rest of our men will meet us there.'

'Sounds like we have time then,' Zim said. 'Let's find a McDonald's drive-through. I'm starving.'

Two guitarists pounded out a rock ballad that Tyler didn't recognize, the sound masking the conversation he was having with Brielle, Alexa, and Grant from potential eavesdroppers. The pub, called Prince Alfred, was close to their hotel in the Bayswater area of London. They'd scarfed down a deli board spread, famished from a long day that was nearing ten p.m. All of them were itching to move on to the next step, but without a destination, they were stuck, so they decided to grab a quick dinner while they discussed their options.

Thanks to the chit they called in from Minister Fournier, he and Brielle were able to get out of France with a minimum of questioning by the police. Grant and Alexa had to spend more time with the Cambridge police explaining their part in the melee. According to Grant, Ashburn's cheerful demeanor had dissipated upon learning that two of his carefully crafted go-karts had been destroyed, but a call from Miles promising two more years of research funding soothed any frayed nerves.

Grant was trying to hide a limp now, and Tyler was worried that his condition was worsening quickly. His outward appearance was no longer something he could effectively hide: Grant's five o'clock shadow was a grizzled gray, he moved with the stiffness of a man thirty years older, and he had to ask for things to be repeated to him in the noise. Of course, Grant had waved off any notion of returning home when Tyler took him aside privately, but he didn't know how long his friend would be able to continue fighting off the effects of the poison. Brielle and Alexa attacked the selection of meats and cheeses with gusto, but Grant merely picked at it. On most other days, they'd have had to order a whole second board just for him.

As they ate, Alexa recalled the information she could from the taxidermy book. Tyler agreed that there was a reason Laroche had sent them on this expedition. Finding a stag head stuffed by John Edmonstone, however, was a tall order. They couldn't ask Laroche where it was, so Tyler did the next best thing and set Aiden MacKenna loose to use his computer skills to track it down. Now they were waiting to hear the results.

'These people are crazy,' Alexa said, munching on cheese and biscuits. 'Attacking us in broad daylight in the middle of Versailles and Cambridge? That's nuts.'

'They don't care if they get caught or killed,' Tyler said. 'I've seen it before with fanatics. They'll do anything to further their cause. And Zim is the most dangerous one. I don't see him ever giving himself up and going back to prison. He'll go down fighting.'

'Not before he kills me.'

'That's not going to happen. I'm not letting you out of my sight from now on.'

'Do you really think the Loch Ness monster exists?' Grant asked Alexa.

'There's something in that loch, and now we have a tangible link between it and John Edmonstone, who happened to be friends with Charles Darwin. The Nazis thought it was real, too, so we might be searching for a descendant of the creature Darwin discovered.'

'If that's the case,' Grant said, 'there could be a whole family of Nessies breeding down there.'

'I suppose that's possible. It would explain why I spotted one two hundred years later. The Nazis were always meticulous in their research, and they seemed sure Darwin was the source of the tissue sample they had.'

Brielle nodded. 'It's not so hard to believe. The Nazis looked up to Darwin.'

'That's a common misconception,' Alexa said. 'Creationists like to trot out the falsehood that Hitler and his buddies were evolutionists to help bolster the spurious thought that evolution leads to eugenics and the justified slaughter of whole races.'

'I'm not a scientist, but isn't Darwin's theory about survival of the fittest?'

'Of course. But the Nazis abhorred the idea that people they considered inferior could possibly have originated from the bloodline that spawned the Aryan race.'

'So the Nazis didn't believe in evolution?' Brielle asked.

'I hate that phrase,' Alexa said, slamming her hand on the table. 'Evolution isn't a faith, it's a scientific theory, one of the most elegant ever created. It's the backbone of biological study, accurately describing everything from the family trees of dinosaurs to the prediction of genetic traits in fruit flies bred in a lab. The empirical evidence is so overwhelming that only the willfully ignorant think evolution isn't true.' She took a breath. 'And it's correct to say that the Nazis rejected Darwin's theories.'

She was getting so heated that biscuit crumbs were spewing from her mouth. Nothing worked Alexa up more than people who tried to argue the merits of evolutionary theory using non-scientific religious dogma. Even though Brielle's question hadn't come from that angle, it had been enough to set Alexa off. Tyler had seen her nearly get into a fistfight with an evangelical minister who'd come to debate the subject when she was in college.

'Then what's the connection between Darwin and Germany?' he asked to defuse the growing tension.

Alexa sipped her cider and went on. 'There are two I know of. Hitler's thinking was influenced heavily by an ex-pat Brit named Houston Stewart Chamberlain. He espoused Teutonic superiority and wrote a book called *The Foundations* that said all of western civilization descended from the German people. In a weird coincidence, he was raised in Versailles by his grandmother and later in life moved to Dresden.'

'Dresden,' Grant repeated. 'Maybe he gave the Nazis Darwin's specimen.'

'Possibly, but he was vehemently anti-Darwin. Still, a British-German connection might have been important. My money is on Ernst Haeckel.'

'Who's that?'

'A German biologist who actually met with Darwin. If Darwin had collected something strange and unexplainable, he might have shared it with Haeckel, who took it back to Germany with him. He died long before the Nazis came along, but they might have found his notes and the specimen and done something with it.'

'*Altwaffe*,' Tyler said.

'Is it possible that the Nazis could have developed something so sophisticated?' Alexa asked.

'Yes,' Brielle replied, her voice weighted with the enormity of the word. 'They had one of the most advanced chemical warfare industries in the world. Although Hitler was afraid to use chemical weapons because of his experiences with mustard gas in World War I, that didn't stop his scientists from developing sarin nerve gas and using Zyklon B in the death camps.'

At that the conversation abruptly stopped, as did the music. The guitarists packed up their instruments, and patrons started to file out. A TV above the bar showed explosions tearing through neighborhoods in both Gaza and Tel Aviv. The next shot featured lines of tanks barreling down a road.

'A lot of Jews are going to be killed again unless we find an antidote for the poison,' Brielle said.

'What do you think the chances are that Edmonstone could have left us something useful to find the Loch Ness monster?' Grant finally asked. 'Even if he did see it, that was two hundred years ago.'

'If we can find his journal,' Tyler said, 'let's hope his record about the encounter has something to go on. If these clues are all a hoax, we have the GhostMantas ready to search the loch starting tomorrow morning. Assuming there is something below the surface, we'll find it.' *Eventually*, he didn't add, *but maybe not in time*.

His phone rang, and Aiden's name came up on the display. The pub was empty enough now that they wouldn't be overheard. He touched the screen and laid the phone on the table.

'Aiden, I've got you on speaker. We're all here.'

'Hello, everyone. I've got some good news. I think I've found Edmonstone's stag heads.'

Tyler felt his first blush of optimism. 'Heads?'

'Yes, there are two of them. They aren't definitively from John Edmonstone, but they're marked by his initials. They were up for auction a few months ago, but it was put to a stop when the authorities figured out they had historical value.'

'Where are they?' Grant said eagerly.

'They were taken to the National Museum of Scotland in Edinburgh for restoration before being displayed. Good luck talking them into letting you examine them.'

'There might be a way,' Brielle said. 'Remember, I went to the University of Edinburgh. I still have contacts up there.'

'The museum doesn't open to visitors until ten in the morning,' Aiden said, 'but I'm sure they get to work earlier than that.'

'Then we know where we're going next,' Tyler said.

'But I can't fly,' Alexa said. 'Marlo Dunham has my passport. I don't have any ID.'

'I heard about your troubles,' Aiden said, 'so I took the liberty of booking you all on tonight's sleeper train to Edinburgh, arriving at seven thirty tomorrow morning. It leaves from Euston station in an hour.'

'You're a lifesaver, Aiden,' Tyler said with literal emphasis. 'I'll call you back when we get to the station.' He hung up.

Tyler dropped a fifty-pound note on the table, and they all stood. After a quick stop at the hotel to collect their belongings, they would have eight hours to figure out how to convince a museum curator to let them examine a pair of two-hundred-year-old historical relics.

THE ROYAL MILE

WORLD NEWS

Ultimatum delivered to Israel at United Nations

By CHARLES BRAVERMAN

June 21, NEW YORK –The US State Department acknowledged yesterday that a poison was released during the Eiffel Tower incident on June 12, but it won't comment on the type or source of the chemical used, fueling allegations that the Mossad, Israel's intelligence agency, was behind the attack. Officials state that researchers at labs in London, Paris, Frankfurt, and Washington are working feverishly to isolate an antidote, but they have no timetable for when it will become available.

As more leaders fall ill in Muslim countries, with six dead already, their citizens' thirst for war has grown exponentially. Protests in Cairo, Amman, Damascus, Tehran, and Baghdad have seen hundreds of thousands of people taking to the streets demanding retribution for what they consider an act of war against their countries.

Twelve countries joined together to propose a resolution forcing Israel to supply an antidote to a rumored chemical attack or suffer the consequences of a full-scale assault. Israel's top diplomat at the United Nations responded by saying that the allegations are false and nothing more than a blatant attempt to justify invasion of the Jewish state.

An unnamed source in the administration revealed that the US military is on high alert and preparing for escalation of this volatile situation, which could become inevitable if Egypt and Syria's leaders, now hospitalized, succumb to the lethal poison.

THIRTY-ONE

Upon arrival in Edinburgh, Brielle was immediately taken back to her college days. As she walked out of Waverley station, the brisk wind nipped at her thin jacket, but the cold, cloudy day was nothing unusual for June. Despite the frigid weather and his worsening condition, Grant wouldn't hear of hailing a taxi, insisting that he could make the ten-minute walk to the National Museum of Scotland.

Alexa and Tyler, having checked all the bags at the left-luggage stand, joined them outside and bundled up against the breeze. All four cradled steaming cups of coffee, trying not only to ward off the chill but to wake up from a long night on the train. Brielle had been worn out from the events in Versailles and went to sleep as soon as her head hit the pillow, waking only grudgingly. From the groggy looks that greeted her when the train pulled into the station, she assumed the other three had as well.

Brielle led the way across the bridge spanning the park and tracks nestled within the ravine that separated the old town from the main shopping district. Above the forested gorge, Edinburgh Castle dominated the city from its perch atop craggy Castle Rock, a steep volcanic outcrop that provided unobstructed views of the city in all directions. Brielle knew the castle had been attacked on many occasions during its nine hundred years of existence, but she could imagine the trepidation of attackers contemplating going up against such a formidable bastion.

Alexa fell into step alongside, and Brielle nodded to her. Because they'd been so tired, they hadn't spoken much in the train berth other than to situate their luggage and turn out the lights. Tyler and Grant kept pace behind them, their conversation inaudible in the blowing wind.

'Beautiful city,' Alexa said. 'I wish I had time to explore it.'

'You've never been?'

'I've flown into the airport, but we went straight to the Highlands. I understand you went to school here.'

'Me and Darwin.'

'I'm sorry about last night,' Alexa said with an rueful smile. 'I didn't mean to blow up about that. The subject of evolution just gets me riled.'

Brielle waved her hand. 'No worries.'

Alexa cleared her throat in a way that made Brielle wonder if something uncomfortable was coming.

'I heard about your friend, Wade Plymouth. I'm sorry.'

'Thank you. He was a *mensch*.' Brielle's throat tightened at the thought of her friend now gone. 'We went to school together here. We made this walk a dozen times when we'd travel back to London to see our families on holiday.'

'Do you have any brothers or sisters?'

'I'm an only child.'

'Are you close to your parents?'

'Very.'

'I wish I had that. Our father is a retired Air Force officer, commanding but distant. I don't see him much now. Our mother left us when we were young, so we were essentially raised by our grandmother. She passed away ten years ago.'

Brielle saw where this was going. 'You and Tyler seem to get on well.'

'Always have. We don't visit as much as I'd like, but we talk a lot on the phone, especially since Karen died.'

'And you don't want me to hurt him.'

Alexa snorted. 'Please. Tyler's not going to get hurt.'

Brielle was unexpectedly miffed, interpreting the response as a suggestion that she meant nothing to him. 'What do you mean by that? I'm not good enough for him?'

Alexa looked at her in confusion and then her eyes widened. 'Oh! No, that's not where I was going. No, I've seen the way Tyler looks at you. He likes you, but I know about your religious incompatibility. I just meant . . . well, Tyler's a resilient guy. After what he's already been through in his life, I think he can handle anything. He's the strongest man I know.'

Brielle's hackles lowered. 'And I've seen the way he looks at you. He's a proud big brother. There's one thing that would destroy him, and that would be losing you.'

'How much farther?' Tyler yelled out. They'd fallen behind the fast pace that Brielle had set, so she and Alexa waited for them to catch up. She could see Grant pushing himself. The Nazi poison was taking its toll.

'Just a few more blocks.'

They turned onto the Royal Mile, the inclined road that connects Edinburgh Castle at the top of the hill to Holyroodhouse, the palace that serves as the UK monarch's official residence during stays in the Scottish capital. After a short walk, they made another left and arrived at the National Museum of Scotland.

The museum wasn't yet open for visitors, but Brielle had pulled a few strings with a professor she knew and arranged an audience with the keeper, or head curator, of the department of Scottish history and archaeology.

A tiny woman with gray hair and an angular face met them at the door.

'Ms Cohen?' she asked in a chirpy voice that crammed Brielle's last name into one syllable.

Brielle nodded and introduced the rest of the group.

'Pleased to meet you. I'm Audrey MacNeil, keeper of the Scottish historical collections. Do come in. When Professor Campbell called and mentioned that you had an emergency, I was only too happy to help.'

She led them through several galleries and onto a lift.

'The nineteenth-century artifacts are located on level three.'

'Dr MacNeil,' Tyler said, 'what do you know about John Edmonstone's relationship with Charles Darwin?'

MacNeil raised an eyebrow. 'Well, that's an interesting question. Edmonstone lived very close to Charles Darwin and his brother Erasmus while Charles was here at the medical college. We believe Darwin may have learned some of his methods for preserving specimens from Edmonstone.'

'Do you know if they ever went to Loch Ness together?'

The door opened and she ushered them out. 'What an odd thought,' she said as she walked. 'Why would you ask that?'

Alexa jumped in. 'We have reason to believe that Mr Edmonstone wrote a journal about a trip he took with Darwin. It's possible the trip took them all the way to the Scottish Highlands.'

'I don't know of any journal like that. Where did you say you saw it mentioned?'

They walked into an airy gallery labeled Kingdom of the Scots and stopped just inside.

'We haven't seen it yet,' Brielle said. 'You acquired two stag heads three months ago from an estate sale in Glasgow.'

MacNeil brightened at that. 'Oh, yes. Magnificent pieces. Both ten-point bucks. Although we haven't been able to confirm it, we suspect John Edmonstone mounted them.'

Grant snickered at that but quieted when he realized no one else was laughing.

'How do you know?' Brielle said.

'A small plaque on the back of the trophy mount is etched with his initials.'

'Would he have had these in his home?' Tyler asked.

'We don't know, but I wouldn't think so. Trophies such as these would be quite expensive in the early eighteen hundreds. Whoever shot the deer might have hired him to stuff them, but it's unlikely the owners would have given them to him.'

'They would make good advertisements, though,' Grant said. 'What if he bagged them himself?'

'I suppose it's possible, but that meant he would have poached them. Why all these questions about the stag heads?'

'Because we think Edmonstone may have hidden something inside one of them,' Tyler said. 'Did you take them apart when you restored them?'

'There was no reason to. They were maintained in excellent condition, and the wooden mounting board showed no rot. A thorough cleaning was all that was required. If there were some kind of secret panel, I assure you we would have seen it.'

'I know this is asking a lot,' Alexa said, 'but may we take a look at them?'

MacNeil frowned. 'You certainly are asking a lot. Those trophies are artifacts of great historical significance, both because of the possible connection to Edmonstone and because of the royal ownership. I would need more evidence than simply your theory before I allowed you to inspect them.'

'Dr MacNeil,' Tyler said, 'this is truly a matter of life and death.'

'How so?'

'That's hard to explain.'

'Try me.'

'Please. We won't touch them. We just want to see them. Maybe we'll notice something you overlooked. If we do spot anything, we'll point it out to you and let you decide how to proceed.'

MacNeil tapped her finger against her lips. 'Since this is a favor for Professor Campbell, all right. But it will take a few days to arrange.'

Brielle choked. 'A few days? We need to see them right now.'

'I'm afraid that's impossible.'

'Why?' Tyler asked, putting his hand on Brielle's shoulder in a calming gesture.

'Because they aren't here. We moved them last week to temporary exhibits.'

'Plural? Where?'

'We're putting on two special exhibitions as promotions to get the tourists who might not otherwise know about us to visit the museum, and we thought the stag heads would be spectacular additions. One exhibition is at Holyroodhouse. The other is at Edinburgh Castle.'

THIRTY-TWO

Thanks to the extensive research she'd done for Laroche, Dunham knew exactly where to find the two stag heads. At the time she had done the research, she had no idea why the old man was so interested in the trophies. She figured he was hoping to add another odd display to his menagerie, but he knew all along that they were the key to finding the Loch Ness monster and the antidote to the *Altwaffe* chemical.

On the drive up, Zim proposed separating into two teams to destroy the contents of the trophies within minutes of each other. Once one of the exhibits was tampered with, the other location would be on alert, making the task much more difficult.

The unique settings required different approaches. Zim would take two men and go for the one at Edinburgh Castle, while she and a man whom she now knew as Cooper, posing as her boyfriend, would go to Holyrood Palace. Since the tourist attractions both opened at 9:30 in the morning, their operations could be synchronized.

Parking in the Old Town section of Edinburgh was a

nightmare, so Dunham and Cooper, whose scruffy beard and long stringy hair made her feel as if she were slumming it with a reject from a grunge band, were dropped at the entrance to the palace by Hank Pryor. He would be in charge of the six men in reserve in case anything went wrong at either location.

The entry building at the front of the palace served as the gift shop, café, and gallery for traveling exhibitions. The gallery was currently closed in preparation for a new exhibit, so the stag head had to be somewhere in the palace itself.

She and Cooper would have brought weapons with them, but a vandalism incident at Windsor Castle had tightened security at all royal installations. Before they were allowed in, they were frisked by attendants looking for spray paint cans.

Once they were cleared, they stood in line with the early birds waiting to be the first people inside that day. As they paid for their tickets, Dunham asked the woman, 'I understand you have some items from the National Museum of Scotland on display. I hear they have some fascinating objects. Where would we find those?'

'In the Great Gallery. It's a long hall toward the end of the self-guided palace tour. You can't miss it. Here's a map. Would you like an audio guide?'

'No, thanks. The map will do fine.'

Dunham took Cooper by the arm and led him out of the building into the vast open-air forecourt, where she got her first good view of the palace. The weathered stone façade was flanked by two turrets on either side. The ruins of an abbey abutted the left edge of the square building, which wrapped around a central quadrangle. Though she imagined that the pomp and circumstance of a royal visit would give the building a certain majesty, Dunham recognized the pragmatic Scottish temperament in its design.

They crossed the forecourt and entered through the door at the center. Numbered placards indicated the direction of the tour. Dunham consulted her map and saw that the gallery was located on the left side of the building. With the security personnel situated in every room, there would be no hurrying there directly. They had to seem as if they were simply tourists taking in the grand appointments of the palace.

She pretended to gawk at the furniture and décor, prompting Cooper to do likewise. As they strolled, she rehearsed the plan in her head.

Once they reached the gallery, they would see how the stag head was displayed. They'd step aside and pretend to look for something in her purse while they decided on the final details of the plan. In addition, she would be handing him one of the two small bottles she was carrying. Although the liquid was clear and in disposable water bottles, it was actually a highly flammable form of alcohol they had bought at a local pharmacy.

When they were ready, Cooper would wander away from her in the gallery and place his open bottle on the floor in a location far away from the trophy. Then he would knock over the bottle so that the liquid spread across the floor. He would drop a lighter on it to ignite it, sending the security people running for a fire extinguisher.

While they were distracted, Dunham would search for the latch on the stag head. Failing that, she'd cut it open with the ceramic knife she had hidden in the lining of her purse. If she found the journal and it was small enough, she would pocket it and leave. If it was too large to carry inconspicuously, she'd have no other choice but to destroy it right then, no matter how curious she was to see what the journal's contents revealed. Dunham would douse it with her bottle of alcohol and burn it, incinerating any chance of ever finding the monster.

After Zim was patted down, a pretty attendant pointed him to Edinburgh Castle's outdoor ticket counter, but it was obvious where to go by the crowd shuffling ahead of him. Two of his men, Smith and Creel, were ahead of him in line. Both were medium height and build, though Smith was blond and wore glasses while Creel had a thick brown mop and a mustache. He would keep an eye on them, but the three of them wouldn't interact until they put their plan into motion.

Zim got his ticket and map and walked past the gift shop through the portcullis gate, its spikes aimed ominously downward. His two men lagged until he passed, and then trailed him discreetly.

The castle was actually a mighty citadel, containing a huge complex of stone buildings surrounded by a series of stout walls. The grounds consisted of a church, barracks, the governor's house, a prison, the National War Memorial, the crown jewels, royal residences, administrative offices, and museums. A central driveway wound through the complex until it ended atop the plateau where the oldest buildings were situated.

There was no need to stop and ask anyone where the stag head was being displayed. Smith and Creel had done reconnaissance in Edinburgh before Zim and the rest of them arrived. Holyrood turned out to be too small for the more elegant tactic they'd be using at Edinburgh Castle. In preparation for today, the two men had followed one of the male employees to his flat after the castle closed the previous night.

He turned out to be a Spaniard, one of the many foreigners the castle hired to interact with tourists from other countries. It didn't take much persuasion at all to get him to reveal that Edmonstone's trophy was on display inside the Great Hall on the castle complex's top plateau. More importantly, he also provided them with information about the operation of the castle and the names of key managers.

The Spaniard also had several uniforms to borrow, black pants and sweaters with the castle's logo, plus name tags that could be altered easily. Zim was too muscular to fit into the outfits, but Smith and Creel matched his size. The sweaters were on underneath their zipped jackets.

When they had all the information they needed, Creel smothered the Spaniard with a pillow while Smith held him down. Although the castle might wonder about the absence of the missing employee, Zim was sure the body wouldn't be found until after their mission was complete.

Zim followed the path as it curled through the massive complex, impervious to the breeze whipping flags atop several of the buildings. Tourists posed for photos next to ancient cannons lined up along one of the outer defenses. Next to an outdoor café was a modern howitzer pointed at the northern part of the city. According to the map, its gun was fired at one o'clock every day except Sunday. One less soldier to worry about today.

The operation wasn't without risk. The castle was one of the few in Britain that still maintained a military garrison, although it was largely ceremonial. However, the presence of the crown jewels of Scotland made security at the castle a prime concern. The Great Hall was positioned adjacent to the old Royal Palace, which housed the jewels. They'd have to complete the operation quickly before anyone realized what was happening.

On the castle grounds' top plateau Zim passed the National War Memorial and walked into Crown Square. He stopped in the center and acted like he was checking his map. Smith and Creel wandered past without looking at him. They headed to the bathroom next to the café, where they would dispose of their jackets and come back out in the guise of employees.

Zim strolled into the Great Hall's antechamber, then into a long room with a vaulted hammerbeam ceiling high above. Chandeliers hanging from the timber crossbeams lit up the dazzling array of weaponry and armor lining the walls. Swords, knives, pikes, axes, and flintlock pistols hung from the ornate carved paneling that ended at a huge stone fireplace illuminated with the fiery red glow of an electric simulation.

Two employees, a man and a woman, stood behind a velvet rope, chatting and observing the visitors to make sure they didn't touch the displays.

The stag head was to their left. It was among a dozen items supported by pedestals and identified by placards stamped with the National Museum of Scotland logo. The deer peered forward with a glassy stare, as if it were still on the lookout for the hunter who had felled it, the rack of antlers at the ready to defend itself.

Zim dawdled at the midpoint of the hall and saw Smith and Creel enter wearing their uniforms. They headed straight for the two employees, and Zim could overhear their conversation.

'Douglas,' Smith said, using the man's name, 'Mr Cobham wants to see you at the information desk.' He used the name of a manager that the Spaniard had told them. The 'Canada' label under Smith's tag meant his American accent wouldn't seem strange.

'Me?' Douglas said, nonplussed. 'What for?'

'Not just you. He wants both you and Mary down there

now. He said he may be a few minutes, so you should wait for him if he's not there when you arrive.'

'That's odd,' Mary said. 'Did he say why?'

'No,' Smith said. 'But he asked us to cover for you while you're gone.'

'This can't be good,' Douglas said. 'All right.' He and Mary hurried away, never questioning the fact that they hadn't seen Smith and Creel before. Zim had counted on the castle being big enough that the employees wouldn't all know each other.

Smith and Creel stepped behind the rope. They needed to give Douglas and Mary a little time to clear the square. Then they could start herding the tourists out, claiming the hall was being closed for maintenance. A 'Closed' sign that they'd purchased would keep the curious at bay long enough for Zim to tear open their prize.

And if Douglas and Mary did return early, they wouldn't get a second chance. Given how easily Smith and Creel had dealt with the Spaniard, Zim had no doubt that the two of them could kill a couple of lowly security guards with their bare hands.

THIRTY-THREE

Grant was glad Brielle had finally talked him into taking a taxi. He leaned his head against the back of the seat and closed his eyes for the short ride to Holyrood Palace.

Although Dr MacNeil was making inquiries about getting access to the stag heads after hours that evening, Tyler thought they should split up to see if they could spot anything unusual about the trophies with a visual inspection. Tyler didn't want to separate from Alexa, so he took her to Edinburgh Castle while Grant and Brielle paired up to explore Holyrood.

Even though MacNeil told them that no one else had inquired about the stag heads, they were worried that Zim and Dunham had some inside knowledge that they weren't aware of. It would be bold of them to try anything in such well-trod and protected places, but boldness hadn't been a problem for those two so far. All Grant and his group could hope to do was scare them off until they could see if there was anything to the taxidermy book's tale.

The cab came to a stop and Grant opened his eyes.

'We're here,' Brielle said. 'Are you sure you wouldn't rather check into a hotel and get some rest?'

Grant straightened up and forced himself to keep from yawning. 'Why? I'm fine.'

'Bollocks. You don't have to pretend with me. I know what's going on. I've noticed you creaking around like an old man when you think no one's looking.'

'I've felt worse.' Which was true to a point. During his wrestling days, he once wrenched his back so hard that he couldn't move for three days. This pain was a slightly lower grade, but it was attacking every joint in his body, as if he'd been stretched out on a rack. He knew it was the advanced symptoms of arthritis, another indication that the *Altwaffe* was doing its work, aging his body beyond his years and making every movement a chore. No one had mentioned the gray hairs he was shaving from his chin and scalp every day. Combined with the constant fatigue, muscle weakness, blurring of vision, loss of hearing, and inability to focus on a task for longer than a few minutes, he could tell that he didn't have much time before he wouldn't be able to power through it any longer.

When he saw Brielle staring at him, he said, 'Really. It's not as bad as you think.'

She narrowed her eyes. 'You're certainly not a *kvetch*, as my mother would say. All right. Let's see if we can find this thing.'

They made their way inside the palace, and every step Grant took required concentration so that he could keep up with Brielle's pace. The rooms were numbered, leading them in a counterclockwise path to the gallery where MacNeil had told them they would find the trophy.

They passed through ornately decorated dining rooms, drawing rooms, and bedchambers, not even pausing to give the appearance that they were interested in the splendor of royal accoutrements. They exited the King's Closet and entered the Great Gallery.

A few tourists wandered along the red carpet splayed across the length of the gallery, which featured over a hundred portraits of what Grant thought of as 'men in tights'. Light filtered in from windows along the inner courtyard, but each of them was obscured by a display set up to show off a distinct part of Scottish history. A TV at the other end was playing a video where several people watched.

The stag head was at the far end of the hall, its antlers reaching toward the ceiling.

'There it is,' Brielle said and walked toward it. Grant followed for a moment, then stopped.

A solo man turned away as Grant had passed, his long hair obscuring his face. Something about him seemed familiar, and suddenly Grant recognized him as the man driving the Range Rover in Cambridge. He turned and saw the man crouch on the ground as if tying a shoe.

Liquid flowed from his hand onto the carpet. The man had a lighter in his hand.

He was going to set the room ablaze. With the amount of wood in the room, half the palace could go up in no time.

'Fire!' Grant shouted. His reaction time felt like it had slowed to a glacial rate, but he ran at the man and tackled him just as the lighter flicked on. He caught the guy in the back, sending the lighter flying before it touched the liquid.

As Grant rolled on the carpet, his face pressed against his adversary's jacket, the smell of alcohol stung his nose. The arsonist hadn't finished pouring the solution from his flask, and Grant's tackle had caused the remainder to soak the man's clothes.

An elbow caught Grant in the solar plexus, causing him to double over in pain. Grant lashed out with a fist but hit only air as the man dodged the weak thrust. The guy twisted away and sprang to his feet.

Grant wasn't as quick to get up, but he managed to block a kick before it smacked his head. A roundhouse punch did get him in the temple, and Grant realized that he was about to endure something that had never happened before.

For the first time ever, he was going to lose a fight against a single opponent.

Brielle was already halfway down the gallery when she realized that one of the women watching the video was Marlo Dunham, dressed in trousers instead of a skirt, but otherwise looking exactly the same as when they'd last seen each other in Laroche's mansion.

Then Brielle heard Grant shout 'Fire!' She whipped around and saw him launch himself at another man. In a split second, they were on the floor throwing fists at each other.

She'd seen Grant wade into a fight with three other men and come out without a scratch, but it was obvious he wasn't himself, taking hits left and right. She was about to go help him when he struggled to his feet and seized his foe in a headlock.

'Get . . . her!' Grant yelled.

Brielle turned back around to see Dunham fumbling with the bottom of the stag head where it was mounted to the pedestal, searching for the secret latch.

Brielle sprinted toward her. Dunham threw open the latch, and the stag head swung to the side on hidden hinges. Before she could extract anything from the interior, she saw Brielle approaching and took a bottle from her purse, upending the contents onto the floor in an arc between them. She flicked open a lighter and threw it onto the rug.

Flames leapt into the air in a wall that spanned two-thirds of the gallery, and Brielle had to jump back to keep from getting burned. The two other visitors who'd been staring dumbfounded at the events in the room ran screaming. It gave Dunham enough time to stick her hand into the trophy and withdraw a small notebook from its cavity. Her eyes went from Brielle to the notebook and back as if she were deciding what to do next.

Brielle wasn't going to wait to find out. She went around the inferno intending to give chase, but Dunham hurled the journal past Brielle into the fire.

Brielle wanted Dunham badly, but the journal was more important. If it were destroyed, then Zim would win. She couldn't let that happen.

Brielle turned and raced toward the fire.

Grant was just about spent. He'd managed to stop the long-haired man from going to Dunham's aid, but the effort was sapping his strength rapidly.

His opponent finally slipped from his grasp and ran toward the flames that were now spreading across the carpet. A fire klaxon shrieked overhead, but it would take a minute for the emergency crews to get there.

Grant mustered every reserve he had and gave chase. He saw something sail out of the fire and then Brielle followed in a tuck, rolling to put out the flames that licked at her coat. She popped to her feet and stamped on the burning object, smothering the flames.

She was oblivious to the man headed right for her.

Grant forced himself into another gear he didn't know he had and barreled toward the fire. Just as the man reached Brielle and was about to launch a vicious kick to her head, Grant caught up to him and shoved him from behind.

The momentum carried Dunham's accomplice stumbling past Brielle and into the fire. His clothes, soaked with the flammable liquid, erupted in flames, and the man lurched around shrieking in agony as he sought to put out the blaze that enveloped him.

Brielle snatched up the charred notebook with her sleeve

and put her other shoulder under Grant, who was now almost too weak to carry on.

'Come on, Sergeant,' she said, calling him by the rank he'd had in the Army. 'We need to get out of here before they start asking questions.'

As they tottered away, employees with fire extinguishers charging into the room, Grant said, 'The journal—'

'We won't know until we look at it, but I think the outside got the worst of it.'

Grant didn't say more, trying to stay upright and maintain the impression of a panicky tourist until he could get outside the palace and curl up in the fetal position.

THIRTY-FOUR

Alexa was subdued as she and Tyler reached the top of the Edinburgh Castle grounds, as if her enthusiasm for the quest they were on had been dunked in an ice bucket. During the walk from the museum, she had tweaked Tyler about his relationship with Brielle.

'We're not serious,' he'd said.

'I know,' Alexa replied. 'Ever think about converting to Judaism?'

'Come on, Alexa. I've known her for a total of two weeks.'

'How long did you know Karen before you were exclusive?' Alexa knew the answer. Tyler and the woman who would become his wife had three dates over the course of a single weekend while he was at MIT. Neither of them dated anyone else after a night watching the Red Sox beat the Yankees at Fenway Park.

'That was different,' Tyler said.

'Why?'

'For one, Brielle's British and I'm American. I'm not up

for a long distance thing. I tried it with Dilara, and that didn't work out so well.'

'Maybe she would move to the US.'

'And she's made it very clear that her parents wouldn't approve of their little girl marrying a gentile.'

'Tyler, you're a genius in many ways, but you are really thick-headed sometimes. Don't you think it's possible that she's using that as an excuse? I mean, you haven't actually met her parents have you?'

'No. So you're saying she doesn't actually like me?'

Alexa shook her head. 'Boy, you need me around more than I thought. I'm saying she might like you too much. I don't know her history, but I know yours. You don't want to get hurt again, and it's quite possible she doesn't want to either. I can tell she's got some stuff going on underneath just like you do.'

Tyler smiled. 'Since when did my little sister become my shrink?'

'Since you became a confirmed bachelor.'

'You sound like Grant. He's always trying to play matchmaker, which is rich coming from the original confirmed bachelor.'

'You don't think he'll ever settle down.'

Tyler laughed loudly, drawing the attention of some tourists as they walked toward the castle entrance. 'Grant? Do you know how many women he's dated in the last five years?'

Alexa shrugged. 'Maybe he's still looking for the right person.'

Tyler stopped smiling and his eyes took on a tinge of sadness. 'He did find one woman he cared for.'

'Who?'

'Someone who was a great fit for him.'

'What happened to her?'

He sighed. 'She was killed. Grant saw it happen.'

'That's terrible.'

'He took it pretty hard. I think he's been a little gun-shy about relationships ever since.'

'He seems like a great guy,' Alexa said. 'He'll find someone.' She didn't mention that the someone might be her.

The sadness on Tyler's face deepened. 'I hope he has the chance.'

'What do you mean?'

He didn't answer as they waited in line for tickets. Once they were through, Alexa asked again. 'What's wrong with Grant? He won't tell me anything.'

'He didn't want you to know, but the symptoms are getting too noticeable.'

'You mean the aches and pains? The tired look that seems to be getting worse?' Alexa felt her stomach roil with nervousness. A serious face from Tyler wasn't to be taken lightly. 'What's going on, Tyler? Tell me right now.'

Tyler paused as if searching for the right words. His expression was pained as he finally spoke.

'Grant's been poisoned. It happened last week at the Eiffel Tower when all of the leaders who have been getting sick and dying were exposed.'

She stared at him, dumbstruck for a moment. 'I can't believe it.'

'You've seen how sick he's been getting over the last couple of days. It's worse than he's letting on.'

'This is ... it's horrible. How long has he got?'

'Days maybe. We don't know for sure.'

'My God! He should be in a hospital!'

'I told him the same thing, but he wouldn't do it. You think *I'm* stubborn.'

'What can we do?' Alexa asked.

'We're doing it. The toxicologists are working on an antidote, but without a better understanding of the poison's chemical structure, I'm not convinced they can create one in time. If that Nazi notebook is right, finding the Loch Ness monster and getting a sample of it might be his only chance.'

Alexa could see the toll Grant's illness was taking on Tyler. She hadn't seen him this distressed since the aftermath of Karen's funeral. 'How long will it take them to synthesize an antidote?'

'Once they have the sample? I spoke to Agent Harris yesterday. She said the toxicologists think it will only take a matter of hours to manufacture the antidote. If the Nazi formula is correct, that is.'

'Does she believe Laroche now?'

'She's still pretty skeptical, but they're getting desperate enough to try it if we come up with the goods.'

'Desperate enough to get the British authorities to crack open the stag heads?'

'We'll see,' Tyler said.

'And even if we find something that helps us track down Nessie, do we have the resources to do it?'

'Miles gave us carte blanche. The *Sedna* passed through the Caledonian Canal from the North Sea last night, and they've begun a grid pattern search from the midpoint of the loch. But with nothing else to go on, the search could take weeks and still not find a trace of the creature.'

'Then John Edmonstone is our best chance.'

'No,' Tyler said, 'he's our only chance.'

The rest of the walk through the castle grounds had been silent. Alexa hugged her jacket close to her body to fend off the wind. She thought about all the teasing she'd done with Grant and now felt guilty about it. He'd known all that time that he was dying and didn't say a word.

They crossed the courtyard to the Great Hall, but she stopped when she saw a CLOSED sign on the door.

'That's odd,' she said. 'Are they still setting up the exhibit?'

'Doesn't seem likely. Dr MacNeil said that they installed it last week.'

'Then why would it be closed?'

'I don't know. Dammit. We need to get in there now.' Tyler turned and pointed to a man crossing the courtyard. 'There's an employee. I'll find out what's going on.'

He made a beeline for the worker. Alexa pressed her ear to the door. She heard voices inside.

'Wait, Tyler,' she called to him. 'Someone's in there. Let's ask them.' He turned and jogged back toward her.

She pushed the door and found that it wasn't locked. She eased it open and saw two men in employee's uniforms.

'Excuse me,' she said, entering the antechamber.

One of the men, a humorless blond with glasses, put up his hands and rushed over to her. 'I'm sorry, ma'am. We're closed for renovations.'

'I just wanted to look at one of the exhibits—'

'You'll have to come back later.' He made a shooing motion with his hand.

'Well, when are you reopening?' By this time, Tyler had joined her, the door closing behind him.

'I don't know, ma'am. You have to leave.' He put his hand on her shoulder and turned her forcefully while the other man moved to the door.

'Hey! You don't have to shove me.'

She ran into Tyler, unyielding as granite. He was fixated on the interior of the Great Hall, his eyes filled with a rage she'd never before seen in her brother.

'Zim,' he whispered.

THIRTY-FIVE

During the milliseconds it took Tyler to process that Zim was in the empty Great Hall prying apart the stag head trophy, he assessed his predicament. Not only was he outnumbered three to one, but Alexa was now in harm's way. But if he simply ran out with her in tow, he'd leave Zim to destroy possibly the only chance to find Grant's cure.

Alexa's immediate safety won. Tyler turned and punched the blond man who had pushed Alexa, breaking his glasses and sending him sprawling. He grabbed Alexa's hand and went for the door, but the blond guy's partner was already there. The man tackled Tyler, and they went tumbling through the archway into the cavernous Great Hall. Tyler went down hard on his recovering arm, but the rush of adrenaline helped him ignore the sudden stab of pain.

He rolled and sprang to his feet next to a suit of armor. He plucked the helmet from its stand and swung it around, connecting with the guy's skull. The glancing blow sent him to his knees.

Alexa was tripped by the blond and scrabbled her way

into the hall, the man tugging at her pant leg in an attempt to stop her. She threw a kick at his face, hard enough for him to release her. She ran for Tyler, and he placed her protectively behind him.

Zim was paying scant attention to the fight. He dug into the neck of the deer and extracted a cylindrical object, letting the crumpled paper around it fall to the hardwood. Zim looked puzzled as he drew the object out, obviously not the journal they'd been looking for.

It was a clear glass jar. There seemed to be something floating in a liquid.

Zim stared at it in confusion, then a look of comprehension came over his face and he smiled at Tyler, a sinister grin that sent a chill down his spine. He needed a better weapon than the helmet if he and Alexa were going to survive this.

That's when Tyler noticed the hall was literally brimming with blades. He nearly let out a whoop of joy when he realized that they had a fighting chance. It wasn't great, but he was elated to have any chance at all.

He snatched a five-foot-long halberd from its clamp on the wall and shoved it into Alexa's hands. With a spear on the end, a spike on one side and a cleaver-shaped blade on the other, it was a menacing weapon. Although Alexa looked terrified, she stuck it out in front of her. He hoped she didn't actually use it as anything but a bluff. An errant swing would slice him just as easily as it would the bad guys.

Tyler drew a saber from the rack and took a defensive

posture next to her. He'd never fought with a sword in his life, but he was betting Zim and his men hadn't either.

The blond grabbed two short swords and criss-crossed them like he was sharpening knives. The mustached man selected a huge claymore, a two-handed broadsword that lent its name to a type of explosive mine. Zim picked a saber of his own, the jar held gingerly in his other hand. They circled around Tyler and Alexa.

'Zim,' Tyler said as calmly as he could, 'why don't you put that specimen down and leave?'

'Because it's three to one and a half.'

Alexa sounded peeved. 'I'm supposed to be half?'

'Besides, why would I give up my best chance to take care of you both at the same time?'

'Because we're not out on some isolated country estate,' Tyler said. 'There's no way you're getting out of here without being caught.'

'Oh, you're wrong about that,' Zim said, then barked at his men. 'Kill them.'

Blond and mustache rushed at them.

Tyler thought this would be a good time to raise the alarm. He howled with his best battle cry as he steeled himself for the assault. Alexa followed suit with a guttural scream. No one in the courtyard outside would fail to hear them. They had to hope the cavalry would arrive before there was nothing to do but mop up their remains.

Either through miscommunication or not taking Alexa seriously as a threat, both men went after Tyler. The blond's short swords swirled, but his aim was off due to his missing glasses. Metal clanged against Tyler's saber. He had to leap back to avoid a swipe from the second sword, and then sidestepped an overhead chop of the mustached man's claymore, which took a massive chunk out of the floor.

Tyler was hoping Alexa would take the opportunity to make a run for it, but he should have known she wouldn't leave him to be slaughtered. Gripping the handle of the halberd like the bat she'd used in college softball, she swung the weapon around, her eyes locked onto her distracted target.

The spike pierced the blond man's ribs, and his swords clattered to the floor. He collapsed backward, wrenching the halberd from Alexa's hands. She stood there staring at what she'd done, mute.

The mustached man sprang back to action. He reared back for another strike of the claymore. It was only when he experienced the inertia involved with the backswing of such a huge weapon, though, that his face registered he might have selected not only an intimidating weapon, but also one that was unwieldy.

Before the man could swing the claymore on its down stroke, Tyler thrust forward and stabbed the saber through his heart. The mustached man looked down in surprise at the blood soaking his shirt and then fell backward, motionless as soon as he hit the floor, the claymore clattering to the ground next to him.

Zim stalked toward them, a menacing sneer on his face,

and Tyler honestly didn't know whether he could win. He was already huffing from the battle so far, while Zim was fresh. And by the looks of her, Alexa wasn't going to be able to repeat her prowess with the blade. Tyler not only was on his own, but he had to protect her as well.

Zim slashed his sword toward Tyler, who blocked it with the saber. He grabbed Zim's wrist, drawing him into a clinch, Zim's fetid breath hot on Tyler's face.

In the brief glimpse Tyler got, he could see two things: an organic piece of skin and flesh floated in the clear liquid, and a label on the jar clearly spelled out 'Loch Ness'.

Zim might be holding the only known tissue sample from the Loch Ness monster, hidden by John Edmonstone two hundred years ago. If Tyler could get it from him, their search would be over.

'This isn't going to get your brother back, Zim,' Tyler said. 'Either one of them.'

'This isn't about getting them back. It's about justice.'

'You mean revenge.'

Zim's lips spread in a vile grin. 'Semantics.'

The door to the hall flew open. Four men rushed through holding batons, their radios cackling.

'Gotta go,' Zim said and heaved Tyler back. Still gripping the jar, he ran for the door, swinging the sword wildly, creating a wide path through the outmatched rescuers.

'Stay here,' Tyler shouted to Alexa and took off in pursuit.

He exploded out of the door. Instead of the exit, Zim was

angling toward the café. Tyler sprinted after him, the saber still in his hand.

He burst through the café door and saw another door closing inside. Tyler gave chase and flung the door open, his weapon at the ready.

As he entered, he realized it was the men's lavatory. He found Zim inside, the jar poised above the toilet. Zim turned it over, and the contents splashed into the bowl.

'No!' Tyler yelled, but he couldn't stop Zim as he flushed the last known bit of the Loch Ness monster into the sewer.

'You bastard!' Tyler shouted, and raised his saber for the final battle. The only thing that stopped him was the pump action of two shotguns.

'Police!' one of the men called out. 'Drop your weapons!'

Tyler grimaced and dropped the saber only after Zim let go of his sword. They each put up their hands and were thrown against the wall.

As handcuffs were laced around his wrists, Tyler was face to face with Zim. The former prisoner didn't seem to have a care in the world as he smiled at Tyler with undisguised glee.

THIRTY-SIX

Brielle was able to get Grant out of Holyrood Palace and into a taxi before they could be detained by the police. Tyler's phone hadn't yet been replaced, so she tried Alexa repeatedly, but the call kept going to voicemail. No reason to panic yet, but troubling nonetheless.

With Edmonstone's journal in hand, they had to head straight to Loch Ness, so she and Grant went to the nearest rental facility and hired the only standard sedan in the lot. She raced over to the train station to retrieve their bags and purchased a disposable mobile phone from a kiosk.

For the next fifteen minutes, they tried calling Alexa and got no answer. By that time, Grant was feeling well enough to drive, so he let Brielle out as close to the castle as he could and went off to find a place to wait for her call.

She walked the block to the esplanade in front of the castle and was stopped by a cadre of armed policemen. Tourists streamed out of the castle, and none were being let inside.

She waved to a policeman. 'Sir, why can't we go in?'

'There's been a death inside the castle.'

Brielle's stomach dropped. 'Who was it?'

'We don't know yet. Please step back.'

She called Grant, her heart hammering.

'Did you find them?' he asked.

'No. The castle's closed off because of a death inside.'

'Are Tyler and Alexa okay?'

'I don't know. They won't let anybody in or answer any questions.'

'Dammit! I'll be right there. I have to make a call.'

He hung up. The policemen pushed the crowd back, allowing a convoy of three patrol cars to pass out of the castle, their sirens wailing. Brielle strained to see who was inside, but they flashed by too quickly to get a good look. They were followed by two ambulances, leaving a dozen emergency vehicles at the entrance.

Brielle dashed back to where Grant dropped her off, arriving just as he did. He hopped out and got in the passenger seat.

'You know how to drive here better than I do,' he said. 'And I have to navigate.'

'Why?' she asked as she got in and stepped on the gas.

'After we thought Alexa went missing in Seattle, Tyler got her permission to track her phone, and Aiden set it up. He transferred the software to my phone.' He showed her a map of Edinburgh with a moving green dot.

'Is she on foot?'

'It's moving too fast,' Grant said. 'She must be in a vehicle.

I got them pulling away right after you called me. Did you see anything?'

'My God! I saw police cars and ambulances coming out of the castle.'

'I saw two ambulances pass me on my way to pick you up, but Alexa wasn't in them. Or at least her phone wasn't.'

'But what about Tyler?'

He pressed his lips together.

'Where do I go?' she asked.

'You're on the right route. They've turned onto a road called A700. Make the next right.'

Brielle turned onto King's Stables Road. They both were quiet as they contemplated what could have happened to Tyler and Alexa. Since she and Grant had come across Marlo Dunham, it was very likely that Tyler and Alexa had a run-in with Victor Zim. If that were the case, then someone was killed in the encounter.

Brielle could barely keep her hands from shaking on the steering wheel. Of course, she had gone through Tyler being injured before, but that was after the fact, when she knew he would be all right. For the first time she was really afraid of Tyler dying.

She sped past dawdling vehicles, yelling obscenities at each putz slowing her down. She wanted to be there as soon as Alexa arrived at wherever she was headed.

Grant guided her onto another road and then through an interchange to Queensferry Street.

'They've stopped,' Grant said with a confused look.

'They're at the station?'

'No. That's strange. The map says they're in the middle of a bridge.'

'Where?'

'Just up ahead.'

She rounded a crescent of buildings and saw lights flashing on the road in front of her. The unmistakable sound of automatic weapons shattered the air.

'What the hell?'

'Ambush!' Grant yelled. 'They've got the police in a crossfire.'

The police cars were sprawled across the road, boxed in by two SUVs blocking their path in either direction. Two ski-masked men on each end poured withering gunfire into the policemen, who were dropping right and left.

Instead of putting the car in reverse, Brielle jammed her foot on the accelerator.

She went up on the sidewalk and around the stopped cars, their drivers ducking as low as they could to avoid stray rounds. The police seemed to have been finished off, so the gunmen by the Range Rover closest to her lowered their weapons and walked around the vehicle to mop up. They were so focused on their targets that they didn't notice her coming.

At the last moment, the gunmen heard the roaring engine behind them. They turned in time to face her as she plowed into them. One of the men went flying over the side of the bridge. The other sailed into the boot of the rear police car and didn't get up.

Screeching to a halt, she jumped out and grabbed the weapon from the downed gunman, the habits from her service in the Israeli Army coming back instantaneously. The gun was an Enfield L85 assault rifle used by the British military and Ministry of Defence. She took cover behind the bonnet of her car and lifted the weapon to her eye, aiming with the red dot sight. She shot twice at the attackers behind the vehicle at the other end, but they took cover while replying with errant potshots that kept her down.

She heard two people banging on the back window of the rearmost police car. Brielle took a quick peek, and to her surprise and relief she saw Tyler and Alexa, both in handcuffs.

'They can't get out!' Grant yelled to her.

'Did you get the other weapon?'

'No. It went over the side with Peter Pan.'

'You get them! I'll cover you!'

She laid down suppressing fire as Grant crabbed his way to the police car. He opened the door, and Tyler and Alexa scrambled out. They got back to the cover of the SUV just as they were bombarded with fire from up ahead.

She didn't take time for greetings, although she wanted to throw her arms around Tyler.

'Are you both all right?' she asked them.

'We're fine,' Tyler replied.

'We have the journal,' Grant said as he unlocked their cuffs with a key he'd plucked from a dead policemen.

'Then we need to get out of here.'

One of the gunmen at the other end of the bridge ducked low to get to the first police car. He opened the rear door, and someone got out. He poked his head up once to look and then dropped again, but it was enough for her to see that it was Victor Zim.

Brielle was about to debate the wisdom of leaving the scene of a police ambush when more shots pelted the Range Rover, from three weapons this time. Zim was now armed, and she had to be down to the bottom of her magazine. Continuing with a gunfight when outgunned wasn't a smart strategy.

'Tyler's right,' Alexa said. 'If the police take us in, we'll be questioned for days. We'll never get the antidote in time.'

Brielle nodded reluctantly. 'Okay. Let's go.'

They jumped into the sedan and peeled away. Brielle was still hopped up on adrenaline, but the rest of them slumped in their seats from exhaustion. In the rearview mirror, she could see Zim's car tear off as the sound of more sirens headed their way.

Now all of them were fugitives from the law.

THIRTY-SEVEN

Getting out of the Edinburgh metro area was a challenge for Zim and Dunham. Zim ditched the Range Rover that was pocked with bullet holes from the gun battle with the police, and they piled into the one Pryor was driving, with Dunham in the passenger seat. Zim certainly wasn't going to sit in the back, so he made Pryor switch.

The only advantage they had was that the police were overwhelmed with three extensive crime scenes – Holyrood Palace, Edinburgh Castle, and the bridge. Few were left over to throw up any roadblocks on the myriad highways and back roads leading out of the city. Still, they prepared themselves to fight the few times they spotted a police car.

By the time they got to Stirling, an hour's drive west of Edinburgh, Zim felt confident that they were out of immediate danger of being caught. He and Dunham would have to wear their disguises in public from now on, knowing sketch artists would soon be blasting their faces out to the world.

Zim was glad that he'd taken the precaution of having Pryor monitoring the police bands. As soon as Pryor heard that a muscle-bound Caucasian man had been taken into custody and would be transferred to the Lothian and Borders Police headquarters, he had quickly drawn up the likely route that would be followed and sent the Scottish part of his team to ambush the convoy.

What Zim wasn't happy about was losing men one after the other. Five more were either dead or injured because of Tyler Locke and his group. Their persistence was infuriating.

Dunham's whining was almost as bad.

'Why are we still going to Loch Ness?' she asked. 'I burned up the journal.'

'Did you see it burn?' Zim countered.

'I saw it start to char, yes.'

'Start to char . . . Did you see it finish charring?'

'Well, no.'

'Then they might have it. Even if they don't, Locke won't give up. I saw him get away.'

'You should have—'

Zim raised a fist. 'So help me God,' he growled, 'if you say I should have killed him when I had the chance, I will kill *you* right now.'

For the first time, Dunham looked meek. She swallowed and licked her lips. 'Fine. We both could have done better. And you did well to get rid of the sample from the other deer trophy. That was quick thinking. You must have been shocked to see it.'

'Thank you. See? A little compliment doesn't hurt anyone now and then.'

Pryor got a phone call.

'Yeah? Uh huh. Okay, hold on.' He looked at Zim. 'It's the captain of the *Aegir*. They want to know where they should meet us.'

'Send him the GPS coordinates I gave you. Tell him to send the Zodiac to pick us up.'

Pryor conveyed the plans and told the captain they'd be there in two hours. Before he hung up, Zim asked another question.

'Have they been keeping an eye on the other ship?' The *Aegir* had two men in the Zodiac observing an odd ship that had entered the loch the day before.

Pryor relayed the question and after a long pause said, 'They've kept their distance like you told them, watching with binoculars all morning, but they haven't been able to figure out what they're doing.'

'Is it a fishing vessel?'

'No. It's like no boat the captain has ever seen.'

'Have them record some video of the ship. I want to see it when I arrive.'

Pryor gave the instructions and signed off.

'What do you think Locke is up to?' Pryor asked.

'He's going to have to assume Nessie is real and alive, just like we do. If he's got Edmonstone's journal, he has to be coming up with a plan for capturing the creature.'

'I think it's about time I hear your plan for *destroying* the creature,' Dunham said.

'I thought you trusted me to spend the money wisely.'

'I did. Now I want to hear the rest of the story.'

She already knew that Zim had paid a Norwegian crew more than a year's wages to bring their whaling vessel over to Loch Ness disguised as a regular fishing boat. For that much money, the captain hadn't asked any questions, even when he took on the remainder of Zim's men as additional crew. Hunting minke whales in the Arctic Ocean was not only a rough business with hot and cold streaks, but because Norway was one of the only countries in the world still whaling, frequent run-ins with protesting ships made it even harder to catch their quota.

The hundred-foot-long ship was small enough to get through the locks into Loch Ness. The Caledonian Canal, built almost two centuries ago, slices all the way from the North Sea through the four lochs making up the Great Glen – Loch Dochfour, Loch Ness, Loch Oich, and Loch Lochy – to its outlet just above the Irish Sea. Built as a bypass around the rough waters off the aptly named Cape Wrath, the canal could handle vessels up to 150 feet long, making it no problem to bring the *Aegir* through.

'The whaling vessel was a nice idea,' Dunham continued. 'But if we find the Loch Ness monster, how are we going to destroy it?'

'We're not going to destroy it.'

Dunham was flabbergasted. 'What? All they need is a few ounces of flesh, and they can synthesize the antidote.'

'I know,' Zim said.

'We have to make it so they can't recover any part of the creature.'

'I know.'

'If we don't kill it, all of this has been for nothing!'

'Calm down. I didn't say we weren't going to kill it.'

'So we're going to haul it up onto the *Aegir* and sneak it out of Loch Ness? That's insane.'

Zim was rather enjoying egging her on like this. They still had a long drive ahead of them, so he may as well be entertained.

'You're correct. If Alexa Locke's video is accurate, then Nessie is at least thirty feet long. I think it would be difficult to smuggle something that big out of the area.'

'Then what are we going to do? Just leave it there?'

Zim smiled and nodded. 'That's exactly what we're going to do.'

THIRTY-EIGHT

Alexa was nauseated. Trying to read John Edmonstone's jagged handwriting while swooping through the curves on the road to Loch Ness finally ended up being too much. When they reached the broad Glen Coe valley, she asked Tyler to stop the car at a scenic overlook so that she could decipher the journal without losing her lunch.

She still felt guilty for freezing up back at Edinburgh Castle. Just yesterday morning, Alexa had never even seen someone die before, let alone killed anyone. Now that seemed so long ago. First, she'd watched the two men killed on the go-karts, contributing to the death of one of them. Then she'd actually done the deed herself. The sickening feel of the blade sinking into flesh made it seem like she'd crossed some unseen threshold that she could never step back over again. The responsibility of ending a life was more than she had been ready to bear, even if it had been in self-defense. All those thoughts overwhelmed her so much that she couldn't finish Zim when she'd had the chance, and the remorse gnawed at her.

Now Tyler's reluctance to talk about his experiences in war made sense to her. In abstract, killing someone to save your own life or someone else's might be a heroic deed, but reliving the carnage and celebrating the event wasn't a prospect she would relish. If there were a pill she could take to completely forget that moment, she would swallow it in a heartbeat.

She stepped out of the car to get some fresh air. Tyler and Brielle followed suit, while Grant stayed in the car to rest. Alexa walked over to a fence and leaned against it for support as she tried to calm her queasy stomach.

Unlike cloudy Edinburgh, the canyon was awash with sunlight. The sloping valley walls, hollowed out by a glacier millennia ago, were painted green with grass and a handful of trees. The scent of earth and flora on the mild breeze bathed her in a revitalizing medley, spoiled only by the tinge of car exhaust from the multitude of vehicles traversing the pass through the rugged highland mountains.

Tyler sidled up and leaned on the fence next to her. 'How are you doing?'

'The sandwich Brielle got me at that convenience store will remain consumed.'

'I meant about the castle. I thought I'd lost you there.'

Alexa massaged her temples to fend off a nausea-induced headache. 'Do you ever get used to it?'

Tyler shook his head, knowing what she was referring to. 'Getting used to it implies it becomes routine. Killing someone is never routine. Not for me, at least.'

'How many people have you killed?' she asked and then immediately regretted the question when she saw the pained look on Tyler's face.

'More than I want to think about. I'm sorry you have to think about it now.'

'But you do it anyway. You chose to go into the Army knowing you might have to kill people. Why?'

Tyler was silent a long time before responding. 'It was my job, my duty to a greater cause than myself. I guess the real answer is that I went into the Army *despite* knowing I might have to kill someone. Some of the soldiers under my command went into the military with a different attitude. They wanted to get into battle as soon as they graduated from boot camp. For everyone except the very few sociopathic recruits, that eagerness lasted until the first firefight. It was nothing like they'd expected it to be. Confusion, terror, and remorse had never been part of their idealized mental image of battle. After that initial experience, most of them just wanted their buddies and themselves to get back alive.'

Alexa shuddered. 'It sounds horrible.'

'It is. Bloody, messy, and brutal. As you've seen first-hand.'

'I've always bragged about you to my friends as a hero, but I never really understood what that meant until now. You're a hero for putting that uniform on in the first place, knowing the piece of yourself you'd have to give up.'

'I'm lucky. Lots of guys I knew couldn't let it go. For some reason, I can compartmentalize. I think that's why I could eventually go on after Karen died.'

'I hope I can do that, too. Compartmentalize it.'

Tyler turned to face her. 'I think you will. I don't see the thousand-yard stare or the jitteriness that doomed some of my guys.'

'Must be our Locke genes.'

'You'll be all right. But remember I'm always around to talk if you need to.'

'Thanks.' She gave him a hug. 'You, too.' She felt like they had closed a distance between them, as if Tyler now trusted her with something she didn't understand before. She couldn't imagine him talking like this with Grant. Their way of communicating was more subtle, the jokes and macho posturing easier for guys like them to deal with.

She stood up. 'Let's see what Edmonstone has to say.'

They all got back in the car, and the others dozed or contemplated quietly while Alexa laboriously read through the journal looking for the relevant passages, carefully turning the singed and yellowed pages so as not to tear them. After thirty minutes of scanning, she finally found it.

'Listen to this,' she said, her heart pounding as she read Edmonstone's notes to them.

Mr Darwin and I returned from Loch Ness, and I hardly believe myself what happened. I've never been scared like that, not even when I was set free and had to fend for myself.

We were camping on the east shore of the loch where Mr Darwin was collecting specimens. I spent my time hunting for animals to add to my taxidermy collection and fishing for our dinner. I caught some big salmon using the Guyanese blue shark saltfish my cousin sent me as bait, and I think that's what did it.

We were coming back across the loch to start the journey back to Edinburgh. I was trolling for one last fish for the trip home while I rowed, and that's when we spotted the beast for the first time. The wake it left behind was bigger than ours, and it slapped against the bottom of our boat to give me the biggest fright.

I rowed with all my strength, but we couldn't outrun it. Just in sight of Urquhart, it rose from the water like some great ghost haunting the dark waters. I only saw shadows until the beast attacked and Mr Darwin fought back. Using his ax, he hacked off a piece of the creature's tail. I stabbed it with the only thing I had by my hand, a gaff hook, and lost it in the combat.

The creature went under never to be seen again, and we made it to shore while I thought my chest would burst. The only thing we had to prove what happened was the fleshy bit Mr Darwin kept.

On the trip back, we agreed never to speak of it – Mr Darwin to protect the wretched creature and me to keep my business. I didn't think anyone would believe us even though Mr Darwin let me keep a piece of the beast. I knew it was the spawn of the devil as it wouldn't die, but I kept it safe all the same because Mr Darwin asked me to.

I don't abide ever going to Loch Ness again, but if I do, I know what would bring the beast calling. This demon craved the taste of shark.

Alexa looked up and saw Grant gaping at her.

'Could it be that simple?' he asked. 'Shark is like catnip to the Loch Ness monster?'

Tyler borrowed Brielle's new phone to use its web browser. 'According to this site, saltfish is a salt-cured and dried dish and was commonly eaten by slaves in the Caribbean in the eighteenth and nineteenth centuries because it was cheap and easy to preserve and transport.'

'Why would a freshwater animal like shark?' Brielle asked.

'The Loch Ness monster may not be a strictly freshwater species,' Alexa said, 'although it's now stranded in the loch. Shark may be one of its favorite foods, but it makes do with fish like salmon.'

Grant looked dubious. 'Don't you think someone would have come across this affinity by now?'

Alexa shook her head. 'Not necessarily. I would never think of using shark as bait, and I'm sure few highlanders would either. The uncommon scent of shark meat might have been irresistible to Nessie. Sharks themselves can detect a few drops of blood in the water from miles away. Edmonstone's trolling might have acted like an underwater beacon.'

'Then it's pretty apparent what we need to do,' Tyler said. 'We have to find us some pickled shark.'

He called Aiden and laid out the unusual request. Aiden said he'd call back as soon as he had an answer.

'This journal entry verifies everything,' Brielle said. 'Darwin did come away with a sample of the Loch Ness monster. His portion somehow ended up in the hands of the Nazis over a hundred years later, while Edmonstone's half was flushed away by Zim today.'

Alexa nodded. 'If we can find Nessie again, an antidote is truly possible.' She squeezed Grant's shoulder. He looked at her in confusion and then read her eyes and knew that she was aware of his plight. He took her hand and laced his fingers with hers in a reassuring gesture.

'How big did you say Nessie is?' Brielle asked.

'At least thirty feet long,' Alexa said. 'If the mass is commensurate, maybe over two tons.'

'Are we able to catch something that big?'

'We don't have to catch it,' Tyler said. 'We only need a piece of it.'

'And we can do that?'

'We've got just the thing. I'll show you when we get to Loch Ness.'

'What did Edmonstone mean when he said that the "spawn of the devil" wouldn't die?' Grant asked. 'Is it immortal?'

Alexa scrunched her brow and looked at the relevant

passage again. 'You said that the *Altwaffe* acts by aging people prematurely,' she said to Tyler.

He nodded. 'I've seen the effects myself.'

'That can't be a coincidence.'

'Why not?'

'The weapon must attack the telomeres in some way.' When she saw blank looks, she continued. 'Telomeres are nucleotide sequences at the end of each chromosome. As cells divide, these telomeres get shorter and shorter until they disappear, which means the chromosomes can no longer duplicate. That's what happens when we get older. The telomeres deteriorate. If the *Altwaffe* destroyed the telomeres, it would replicate the effect of rapid aging.'

'Biology was a long time ago for me,' Brielle said. 'How does that relate to Edmonstone's observation about it not dying?'

'If he saw something unusual in the tissue sample that he had – say tissue repair – then the Loch Ness monster's body might have some way of regenerating its telomeres. Lizards and starfish can grow new tails and limbs after they've been amputated, so the Loch Ness monster may have a similar ability. Essentially, it wouldn't age. The Nazis could have figured out how to reverse the process using the tissue sample from Darwin.'

'Bastards,' Brielle spat. 'They had something that could help mankind, and instead all they did with it is create another way to kill.'

'Except they were more interested in poison gasses for

battlefield use or the extermination camps,' Alexa said. '*Altwaffe* may have worked too slowly for their purposes, and that's why they never used it.'

'And all it took from the monster itself was a bit of flesh it probably re-grew in a few days,' Grant said. 'A week later you probably wouldn't even see any scars. I have to say I like mine. They're good reminders of what I've been through.'

Grant's words struck a chord with Alexa. *They're good reminders.*

Brielle's phone rang. Tyler answered with, 'What have you got, Aiden?'

'Grant,' Alexa said, waving her hands at him, 'let me see your phone.'

'Sure,' he said, handing it to her. 'What's up?'

'I have to check something.'

She brought up her YouTube video and fast forwarded to the sighting of the monster. She played it three times, holding it as close to her eye as she could until she was sure she wasn't hallucinating. She dropped the phone to her lap and stared at Tyler.

'You're the man,' Tyler said into the phone. 'Ship the package to Inverness airport. Brielle will pick it up there since I'm a known fugitive. I'm hoping the police don't realize yet that she's an accomplice.' He hung up.

'What package?' Brielle asked.

'Aiden found a market in London that specializes in food from around the world. They have twenty pounds of Caribbean blue shark saltfish. He's getting an expedited shipment of the whole thing to Inverness in the next two hours. Then we'll see if Edmonstone's theory is correct or if we—' He paused when he saw Alexa staring at him. 'What's the matter?'

'I think the cell regeneration theory is right,' she said. 'Look at this.'

They huddled around the phone as best they could. Alexa played the video, which showed the surfacing flipper.

'What are we supposed to be looking for?' Grant asked.

'The glint of light. It's faint, but once you notice it, the outline becomes obvious.'

Brielle squinted and then gaped as it was replayed.

'Is that what I think it is?' she gasped.

Alexa nodded. 'That's a gaff hook embedded in the flipper.'

She shook her head in disbelief at the revelation. They weren't searching for a descendant of the creature that Darwin and Edmonstone had encountered. There was only one Loch Ness monster, and it was over two hundred years old.

LOCH NESS

WORLD NEWS

Arab Countries Indicate War Is Imminent

By PHYLLIS CROUCH and MARCUS THUNE

June 22, JERUSALEM – As forces mass along the eastern and western borders of Israel, residents of this ancient city have flocked to the holy sites of the Western Wall and the Dome of the Rock, praying for a miracle to avert an invasion that seems nearly inevitable.

With the leaders of Egypt, Syria, and Jordan rumored to be in intensive care, the more hawkish ministers in those countries have garnered support for a retaliatory strike against the perceived aggressor, the Israeli government. With the support of other Muslim nations whose leaders are also in dire straits, and bolstered by new missile technology purchased from China and Russia, the armies arrayed against Israel are the most formidable they have faced since the Yom Kippur War of 1973 nearly drew the United States and the Soviet Union into a nuclear standoff.

The massive military buildup has caused the United States to raise its threat level to the highest it has been since the 9/11 attacks. Countries in western Europe are undertaking similar preparations for possible terrorist strikes. Some analysts believe Israel may call on its allies if it fears being overwhelmed in an assault, which could draw the western powers into wider war.

Authorities are racing to identify the true perpetrators of the Eiffel Tower attack that set these events in motion, but even if Israel is proven not to be culpable, the deaths of the Muslim nations' ailing leaders may tip the crisis past the point of no return.

THIRTY-NINE

Dunham yawned and opened her eyes when she felt the Range Rover slow and turn onto a dirt road with a rutted track that looked like it saw no more than two vehicles a week. The clock on the dashboard read 2:34 p.m.

'Where are we?' she asked, rubbing the sleep from her eyes.

'The east shore of Loch Ness,' Zim said.

Dunham made careful note of the location since it was going to be their way out when the mission was over. Zim parked in a turnout, and they all climbed out of the Range Rover, stretching their legs and removing their disguises before making the short hike to the point where the Zodiac outboard from the *Aegir* picked them up.

In contrast to the sheep pastures and scrub brush they had passed for much of their way up, the loch was surrounded by thick forests. Dunham peered over the side of the boat and could see nothing beneath the rippling black surface of the water. Three white boats were visible in the distance, all of them cruising around the ruins of Urquhart

Castle clinging to a rocky promontory. Its jagged stone walls and crumbling tower were only shells of the redoubt it used to be, damaged in an explosion long ago to prevent it from falling into enemy hands.

As they approached the whaling vessel, Dunham could see two seamen cutting a net away from an object floating on the water. Most of it was hidden from view, a concealing tarp hastily thrown over it. All she could spot was the black fin of a sleek craft knifing out of the water. Zim called it a gift from Gordian Engineering.

The *Aegir*'s cobalt blue hull was topped by a white superstructure, and the ship looked indistinguishable from any other fishing vessel to Dunham's untrained eye. Fresh paint and a new registry number had been applied so that it wouldn't be recognized as a whaler. The yellow foremast was equipped with a boom crane and topped by a crow's nest for spotting whales. The harpoon launcher at the bow was covered by another tarp.

Once they were on board, they got the rundown from the captain, who finally realized he was in over his head but could do nothing about it now that he had armed men on the ship. The remainder of Zim's men had boarded the *Aegir* in Inverness, and the equipment he had told them to bring with them was stowed in a locker in the crew quarters. The odd-looking ship they'd been spying on – a vessel called the *Sedna* and confirmed as property of Gordian – was anchored near the south end of the loch by the town of Fort Augustus. As instructed, Zim's men forced the *Aegir*'s captain to capture one of the search craft the *Sedna* had sent out, and its two operators were currently being held under guard below decks.

Zim made a move to head down there, but Dunham said, 'We need to talk.'

'Why?' Zim asked. 'We need to question Locke's men.'

'Not until we settle our strategy.'

'I told you what it was on the way up.'

'I have some problems with it.'

'You have problems . . . ' Zim clenched his fists and tilted his head at Pryor. He and the other two men from Edinburgh left them in the galley alone.

While she munched on a sandwich, Zim poured two cups of coffee and handed her one of them. She took a sip of the bitter brew and made a face, but the warmth of the liquid made it go down well.

'What about our strategy do you not like?' Zim asked.

'You're betting everything on Locke finding the monster.'

'Believe me, I know the man. He won't give up. He's a pro.'

'But then we have to make sure that not only do we kill the monster and dispose of it, but we also have to make sure Locke doesn't get away with a tissue sample.'

'That's why we need to question his men. That GhostManta under the tarp may be our ticket to making this all work.'

'See? You're thinking too narrowly. All we need to do is prevent him from finding the monster in the first place.'

'You're insistent you torched the journal,' he said sarcastically, 'so that's taken care of, isn't it?'

'I'm open to the possibility that they may have been able to reconstruct it even if it was partially burned. That's why we need to be thinking offensively as well as defensively.'

Zim slammed his fist on the table. 'I am not thinking defensively! I'm beating Locke at his own game. I'm letting *him* do the work for me.'

Dunham rolled her eyes. 'Yes, yes, you're a brilliant mastermind. But it didn't occur to you that we can stop him before he even gets onto the loch.'

'How?'

'Can your phone be traced?'

'Not if I route it through an internet anonymizer that Pryor set up.'

'Then give it to me.'

'Why?'

'So you can learn a lesson in alternative thinking.'

Zim bellyached, but he handed over the phone and told her how to dial so that the call couldn't be traced.

She dialed the Inverness operator and asked to be connected to the police.

Zim stared at her, incredulous. 'What the hell are you doing?'

'You'll see.'

The line picked up. 'North Constabulary,' a woman said. 'How may I help you?'

Dunham put on her best freaked out voice. 'Oh, my God! I just saw the man who escaped after being arrested at Edinburgh Castle this morning.'

That got the call center operator's attention. The events in Edinburgh had blanketed the national news all day.

'Which man, ma'am?'

'Tall, brown hair, good-looking. He's with three other people: a red-headed woman, a dark-haired woman, and a huge, bald black man.'

Zim sat back and fumed at her.

'Where did you see them, ma'am?'

'I was passing through Fort Augustus and saw them get into a small boat that went out to a ship. I think it's called the *Sedna*.'

'When was this?'

'Just a few minutes ago. And they had guns with them.'

'Guns? Are you sure?'

'Oh, yes. Big ones, like the military carry. You know, machine guns.'

'How many people are on the ship?'

'I don't know. A lot. And they looked dangerous.'

'And what's your name?'

'Oh, I'm just a tourist. I don't want to get involved. But please hurry. I'm very worried about our safety here with people like that roaming around.'

She hung up.

'What the hell was that about?' Zim asked. 'What if Locke isn't even on the ship yet?'

'Then he won't be able to get on it. The police will realize that it's a Gordian-owned vessel and make the connection. It'll take hours for them to search it and question the crew.

They'll probably even leave police behind in case he shows up here.'

'I don't like it.'

'Why? Because now you aren't able to carry out your little revenge angle? Do that on your own time.'

Zim glowered at her, then held out his hand. 'My phone.' She gave it back.

He stood and drained the rest of his coffee.

'Where are you going?' she asked.

'I was under the impression that we were done. I'm going to do some of my own questioning.'

'Why?'

'I have to work on the assumption that your clever little idea won't work. The men we captured are going to show me and Pryor how to use Locke's own technology against him.'

FORTY

Tyler drove through the tiny village of Fort Augustus at a steady pace to give the impression that they were a group of travelers passing through on their way to a destination in western Scotland. The flashing lights of parked police vehicles in town had been visible from a mile down the road.

Alexa stared at the array of patrol cars and vans lined up at the dock. 'What's going on here?'

'Someone ratted us out,' Grant said.

'I think we can all guess who,' Tyler said.

'Looks like we're not getting on the *Sedna* tonight.'

'But we have to!' Alexa protested. 'We don't have time to wait around.' Tyler saw her eyes focus on Grant.

'The longer we stay on the run,' Brielle said, 'the likelier it is that you or Tyler will be recognized.'

'We'll figure out something,' Tyler said, already forming the outline of a plan.

They could only dare one pass through the town, so he noted as many details as he could during the short trip along its main thoroughfare. The quaint village consisted of a few dozen small buildings holding businesses that catered to tourists coming by car or boat. The canal split Fort Augustus in half, and Tyler crossed it by the only route, a swing bridge that could be opened to let boat traffic from Loch Ness access the water staircase of five locks leading south. Tyler counted three boats in the middle lock slowly rising to the level of the lock above it.

To the north, Tyler could see the *Sedna* approaching a dock along the canal, a phalanx of policemen in body armor ready to board. The white ship looked unbalanced with the command deckhouse located at the very bow of the ship. The aft portion of the ship consisted of a stowed crane and a retractable covering that angled down toward the stern, giving the boat an aerodynamic appearance. The covered area was useful for protection against the elements when launching its craft.

This had to be the most excitement the town had experienced in years. Tourists gathered to watch the proceedings, and others wandered amongst the shops or stood in line for one of the loch tours ready to set sail. A policeman directed traffic around the parked police vehicles. Within a minute, they were out of Fort Augustus and on the road leading along the western edge of Loch Ness.

'Now what?' Brielle asked.

'Alexa,' Tyler said, 'when did you say Darwin and Edmonstone had their encounter with Nessie?'

'At twilight.'

'And you saw the creature at sundown?'

She nodded. 'Right. Our best chance to find it is to go out at dusk.'

At this northerly latitude, sundown in June was around 10:20 p.m.

'That gives us seven hours,' Tyler said. 'If the police are gone by then, we can continue with the original plan.'

'We should be so lucky,' Grant said. 'You know they'll leave some forces behind in case we show up. We destroyed two landmarks and participated in a gun battle in broad daylight. It won't matter that we were on the side of the good guys.'

'Which means we need to go to plan B.'

Brielle leaned forward. 'Which is?

'It's an hour's drive to Inverness airport,' Tyler said. 'We head there and pick up the bait from the courier. We also arrange for a sunset boat tour.'

'Why?'

'You're going to have to chum the water for me using the saltfish.'

'You mean, for us,' Grant objected. 'There's no way I'm not coming with you.'

'Grant, you're . . . ' Tyler stopped himself from saying the unintended pun 'dead tired' and chose something less cringe-inducing. 'You're exhausted as it is. Are you up for it?'

Grant straightened in his seat, unsuccessfully hiding a wince. 'You may be the pilot, but I know more about the GhostManta than you. If we're going to use it, you need me there.'

Tyler couldn't argue with that, and normally he wouldn't even question Grant coming along for the ride. But Grant's face was sagging and drying out, the wrinkles more obvious. He was decaying right before their eyes. However, he was also a fighter. Sitting on the sidelines wasn't his nature, and he'd have to be unconscious for Tyler to leave him behind.

'All right,' Tyler said. 'But if you aren't feeling up to it, let me know. We'll only get one shot at this tonight.'

'If I keel over, just dump my ass overboard.'

Tyler smiled. 'Well, of course. That goes without saying.'

'What about us?' Alexa asked. 'We're doling out the bait?'

'Yes,' Tyler replied. 'There's a town called Drumnadrochit about two-thirds of the way up the loch. It's right across from Urquhart Castle, which is where both you and Edmonstone spotted the creature. That location seems like our best shot for finding it again. The town has a few boats that give tours.' He had researched the options on Brielle's phone.

'We'll make them an offer they can't refuse?'

'Right, but we'll use cash instead of a horse's head.'

'That doesn't explain how you'll get onto your ship,' Brielle said.

'That's where you come in. We'll have to stop and get you some warm wool clothing.'

'Why?'

'Because you're going to be a bit chilly.'

Brielle met his gaze in the mirror with a confused and

suspicious stare. Tyler had an hour's drive each way to and from the airport to convince her to give an encore performance of her experience at Lake Shannon.

By eight thirty in the evening, they were approaching Fort Augustus again, this time from the north, and Brielle was not pleased with the plan. However, she strained to think of anything better and failed, so she agreed to go along with it. A towel and a change of clothes were waiting for her in the boot. The car now sported a license plate pinched from a similar model in an Inverness car park.

It was less than two hours to sundown, so they had to act quickly. She was driving since she was the least conspicuous of the group. Tyler and Alexa had identified themselves to the police at Edinburgh Castle. A search of the internet showed that their photos were being broadcast as persons of interest in the Edinburgh events that left three unidentified men and six policemen dead that morning, one of the worst mass killings in Scotland's history. And Grant stood out because of his size and skin color. As Brielle drove into Fort Augustus, they ducked low, all of their heads covered in woolen ski hats. The police presence was diminished, but she spotted the tactical team's van on a side street. She cruised past the dock where the *Sedna* was tied up and saw an unmarked car watching the vessel.

She turned around and headed back to the car park next to the closed information center. They left the rental car there and split up into two groups. Tyler and Grant headed south along the river that paralleled the canal, while she and Alexa wandered into town as if they were looking for a place to eat. Alexa wore her hair tucked under her hat with a pair of oversized tortoiseshell glasses to mask her face.

When they got to the swing bridge, Brielle pointed at the boats along the dock and they ambled down the road past the stakeout police car as if they were a couple of tourists. Alexa made sure to keep her back toward them.

Brielle handed Alexa her phone and mimed taking a picture. She made a big deal of pointing out what she wanted in the background, keeping an eye on the trees that abutted the path next to the dock. Only because she was looking right where she had to, she saw Tyler and Grant creep up to the edge of the woods, ready to make a dash for the *Sedna*.

When they were in position, she nodded at them and began posing in outrageous positions, putting on quite a show, sticking her bum out and cocking her hips in such a way that the two officers couldn't resist watching her.

As she posed, she inched her way backward until she felt the edge of the dock under her heel. She winked at Alexa, and they both laughed as if she'd said some something hilarious.

Brielle took another step back, her toe on the edge. She pinwheeled her arms as if she were trying to catch her balance and then launched herself backward.

She hit the water. Brielle had prepared herself for its icy embrace, but the cold knocked the wind from her just the same. The replay of her escape into Lake Shannon was improved by the layers of wool wrapped around her, though the sudden immersion was more shocking.

She surfaced and screamed as if she were drowning, the cold doing all the work of getting her into character. On the dock Alexa acted like a panicked schoolgirl and shrieked for help.

The doors of the police car flew open and the officers came running toward the dock, their original duties momentarily forgotten. Brielle was glad she could count on good old-fashioned British gallantry, but she felt a tad guilty for taking advantage of it.

As she thrashed in simulated terror, she glanced farther down the dock and saw Tyler and Grant hustle across the open space and climb onto the *Sedna*. When they were safely aboard, Brielle acted like she had gotten her wits about her and paddled toward the outstretched hands above her.

She reached out and was pulled from the water, coughing and trembling as they sat her down. Alexa crouched next to her and whispered in her ear. 'Did it work?'

Brielle nodded and coughed again.

'She's okay,' Alexa said to the gathered crowd. With the glasses, her red hair covered by the hat, and the cops' focus on the near-drowned woman, no one gave her a second glance.

'Oh, my God,' Brielle croaked, latching onto the attending policemen. 'Thank you so much!'

The two men beamed at her, and one said, 'We're just glad you're all right, ma'am.'

After an attempt to convince Brielle to seek medical attention, they accepted her decision to decline and went back to their stakeout, unaware that they'd helped the two women they were looking for. She and Alexa hurried back to the car.

Under a blanket, Brielle changed out of her wet clothes and into a dry set, depositing the dirty and smelly togs in the car park's dust bin. She was still shivering as Alexa drove them away, headed back to Drumnadrochit for their sunset cruise.

FORTY-ONE

Jerry Yount, the captain of the *Sedna*, listened to Tyler and Grant tell their story, the creases in his ruddy face deepening with every new revelation. He'd been a ship's master for more than twenty years and sailing on boats for twice that long, so Tyler was sure the old sea dog had thought he'd heard it all. Yount was being disabused of that notion quickly.

'You're telling me that you two think the Loch Ness monster is real?' Yount said when they were finished telling him why they'd had to sneak on board. Grant leaned against the wall of the captain's cabin and sipped a cup of tea, his hands quivering.

'Not only real,' Tyler said. 'We need to find it. Tonight.'

'I thought we were out here doing a sounding survey. At least your odd request for outfitting the GhostMantas makes sense now.'

'Sorry about the deception. I was hoping you'd come across something in your search.'

'The closest we got was a few logs floating on the surface.'

'When can we leave?' Grant asked.

Yount shook his head. 'Can't. The police ordered me to stay docked here until tomorrow. They've even got the loch's only rescue boat stationed in Fort Augustus temporarily to keep an eye on me in case I cast off without permission.'

'They're hoping we'll show up here,' Tyler said. 'They probably also have the Gordian offices in London or Glasgow staked out. They probably think you have a better chance of smuggling us out of the country.'

'Just say the word.'

'I appreciate the offer, but we're not criminals. However, it could take days for them to sort out what happened, and we don't have that kind of time.'

'Then what do you need?'

'Grant and I need to borrow one of the GhostMantas.'

Yount shrugged. 'It's your company. You can do what you want with it. There's only one here, but it's charged up and ready to go.'

'Where is the other one?'

'That's a good question. It should have been back an hour ago. We haven't been able to contact the operators. I'm starting to get concerned.'

Tyler frowned at Grant. Coincidences hadn't been good to them lately.

'Where was it searching?' Tyler asked.

Yount showed them on a map of the loch. The grid section where it was last heard from was near Urquhart Castle.

'Let's hope it's just a busted radio,' Tyler said. 'We'll keep an eye out for them.'

'It's a big lake. What about calling in a helicopter for the search?'

'If we call in a rescue chopper,' Grant said, his voice a husky rasp, 'it'll mean giving up on the search for Nessie. We'll have boats all around us.' His ability to speak had been deteriorating rapidly throughout the day, causing Tyler to reconsider whether he should bring Grant along on the mission. He felt damned either way.

'My men might be in trouble,' Yount said.

Tyler wrestled with the decision, weighing the need to search for Yount's men with the consequences of not finding the *Altwaffe* antidote. If Zim was responsible for the disappearance, they could be dead already. A damaged radio wasn't serious, but if it were a major equipment malfunction, the odds of finding the men in time to save them was a million-to-one. Tyler had to play the odds.

'It won't be long until dark,' he said, 'and by the time the police believe you aren't trying a ruse to distract them, the sun will have gone down. Give us until an hour after dusk. If you haven't heard from your men by then, bring in the police to scour the loch.'

After going a few more rounds, Yount grudgingly agreed with Tyler's logic.

'All right, then,' Yount said. 'Come on.'

They left his cabin and took a circuitous route below decks so they could come up within the covered section of the ship unseen from the outside.

Tyler felt the weight of the moment as they walked. Grant

was shuffling along doing his best to hide his illness. Yount might not have noticed, but it was painfully obvious to Tyler. Then there was trying to avert the war brewing in the Middle East, and the fact that he had dragged Alexa along into this mess. He was so wrecked about turning her into a killer that he hadn't had the heart to tell her Michael Dillman's body had been recovered from Puget Sound with two bullets in his head. Aiden mentioned it when Tyler got the update on Laroche's status, which was that he was still comatose but showing some response to stimuli.

All Tyler could do was focus on the task at hand, which at least provided some distraction from his morbid thoughts.

They entered the launch bay to find the GhostManta nestled in its cradle. Tyler hadn't seen it since they began testing it last winter, so he admired anew the sleek lines of the submarine.

Modeled on the form of a manta ray, the Ghostmanta was the brainchild of a design student named Caan Yaylali. Originally meant to be used as a camera platform for documentary videographers interested in recording sea creatures at great depths, Gordian had modified the design to create a multi-purpose sub that could be used for underwater maintenance and surveying, particularly for the oil and gas industry. After the blowout of the Deepwater Horizon drilling platform in the Gulf of Mexico, in which it had taken months to cap the sea-bottom well, Gordian saw the opportunity to produce a speedy and flexible vessel for performing undersea repairs. The two GhostMantas aboard the

Sedna were headed to a North Sea oil rig for testing when Tyler had requested that Miles divert them to Loch Ness.

The black sub's wings were used to stabilize the craft and pitch it up and down underwater while the fin-like rudder steered it. On the surface, the GhostManta performed like a boat, but when it dived, it flew like an airplane. Tyler had taken it out for several test runs. Although that had been six months ago, it wouldn't take long to familiarize himself with the controls again.

The sub's operators met them in the shed, as the rear covered hangar was called, and talked Tyler and Grant through the latest updates. The sub was propelled by two battery-powered pump jets similar to the ones on the US Navy's new Virginia-class nuclear subs and could reach a speed of twenty knots. That would get them to their pre-arranged rendezvous by Urquhart Castle in little more than thirty minutes, just as darkness was falling. Of course, the sub's regular pilots would have been much more adept at handling the craft, but Tyler couldn't ask them to defy the police or risk another run-in with Zim.

While Tyler would pilot the sub, Grant's main job would be to operate the firing controls. The additional modification Tyler had asked for from Yount was a spear gun, one mounted on each side of the cockpit. But this spear wasn't for killing. It had two purposes. The first was as a biopsy tool. The spear was a customized soil sampler that had been altered to capture a tissue sample from Nessie. It had a high-tensile filament lead which would be used to retract it once it had lanced through skin, bringing back a piece of flesh the size of a toilet roll tube.

The second purpose was to implant a low-frequency radio transmitter. If the sample retrieval failed, they would be able to follow the creature in an attempt to get another.

Once they were brought up to speed on the controls, Tyler and Grant squeezed into the tandem cockpit, Tyler in front and Grant in back.

Before they closed the canopy, Yount handed Tyler a short-barrel rifle and some extra ammo.

'We keep this hidden on board for when we travel through unsavory parts of the world.' When he saw Tyler's surprised look, he added, 'Pirates are getting bolder these days. You might need it if you run into this Zim character. I don't want to lose any more people.'

Tyler thanked Yount and stowed it in the footwell beside him. He closed and latched the canopy, while Grant made the final checks on their environmental systems.

'How are you doing back there?' Tyler asked through his earpiece.

'Ready for warp speed, Cap'n,' Grant said, trying to sound jauntier than he had looked, the words coming out like they'd been spoken by a buzz saw. However, as long as Tyler heard him say something, he wasn't going to doubt Grant's ability to carry out the mission.

The shed's rear door rolled open, revealing the fading light outside. The unique configuration of the ship was designed to facilitate launching and capturing the subs. An inclined ramp extended into the water as the door raised. The GhostManta was latched onto a dolly that descended the ramp until the sub was in the water, at which point the latch would release. When the sub was ready to be pulled back in, it would simply maneuver to the stern and mate with the dolly, which would draw it back up the ramp and into the ship. Based on the well decks used by amphibious assault ships, the system made the launch and capture process go faster, more smoothly, and with less potential for damage than with a traditional crane.

Tyler gave a thumbs up to Yount, who nodded for the dolly to be lowered. The GhostManta eased down the ramp, and Tyler could see a couple watching them from a sailboat docked behind them. As long as they didn't raise the alarm, the policemen watching the bow would never know the sub launched. The boaters watched intently and seemed content to snap a few photos with their phones.

Water surged around the sub as it reached the aft end of the ramp.

'All systems are nominal,' Yount said into Tyler's ear. 'Are you a go?'

'We're ready. We'll submerge as soon as we're free.'

'Understood. Good luck, gentlemen.'

Tyler felt a lurch as the dolly released, and the GhostManta eased into the water. Tyler filled the ballast tank, and the sub sank until the canopy was covered. The sonar told him he had only a few feet of clearance above the canal bottom until they reached the open loch, so he'd need to be careful not to ground the vehicle. Tyler pushed the throttle, and the propellers whirred to life.

With a muted whine, the sub cruised into the darkness ahead.

FORTY-TWO

Zim was impressed by the technology packed into the GhostManta, particularly the fiber-optic periscope that allowed him to observe the Gordian ship while submerged. A dozen boats had already passed him and Pryor without noticing the tiny scope protruding from the water.

The view revealed Locke's surreptitious boarding of the *Sedna*, frustrating Dunham's futile attempt to prevent him from going forward with his search for the monster. Zim knew it wouldn't work; Locke was too resourceful. He silently patted himself on the back for his wisdom in using the sub to spy on his nemesis.

Then he'd seen the second GhostManta launch from the rear of the sub tender, and Zim was sure Locke and Westfield were inside. He let them go by before swinging around to follow with Pryor acting as the sub's pilot.

Although the sub was a marvel of sophisticated equipment, it did have one weakness. The passive sonar was processed by a computer that projected a head-up display for the pilot and navigator. Any object that was in the sonar's field of view was shown on the three-dimensional image collimated for the operator's eyes so that glasses weren't necessary. The disadvantage was that it showed only what was in front of the sub. Since it wasn't a military vessel, it wasn't a critical problem, and the view was supplemented by a rear-view camera, although it could penetrate just a few feet through the peat-rich water. As long as Pryor kept them in Locke's baffles, he'd never know he was being followed.

Pryor accelerated until Locke's sub was visible on the display, its outline perfectly rendered in the HUD. He slowed to keep a respectable distance behind as they cruised up the loch.

The sub's original pilots had been convinced to be helpful in explaining the GhostManta's operation, which Pryor had absorbed easily. By the time they had reached the southern portion of Ness, he had become proficient enough in piloting the sub, but Zim credited that primarily to the designers. Care had been taken in making the controls simple to use, modeling the stick, rudders, and throttle on the ones in an airplane's cockpit. Important switches and knobs unique to a submarine were well-labeled, and the rest were accessed by touch screens that looked like those found on a smartphone.

Zim was uneasy about leaving Dunham to coordinate the preparations on the *Aegir*. Her constant questioning of his tactics had become intolerable, but at least he could be satisfied that she would get hers when they were done here.

What he hadn't figured out yet was Locke's strategy. If the journal had been incinerated, the Lockes would have no way to know what Edmonstone had divulged about his encounter with the creature. But the fact that they were here must have meant they had some clue about how to find Nessie.

Which is why Zim had to be ready to respond if Locke were successful. Zim was sorely tempted to take him out right now, but the uncertainty of what Locke was up to prevented him from taking the shot. Soon, though.

Zim had the means to sink him, thanks to a modification that had been made to the sub. In addition to the retractable claws that could be extended from the streamlined body for maintenance work, the sub had been equipped with two launchers that were aimed like torpedo tubes. They'd been designed to be loaded with some kind of spear, which was ejected by compressed air.

But Zim had a better idea of what to load in them.

The whaler had a full complement of harpoons used to hunt minke whales. Thanks to international pressure, each harpoon was tipped with an explosive penthrite grenade to minimize the suffering of the whales. The round would go off once it penetrated a foot of flesh. With a well-placed shot to the Minke's head, death was designed to be instantaneous.

Zim was looking forward to seeing what kind of damage it would do.

Using a 'cold' nonexplosive harpoon, they'd tested shooting it from the launcher on the sub. In the water it had barely a quarter the range of one fired from the cannon mounted on the *Aegir*'s forecastle, but it would be able to hit Nessie if they got close enough. It also packed enough of a punch to sink a small vessel.

With two harpoons ready to fire, Zim had one for the monster and one for Locke.

Once the monster was dead, they would haul it up onto the deck of the whaler. With the cloud cover, the darkness would shield their activities from prying eyes on the shore. They'd tack it to the deck, ready for the final phase.

Dunham had suggested sailing out of the loch during the night, but the canal at the north end wouldn't reopen until morning, meaning they'd have to motor past Inverness and into the North Sea in broad daylight.

Too risky. They had an entire loch to dispose of the creature. Ness averaged seven hundred feet deep. It might take weeks to find the location of the sinking and then would require special equipment to get to it that far down. All they needed to do was weigh down Nessie, a beast that could tip the scales at a couple of tons. Something very heavy would be required to assure the job would be done.

'Pryor,' Zim said, 'how long do you need once we have the creature locked down?'

'Say, three minutes to set everything. How much time should we allow to get away?'

'I think five minutes should do it. You're sure of the detonators' placement?'

'While you were talking to Dunham, I set them all up exactly as you directed. No way the Norwegians will find them unless they're looking for them.'

'Good. Then while we've got some time, let's go over the plan again. We'll have all the whalers on deck during the tie down process. Once it's secure, I'll waste them while you start the timers.'

'Seems a shame,' Pryor said. 'They're Scandinavians. Our kind of people.'

'They're already chafing at holding two men hostage. They'll talk, and we don't want witnesses to lead anyone back to the point where it sank.'

'What about the submariners?'

'They're locked up. That problem will take care of itself.'

'And Dunham?'

'She comes back with us. She still has to pay us.'

'And after that?'

Zim smiled. 'I want to make sure she gets away alive.'

'Why? You hate her. I can tell.'

'She'll understand.'

'All right,' Pryor said. 'Hey, they're slowing down.'

'Match their speed. I want to see what they're planning. Make sure to stay behind them.'

'Will do.'

Zim could feel the tingle of excitement he remembered when he'd sabotaged the chemical plant. The endgame was near. Locke and his sister would soon be dead, and the explosive charges on board the *Aegir* would scuttle the whaling vessel, sending the Loch Ness monster down to the icy depths once and for all.

FORTY-THREE

As she peered through the window of the gift shop in Drumnadrochit, Alexa was amazed at the number of Nessie-related items that could be squeezed into one store. It was packed with all manner of toys, books, and clothes emblazoned with the creature's likeness. In the window display was a plush Nessie stuffed animal, a Disneyfied version with a goofy smile and doe eyes. If only the real thing ended up being as friendly and tame.

Alexa moved away from the window and checked her watch. The sunlight was fading, only twenty minutes until their preset rendezvous with Tyler and Grant. Brielle rubbed her arms and stood quietly at the door where the skipper of the *Nessie Seeker* would meet them to take them to his boat. The shop, now closed, was the final stop for patrons of the Loch Ness Centre and Exhibition, so the tour operator had contracted to sell his trips from the store.

'Are you warm yet?' Alexa asked.

'I don't know if I'll ever be warm again after that

dunking,' Brielle replied. 'My whole view of swimming has been radically altered in the last few days.'

'You should try Lake Michigan in winter. I did a polar bear plunge while I was in college to support the Special Olympics. It was mid-January, and we'd just gotten twelve inches of snow.'

Brielle rolled her eyes. 'You Lockes are a bit touched, aren't you?'

'If you mean crazy, then yes. I'll never get in water that cold again.'

A white van with the logo of Loch Ness Voyages pulled into the parking lot and circled around to the front door of the shop. The driver, a tall man with a paunch, a grey beard, and a sailor's cap, lumbered around the van and stuck out his hand.

'Greg Sinclair, skipper of the *Nessie Seeker*,' he said in a Scottish brogue thick enough to pour on pancakes.

Alexa and Brielle introduced themselves using false last names only in case Sinclair had caught a radio report about them while he was on the loch.

'As you know from our phone conversation,' Alexa said, 'we have a special request.'

'Doubling my usual fee takes care of anything you'd like, barring any illegal activities, of course.'

'We want to go fishing.'

Sinclair rubbed his beard. 'I don't have any fishing tackle, so you'd have to be bringing your own. Is it salmon you're after?'

'Something bigger. We're looking for Nessie.'

Sinclair laughed. 'I've been sailing Loch Ness for thirty-five years, and I've seen Nessie once in all that time.'

'You've actually seen it?' Brielle asked.

'"Her" is what I call Nessie. Fifteen years ago, she surfaced about five hundred yards away while I was out on my own.'

'What did she look like?'

'A black hump with a snake head, just like the surgeon's photograph. I didn't have a camera with me to record it, but you can be sure I carry one now. How is it you'll be expecting to find her?'

'We're going to chum the waters,' Alexa said.

Sinclair furrowed his brow at the two of them. 'You're serious about this?'

'Yes.'

He shrugged. 'I won't be telling you how to spend your money. But I hope you don't come away disappointed.'

Alexa looked at Brielle with concern. 'I hope we don't, either.'

They lugged the shipping box full of saltfish from the trunk to the back of the van. When they were belted in, Sinclair drove the minute it took to get to the boat dock.

He pulled up next to a crisp white power cruiser with 'Nessie Seeker' on the side. The forty-foot-long boat had a railing around the bow, an upper deck above the wheelhouse, and an open-air aft area. It was perfect for their needs.

Once they had hauled the box on board, Sinclair cast

off. He fired up the engine and sailed into Urquhart Bay. The castle was resplendent across the bay in the waning light. The floodlights used to illuminate the ruins at night were already visible, and the Grant Tower smoldered with an ethereal glow.

Alexa donned the rubber gloves they'd bought while Brielle opened the box. She uncapped the plastic container inside, and the pungent odor of cured fish assaulted their noses.

'Mind not to spill any of that on the cushions,' Sinclair called out from his position at the helm. Alexa had asked him to take the boat out to the open loch and cruise back and forth three hundred yards offshore of the castle.

Alexa and Brielle put a towel on the bench seat and rested the plastic container atop it. Alexa retrieved another purchase, an ice scoop. She dug it into the pile of fish and drew out a heaping scoopful.

'Here we go,' she said and tossed it into the water.

'You think this will really work?' Brielle asked.

'I don't know. It was a fluke that we got to see it the first time.'

Brielle shook her head as Alexa threw another scoop into the loch. 'I don't understand why Nessie would be interested in shark meat.'

'Remember the coelacanth?'

'That ugly fish in Laroche's vault?'

Alexa nodded. 'That species evolved into its current form four hundred million years ago. Maybe Nessie's species is just as old, although not a dinosaur. Shark may very well have been part of its diet since they've been around for four hundred and fifty million years.'

'How could Nessie still be around after all that time?'

Alexa had gotten into a rhythm of doling out scoops as she talked. 'If she's not a sturgeon – which I still think is the best explanation for the legend – she could be the last of her species, isolated here hundreds of years ago.' She shook her head and scanned the desolate loch. 'It's actually sad when you think about it. Alone all that time.'

'That would explain why it's rarely seen,' Brielle said. 'But if it's a sturgeon, how could it be the source of the *Altwaffe* chemical? There are sturgeons in other parts of the world, and nobody has made weapons out of their flesh.'

The question of how it could be the source of the Nazi *Altwaffe* was definitely a puzzle for Alexa. She couldn't reconcile that aspect of the creature's anatomy with what she knew about the most likely candidate for all those Nessie sightings over the years.

'The other possibility, of course, is that it's a unique species,' Alexa said, 'one not discovered yet in the fossil record.'

'And in all these years, we've only had apocryphal stories? Why haven't we ever seen one wash up on shore or get caught by a fisherman?'

'Giant squid have been reported by sailors for centuries, but it's only in the last couple of years that we've gotten actual videographic evidence of living specimens.'

'We can't wait that long,' Brielle said, 'so let's hope this works.'

Alexa flashed on Grant's drawn face and silently agreed with Brielle as she tossed another dollop of chum in the water.

They continued trolling for twenty more minutes while the sky went from gunmetal to charcoal. Alexa had kept an eye out for Tyler's sub, but she hadn't seen it. It had to be out there, though, because Tyler would have called her if he couldn't get the GhostManta into the water.

Despite the stench of the saltfish, the unique smell of the peat and highland air and the dimming light brought Alexa back to the last time she'd been on the loch with Michael Dillman. She happened to be looking at the opposite shore and saw a sinewy black form on the water.

'Oh, my God!' She cried out. 'Look!'

She and Brielle rushed over to the starboard side and leaned out as far as they dared. Sinclair wheeled the boat about and headed for the humped shape. Alexa's knuckles were white on the railing. They were actually about to come face to face with the monster.

The black shape remained motionless, and Alexa hoped it wouldn't dive before they had a chance to approach it. She got a scoop of saltfish ready to throw at the creature to lure it closer.

Sinclair suddenly slowed the *Nessie Seeker* and began turning away from their target.

'What are you doing?' Alexa yelled.

'Sorry, miss,' Sinclair said. 'It's not what you're looking for. It's just a log.'

'What are you talking about? I saw it move when ...' Alexa's voice trailed off. The black shape was now close enough for her to see it for what it really was. Sinclair was right. It was a rotten log bobbing in the water.

The rush of disappointment was overwhelming. She was so sure they had found it. Now Alexa felt like a fool. She'd fallen for the same optical illusion that had tricked so many other observers hoping to spot Nessie before her.

'I'll keep trolling if you'd like,' Sinclair said.

Alexa nodded her assent, but her enthusiasm was shot.

They went on for another ten minutes, until the sun was below the mountains, leaving only a diffuse light in the clouds to illuminate the loch. Darkness would be total soon, effectively ending the expedition.

Alexa was methodically doling out the chum when Brielle, who had been keeping an eye on the boat's wake, stiffened in her seat. Alexa looked back, trying not to get her hopes up, but could see nothing. She'd been so busy with the chum that she hadn't been watching the water closely.

'What is it?' she asked.

'I thought I saw movement.'

'Tyler's sub?'

Brielle pursed her lips. 'It was a disturbance in the water that didn't look like our normal wake.'

'Tyler said the sub would be black.'

'I couldn't see anything come out of the water, just a difference in the surface pattern.'

They waited, but Alexa couldn't see anything. She felt them both deflate, the anticipation subsiding again.

'Must be another false alarm,' she said dejectedly. 'It's almost dark, and I don't have much bait left—'

Brielle stood and pointed. 'There! You see it?'

Alexa followed the line of her finger, but it took her a moment to see what Brielle meant.

A swirl of whitewater where it shouldn't have been.

And it was closing on them.

Alexa's heart pounded at the sight. Something was definitely out there.

'Keep chumming,' Brielle said.

Alexa sped up the pace of her scoops. The breadth of the whitecap grew wider and closer.

'My God,' Alexa breathed.

She kept tossing saltfish behind the *Nessie Seeker* until the unusual wave was forty feet from the boat's stern. It was only then that Alexa realized that the extra wake wasn't necessarily created by the creature's head.

Brielle was leaning out over the transom trying to get a better look, her head close to the water.

'Brielle!' Alexa shouted, and dropped the scoop. She yanked Brielle back by the shoulders just as a great maw of jagged teeth broke the surface of the water, yawning wide to take its next gulp.

FORTY-FOUR

Tyler was speechless.

There it was, the 3-D image of the Loch Ness monster on his sonar, but he still couldn't believe his eyes. Until this moment, he hadn't realized how much he'd doubted the existence of the Loch Ness monster, how close to resignation he was that they were on a fool's errand and that Grant would die. The awe and incredulity lasted a few moments more and then were swept aside by the sense of relief and elation that cascaded over him. Grant had a chance.

The creature's sinewy form foiled the sophisticated computer's ability to generate a cohesive image, but there was no longer any reason to be a skeptic. Tyler could make out the jaw-dropping creature's general shape: a large, wide head, humpbacked body, four lateral appendages that could either be flippers or feet, and a long tail that swished back and forth as it swam. Overall, the animal had to be at least thirty feet in length.

The bait worked exactly as Edmonstone had said it would.

'We found it, man!' Tyler shouted over his shoulder to Grant. 'You're going to be all right.'

'As long as the fat lady finishes warming up and starts crooning,' Grant replied, his hoarse voice thin and weary but hopeful. 'Get us a little closer and I'll take the shot.'

Grant was in control of the spear that would insert the tracking transmitter and the tissue collection device. Once it hit the creature, they would retract it, leaving the tracker embedded in its flesh. Then they would return to the *Sedna* with the sample and call the authorities to whisk it away to the toxicologists for processing into an antidote.

Tyler inched the throttle forward to get within two dozen yards of the creature, point-blank range.

'Keep her steady,' Grant said. 'One, two . . .'

Something whizzed past them like a torpedo, its shape barely registering on the sonar.

'What the hell?' Grant said.

Tyler didn't know where the object had come from, but it threatened to disrupt their only chance at tissue collection.

'Launch now!' he shouted.

The torpedo sliced on through the water, missing Nessie and continuing on toward the power cruiser.

'Away!' Grant called out. The spear hissed from its tube, but it was too late. The Loch Ness monster, spooked by the unknown object, veered away, and the spear lanced through open water.

The torpedo collided with the aft underside of the tour

boat, where it detonated, pummeling the sub with a deafening shock wave. Tyler wrestled with the stick to keep from going into a spin. When he had it under control, he pulled back, heading for the surface.

'Was that Zim?' Grant asked.

'Had to be.'

'Where did they get torpedoes?'

'No idea.'

Tyler circled around and saw the enemy sub speeding away. No longer in immediate danger, he pulled back on the stick. The GhostManta broke the surface, and Tyler could see the *Nessie Seeker* dead in the water. There was no smoke, but the boat listed to one side. He motored forward and raised the canopy.

He couldn't see anyone, and his chest thumped in fear.

He pulled the sub next to the boat and cut the throttle. His low position in the water didn't afford him much of a view into the cabin, so he stood awkwardly in his seat.

'Alexa! Brielle!' he called out. 'It's Tyler!'

Alexa and Brielle poked their heads above the transom. When they saw it was clear, they stood, and Tyler breathed a sigh of relief.

'Are you both okay?'

'Yes,' Alexa said. 'What about you?'

'No damage. How's the boat?'

'Sinclair's below checking the engine,' Brielle said, 'but we're taking on water. What the bloody hell was that?'

'Zim. He's got the other sub and equipped it with some sort of weapon.'

'Did the spear work?' Alexa asked. 'Did you get the sample?'

'That asshole made me miss,' Grant said.

'Then what are you still doing here? Go get it!'

'But you—'

'We'll be fine. You may never get another shot.'

Tyler noticed a large fishing boat headed their way. Its crew might have heard the explosion and come to help or it might be Zim's men. The least he could do was give Alexa and Brielle a little protection.

'Here,' he said, handing Brielle the rifle and ammo. He pointed at the approaching fishing boat. 'Make sure you know who that is before you let them help. When you get the boat moving again, head back to the harbor and call the police.'

'Thanks. Now go.' She pointed at a spot south of them on the loch. 'I think I can make out Nessie's wake about two hundred yards that way.'

The concern etched on their faces nearly kept him from leaving, but Tyler nodded at them and got into his seat. He pressed the button to lower the canopy. A green light indicated when it was sealed.

'They'll be all right,' he said, more to reassure himself than Grant.

'Yeah, they will,' Grant replied, but he didn't sound any more confident than Tyler felt.

He slammed the throttle forward and submerged. Within seconds the GhostManta was at full speed.

Zim and the creature had a head start, but Nessie was slower than the sub. Even if Zim were able to torpedo the animal and kill it before they reached it, they'd still be able to secure a tissue sample as long as it didn't sink into the deep sediment at the bottom of the loch.

Two small dots appeared on the sonar display and grew rapidly. The creature was swimming in a zigzag pattern in an attempt to get away from the pursuing sub. Suddenly, it reversed course, and Zim's sub swung around. A few moments later, the creature veered left, and Tyler realized it wasn't randomly taking evasive action.

It was being herded.

Tyler slewed left and saw where they were headed.

Toward the fishing boat.

'What are they up to?' Grant asked.

'I don't know. But something tells me we don't have much time.'

Tyler was on an intercept course. At their present speed, he calculated that they would reach the monster just before it got to the fishing boat.

'You ready with the other spear?' Tyler asked.

'Locked and loaded.'

'Good. We're only going to get one more pass.'

Tyler wracked his brain for a way to save the creature from Zim after he got the sample. Alexa would be devastated if Tyler let it die, but he couldn't think of anything other than getting help from the police once he and Grant were docked on the *Sedna*. His GhostManta was unarmed, so he couldn't fight back against Zim.

He would have to leave the creature to its fate. He was sick about having to sacrifice Nessie, but he had no choice. Retrieving the tissue specimen was more important than rescuing the monster, despite how he felt about it.

Tyler suppressed his qualms about sacrificing this unique creature and focused on the mission. Instead of aiming directly for the animal, he altered the sub's course so that he was leading it like a clay pigeon.

'I'll count down,' he said. 'On my mark.'

'Ready,' Grant replied.

Nessie's outline in the sonar grew large as they approached to intercept.

'One.'

Closer.

'Two.'

The creature nearly filled the sonar image.

'Three.'

Its torso was dead center on the screen.

'Mark!'

'Away!'

The spear launched. Tyler held his breath until he saw the red light that indicated a hit.

'Contact!' Grant shouted triumphantly.

Before Tyler could tell him to retract the sample, the creature suddenly stopped and began thrashing in place.

'Reel in the spear,' Tyler said.

After a pause, Grant said, 'I can't. It's stuck in something.'

After a moment, Nessie seemed to curl up into a ball. It started to rise to the surface, and Tyler understood what was happening.

'They've caught it in a net,' he said. 'Hurry.'

The winch whined, straining to retract the spear. Then Tyler heard a pop.

'Dammit,' Grant said. 'The line snapped.'

Something splashed into the water from above the surface and impaled Nessie, followed immediately by a muffled explosion.

Locke realized it wasn't a fishing boat he'd been seeing. It was a whaler. Zim didn't have torpedoes. He had harpoons like the one just shot from the boat.

Nessie stopped moving.

The next harpoon would be aimed at them.

'Let's get out of here,' he said, wheeling the sub about. 'We'll go back to the *Sedna* and track Nessie from there as long as the transmitter wasn't damaged in the explosion.'

'Agreed,' Grant croaked. 'Not feeling too good.' He sounded spent.

Tyler was about to throttle up when he saw an image appear on the sonar. It was the other GhostManta banking toward them.

And if Zim had installed harpoons in both spear ejection tubes, that meant the other GhostManta was still armed.

FORTY-FIVE

Zim wasn't going to let Locke get away, not when he had the means to finish him off.

'Follow him,' he said to Pryor.

'But we have the monster—'

He reached over the seat back and grabbed Pryor by the neck. 'Do it or I'll shoot you myself when we get back.'

'All right! Back off!'

Zim let go, and the sub took off in pursuit.

Locke weaved back and forth trying to shake them, but Pryor was an accomplished pilot and stayed glued to the other GhostManta's tail.

'I just need one clear shot,' Zim said.

'He may not give it to you,' Pryor grunted as he whipped the stick sideways. 'This guy is good.'

'But he can't see us. He can't know if he's lost us or not, and his evasive tactics are slowing him down. When we're close enough, there's no way I'll miss.'

They continued edging closer until Locke's sub took an abrupt dive, and Zim's stomach rose in his throat as Pryor matched the maneuver, a forty-five-degree angle down.

Zim hung from his harness, keeping his finger near the LAUNCH button for the right moment.

At three hundred feet, Locke pulled out of the dive and swooped up, aiming for the surface. Pryor matched him again. The sub rocketed up, compressing Zim against his seat.

The desperation move was slowing Locke, bringing Pryor and Zim closer. He'd lose all momentum if he broke the surface, making him easy prey.

Zim rested his finger on the button. Any moment.

Then Locke's sub twisted as it dodged another shape it had been masking on Zim's sonar.

'Look out!' Zim shouted.

Pryor wrenched the stick to the right, but not in time to prevent the sub from sideswiping the obstacle. The canopy bounced against it with a crunch. The polycarbonate held, but the impact broke part of the seal loose. Pinpricks of water jetted into the cockpit.

Pryor surfaced, and the sub came to a stop. Zim could see the object they'd collided with.

A drifting log. Locke must have seen it and led them directly into it.

Zim swiveled around and saw the other sub only a few yards to his right. Locke stared back with an icy glare, his control panel casting a menacing glow. Westfield was in the back seat and looked like he was about to pass out.

Their sub began to submerge.

'Go after them.'

'With all these leaks? We can't—'

'Do it!' Zim screamed.

Pryor turned the sub, and as they sank the jets of water returned with greater force. They'd only have a minute or two before the cockpit was full of water, but Zim was determined to take his shot.

Locke began the evasions again.

'Don't match his weaves,' Zim said.

'What?'

'Give me a straight line.'

Pryor did as he was told, and they caught up quickly. The freezing water was accumulating around Zim's feet, seeping into his boots, but he ignored the shocking cold.

The weaving seemed to occur at a random pace and cadence, but Zim thought he had a pattern figured out. They were within twenty yards. On the next swerve, Zim would have him.

As he expected, Locke banked right, directly into their path. Zim's finger stabbed the LAUNCH button, and the harpoon shot out of the tube. The aim was dead-on, a perfect intercept course.

The tip of the harpoon entered Locke's starboard impeller intake and detonated with a satisfying thump.

Because its battery-powered engines had no fuel to trigger a secondary explosion, the GhostManta wasn't ripped apart, but the damage was severe enough.

The sub spiraled away and began an uncontrolled descent toward the bottom.

Seeing the successful hit, Pryor didn't need to be told to surface. He tilted the sub up. Zim smiled as Locke and Westfield disappeared from his sonar display and into the inky abyss.

Dunham ducked as another round fired from the tour boat pinged off the whaler's superstructure. She had ordered the *Aegir* closer to the powerless cruiser in order to finish them off, but a couple of surprise shots from Brielle Cohen killed two of their men before they could get in range to use the harpoon grenades on it.

The Norwegian crew had completed lashing the Loch Ness monster to the deck. Dunham had taken only a few moments to look at the creature that had fascinated legend hunters for generations. Even though she had to destroy it, she was still in awe of the animal, a beast like none she'd seen before. The image that would stay with her was its eely tail hanging limply from the rear. From what she could tell, Nessie was dead.

To make sure it remained at the bottom of the loch, they had to make sure no one could find it, which meant leaving no witnesses. The harpoon cannon was in an exposed position on the bow, so there was no way for Dunham to get to it without coming under Cohen's fire. She went to the wheelhouse and ordered the captain to ram the other boat. When he refused, she took out her pistol and aimed it at him.

He eyed her with contempt, then twisted the wheel and ran up to full power.

The *Aegir* plowed forward on a collision course. Dunham could see the *Nessie Seeker*'s captain furiously trying to start the engine. Flashes of light from the upper deck preceded bullets that crashed through the *Aegir*'s windshield, but by this time there was no stopping the whaler even if Cohen hit the captain.

Once the *Nessie Seeker* was gone, they could sink the *Aegir*, and this whole business would be over. Israel would cease to exist.

Dunham couldn't help grinning as the bow loomed over the smaller boat.

The grin disappeared when she heard its engine roar to life, and the boat crawled forward.

The *Aegir*'s captain spun the wheel to compensate, but the inertia was too great. The *Nessie Seeker* slid forward in time to escape the attempted ramming with nothing more than a scrape to its stern.

'Turn around!' she yelled, but it was a lost cause. Although the smaller boat seemed to have sustained enough damage to keep it from reaching its top speed, it was far more maneuverable than the whaler.

It circled around them once, peppering them with bullets, and then veered off toward Urquhart Castle.

Dunham ordered the ship back toward the center of the loch.

Zim's sub pulled alongside the *Aegir* and was tied up. Zim and Pryor climbed the rope ladder to the deck, and Zim stalked over to her, stepping over bodies as he walked.

'What the hell are you doing?' he demanded.

'I was trying to get rid of them.'

'Yeah, and how'd that go? Now they're getting away.'

Dunham gave him a dirty look. 'Did you get Locke?'

'He's dead.'

'Good,' she said, and nodded at the motionless beast on the deck. 'Then it's time to get rid of that.'

He nodded to Pryor, who went below decks. Zim took an assault rifle from his nearest man and leveled it at the captain. The captain put up his hands in a supplicating gesture and pleaded desperately in Norwegian.

Zim pulled the trigger, and the captain collapsed to the deck. Zim's men took their cue and gunned down the other crewmembers. After Dunham's experience in Gaza, the sight of blood and dead bodies no longer disturbed her. She had hardened her heart to it. Nothing could be worse than seeing her fiancé's mangled body.

Zim shoved the rifle into her hands. 'Now take my men in the Zodiac and go after Locke's sister. And this time finish them off. Pryor and I will follow in the sub.'

Dunham had the impulse to mouth off at him, but bit her tongue. Just another few hours of Zim, and she'd be on her way to Indonesia – her new home and, not coincidentally, a non-extradition country.

FORTY-SIX

Tyler was able to pull the GhostManta out of its spin, but there was nothing he could do about its trajectory. He and Grant had less than two minutes before the sub hit the bottom of the loch, and his control panel was completely dark. Only the HUD was still working. At least the blast hadn't compromised hull integrity.

He hadn't heard anything from the back seat since the harpoon hit.

'Grant, are you still with me? Grant!'

After a few more tries, he got a groggy reply. 'I'm right here. You don't have to shout.'

'We're in trouble.'

Grant cleared his throat. 'What's our status?'

'We've lost pitch control, and the starboard impeller is dead. The port impeller is operational, but I can't get us out of our descent. Reversing thrust would put us into another spin.'

'If we hit bottom, we'll get buried in silt.' If that happened, they'd never get free. The muck on the bottom would act like a giant suction cup. They'd run out of air long before a rescue sub arrived.

'I know. The throttle and stick are still working, but the explosion must have taken out the electrical feed to my control panel. I can't jettison the emergency ballast. Does your control panel have power?'

There was a moment of silence, and Tyler was about to repeat the question when Grant said, 'It's lit.'

'We only have a minute left.' The 3-D display of the loch bottom approached quickly on the HUD. 'You have to activate the emergency drop.'

'Can't see. Everything's blurry.'

'Do it by touch. It's the switch on the lower left-hand corner of the panel. It has a safety cover that you have to flip up.'

The bottom rushed toward them, thirty seconds away now.

When he didn't hear anything, Tyler said, 'You can do it, buddy. Time is a factor here.'

'Found it,' Grant said. 'Activating.'

Two heavy weights dropped from the bottom of the sub, and Tyler felt the sudden buoyancy. The sub's angle started to flatten, but it was taking time to counteract the downward momentum.

Tyler braced himself for impact.

The sub leveled off just as they reached the loch bottom. The underside of the sub scraped along the sediment, and the GhostManta came to a stop.

The silence was total, and Tyler could feel the weight of the crushing darkness outside.

He waited with his hands grasping the armrests, holding his breath for any sign of them sinking further into the silt. They remained motionless. Tyler briefly considered a desperation move: blow the canopy and swim to the surface. But he knew it wasn't desperate; it was suicidal. No way they'd be able to go seven hundred feet up on one lungful of air. Better to go out of this life peacefully breathing their own carbon dioxide.

Then Tyler felt a slight nudge. It hesitated for a moment, and he wasn't sure if he'd imagined it until he heard the sucking sound of the muck releasing them. The sub slowly pulled away from the bottom, the dropped emergency ballast making it buoyant.

The GhostManta began its ascent. Tyler inhaled at the reprieve. They were free.

'We made it, buddy,' he said, but got nothing in response. He turned to see Grant's head lolling back. He was conscious, but barely.

Now that Tyler was confident they weren't going to be entombed on the bottom of Loch Ness, he started formulating a plan about how to get the tissue sample he needed from Nessie.

He figured Zim had only two choices: cart Nessie away or sink it somewhere in the loch. Tyler couldn't imagine him trying to smuggle it back through the canal, so sinking it was the likeliest course of action. But the loss of the ballast meant the sub wouldn't be able to dive again. If Zim were successful in sinking the monster, it would be game over. They'd never get to the creature in time to avert war and save Grant.

As the sub rose, it accelerated toward the surface. In the spiraling descent, Tyler had lost his bearings, so he had no idea where they would pop up. He had his hand on the throttle, prepared to make a getaway in case they surfaced anywhere near Zim's boat.

Tyler checked his watch. It was now 10:40 p.m., well past sunset. If they were a reasonable distance from the whaler, it was unlikely that the black sub would be seen as it surfaced.

'Grant, if you can hear me,' he said, 'shut off all the lights in the cockpit.'

He detected a grunt, and the cockpit went dark. The blackness was total, and Tyler felt as if he were floating in the void of space, the stars somehow erased from existence.

There was nothing to do now except wait. At least his eyes would be dark-adapted once they were topside.

When the sub broke the surface, he quickly looked around to get his position and saw the luminous tower of Urquhart Castle to his right. Directly ahead of him, he could see the illuminated outline of a familiar boat a hundred yards away, moving perpendicular to him.

It was the *Nessie Seeker*. It was limping back to the harbor at Drumnadrochit, its list now ten degrees and worsening.

He threw the throttle forward and headed for the foundering boat.

As he brushed the sub up against the hull of the tour boat, Brielle rushed over to the transom and aimed her rifle at the sub. Tyler raised the canopy and called her name.

'My God!' she exclaimed, lowering the weapon. 'We thought you were dead.' She tossed him a line, which he lashed to one of the handholds on the sub's flat manta wing, normally intended to be used by divers being transported underwater.

'We almost became a permanent part of the loch.'

Alexa ran over and leaned against the rail.

'Are you all right?'

'I'm fine,' Tyler said, unbuckling his harness, 'but Grant's in bad shape. Help me get him out.'

Alexa jumped down onto the sub's wing. 'I knew he shouldn't have been pushing himself so hard.' She bent and patted him on the cheek. 'Grant. Come on, wake up.'

He shook his head, came to, and looked up at her. 'You're a sight for blurry eyes.'

Tyler took one arm while Alexa steadied him with the other, but unless Grant was able to stand on his own, there was no way the two of them would be able to lift his deadweight. Fortunately, Grant managed to get up under his own power. They helped him over the railing, and he collapsed onto the bench.

'That's better,' he said and leaned back. Even in the dim light of the boat, Tyler could see the deep lines on his face.

The hair that had grown in since his last shave was fully gray, and some of it was falling out.

'Oh, my God,' Alexa said.

'He hasn't got much time left,' Brielle said.

'Neither have we,' came a Scottish brogue from the cabin. Tyler turned to an authentically older gentleman at the helm. 'We're taking on water so quickly that I don't think we'll make it back to the harbor.'

Brielle pointed to Urquhart Castle. 'Can we go ashore there?'

'Aye,' the skipper said. 'There's a short pier where the loch cruises tie up. We'll have to make a go of it.'

The whaler hadn't been visible from the side of the *Nessie Seeker* where the sub was idling, but now that he was standing, Tyler saw its lights in the distance and could make out the bulbous shape of the Loch Ness monster on its deck. The Zodiac had cast off and was racing toward them.

'Okay,' he said, 'you all head for the pier.'

'Where are you going?' Alexa protested.

'We lost the tissue sample. I have to try to get it back.'

'Not on your own, you're not,' Brielle said. 'I'm coming with you.'

'Do you have any ammo left?'

'Seven rounds.'

'Then you have to stay and provide protection for them. With Grant out, you're the only one who can handle a gun.'

'Then I'm coming with you,' Alexa said.

'Absolutely not.'

She didn't argue, but before Tyler could stop her, she hopped down onto the sub and into the rear cockpit.

'You know you need me,' she said, belting herself in. 'Now we can either get going or you can try to pull me out of this sub. What'll it be?'

Tyler shook his head, equal parts frustration and admiration. The Locke stubbornness was strong in this one.

He patted Grant on the shoulder while looking at Brielle. 'Keep him safe.'

'I will.'

Then Tyler did something that surprised even himself. He pulled Brielle to him and planted a kiss on her, holding her body against him in a passionate embrace.

When he backed away, Brielle looked stunned, pleased, and slightly embarrassed. Exactly what he wanted to see.

Tyler jumped onto the sub and saw Alexa staring at him with a mischievous smile.

'What?'

'Oh, nothing,' she said.

Tyler got in and latched the canopy. He threw the throttle forward and circled around the *Nessie Seeker*, planning to give the Zodiac a wide berth as he and Alexa cruised toward their final meeting with the Loch Ness monster.

FORTY-SEVEN

Brielle was glad to see that the cold air revived Grant. His eyes fluttered open and he sat up massaging his head as he looked around.

'Where are Tyler and Alexa?' he asked.

'They went to get a tissue sample from Nessie.'

'Where are *we*?'

'About a hundred yards from the pier. Will you be able to walk when we get there?'

He nodded.

'Good. Actually, we may have to run.' She tilted her head at the sound of the Zodiac fast approaching.

Grant steadied himself on the seat. 'Is it me or is our boat slanted?'

'We're taking on water.' As if to punctuate her statement, the engine conked out.

'That's it,' Sinclair said from the wheelhouse. 'The engine bay's flooded.'

They were still fifty yards from the pier but coasting steadily.

'Can we make it?'

'Aye,' the skipper said. 'But we'll have to be ready to get off in a hurry.'

Brielle didn't have to ask why. Water sloshed around her feet and grew deeper by the second.

'Stand up,' she said to Grant, slinging the rifle over her shoulder.

He got to his feet, and Brielle groaned at trying to hold his bulk steady.

'Mr Sinclair, a little help if you please.'

He didn't move from his position at the wheel. 'Can't, dear. I've got to steer us just so.'

'Looks like we're on our own,' she said to Grant.

'We'll be fine,' he replied, and stepped up onto the port side of the transom. With Brielle's help, he was able to stay upright by holding onto the railing next to him. The boat was now listing precariously toward the pier.

'Get ready!' Sinclair yelled.

The wooden pier jutted out into the loch perpendicular to shore, so they were coming in on a parallel course. The boat's bow reached the end of the pier and edged along it. When the stern of the boat was beside the pier, Grant jumped off, pulling Brielle out with him. They fell on the planks and rolled to a stop.

The boat kept going and Sinclair abandoned his post. He nimbly hopped over the transom and landed on his feet.

The boat smashed into the rocks and rebounded backward. The impact was literally the tipping point for the stricken boat. Its hull creaking from the strain, the *Nessie*

Seeker capsized. The wide hole below the waterline was visible for a count of three, and then it gurgled as it slipped beneath the surface of the loch.

'*Mo chreach*!' he yelled, followed by a muttered, 'Excuse my language.'

Brielle heaved Grant to his feet and said, 'Sorry about your boat, Mr Sinclair, but we have to get out of here.' By her estimation, the Zodiac was only a minute away.

'It's not just the *Seeker*,' he said, putting a shoulder under Grant's other arm. 'I've got insurance to cover the loss, but I forgot to take my camera. I got two good pictures of Nessie while she was following us, and now no one will ever see them.' He swore again softly.

They hoofed it up the pier and onto the sidewalk that led across an expanse of lawn to the entrance into the castle grounds. To their right, past an ancient trebuchet and up a long hill, was the closed visitor's centre and the parking lot.

Shots rang out behind them, throwing up pieces of sod, and Brielle looked over her shoulder. The Zodiac was nearing the pier. With Grant slowing them down, they'd never make it up the hill to the visitor's centre without getting killed. The castle entrance was nearer and looked like the better choice. The place was a fort, after all.

'Where's a good defensive position in the castle?' Brielle asked Sinclair as she steered them toward the small bridge over the grassy dry moat that surrounded the castle.

'There's a platform atop the gatehouse at the entry to the

castle. It has a good view of the grounds inside and outside the castle.'

'Leave me behind,' Grant croaked.

'Don't be so noble,' Brielle said. 'Now hurry your arse.'

She heard shouts behind her as she hauled Grant across the bridge and through the arched stone gateway. Sinclair guided them left into a small room in the reconstructed gatehouse where they found a modern spiral staircase behind a closed glass door.

It was locked.

She unslung the rifle and aimed it at the lock at the top of the door. Shooting out the glass would take more shots, and she needed to conserve every round.

Brielle blasted the lock and yanked the door open. She ran up the stairs, leaving Sinclair to usher Grant up behind her.

Once she was up top, she peeked from behind a crumbling stone wall. Four men and one woman were hustling toward the castle entrance. Brielle picked the man in the lead and fired a shot that took him down.

The others dropped to their knees and returned fire, forcing Brielle to crouch. She popped up in a different location to shoot, but the attackers had taken shelter behind a berm close to the trees that lined the shore. More bullets pinged off the stones. She crabbed over to the back wall of the gatehouse roof and poked her head up to survey the interior grounds of the fortress.

The flood lights illuminating the tower walls cast a

ghostly hue on the whole complex. Although the perimeter walls were fairly intact – and tall enough to prevent Zim's men from scaling them – most of the inner buildings had been razed to their foundation centuries ago. She could see there was little shelter for hiding.

Opposite her, a small archway in the center of the back wall had a wooden gate that opened onto a set of steps leading down to the loch, which bordered the castle grounds on two sides. To her right was an undulating series of mounds covered with manicured grass and sidewalks. To her left was a path leading to the cobbled yard in front of the Grant Tower, the imposing five-story ruin they had used as a landmark while cruising Loch Ness.

Neither direction provided any better stronghold than what they had now.

She crossed over to the front and waved for Grant and Sinclair to stay low. She raised her head and saw one of the men making a break for the castle entrance. She fired a shot that hit only grass, but it made the man dash back to his hidden position.

Her tactic wouldn't work for long, though. She only had four rounds left. Once she was out, they would soon realize it and rush the castle, reminding Brielle of two other famous sieges that didn't end well for the defenders inside the fort.

One was Masada in Israel. The other was distinctly American.

The Alamo.

FORTY-EIGHT

Riding on the surface of Loch Ness in the darkened and whisper-quiet GhostManta felt odd to Alexa, as if she were adrift on the open ocean, but she understood the benefit when she saw the other sub pass them on its way toward Urquhart. It was visible only because of the reflected glow of its canopy, the two occupants oblivious to its twin going in the other direction.

When she and Tyler reached the whaler, he circumnavigated it and found a rope ladder on the side away from the castle. He tied up the sub.

They knew Dunham and Zim were out of the way, but they weren't sure how many crew had remained on the *Aegir*. With a boost from Tyler, Alexa raised herself up so she could peer over the edge of the deck. She gasped when she saw a corpse riddled with bullet holes. A half-dozen others littered the deck around the Loch Ness monster. It looked like they wouldn't have to worry about the rest of the crew.

When she felt confident the coast was clear, Alexa heaved herself onto the deck and got her first up-close look at

Nessie, which lay prone and unmoving. She forgot her dire circumstances as she marveled at the sight.

The charcoal-colored creature was covered by netting that was tacked down at four corners. The scale was apparent now that she was next to it. The animal rivaled an orca in size, its body stretching all the way from the boom to the wheelhouse. From her vantage point at its rear, she could make out the humped dorsal spine but saw no signs of activity.

Under the boat's lights, the creature's skin glistened. She reached out and touched it. The surface had a smooth, tacky feel, neither like the hard scales of a reptile nor the rubbery give of a dolphin's hide. The tail curled around and rested against the gunwale so that the tip was close to her. She stooped and saw a pale scar across the tip where Darwin's hatchet had sliced off a piece.

It had grown back. Other than the scar, the tail was completely intact, ending in the shape of a shovel blade. From this angle, she could see how it could be mistaken for a head from a long distance, like in the surgeon's photograph.

Tyler hopped onto the deck and froze when he saw the legendary beast.

'Wow,' he said in hushed awe. 'Incredible.' Then he noticed the dead bodies, and his jaw set in a grim expression.

'I know. I've never seen anything like it. Any of it.'

Their quiet contemplation of the tableau was shattered by muffled explosions beneath them. It wasn't enough to throw them off their feet, but they stumbled against one another.

'What was that?' Alexa asked.

She could see Tyler's gears working, culminating with an aha moment.

'Zim's sinking the boat,' he said. 'He must have placed charges to scuttle it.' The ship was already showing the first traces of a list.

Tyler gave her his Leatherman tool. 'Here. Find the sample capsule and pull it out with the pliers. I think we hit it on the left side. If you can't find it or it's too hard to remove, there's a small saw on the tool to cut off a piece of the animal.'

He hurried to the nearest bulkhead hatch.

'Tyler, where are you going?'

'To see if our pilots from the other sub are still alive. I'll be right back.' He cautiously surveyed the interior, then disappeared through the opening.

Alexa stepped over the tail and walked around until she was on its left.

An appendage was splayed out to the side. She hadn't noticed one on the right because it must have been tucked under the body. She bent and saw that the limb had the outline of a flipper but possessed vestigial toes poking from the edge, like those of a sea lion.

Embedded in the flipper was the wooden handle of a gaff hook impaled through the meatiest part, confirming what she'd seen in the video. Nessie having no way to remove it,

John Edmonstone's defensive weapon was still stuck in the animal two hundred years later.

She stood and drew a sharp breath when she saw the damage caused by the harpoon grenade. A two-foot-diameter crater had been carved out of its back. However, the injury looked odd. Instead of raw chunks of meat hanging by sinew from the gaping wound, it looked as if had been cauterized. No blood dripped from the opening. The surface of it had the same smooth look as the skin, although the coloration was a dull red.

Alexa continued on toward the head, struggling to figure out what kind of animal it was. She reached the neck and saw no gills, which meant it couldn't be a fish.

The flat head, which had the outline of a broad chisel, rested to one side. She nearly jumped back when she saw a black saucer-sized eye staring back at her, lidless and unmoving. As with the squid, the gigantic optical organ must help the creature navigate the dark depths of the loch.

The wide jaw that she'd seen earlier lay open. She could make out rows of sharp teeth curving back toward the throat, which would aid in the capture of fish.

Her eyes drifted back and rested on an unusual stalk of feathery filaments that extended from its head like a horn. An identical stalk was on the opposite side of the head.

Alexa put her hand to her mouth to stop herself from shouting in revelation. She knew what kind of animal this was.

The stalks were external gills. The Loch Ness monster was an amphibian.

In fact, it had many of the characteristics of an axolotl, a rare fully-aquatic salamander found only in lakes around Mexico City and now almost extinct in the wild. The axolotl was prized by biological researchers because of its uncanny ability to regenerate limbs.

Suddenly, everything made sense. As an amphibian, it didn't need air to breathe, getting all its oxygen from the water, so it rarely had cause to surface. The regenerated tail and cauterized wound was consistent with a salamander's capability, but Nessie seemed to have an even more advanced ability to heal itself, perhaps even preventing the cells themselves from aging. Its body could have a genetic method for preventing telomere shortening so that its cells were essentially immortal.

Alexa practically shook with the exhilaration of her discovery, but her excitement was immediately dashed when she realized that the dead creature would never be studied in its natural habitat.

If nothing else, she could preserve part of this animal for posterity, so she worked back toward the creature's rear, stooping to palpate the skin for any rupture. Just behind the front flipper, she felt the nub of a metal protrusion almost at the level of the deck. That had to be it.

She opened the pliers on the Leatherman and gripped the end of the object. With a gentle touch, she pulled with the pliers, but the angle made it difficult to get any leverage.

She sat on her butt and put the soles of her shoes against the animal's body on either side of the pliers. When she thought she had a good grip, she yanked the tool backwards.

Two things happened simultaneously. She extracted a gleaming five-inch-long aluminum tube, and Nessie woke up.

The pain of the tube's removal must have brought the animal out of its comatose state. It thrashed around in the confines of its restricting shackles, the tail whipsawing back and forth.

Alexa screamed and scrambled against the gunwale. She heard a high-pitched mewl, like the sound of a baby crying, and realized it was coming from Nessie. She'd heard something similar from a recording of the Chinese giant salamander's vocalizations. Nessie's whine was uncannily distressing, as if it were advertising its suffering.

The animal flailed a moment longer and then came to rest, either exhausted or comatose again.

Alexa stood, the tube still in her hand and tears brimming in her eyes, and realized she had to save the poor creature. If she could free it, it might be able to survive its wounds. Lashed to the deck, it would certainly starve to death no matter how efficient it was at regenerating.

She flipped the Leatherman open to its saw and hacked at the nylon tie-down near its head.

Tyler appeared on deck with two men dressed in sweatshirts and jeans. One of the Gordian employees was holding up the other, who looked badly beaten and was supporting himself with only one leg.

Tyler rushed over to her. 'Are you all right?'

'Yes. Get them onto the sub.'

'What are you doing?'

'Freeing her.'

'Isn't it dead?'

'No, just wounded. Go.'

'You know what they say about a wounded animal being the most dangerous kind.'

'I know. Be ready for me.' She gave him the tube.

Tyler glanced at the men struggling to get over the side and then back to Alexa.

'Hurry up. The ship is sinking fast,' he said, and ran around to the other side out of sight behind Nessie's tall back.

Alexa finished sawing through the strap and braced herself in case the animal thrashed again. It remained still. Her hope was that it would stay in place as long as it wasn't disturbed, and then swim free once it was in the water.

She moved back to the rear strap and sawed again. Two would be enough to release it.

When the strap was cut, she stood and put the tool in her pocket.

Out of the corner of her eye, she saw movement, a person climbing over the gunwale. At first she thought Tyler had circled around to pick her up on this side, but a head with a crewcut rose into view.

Victor Zim. He'd come back.

He vaulted over the side and lunged at her. She stumbled backward and tripped over Nessie's flipper.

She tried to crawl away, but Zim grabbed her by the hair to pick her up.

'No, no,' he said. 'I need you for my negotiation with your brother.'

Alexa screamed and grabbed for anything to resist his pull. Her hand settled on the handle of Edmonstone's gaff, the wood preserved perfectly by the cold depths of the loch.

Alexa tried to loosen his hold by shaking her head as she worked the hook free. The pain set Nessie going again, squealing and thrashing about, and in raising its flipper, the gaff came loose. At the same time, Zim lost his grip on her hair. She turned and saw him momentarily paralyzed by the movement and sound of the creature he thought was long dead.

With a war whoop to give her strength, she lashed out with the hook and stabbed Zim in the thigh.

The gaff sank into his flesh until it hit the femur. This time it was Zim who screamed.

Alexa let go and he stumbled backward toward the bow, where he was knocked over by the swinging tail.

'Pryor!' Zim shrieked. 'Help!'

She wasn't going to stick around to find out what that meant. She got to her feet and ran in the other direction.

A skinny man wielding an assault rifle faced her at the opposite end of the ship near the wheelhouse. He stood safely away from the writhing head of the animal. He had to be Pryor.

Alexa was at serious risk of being crushed against the

gunwale if Nessie decided to roll in her direction, but she put up her hands. If she tried to jump overboard, Pryor would kill her before she got one foot over the side.

He smiled and nodded that she'd made the right decision. Then he aimed the gun at Nessie.

'No!' Alexa screamed.

Bullets poured from the gun into Nessie's side, the vicious man's smile only growing wider as the animal barked in agony, wailing like a stricken infant.

The animal's mouth gaped, and its throat convulsed. An enormous tongue shot forward at lightning speed, hitting Pryor's body with a splat. The mucus adhered to his clothes, and he yelped as he was reeled back toward Nessie's mouth.

He fell to his knees and was dragged the rest of the way screaming. The giant salamander clamped its jaws around Pryor and bit hard, bones crushed with a sickening crunch. Pryor's screaming abruptly ceased.

Nessie spat him out, apparently unhappy with the taste.

Tyler appeared near the body, then ran over to Alexa, his panicked eyes searching her for wounds.

'Are you shot?'

She shook her head.

'Thank God,' he said, putting his arm around her. 'We better leave. The ship's about to go under.'

'Zim is here,' she said.

Tyler's head swiveled around. 'Where?'

'I don't know. He was at the bow.'

'We'll worry about him later. Let's go.'

He escorted her around Nessie's head and they scrambled down the ladder. Alexa saw how Tyler planned to get them all to safety with the small sub. The Gordian submarine pilots lay on the wings gripping the handholds. It didn't matter that the GhostManta could no longer dive; the sub would have to remain on the surface.

Tyler cruised away from the ship. Alexa turned in her seat so she could see Nessie swim free.

Instead, she watched in horror as Zim climbed onto the *Aegir*'s harpoon cannon pedestal. He was limping, blood pouring down his leg from where he'd removed the gaff hook, as he loaded a fresh harpoon.

'Tyler!' she yelled. 'Go back!'

'We can't. We don't have any weapons.'

The stern of the *Aegir* descended into the water, and the deck was immediately awash.

'Come on, Nessie,' Alexa chanted. 'You can do it.'

At the feel of water on its skin, Nessie struggled to free itself of the netting.

Zim finished loading the harpoon and moved back to the trigger. With both hands on the grips, he swiveled it around to aim it at Nessie.

The animal flopped over the gunwales but it was too late.

Zim fired.

The harpoon speared Nessie through the base of the tail but didn't explode, and Alexa understood what Zim's plan had been. He'd loaded a cold harpoon, one without a grenade and trailing five strands of the strong nylon rope.

Zim wasn't trying to kill Nessie. He wanted it to go down with the ship.

The other end of the rope was securely lashed to the welded pedestal holding the cannon. Nessie was big, but if she couldn't loosen a gaff hook in two hundred years, she wouldn't be able to pull out a huge harpoon. She struggled to swim away, but the harpoon was lodged too deeply.

Zim staggered off the pedestal and sloshed along the deck to pick up Pryor's assault rifle, which she had stupidly left behind in her shock. He jumped back in the sub he had commandeered and came after them.

'Tyler,' she said, 'Zim's on his way. It looks like he's faster than we are.'

'We're running on only one impeller and weighed down by four people. I'll make a run for that little beach in front of the castle and hope we can get there before he catches us.'

Alexa watched the *Aegir* founder. Its bow went up in the air, dragging Nessie backward.

She sobbed when the fishing boat disappeared beneath the water, dousing the last light illuminating the creature. All she could do was listen to the animal's final haunting cry burble into silence as Loch Ness reclaimed its monster.

FORTY-NINE

Zim's throbbing leg only fueled his rage at the Lockes, not only for injuring him but for killing Pryor, who was a good supporter of the white cause even if he'd been annoying at times. Zim would savor the success of getting rid of that ugly animal later. First, he was going to show Alexa and Tyler that a hook through the leg was a pinprick compared to the pain they'd endure.

He held the rifle above his head and loosed some rounds in their direction, but at this distance any hit would be luckier than winning a lottery jackpot.

Zim withdrew the rifle and used the strap to tie a tourniquet around his thigh. It slowed the blood loss to a trickle and alleviated some of the agony. He convinced himself he'd be able to walk.

Trailing by only a hundred yards, he saw where Tyler was headed: a small rocky beach with a staircase leading up to a stone archway and a wooden gate flanked by low walls on the back side of the castle grounds.

With Dunham and his well-armed men positioned at the

opposite entrance, Zim could catch them all in a classic pincer movement.

Tyler ran the GhostManta up onto the beach, where it tilted to one side. The two pilots on the wings slid off and clambered up the staircase.

This might be Zim's best chance to kill them. Tyler and Alexa climbed out of the sub and scrambled for the steps. Zim stood, ignoring the sudden lightheadedness, and loosed a volley at them. Tyler was hit in the left arm and went down. Alexa stopped to help him get to his feet.

Zim shot again, this time hitting the gate as the two rescued pilots squeaked through. Tyler and Alexa veered to the right and tore up the hill, where they climbed over the railing.

Zim beached his own sub next to Tyler's, running it so far onto the rocks that it would be impossible to launch again. He didn't care. Once they finished off Tyler and his friends, they'd take the Zodiac back across the loch to the stashed Range Rover and freedom.

He eased himself out of the cockpit. The pain flared up again in an excruciating jolt, but he did his best to tamp it down for now. It reminded him that he had a special present for Tyler and Alexa.

He picked up the gaff hook and tucked it in his belt. Getting off the sub was even worse, and he took a moment to gather himself before continuing on, his rifle at the ready.

He considered yelling that he was coming for Tyler and

Alexa, then thought better of it as he set off up the stairs. Fear of the unknown was always scarier.

Grant snapped out of his stupor when he heard rifle fire not only in front of him, but also behind him as well. Something primal from his long stint in the Army gave him a sudden burst of adrenaline. He felt more alert than he had in days, but he knew it wouldn't last long.

He peeked over the back wall and saw Tyler and Alexa creep out of hiding behind a crumbling retaining wall. Tyler would know that Brielle had chosen the gatehouse for their last stand and would lead Alexa in that direction.

As he watched, they kept low and were about to dash along the sidewalk to the gatehouse when another man burst from the loch gate behind them. The hulking figure in the shadows had to be Zim. He fired from the hip, sending Tyler and Alexa running away from him toward the tower.

Grant called to Brielle. 'I need the rifle!'

She shook her head and whispered, 'I ran out of ammo two minutes ago.'

Grant couldn't sit there while Tyler and Alexa were killed.

'Keep showing the rifle over the wall,' he said. 'Since you're such a good shot, the bluff should give us another minute or two.'

He crawled toward the stairwell, willing the energy to move.

'What are you going to do?' she asked.

'Whatever I can,' he replied, and went down the stairs.

Dunham couldn't convince either of the remaining men to make a run for the gatehouse. They were too afraid of Brielle's sharpshooting skills to venture out, so they kept taking potshots at the balcony.

A distant sound pierced the silence between gunshots. Dunham was the only one not firing, so she doubted the men heard it. But as it grew closer, the source was unmistakable.

Sirens.

She looked in the direction of the road and saw blue flashing lights heading toward them. The police would be there any minute, responding to the sound of gunshots.

Sticking around was no longer a good idea.

'Keep firing,' she said, and they each shot a few more rounds at the castle.

Sufficiently distracted, they didn't notice when she backed away, got to her feet, and made a run for the pier.

It wasn't until her footsteps were banging against the wood that she heard them shout, 'Hey! Come back!'

She ignored their pleas, instead laying down her own covering fire with the machine gun. It bucked in her hands so much that she hit nothing, but it did the job. The two men dived to the ground.

She leapt into the Zodiac and untied it from the pier.

After a moment of fumbling with the starter, she figured out how it operated. The engine thrummed to life, and she reversed away from shore.

Once she was clear, she twisted the throttle to full and aimed for their drop-off point across the loch. The lights at the front of the Zodiac would show her the reflectors they'd planted on shore. Dunham congratulated herself for having the foresight to swipe the car keys from Pryor before getting off the ship.

She streaked away, passing the Grant Tower to her right. The *Aegir* was nowhere in sight, so she assumed it was on the bottom of the loch with the monster strapped to it. Although her plan to capture Tyler hadn't worked, she felt pretty good about the outcome.

She waved goodbye to the ruins and couldn't help but grin that she was done with Zim even earlier than she had planned.

Tyler winced at every footstep that jarred his re-injured left shoulder. His arm dangled by his side, useless. The pain was far worse than when he was shot at the Eiffel Tower. He wouldn't be surprised if it had shattered bone. Zim's gunshot had hit him so hard it knocked the wind from his lungs. It was only by leaning on Alexa that he could go on without passing out.

They hobbled into the tower and onto a modern wood floor that had been built to cover the open basement.

Bullets bit into the floor, and they hobbled faster, plunging into the darkness of a doorway. It was the landing of a narrow spiral staircase.

'Up or down?' Alexa asked.

'Up,' Tyler said without hesitation. High ground was always better.

Tyler chewed on his lip to keep from screaming as they climbed the stairs. Footsteps pounding across the floor below them hurried their pace.

They reached the top of the tower, a twelve-by-fifteen-foot observation platform constructed for tourists to have an unsurpassed view of the loch, and Tyler realized they were cornered. There was nowhere to run, no other way down. Crawling to one of the other parapets along the disintegrating rampart was suicide, but the alternative wasn't much better.

To the north, Tyler could see the Zodiac speeding away. A woman's long hair streaming backward from the head of the only passenger was barely visible in the running lights. It had to be Dunham.

Zim, who was now on the stairs below, must have seen it too.

'No!' he screamed. 'You bitch!'

He fired a long burst from a window opening in the stairwell until the weapon clicked empty. Tyler listened for the sound of him reloading another magazine, but the rifle clattered down the stairs instead.

'I'm coming for you, Tyler,' Zim cackled with glee. 'I'm coming for both of you.'

Tyler considered jumping over the balustrade and landing on Zim, but decided it was too risky. In close quarters Zim had the advantage of upper body strength, doubled now because of Tyler's injured shoulder. Better to bring him into open space where Zim's wounded leg would hinder him.

Tyler backed Alexa against the railing behind him and readied himself for the fight.

Zim limped up the stairs one at a time, brandishing the gaff hook in front of him. Tyler didn't want to think what landing on that would have felt like.

Alexa pressed something into his good hand.

'I forgot I had this,' she said.

Tyler looked down and saw his Leatherman gleaming in the floodlight. He flipped open the knife and held it out, bending his knees in a defensive posture.

Zim came to a stop at the top of the stairs.

'How's your arm?' he asked with a maniacal grin.

'Nothing but a scratch. What about your leg?'

'I've had worse.'

'Well, now that we've gone through our ritual lies, why don't you go back down the stairs and give yourself up?' Tyler pointed at the flashing blue lights in the parking lot. 'Without your boat, you won't be getting out of here.'

'I don't care. I know you must have gotten a tissue sample, and I want it. Now.'

'Come and get it.'

Even with his gimpy leg, Zim was quick and the platform

was small. He charged forward, swiping with the hook. Tyler dodged to the side and kicked at Zim's leg, grazing it enough to elicit a howl.

Zim whirled around again with the hook but missed. He followed through with his other arm and connected with Tyler's chest close to the shoulder. The vibration jolted the injury, causing a blaze of stars to temporarily obscure his vision. Another hit like that and he'd be down for the count.

Tyler staggered back, waving the knife. Zim came at him again, bringing down the hook in an overhand sweep.

Tyler blocked the move with his right forearm, but couldn't bring his other hand up to ward off Zim's right fist. It crashed into Tyler's shoulder, and this time he buckled to his knees in agony, dropping the Leatherman to the floor as he grasped at his shoulder.

Zim raised the hook to finish him off, then dropped the weapon when Alexa smashed her knee into his wounded leg. He screamed and threw his arm back, catching Alexa with an elbow that sent her reeling.

Pain seemed to provide Zim with superhuman powers. He put one hand on Tyler's shoulder and the other around his neck. Tyler had little strength to fight back. Once he was unconscious or dead, Zim would find the tissue sample in his coat pocket and dispose of it, killing Grant in the process as well.

As his vision tunneled, Tyler reached into his pocket and slid the tube to Alexa, who was looking at him, still on her hands and knees from Zim's massive blow.

Zim heard the skittering metal and saw that Alexa now had it. She got to her feet and made a dash for the stairs, but Zim pushed himself up and grabbed the back of her jacket, whipping her around into the railing that overlooked the deck.

Tyler struggled to regain his footing while he watched Zim pin his sister against the rail. He grabbed the arm that was holding the aluminum tube and drew it to him. He was about to pluck it from her fingers when Alexa flicked her wrist, pitching the tube backward in an attempt to throw it down to the first floor. Instead, the tube bounced along the top of the wall and lodged in the crevice between two stones.

'Bad move,' Zim said.

Tyler staggered to his feet as Zim looked back at him and said, 'Say goodbye.'

As easy as picking up a feather pillow, Zim tossed Alexa over the railing. Her terrified shriek ended with a horrible abruptness.

Tyler felt a savage scream tear directly from his soul, creating a rupture that seemed bottomless. With pure animal fury, he rushed at Zim. He landed one blow before Zim tossed him aside.

Zim crawled over the railing and out onto the top of the outer wall, grasping at the tube. As soon as he had it, he'd throw it into the loch, and Grant's death warrant would be signed.

Tyler was not going to lose him as well. He frantically

looked around and saw the Leatherman with the knife still extended. He scrabbled over to it and picked it up. With the last bit of strength he had, he pushed himself up and hurtled toward Zim, who was snatching the tube from the crevice.

Zim got to his knees and reared back, preparing to throw the last vestige of the Loch Ness monster into the bottom of the loch. He saw Tyler coming and struck out with his good leg, which was exactly what Tyler had been expecting.

He plunged the knife into Zim's foot and twisted his leg sideways, causing enough imbalance to teeter Zim over the edge.

As Zim was going through his throwing motion, he fell off the wall. There was no scream, just a thump when his body hit the platform.

Tyler crumpled to the ground, tears streaming down his cheeks. Alexa was gone. He sensed the same darkness that had descended when Karen died now threatening to overwhelm him.

He forced himself to look down at the first floor through the mesh steel railing, preparing himself to see two bodies laying side by side.

Instead, he saw three.

In addition to Zim's motionless form, he saw Grant cradling Alexa, who pushed herself up and waved to him.

In the grip of despair moments before, Tyler was now seized by a dizzying euphoria he'd never experienced. The rush of adrenaline gave him the energy to stumble down the staircase.

He walked over to Alexa, dropped the knife, and pulled her to him with his good arm.

'I thought you were dead,' he said, his voice cracking.

'I thought I was too. But Grant saw what was happening and caught me. Or at least cushioned my fall.'

Tyler knelt next to him and grabbed his hand. 'Thanks, man. I owe you big time.'

'No problem,' he said with a weak smile and closed his eyes. 'I think I'll take a nap now.'

Brielle came running through the entrance and said, 'Zim's men surrendered to the police, so I left Sinclair to explain what's going on.' She helped Tyler up. '*Oy vey*, you're a mess.'

'I look better than I feel.'

She looked down at Grant. 'How is he?'

'I don't know, but without the antidote he won't make it much longer.'

'Did you get it? The tissue from the Loch Ness monster?'

'I had it, but Zim threw it over the side of the castle. They might find it eventually, but not in time.'

'The police are here,' she said, looking at Zim. 'I suppose they'll take him back to prison.'

Tyler had assumed he was dead, but Zim was still breathing. Tyler picked up his knife and knelt next to him.

'He doesn't deserve to live.'

'Tyler, don't,' Alexa said. 'There's been enough killing for one day.'

'I know. But he still doesn't deserve it.'

Tyler saw a glint in Zim's palm. He opened Zim's fingers, and there was the aluminum tube.

He felt another rush of euphoria, but the adrenaline was gone. He rocked back on his heels and sat down against the wall, laying his head against the cold stone and closing his eyes. Like Grant, Tyler decided that he needed a nap.

WORLD NEWS

Crisis in the Middle East Averted

By PETER HAVERFORD

June 25, LONDON – Scientists at the toxicology laboratory of Imperial College confirmed today that they have successfully synthesized an antidote to the poison that struck down leaders across the Middle East. Doses have already been couriered to all of the affected countries, and the condition of the treated patients has shown dramatic improvement.

The recovering health of the ministers in twelve countries, including Egypt, Syria, and Jordan, along with vigorous diplomatic gestures from the United States and the European Union, has convinced the affected countries to begin a measured drawdown of forces. One reason tensions are easing is that Israel is no longer considered the instigator of the crisis. The source of both the poison administered at the Eiffel Tower and the subsequent antidote have been under intense scrutiny, but authorities have not revealed details of its origin.

Answers about the toxin, however, may eventually be forthcoming if they're able to capture a third mastermind implicated in the Eiffel Tower attack. According to sources at the US State Department, while André Laroche has been exonerated of any role in the plot, an American woman named Marlo Dunham has recently been named a co-conspirator of Carl Zim and his brother, recent fugitive Victor Zim. Ms Dunham's whereabouts are currently unknown, but she is now the subject of a massive worldwide search conducted by Interpol and law enforcement agencies on every continent.

EPILOGUE

Three weeks later

Alexa felt an intense sensation of déjà vu as she rode in Grant's Tahoe down the driveway at André Laroche's estate. It brought back memories of her jittery arrival after being rescued from the kidnapping attempt at Pike Place Market. The difference was that the fear, urgency, and desperation were gone, replaced by calm anticipation.

She couldn't help looking at Grant for any signs of a relapse, but he seemed stronger than ever, the wrinkles and grey hair erased as if they were never there. It seemed the antidote not only stopped the progression of the poison but had a rejuvenating effect as well. The treatment in London had lasted a week, followed by recuperation in Seattle, during which she'd taken care of him. Other than one dinner at a local Chinese restaurant, this was their first foray out into the world since leaving Urquhart Castle.

He parked in front of the mansion and shut off the engine.

'Thanks for coming with me,' she said, putting her hand on his.

'After what you did for me? I would have come if you were visiting a scorpion pit.'

Alexa smiled because for Grant that was saying a lot. Through their long discussions in the last month, one tidbit she'd learned was that he was deathly afraid of scorpions, an aversion forged by a bad experience when he was camping as a child and found one had crawled into his shoe during the night.

'Aw, thanks, honey,' Alexa said. She leaned over, and they shared a hungry kiss that went on for a minute. If they had been at Grant's apartment, she was sure the make-out session wouldn't have stopped there.

When she drew back, Grant stared into her eyes with a pained expression.

'Are you sure we have to tell Tyler?' he asked.

Even though she'd made frequent visits to Grant's place, they'd successfully kept the relationship a secret, which was even easier in the past week with Tyler gone on a well-deserved vacation in the UK. She knew he'd be seeing Brielle and secretly hoped it would lead to something more. She thought they made a good couple.

'I think you're making too big a deal of this,' Alexa said. 'He'll understand.'

Grant shook his head. 'You're not a guy with a sister. I know if anyone messed with my sisters, I'd have some strong words with them.' His balled fists at the thought made it clear that words weren't the only thing the offender would get.

'So you're just messing with me?'

Grant's eyes went wide when he realized how that had come out. 'No, no. It's kind of an unwritten code. You're not supposed to . . . get involved with your friend's sister.'

'So a stranger would be better? Why?'

'I don't know. That's how it works.'

'You want me to talk to him?'

He hesitated. She was amused that Grant would face down hordes of enemy soldiers armed with guns, but admitting something like this to Tyler was terrifying to him.

'No,' he finally said. 'I think we should do it together.'

'So do I,' she said lasciviously.

'See? That is exactly why the rule is in place.'

'It'll be okay. Trust me.'

'I do,' Grant said. 'But if it goes south, I'll tell him it was all your idea.'

'Yes, you were completely helpless under my spell. That'll work.'

Alexa and Grant got out of the car and knocked on the front door. A woman in a nurse's outfit answered and brought them inside. She didn't have Marlo Dunham's panache, but she had a friendly smile.

They walked down the long hallway where Marlo Dunham had shot at Brielle, and Alexa could still see where the bullets had torn out chunks of wood and drywall.

Entering the living room, they found André Laroche seated in a chair, a cane by his side. He'd come out of the coma two weeks ago but had been able to return home only yesterday. Though the left side of his face drooped from paralysis, the doctors hoped that he'd someday regain control of his features. Even so, he looked much better than the last time Alexa had seen him, unconscious in his vault. His color had returned, and he still had the regal bearing she recalled.

He gave Alexa a lopsided smile and held out a wobbly hand. She took the cue and went to him, bending over to give him a traditional French kiss on both cheeks.

'Sit down, please,' he said, his voice slurred and shaky. 'Can I offer you some tea?'

'That would be lovely,' Alexa said. She and Grant sat on the settee opposite him.

'Ms Frost, would you please prepare some Earl Grey for us?'

She nodded and left the room.

'I'm so sorry for what I put you through,' Laroche said. 'Both of you. I hope you can find it in your heart to forgive an old man.'

'Of course, André.'

He shook his head with a look of profound disappointment. 'My trust in Marlo was so misplaced.'

'Justice will catch up with her some day,' Grant said.

'Yes, I suppose it will, one way or another.'

'At least this affair has opened up a whole new line of research into the aging process,' Alexa said. 'Without your contribution to discovering the Loch Ness monster, that wouldn't have happened.'

'It really does exist?' he asked eagerly. 'You saw it with your own eyes?'

She nodded. Her heart was still heavy at the magnificent creature's loss, but she hoped they'd be able to find its remains someday for proper study and display. Alexa wanted to share the exhilaration she'd felt upon seeing it. She'd start by sharing her experience with the person who would appreciate it most.

Laroche leaned forward. 'Tell me everything.'

Dr Wayan Sulastri of Rumah Sakit Wongaya Hospital in Denpasar rushed down the hall in response to the code called on his pager. He entered the patient's room and found two nurses already getting the crash cart ready.

He checked the monitor and confirmed that the elderly woman was suffering another episode of ventricular tachycardia, the third since she'd been admitted to the hospital several days before. He took the paddles and yelled, 'Clear!'

Her chest heaved up in response to the electrical shock. It took two more to revive her. The heart was beating, but thready and weak. One of the nurses collected the cart and left while Sulastri stayed with the other nurse to jot down some notes.

The English interpreter, on call for the many tourists who became ill on their visits to Bali's capital city, appeared in the door.

'Do you need me?' she asked Sulastri. He spoke only Balinese and Indonesian.

He looked at the patient, who was stirring. She was frail, assumed to be in her eighties, with hair falling out in clumps, loose teeth, and severe osteoporosis resulting in a broken pelvis. Nothing they did seemed to reverse her rapidly deteriorating state. Sulastri had no options but to keep her alive as long as he could and make her comfortable.

'Ms Duncan,' he said, focusing on the patient instead of the interpreter, 'you've suffered another arrhythmia, so we had to resuscitate you again. Is there anyone you want me to call?'

The interpreter translated, and then shook her head at the wheezed response. 'She keeps repeating the same thing, that the only way to cure her is by creating some kind of elixir from the flesh of the Loch Ness monster.'

'It must be delirium.' He made a note of the ramblings, and the interpreter left him and the nurse alone with the patient.

'Poor woman,' the nurse said. 'To be alone in her last days. It must be horrible.'

'Any luck finding a relative? Her passport says she's American.'

'We've tried contacting the home of every Marley Duncan in the United States. None of them have ever been here. I'll try the US embassy next, but I don't even think it's a real passport.'

'It's definitely been altered in some way,' Sulastri said, looking at the chart, 'because there's no possible way this fragile old woman is twenty-nine years old.'

*

The only enjoyment Victor Zim got these days was from imagining Marlo Dunham at the moment she would have realized that Zim poisoned her. All it had taken was a quick pour into her coffee on board the *Aegir* when he'd been fed up with her for good. At the time he'd regretted his impulsive use of the remainder of *Altwaffe* he'd retained, but now he was glad he'd had the foresight to do it. She was either dying somewhere or in custody in order to receive treatment. He alternated between gratifying thoughts about each outcome.

Staring at the ceiling from his bed, he didn't know how long such entertaining reflection would stave off the boredom that he was sure would eventually drive him insane. Returned to California, Zim had been denied any kind of entertainment except for one hour a day when he was allowed to watch television. There would be no trips to the exercise yard, and he was allowed no visitors other than his court-appointed lawyer. No trial was forthcoming; it hadn't been deemed necessary since he could still be incarcerated under his original sentence. He longed for his last cellmate at Pleasant Valley, a crass plumber who'd murdered his wife but had amusing stories about his four exes before the one he killed.

At times Zim was filled with rage at his situation, but it was primarily the depression that consumed him. Although he did have a window, all he could see was the sky. It was probably the only outdoor view he'd ever see again, since they'd never let him go. But even if they did, his life was over.

A nurse entered his room and adjusted his arms and legs to prevent bedsores. She might as well have been adjusting couch cushions for all he could feel. He looked down and saw that the muscle tone in his limbs was already drastically reduced. In another few weeks, his arms and legs would look like toothpicks.

When Zim had awoken in an Inverness hospital, he'd been told that the fall at Urquhart Castle had crushed his third cervical vertebra, instantly turning him into a quadriplegic. His situation was irreversible, paralyzing him from the neck down.

Without saying a word, the nurse finished her job and left.

He was as helpless as a baby, suffering every indignity to which a newborn was oblivious. And there was nothing he could do about it. Even if the nurse had left a loaded Glock on the bed, he wouldn't have been able to put himself out of his misery. He'd tried to kill himself by refusing to eat, but they'd put a disgusting feeding tube down his nose.

He looked back at the featureless sky outside the window, and tears rolled down his cheeks as he thought about the reality of the next forty years being confined to the worst prison he could imagine.

Tyler climbed up to the top deck of the *Nessie Seeker II* with two glasses of scotch and took a seat next to Brielle, who was dressed only in a long-sleeved shirt and light pants made possible by the unusually warm breeze blowing across

Loch Ness. She took her tumbler and they clinked them together.

'To Nessie,' she said.

Tyler smiled. 'May her legend live on.'

Tyler took a sip and savored the peaty scotch, which went down oh so smoothly. A little liquid anesthetic would help ease the ache in his shoulder, which had come out of its sling the day before. It would take a few months to get back to ninety percent, but the doctors didn't know if he'd ever regain a full range of motion. Still, it was a small price to pay for Grant's return to health.

They quietly watched the sun descending over Urquhart Castle, the azure sky broken by a few wisps of white cloud. Tyler had to admit that the view from Greg Sinclair's new boat was much better than it had been from the cramped submarine.

After his original boat sank, Sinclair told Tyler that he'd been in the process of searching for a replacement anyway, and the insurance money allowed him to buy the boat he'd had his eye on, a beautiful forty-two-footer. When Tyler had left him at the helm, Sinclair was still playing with the new gadgets that came installed in the control panel.

The leisurely cruise went on for a while without conversation until Brielle turned to Tyler.

'Do you like blintzes?' she asked.

Tyler thought about it for a moment. 'I don't know if I've ever had blintzes.'

'Then I think you should try them.'

'Okay. Do you know a good place?'

She nodded. 'In London. My mum makes the best cheese blintzes you'll ever taste.'

Tyler was genuinely surprised. And pleased. He was beginning to think they might be taking this beyond a fling. 'Are you asking me over to your parents' house?'

'It's not an audition or anything like that. I just think they might like you, even if you aren't one of the chosen people. What do you say?'

'I'd be honored.' They clinked again.

'Has Grant met your father?' Brielle asked.

'Oh, yeah.'

'But not since he started seeing Alexa.'

Tyler shook his head and grinned. 'They don't even think that *I* know.'

'You're going to let them sweat it out?'

'I don't know how serious it is, but they'll tell me when they're ready.' All he wanted was for them both to be happy, and if they found happiness together, that would be great as far as he was concerned.

Another few minutes of silence went by before Brielle spoke again.

'Are you ready to tell me why we're here?'

'A romantic boat ride isn't enough? We *are* his first passengers.'

'I know you well enough now to realize you brought us back up here for another reason.'

She really did know him well. 'You're right. I promised

Mr Sinclair that we'd help him get a photograph to promote his business.'

'A photo of what?'

Tyler pulled a tablet computer from his bag, drawing a quizzical look from Brielle. He opened the cover and tapped on the screen to bring up an app specially designed by Gordian. The app showed a satellite map of Loch Ness. There were three dots on the map – red, yellow, and blue.

'That's us right there,' he said, pointing at the blue dot. He zoomed in, and the dot moved steadily toward the south. The stationary yellow dot was only a few hundred yards off their port bow.

'What does that represent?' Brielle asked.

'That's the wreckage of the *Aegir*. When Gordian did its survey last week with the unmanned submersible, they marked the location with a submerged buoy, far enough beneath the surface that no boat would ever hit it.'

'It's a shame they couldn't find Nessie down there. From what Alexa told me, the animal's carcass could have provided scientists with valuable insight into preventing cell decay.'

'They have enough of a sample for now. I hear they're already making progress.'

'They found the harpoon and nothing else?'

'The official story is that the creature must be buried in the muck, irretrievable without a serious dredging effort.'

'What do you mean, official?'

'I haven't told Alexa any of this yet because I didn't want

to get her hopes up until I'd confirmed it, but the part of the story you haven't heard is that they found the tail with the harpoon still buried in it. Remember when Alexa was telling us about lizards shedding their tails to get away from predators?'

Brielle's mouth fell open. 'You mean . . .'

Tyler nodded and scrolled the screen to the southern portion of the loch, where the red dot representing the Loch Ness monster was located, a three-digit number next to the dot indicating depth in meters. It currently read 045.

'That's her.'

Brielle gasped when she saw the dot change position.

Nessie was moving.

AFTERWORD

One of the things I enjoy about writing Tyler Locke thrillers is researching all the cool technology, history, and settings that I use in the book. As you were reading this, you probably came across a few things that surely seemed made up, but it's likely they're actually real or at least based on reality.

I will admit that the DeadEye targeting system and Mayfly drone are my creations, but quadcopters are absolutely real. In fact, you can buy one for yourself for a very reasonable price and control it using your smartphone. It even does flips, but I don't know of any equipped with a Taser.

Harris Ranch (dubbed Cowschwitz) is a real cattle stockyard in California. I've experienced the smell myself. Pity the poor employees of Pleasant Valley State Prison, which is located just to the south.

If you're one of the lucky buyers of an actual Icon A5 sport plane, I highly recommend checking the option box for the Ballistic Recovery Systems Complete Plane Parachute. Their system has already saved over 225 lives.

Pike Place Market is one of my favorite destinations in

Seattle. Be sure to stop by and watch the fishmongers throw gigantic salmon to each other.

The shadow sculptures of Tim Noble and Sue Webster are really quite remarkable. I'd get one for my own house if I had anywhere to put it.

The remodeled Salle Gustave Eiffel should now be open for parties so make your reservation right away.

If you haven't been to Versailles, it's hard to convey the sheer ostentation of the palace and gardens. I had the good fortune to visit it for the purposes of researching this novel, and serendipity from my tour appears in the closure of the *Bains d'Apollon*, which was shut down for renovation while I was there, and in the surprise appearance of a cat while I was wandering through the gardens.

Although *Altwaffe* is a fabrication, the rare disease its effects are based on is depressingly real. The poor children afflicted with progeria usually don't live far into their teens, and the genetic disease has no known cure.

Fuel-cell cars are beginning to make an appearance on the roads, but I don't know of any go-karts featuring that powerplant.

John Edmonstone, a freed Guyanese slave who lived in Edinburgh, was a friend of Charles Darwin during his time in medical college at the University of Edinburgh and may indeed have trained him in taxidermy.

While Darwin did visit Glen Roy in the Scottish Highlands, there's no record of him ever visiting Loch Ness. I prefer to think he kept that trip a secret.

The interiors of Holyroodhouse Palace and Edinburgh Castle are as I've described them, including the castle's Great Hall lined with hundreds of old weapons.

Urquhart Castle is also described faithfully, down to the glass door in the gatehouse. The Grant Tower really is the bastion's name, and I was lucky to view the loch from its top floor platform (on the coldest May day I've ever experienced).

I was surprised to learn that hunting of minke whales continues to this day in Norway, and the whalers use explosive-tipped harpoons to kill their prey.

The GhostManta sub, designed by Caan Yaylali, hasn't put to sea, but you can find renderings of it on the internet. I would love to fly under the ocean in such a submarine if anyone ever constructs one.

Many theories have been put forth about the Loch Ness monster, first and foremost that it's nothing more than a hoax or wishful thinking. However, coelacanths, axolotls, sturgeons, and Chinese giant salamanders are all real creatures that have characteristics in common with Nessie's alleged behavior.

While I was at Loch Ness, I took a boat tour of the loch guided by George Edwards, captain of the *Nessie Hunter IV*. Although we didn't spot Nessie that day, several months later Mr Edwards snapped a photo of a mysterious shape in the water, and it made worldwide headlines. Few people consider the photograph to be definitive proof of the creature's existence, but it certainly adds more intrigue to the legend. Now that more people than ever are armed with cell-phone cameras, maybe one day we'll get irrefutable evidence that something lives in the depths of Loch Ness.

ACKNOWLEDGEMENTS

Thanks are due to the many people who helped make this book a reality:

To Jade Chandler, my editor, for being such a big fan and champion of my work and for helping me polish the story to the best of my abilities;

To Irene Goodman, my literary agent, for standing by me when the chips were down;

To Danny Baror and Heather Baror-Shapiro, my foreign rights agents, for bringing my books to places I barely knew existed;

To George Edwards, skipper of the *Nessie Hunter IV*, for his expertise on Loch Ness;

To Shelley Innes and Elizabeth Smith of the Darwin Correspondence Project, for providing the solid foundation over which all my wild speculation about Charles Darwin is built;

To Erik Van Eaton, friend and trauma surgeon, for helping me kill people in creative ways;

To Susan Tunis, for all her hard work in pointing out my dumb mistakes;

To Frank Moretti, my father-in-law, for late nights going through the manuscript;

To Beth Morrison, my sister, for suffering through my first drafts;

And to Randi, for being the best wife a guy could ever hope to marry.

After university, Boyd Morrison earned a PhD in industrial engineering, worked for NASA and tested Xbox games for Microsoft. A professional actor and outdoor-sports enthusiast, he is currently at work on his next thriller.

Visit his website at www.boydmorrison.com